TYPHOON

ALSO BY CHARLES CUMMING

A Spy by Nature

The Spanish Game

The Hidden Man

TYPHOON

CHARLES CUMMING

St. Martin's Press   New York

TYPHOON. Copyright © 2008 by Charles Cumming. All rights reserved. Printed in the United States of America. For information, address St. Martin's Press, 175 Fifth Avenue, New York, NY 10010.

www.stmartins.com

Design by Phil Mazzone

Library of Congress Cataloging-in-Publication Data

Cumming, Charles, 1971–
    Typhoon / Charles Cumming.—1st U.S. ed.
        p.   cm.
    ISBN 978-0-312-55852-9
    I. Title.
    PR6103.U484T97   2009
    823'.92—dc22

                                2009024029

Originally published in Great Britain by Michael Joseph

First U.S. Edition: November 2009

10 9 8 7 6 5 4 3 2 1

For Iris and Stanley
and
to the memory of Pierce Loughran
(1969–2005)

The superior man understands what is right;
the inferior man understands what will sell.

—CONFUCIUS

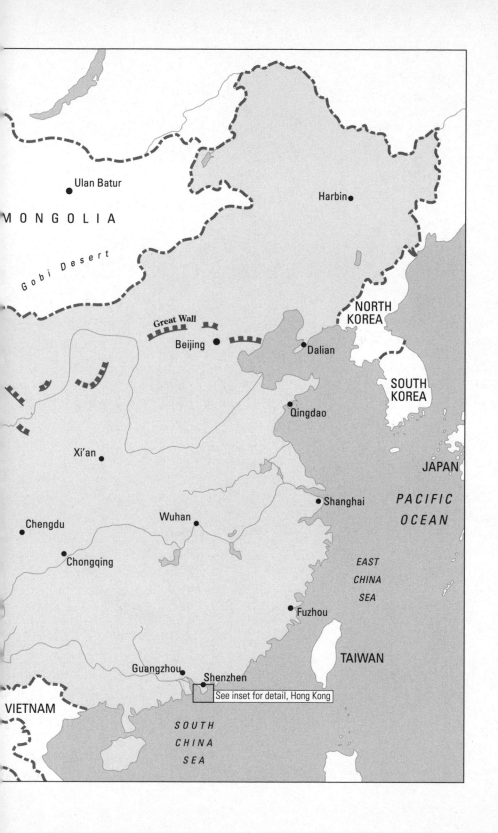

TYPHOON

PROLOGUE

"Washington has gone *crazy."*

I am standing at the foot of Joe's bed in the Worldlink Hospital. Six days have passed since the attacks of 11 June. There are plastic tubes running from valves on his wrists, a cardiac monitor attached by pads to the spaces between the bruises and cuts on his chest.

"What do you mean?"

"Only a handful of people at Langley knew what Miles was up to. Nobody else had the faintest idea what the hell was going on out here."

"Who told you this?"

"Waterfield."

Joe turns his head towards the window and looks out on another featureless Shanghai morning. He has a broken collarbone, a fracture in his left leg, a wound on his skull protected by loops of clean white bandage.

"How much do you know about all this?" he asks, directing his eyes into mine, and the question travels all the way back to our first months in Hong Kong.

"Everything I've researched. Everything you've ever told me."

My name is William Lasker. I am a journalist. For fourteen years I served as a support agent of the British Secret Intelligence Service. For ten of those years, Joe Lennox was my handler and close friend. Nobody *knows more about RUN than I do. Nobody except Joe Lennox himself.*

He clears a block in his throat. His voice is still slow and uneven from the blast. I offer him a glass of water which he waves away.

"If the CIA didn't know about Miles, they'll be going through every file, every email, every telephone conversation he ever made. They'll want answers. Heads are going to roll. David Waterfield can get you those files. He has a source at Langley and a source in Beijing."

"What are you getting at?"

A nurse comes into the room, nods at Joe, checks the flow rate on his IV drip. Both of us stop talking. For the past six days the Worldlink has been crawling with Chinese spies. The Ministry of State Security will be keeping a record of everybody who comes in and out of this room. The nurse looks at me, seems to photograph my face with a blink of her eyes, then leaves.

"What are you getting at?" I ask again.

"They say that every journalist wants to write a book." Joe is smiling for the first time in days. I can't tell whether this remark is a statement or a question. Then his mood becomes altogether more serious. "This story needs to be told. We want you to tell it."

PART ONE | Hong Kong
1997

1 | ON THE BEACH

Professor Wang Kaixuan emerged from the still waters of the South China Sea shortly before dawn on Thursday 10 April 1997. Exhausted by the long crossing, he lay for some time in the shallows, his ears tuned to the silence, his eyes scanning the beach. It was 5:52 a.m. By his calculations the sun would begin to rise over Dapeng Bay in less than fifteen minutes. From that point on he would run the greater risk of being spotted by a passing patrol. Keeping his body low against the slick black rocks, he began to crawl towards the sanctuary of trees and shrubs on the far side of the beach.

He was wearing only a pair of shorts and a thin cotton T-shirt. All of his worldly possessions were otherwise contained in a small black rucksack attached to the makeshift raft which he dragged behind him on a length of twine attached to his leg. The plastic containers that had floated the raft clattered and bounced on the rocks as Wang inched inshore. The noise of this was too much; he should have prepared for it. Twenty metres short of the trees he stopped and turned. Sand had begun to stick to his damp, salt-stiffened fingers and he was aware that his breathing was hard and strained. Two hours earlier, in the half-light of eastern Shenzhen,

Wang had attached a cheap kitchen knife to his calf using a stretch of waterproof tape. It took all of his strength now to tear the knife free and to sever the twine so that the raft was no longer attached to his body.

Kuai dian, he told himself. *Hurry*. Wang cut the rucksack free and tried to sling it across his shoulders. It felt as though he had been drugged or beaten and a grim sense memory of the prison in Urumqi crept up on him like the rising sun. The rucksack was so heavy and his arms so tired from the swim that he felt he would have to rest.

Jia you.

Keep going.

He stumbled to his feet and tried to rush the last few metres to the trees, but the rucksack tipped on his back and Wang fell almost immediately, fearing an injury to his knee or ankle, something that would hamper him on the long walk south across the hills. *Imagine that, after everything I have been through: a tendon sends me back to China.* But he found that he could move without discomfort to the nearest of the trees, where he sank to the ground, sending a flock of startled birds clattering into the sky.

It was six o'clock. Wang looked back across the narrow stretch of water and felt a tremor of elation which numbed, for an instant, his near-constant dread of capture. He reached out and felt for the bark of the tree, for the sand at his feet. *This place is freedom*, he told himself. *This shore is England*. Starling Inlet was less than two kilometres wide, but in the darkness the tide must have pulled him west towards Sha Tau Kok, or even east into the open waters of Dapeng. Why else had it taken him so long to swim across? The professor was fit for a man of his age and he had swum well; at times it was as if his desire to succeed had pulled him through the water like a rope. Wiping seawater from the neck of the rucksack he removed several seals of waterproof tape and withdrew a tightly bound plastic bag. A few minutes later he had discarded his T-shirt and shorts and dressed himself in damp blue jeans, a black cotton shirt and dark sweater. On his feet he wore grey socks and the counterfeit tennis shoes from the market in Guangzhou.

Now I look like a typical Hong Kong Chinese. Now if they stop me I can say that I am out here watching for birds.

Wang removed the binoculars from his rucksack and the small, poorly bound volume on egrets posted to him from Beijing three weeks earlier. The back of his throat was sour with the salt and pollutants of the sea and he drank greedily from a bottle of water, swallowing hard in an effort to remove them. Then he looped the binoculars around his neck, placed the water bottle back in the rucksack and waited for the sun.

2 | BLACK WATCH

Lance Corporal Angus Anderson, 1st Battalion Black Watch, three months into the regiment's final tour of Hong Kong, walked along the path from Luk Keng. This was magic hour, before the heat and the mosquitoes, before cockerels and barked orders and discipline punctured his private dream of Asia. Breathing the cool salt air, he slowed to an easy stroll as the first rays of the dawn sun began to heat the surrounding hills. One of only six Black Watch soldiers assigned to patrol the border in support of the Hong Kong Police, Anderson had been dispatched by an immigration inspector to make a brisk check of Starling Inlet before returning to headquarters for breakfast.

"Sometimes they try to swim," the inspector had told him. His name was Leung. There were purple scars on his hands. "Sometimes they escape the sharks and the tide and make their way on foot to Tai Po."

Anderson took out a cigarette. The sea was calm and he listened to the rhythm of the water, to the cry of a cormorant on the wind. He felt a strange, anarchic impulse to strip out of his uniform and to run, like a streaker at Murrayfield, down into the lukewarm freedom of the ocean. Six hours earlier he had helped to untangle a corpse from the coils of razor wire that stretched all along the land border from Deep Bay to Sha Tau Kok. His commanding officer called it "Chateau Cock," like a bottle of cheap claret, and everybody in the battalion was expected to laugh. The body was that of a Chinese peasant girl wearing shorts and flip-flops and he could not erase from his memory the picture of her pale neck twisted into the fence and the blood from her arms which had turned brown in the sulphur glare of the floodlights. Would this kind of thing end after 30 June? Would the eye-eyes stop coming over? Leung had told them that in 1996 alone the Field Patrol Detachment had arrested more than 5,000 illegal immigrants, most of them young men looking for work in the construction industry in Hong Kong. That was about fourteen coming across every night. And now the FPD was facing a last-minute, pre-handover surge of Chinese nationals willing to risk the phalanx of armed police massed on both sides of the border in the slender hope of vanishing into the communities of Yuen Long, Kowloon and Shatin.

Anderson lit the cigarette. He couldn't see the sense in chogies risking their lives for two months in what was left of British Hong Kong. There wouldn't be an amnesty on eye-eyes; there wouldn't be passports for the masses. Thatcher had seen to that. Christ, there were veterans of the Hong Kong Regiment, men sitting in one-bedroom flats in Kowloon who had fought for Winston bloody Churchill, who *still* wouldn't get past immigration at Heathrow. Outsiders didn't seem to realize that the colony was all but dead already. Rumour had it that Governor Patten spent his days just sitting around in Government House, counting down the hours until he could go home. The garrison was down to its last 2,000 men: everything from Land Rovers to ambulances, from coils of barbed wire to bits of old gym equipment, had been auctioned off. The High Island Training Camp at Sai Kung had been cleared and handed over to the People's Liberation Army before Anderson had even arrived. In the words of his commanding officer, nothing potentially "sensitive" or "hazardous" could be left in the path of the incoming Chinese military or their communist masters, which meant Black Watch soldiers working sixteen-hour days mapping and documenting every fingerprint of British rule, 150 years of naval guns and hospitals and firing ranges, just so the chogies knew exactly what they were getting their hands on. Anderson had even heard stories about a submerged net running between Stonecutters Island and Causeway Bay to thwart Chinese submarines. How was the navy going to explain *that* one to Beijing?

A noise down on the beach. He dropped the cigarette and reached for his binoculars. He heard it again. A click of rocks, something moving near the water's edge. Most likely an animal of some kind, a wild pig or civet cat, but there was always the chance of an illegal. To the naked eye Anderson could make out only the basic shapes of the beach: boulders, hollows, crests of sand. Peering through the binoculars was like switching off lights in a basement; he actually felt stupid for trying. Go for the torch, he told himself, and swept a steady beam of light as far along the coast as it would take him. He picked out weeds and shingle and the blue-black waters of the South China Sea, but no animals, no illegal.

Anderson continued along the path. He had another forty-eight hours up here, then five jammy days in Central raising the Cenotaph Union Jack at seven every morning, and lowering it again at six. That, as far as he could tell, was all that he would be required to do. The rest of the time he could hit the bars of Wan Chai, maybe take a girl up to the Peak or go gambling out at Macau. "Enjoy yourself," his father had told him. "You'll be a young man thousands of miles from home living through a little piece of history. The sunset of the British Empire. Don't just sit on your arse in Stonecutters and regret it that you never left the base."

The light was improving all the time. Anderson heard a motorbike gunning in the distance and waved a mosquito out of his face. He was now about a mile from Luk Keng and able to pick out more clearly the contours of the path as it dropped towards the sea. Then, behind him, perhaps fifteen or twenty metres away, a noise that was human in weight and tendency, a sound that seemed to conceal itself the instant it was made. Somebody or something was out on the beach. Anderson swung round and lifted the binoculars, yet they were still no good to him. Touching his rifle, he heard a second noise, this time as if a person had toppled off balance. His pulse quickened as he scanned the shore and noticed almost immediately what appeared to be an empty petrol can lying on the beach. Beside it he thought he could make out a second container, perhaps a small plastic drum—had they been painted black?—next to a wooden pallet. So much debris washed up onshore that Anderson couldn't be certain that he was looking at the remains of a raft. The men had been trained to look for flippers, clothing, discarded inner tubes, but the items here looked suspicious. He would have to walk down to the beach to check them for himself and, by doing so, run the risk of startling an eye-eye who might care more for his own freedom than he did for the life of a British soldier.

He was no more than twenty feet from the containers when a stocky, apparently agile man in his late forties poked his nose out of the trees and walked directly towards him, his hand outstretched like a bank manager.

"Good morning, sir!" Anderson levelled the rifle but lowered it in almost the same movement as his brain registered that it was listening to fluent English. "I am to understand from your uniform that you are a member of Her Majesty's Black Watch. The famous red hackle. Your bonnet. But no kilt, sir! I am disappointed. What do they say? The kilt is the best clothes in the world for sex and diarrhoea!" The chogie was shouting across the space between them and grinning like Jackie Chan. As he came crunching along the beach it looked very much to Anderson as though he wanted to shake hands. "The Black Watch is a regiment with a great and proud history, no? I remember the heroic tactics of Colonel David Rose at the Hook in Korea. I am Professor Wang Kaixuan at the university here, Department of Economics. Welcome to our island. It is a genuine pleasure to meet you."

Wang had at last arrived. Anderson took an instinctive step back as the stranger came to a halt three feet away from him, planting his legs like a sumo wrestler. They did indeed shake hands. The chogie's closely cropped hair was either wet or greasy; it was hard to tell.

"Are you out here alone?" Wang asked, looking lazily at the

colouring sky as if to imply that the question carried no threat. Anderson couldn't pick the broad face for northern Han or Cantonese, but the spoken English was impeccable.

"I'm on patrol down here at the beach," he said. "And yourself?"

"Me? I stayed in the area over the weekend. To take the opportunity to look for the egrets that are native to the inlet at this time of year. Perhaps you have seen one on your patrol?"

"No," Anderson said. "I haven't." He wouldn't have known what an egret looked like. "Could you show me some form of identification, please?"

Wang managed to look momentarily offended. "Oh, I don't carry that sort of thing." As if to illustrate the point, he made a show of frisking himself, patting his hands up and down his chest before securing them in his pockets. "It is a pity you have not seen an egret. An elegant bird. But you enjoy our surroundings, no? I am told—although I have never visited there myself—that the hills in this part of the New Territories are very similar in geographical character to certain areas of the Scottish Highlands. Is that correct?"

"Aye, that's probably true." Anderson was from Stranraer, a pan-flat town in the far south-west, but the comparison had been made many times before. "I'm sorry, sir. I can see that you're carrying binoculars, I can see that you're probably who you say you are, but I'm going to have to ask you again for a passport or driving licence. Do you not carry any form of identification?"

It was the moment of truth. Had Angus Anderson been a different kind of man—less certain of himself, perhaps more trusting of human behaviour—the decade of events triggered by Wang's subsequent capture might have assumed an entirely different character. Had the professor been allowed, as he so desperately desired, to proceed unmolested all the way to Government House, the name of Joe Lennox might never have been uttered in the secret corridors of Shanghai and Urumqi and Beijing. But it was Wang's misfortune that quiet April morning to encounter a sharp-eyed Scot who had rumbled him for a fake almost immediately. This chogie was no birdwatcher. This chogie was an illegal.

"I have told you. I don't usually carry any form of identification with me."

"Not even a credit card?"

"My name is Wang Kaixuan, I am a professor of economics at the university here in Hong Kong. Please telephone the department switchboard if you feel uncertain. On a Wednesday morning my colleagues are usually at their desks by eight o'clock. I live at 71 Hoi Wang Road, Yau Ma Tei, apartment number 19. I can understand that the Black Watch regiment has an important job to do in these difficult months but I have lived in Hong Kong ever since I was a child."

Anderson unclipped his radio. It would only take ten seconds to call in the sighting. He seemed to have no other option. This guy was a conman, using tactics of questions and bluster to throw him off the scent. Leung's unit could be down in a police patrol boat before seven o'clock. Let them sort it out.

"Nine, this is One Zero, over."

Wang now had a choice to make: sustain the lie, and allow the soldier to haul him in front of Immigration, which carried the risk of immediate deportation back to China, or make a move for the radio, engendering a physical confrontation with a Scotsman half his age and almost twice his height. In the circumstances, it felt like no choice at all.

He had knocked the radio out of Anderson's hand before the soldier had time to react. As it spun into the sand Anderson swore and heard Wang say, "I am sorry, I am sorry," as he stepped away. Something in this surrendering, apologetic gesture briefly convinced him not to strike back. For some time the two men stared at one another without speaking until a crackled voice in the sand said: "One Zero, this is Nine. Go ahead, over," and it became a case of who would blink first. Anderson bent down, keeping his eyes on Wang all the time, and retrieved the radio as if picking up a revolver from the ground. Wang looked at the barrel of Anderson's rifle and began to speak.

"Please, sir, do not answer that radio. All I am asking is that you listen to me. I am sorry for what I did. Tell them it was a mistake. I beg you to tell them you have resolved your problem. Of course I am not who I say I am. I can see that you are an intelligent person and that you have worked this out. But I am asking you to deal with me correctly. I am not a normal person who swims across the inlet in the middle of the night. I am not an immigrant looking for a job. I do not want citizenship or refugee status or anything more or less than the attention of the British governor in Hong Kong. I am carrying with me information of vital importance to Western governments. That is all that I can tell you. So please, sir, do not answer that radio."

"I have to answer." Anderson was surprised to hear a note of conciliation in his voice. The encounter had taken on a surreal quality. How many Chinese mainlanders pitched up on a beach at 6 a.m. talking about David Rose at the Hook in fluent, near-accentless English? And how many of them claimed to have political intelligence that required a meeting with Governor Chris Patten?

"What kind of information?" he asked, amazed that he had not already jammed Wang's wrists into a set of PlastiCuffs and marched him up the beach. Again the voice said, "One Zero, this is Nine. Please go ahead, over," and Anderson looked back across the water at the pale contours of China, wondering what the hell to do. A fishing boat was edging out into the bay. Wang then turned his head to stare directly into Anderson's eyes. He wanted to convey the full weight of responsibility which now befell him.

"I have information about a very senior figure in Beijing," he said. "I have information about a possible high-level defection from the Chinese government."

3 | LENNOX

Joe Lennox left Jardine House at seven o'clock that evening, nodded discreetly at a French investment banker as he sank two vodka and tonics at the Captain's Bar of the Mandarin Oriental, hailed a cab on Connaught Road, made his way through the rush-hour traffic heading west into the Mid-Levels and walked through the door of Rico's at precisely 8:01 p.m. It was a gift. He was always on time.

I was sitting towards the back of the restaurant drinking a Tsingtao and reading a syndicated article in the *South China Morning Post* about the prospect of a Labour victory in the forthcoming UK elections. A ginger-haired Canadian woman at the next table was eating crayfish and throwing out dirty looks because of the cigarette I was smoking. When she coughed and waved her hand in front of her face once too often, I stubbed it out. The air conditioning was on high and it felt as though everyone in the room was shivering.

Joe looked the way Joe always looked in those days: fit and undiminished, his characteristically inscrutable expression becoming more animated as he found my eyes across the room. At first glance, I suppose he was no different from any other decent-looking Jardine

Johnnie in a Welsh & Jeffries suit, the sort who moves millions every day at Fleming's and Merrill Lynch. That, I suppose, was the whole point about Joe Lennox. That was the reason they picked him.

"Cold in here," he said, but he took his jacket off when he sat down. "What are you reading?"

I told him and he ventured a mildly critical opinion of the columnist—a former Tory cabinet minister—who had written the piece. (The next day I went through some cuttings and saw that the same grandee had been responsible for a couple of Patten-savaging articles in the British press, which probably explained Joe's antagonism.) He ordered a Tsingtao for himself and watched as the Canadian woman put her knife and fork together after finishing the crayfish.

"Been here long?" he asked.

"About ten minutes."

He was wearing a dark blue shirt and his forearms were tanned from walking in the New Territories with Isabella the previous weekend. He took out a packet of cigarettes and leaned towards the Canadian to ask if she would mind if he smoked. She seemed so taken aback by this basic display of courtesy that she nodded her assent without a moment's hesitation, then eyebrowed me as if I had been taught a valuable lesson in charm. I smiled and closed the *Post*.

"It's good to see you," I said.

"You too."

By this point we had been friends for the best part of a year, although it felt like longer. Living overseas can have that effect; you spend so much time socializing with a relatively small group of people that relationships intensify in a way that is unusual and not always healthy. Nevertheless, the experience of getting to know Joe had been one of the highlights of my brief stay in Hong Kong, where I had been living and working since the autumn of 1994. In the early days I was never certain of the extent to which that affection was reciprocated. Joe was an intensely loyal friend, amusing and intelligent company, but he was often withdrawn and emotionally unreadable, with a habit—doubtless related to the nature of his profession—of keeping people at arm's length.

To explain how we met. In 1992 I was reporting on the siege of Sarajevo when I was approached at a press conference by a female SIS officer working undercover at the UN. Most foreign journalists, at one time or another, are sounded out as potential sources by the intelligence services. Some make a song and dance about the importance of maintaining their journalistic integrity; the rest of us enjoy the fact that a tax-free grand pops up in our bank account every month, courtesy of the bean-counters at Vauxhall Cross. Our Woman in Sarajevo took me to a quiet room at the airport and, over a glass or two of counterfeit-label Irish whiskey, acquired me as a support agent. Over the next couple of years, in Bosnia, Kigali and Sri Lanka, I was contacted by SIS and encouraged to pass on any information about the local scene that I deemed useful to the smooth running of our green and pleasant land. Only very occasionally did I have cause to regret the relationship.

Joe Lennox left school—expensive, boarding—in the summer of the Tiananmen Square massacre of 1989. He was not an exceptional student, at least by the standards of the school, but left with three good A-levels (in French, Spanish and history), a place at Oxford and a private vow never to submit any children of his own to the peculiar eccentricities of the English private-school system. Contemporaries remember him as a quiet, popular teenager who worked reasonably hard and kept a low profile, largely, I suspect, because Joe's parents never lost an opportunity to remind their son of the "enormous financial sacrifices" they had made to send him away in the first place.

Unlike most of his contemporaries, who went off to pick fruit in Australia or smoke weed for six months on Koh Samui, Joe didn't take a gap year but instead went straight up to Oxford to study Mandarin as part of the BA Honours course at Wadham. Four years later he graduated with a starred First and was talent-spotted for Six in late 1993 by a tutor at the School of Oriental and African Studies, where he had gone to enquire about the possibility of doing a PhD. He went to a couple of interviews at Carlton Gardens, sailed through the Civil Service exams and had been positively vetted by the new year of 1994. Years later, Joe and I had dinner in London, when he began to speak candidly about those first few months as an Intelligence Branch officer.

"Think about it," he said. "I was twenty-three. I'd known nothing but straitjacket British institutions from the age of eight. Prep school, public school, Wadham College Oxford. No meaningful job, no serious relationship, a year in Taiwan learning Mandarin, where everyone ate noodles and stayed in their offices until eleven o'clock at night. When the Office vetted me for the EPV I felt like a standing joke: no police record; no debts; no strong political views—these were the Major years, after all; a single Ecstasy tablet swallowed in a Leeds nightclub in 1991. That was it. I was a completely clean slate, *tabula rasa*. They could do with me more or less as they pleased."

Vetting led to Century House, in the last months before the move to Vauxhall Cross. Joe was put into IONEC, the fabled initiation course for new MI6 recruits, alongside three other Oxbridge graduates (all male, all white, all in their thirties), two former soldiers (both Scots Guards, via Sandhurst) and a forty-year-old Welsh biochemist named Joanne who quit after six weeks to take up a $150,000-a-year position at MIT. On Joe's first day, "C" told the new intake that SIS still had a role to play in world affairs, despite the ending of the Cold War and the break-up of the Soviet Union. Joe specifically remembered that the Chief made a point, very early on, of emphasizing the importance of the "special relationship with our Cousins across the pond" and of praising the CIA for its "extraordinary technical resources," without which, it was implied, SIS would have been neutered. Joe listened, nodded and kept his head down, and within two months had been taken to the spook training centre at Fort Monckton, where he persuaded strangers in Portsmouth pubs to part with their passport numbers and learned how to fire a handgun. From the sources I've spoken to, it's fairly clear that Joe, in spite of his age, was considered a bit of a star. Spies, declared or otherwise, usually operate from the safety of British embassies overseas, using diplomatic cover as a means of running agents in hostile territories. Very early on, however, it was suggested that Joe would be most effective working under non-official cover in Asia, at long-term, deniable length from the Service. It was certainly a feather in his cap. While his fellow IONEC officers were moved into desk jobs in London, analysing intelligence and preparing for their first postings overseas, the Far East Controllerate was finding Joe a job in Hong Kong, ostensibly working as a freight forwarder at Heppner Logistics, a shipping company based in Jardine House. In reality he was a NOC, operating under non-official cover, by far the most sensitive and secret position in the intelligence firmament.

Joe turned twenty-four on the day he touched down at Kai Tak. His parents had seen him off at Heathrow under the misguided impression that their beloved only son was leaving England to seek his fortune in the East. Who knew? Perhaps he'd be back in a few years with a foxy Cantonese wife and a grandchild to show off in the Home Counties. Joe felt awkward not telling his family and friends the truth about what he was up to, but Six had advised against it. It was better that way, they said. No point in making anyone worry. Yet I think there were additional factors at play here. Secrecy appealed to something in Joe's nature, a facet of his personality that the spooks at Vauxhall Cross had recognized instantly, but which he himself had not yet fully come to understand. Lying to his parents felt like an act of liberation: for the first time in his life he was free of all the smallness and the demands of England. In less than a year Joe Lennox had cut himself off from everything that had made and defined him. Arriving in Hong Kong, he was born again.

Heppner Logistics was a tiny operation run out of two small offices on the eleventh floor of Jardine House, a fifty-two-storey edifice overlooking Victoria Harbour and dotted with tiny circular windows, an architectural anomaly which earned it the local nickname "The House of a Thousand Arseholes." Ted Heppner was a former Royal Marine who emigrated to Hong Kong in 1972. For eighteen years he had facilitated the international shipment of "sensitive" cargoes on behalf of SIS, but this was the first time that he had agreed to take on an intelligence officer as an employee. At first, Ted's Singaporean wife Judy, who also functioned as his secretary, wasn't keen on the idea, but when the Cross bought her a Chanel handbag and bumped up her salary by twenty per cent she embraced Joe like a long-lost son. Nominally he was required to show up every day and to field whatever faxes and phone calls came into the office from clients looking to move freight consignments around the world, but in reality Ted and Judy continued to deal with over ninety-five per cent of Heppner business, leaving Joe free to carry out his work for Queen and Country. If anybody asked why an Oxford graduate with a starred First in Mandarin was earning less than £20,000 a year working for a logistics company in Hong Kong, Joe told them that he'd been involved in a failed business venture back home and had just wanted to get the hell out of London. If they continued to pry, he hinted that he saw Heppner's as a short-term option which would allow him, within six or eight months, to apply for a job with one of the larger Taipan conglomerates, such as Swire's or Jardine Matheson.

It was illustrative of the extreme sensitivity of Joe's position that Ted and Judy were two of only a handful of people who knew that Joe was under non-official cover. The others included David Waterfield, Head of Station for SIS in Hong Kong, Waterfield's second-in-command, Kenneth Lenan, and Rick Zagoritis, a legendary figure in the Far East Controllerate who acted as Joe's mentor and go-between in the first few months of his posting. I became aware of his activities when Zagoritis was obliged to fly to London for medical reasons in the autumn of 1995. Up to that point, Rick had been my SIS handler. As a result of an article I had written for the *Sunday Times Magazine* about Teochiu triad heroin dealers, London had become interested in the contacts I had made in the criminal underworld and I had provided Zagoritis with detailed assessments of the structure and intentions of triad groups in the Pearl River Delta. With Rick gone, I needed a new handler.

That was when Joe stepped in. It was a considerable challenge for such a junior player, but he proved a more than competent replacement. Within less than a year of arriving in the colony, he had made a name for himself as a highly effective NOC. Nor were there any concerns about his private life. In two reports commissioned by Kenneth Lenan as routine checks into the behaviour of new recruits, Joe demonstrated himself to be surprisingly self-disciplined when confronted by the myriad opportunities for hedonism which are part and parcel of male expat life in Asia. ("He'll learn," Waterfield muttered glumly. "He'll learn.") Nor was he troubled by the paranoia and duplicity of his double life. One of the more potent myths of the secret world, put about by spy writers and journalists and excitable TV dramas, is that members of the intelligence community struggle constantly with the moral ambiguity of their trade. This may be true of a few broken reeds, most of whom are quietly shown the door, but Joe lost little sleep over the fact that his life in Hong Kong was an illusion. He had adjusted easily to the secret existence, as if he had found his natural vocation. He loved the work, he loved the environment, he loved the feeling of playing a pivotal role in the covert operations of the state. About the only thing that was missing in his life was a woman.

4 | ISABELLA

Isabella Aubert arrived at the restaurant at about twenty-past eight. The first indication that she had entered the room came with a simultaneous movement from two male diners sitting near the entrance whose heads jerked up from their bowls of soup and then followed her body in a kind of dazed, nodding parabola as she swayed between the tables. She was wearing a black summer dress and a white coral necklace that seemed to glow under the lights against her tanned skin. Joe must have picked up on the crackle in the room because he pushed his chair back from the table, stood up and turned to face her. Isabella was smiling by now, first at me, then at Joe, checking around the restaurant to see if she recognized anyone. Joe kissed her only briefly on the cheek before she settled into the chair next to mine. Physically, in public, they were often quite formal together, like a couple who had been married for five or ten years, not two twenty-six-year-olds in only the second year of a relationship. But if you spent time around Joe it didn't take long to realize that he was infatuated with Isabella. She dismantled his instinctive British reserve; she was the one thing in his life that he could not control.

"Hi," she said. "How are you, Will?" Our little hug of greeting went wrong when I aimed a kiss at her cheek that slid past her ear.

"I'm fine," I replied. "You?"

"Hot. Overworked. Late."

"You're not late." Joe reached out to touch her hand. Their fingers mingled briefly on the table before Isabella popped her napkin. "I'll get you a drink."

They had met in December 1995, on Joe's first visit back to the UK from Hong Kong, when he had been an usher at a wedding in Hampshire. Isabella was a friend of the bride who had struggled to keep a straight face while reading from "The Prophet" during the service. "Like sheaves of corn he gathers you unto himself," she told the assembled congregation. "He sifts you to free you from your husks. He grinds you to whiteness." At one point Joe became convinced that the beautiful girl at the lectern in the wide-brimmed hat was looking directly at him as she said, "He kneads you until you are pliant. And then he assigns you to his sacred fire, that you may become sacred bread for God's sacred feast," but it was probably just a trick of the light. At that moment, most of the men in the church were labouring under a similar delusion. Afterwards Isabella sought him out at the pre-dinner drinks, walking towards him carrying a glass of champagne and that hat, which had lost its flower.

"What happened?" he said.

"Dog," she replied, as if that explained everything. They did not leave one another's side for the next two hours. At dinner, seated at separate tables, they made naked eyes across the marquee as a farmer complained to Isabella about the iniquities of the Common Agricultural Policy while Joe told a yawning aunt on his left that freight forwarding involved moving "very large consignments of cargo around the world in big container ships" and that Hong Kong was "the second busiest port in Asia after Singapore," although "both of them might soon be overtaken by Shanghai." As soon as pudding was over he took a cup of coffee over to Isabella's table and sat at a vacant chair beside hers. As they talked, and as he met her friends, for the first time he regretted having joined SIS. Not because the life required him to lie to this gorgeous, captivating girl, but because within four days he would be back at his desk on the other side of the world drafting CX reports on the Chinese military. Chances are he would never see Isabella again.

Towards eleven o'clock, when the speeches were done and middle-aged fathers in red trousers had begun dancing badly to "Come on Eileen," she simply leaned across to him and whispered in his ear, "Let's go." Joe had a room at a hotel three miles away but they drove back along the M40 to Isabella's flat in Kentish Town, where they stayed in bed for two days. "We fit," she whispered when she felt his naked body against hers for the first time, and Joe found himself adrift in a world that he had never known: a world in which he was so physically and emotionally fulfilled that he wondered why it had taken him so long to seek it out. There had been girlfriends before, of course—two at Oxford and one just a few days after he had arrived in Hong Kong—but with none of them had he experienced anything other than the brief extinguishing of a lust, or a few weeks of intense conversations about the Cultural Revolution followed by borderline pointless sex in his rooms at Wadham. From their first moments together Isabella intrigued and fascinated him to the point of obsession. He confessed to me that he was already planning their lives together after spending just twenty-four hours in her flat. Joe Lennox had always been a decisive animal, and Joe Lennox had decided that he was in love.

On the Monday night he drove back to his hotel in Hampshire, settled the bill, returned to London and took Isabella for dinner at Mon Plaisir, a French restaurant he loved in Covent Garden. They ate French onion soup, steak tartare and confit of duck and drank two bottles of Hermitage Cave de Tain. Over balloons of Delamain—he loved it that she treated alcohol like a soft drink—Isabella asked him about Hong Kong.

"What do you want to know?" he said.

"Anything. Tell me about the people you work with. Tell me what Joe Lennox does when he gets up in the morning."

He was aware that the questions formed part of an ongoing

interview. Should I share my life with you? Do you deserve my future? Not once in the two days they had spent together had the subject of the distance that would soon separate them been broached with any seriousness. Yet Joe felt that he had a chance of winning Isabella round, of persuading her to leave London and of joining him in Hong Kong. It was fantasy, of course, not much more than a pipe dream, but something in her eyes persuaded him to pursue it. He did not want what they had shared to be thrown away on account of geography.

So he would paint a picture of life in Hong Kong that was vivid and enticing. He would lure her to the East. But how to do so without resorting to the truth? It occurred to him that if he told Isabella that he was a spy, the game would probably be over. Chances were she would join him on the next flight out to Kowloon. What girl could resist? But honesty for the NOC was not an option. He had to improvise, he had to work around the lie.

"What do I do in the morning?" he said. "I drink strong black coffee, say three Hail Marys and listen to the World Service."

"I'd noticed," she said. "Then what?"

"Then I go to work."

"And what does that involve?" Isabella had long, dark hair and it curled across her face as she spoke. "Do you have your own office? Do you work down at the docks? Are there secretaries there who lust after you, the quiet, mysterious Englishman?"

Joe thought about Judy Heppner and smiled. "No, there's just me and Ted and Ted's wife, Judy. We're based in a small office in Central. If I was to tell you the whole story you'd probably disintegrate with boredom."

"Are *you* bored by it?"

"No, but I definitely see it as a stepping stone. If I play my cards right there'll be jobs that I can apply for at Swire's or Jardine Matheson in a year or six months, something with a bit more responsibility, something with better pay. After university, I just wanted to get the hell out of London. Hong Kong seemed to fit the bill."

"So you like it out there?"

"I *love* it out there." Now he had to sell it. "I've only been away a few months but already it feels like home. I've always been fascinated by the crowds and the noise and the smells of Asia, the chaos just round the corner. It's so different to what I've grown up with, so *liberating*. I love the fact that when I leave my apartment building I'm walking out into a completely alien environment, a stranger in a strange land. Hong Kong is a British colony, has been for over ninety years, but in a strange way you feel we have no place there, no role to play." If David Waterfield could hear this, he'd have a heart attack. "Every face, every street sign, every dog and chicken and child scurrying in the back streets is Chinese. What were the British *doing* there all that time?"

"More," Isabella whispered, looking at him over her glass with a gaze that almost drowned him. "Tell me more."

He stole one of her cigarettes. "Well, at night, on a whim, you can board the ferry at Shun Tak and be playing blackjack at the Lisboa Casino in Macau within a couple of hours. At weekends you can go clubbing in Lan Kwai Fong or head out to Happy Valley and eat fish and chips in the Members Enclosure and lose your week's salary on a horse you never heard of. And the food is incredible, absolutely incredible. Dim sum, *char siu* restaurants, the freshest sushi outside of Japan, amazing curries, outdoor restaurants on Lamma Island where you point at a fish in a tank and ten minutes later it's lying grilled on a plate in front of you."

He knew that he was winning her over. In some ways it was too easy. Isabella worked all week in an art gallery on Albemarle Street, an intelligent, overqualified woman sitting behind a desk eight hours a day reading Tolstoy and Jilly Cooper, waiting to work her charms on the one Lebanese construction billionaire who just happened to walk in off the street to blow fifty grand on an abstract oil. It wasn't exactly an exciting way of spending her time. What did she have to lose by moving halfway round the world to live with a man she barely knew?

She took out a cigarette of her own and cupped Joe's hand as he lit it. "It sounds incredible," she said, but suddenly her face seemed to contract. Joe saw the shadow of bad news colour her eyes and felt as if it was all about to slip away. "There's something I should have told you."

Of course. This was too much of a good thing for it to end any other way. You meet a beautiful woman at a wedding, you find out she's terminally ill, married, or moving to Istanbul. The wine and the rich food swelled up inside him and he was surprised by how anxious he felt, how betrayed. What are you going to tell me? What's your secret?

"I have a boyfriend."

It should have been the hammer blow, the deal-closer, and Isabella was instantly searching Joe's face for a reaction. Somehow she managed to assemble an expression that was both obstinate and ashamed at the same time. But he found that he was not as surprised as he might have been, discovering a response to her confession which was as smart and effective as anything he might have mustered in his counter-life as a spy.

"You don't any more."

And that sealed it. A stream of smoke emerged from Isabella's lips like a last breath and she smiled with the pleasure of his reply. It had conviction. It had style. Right now that was all she was looking for.

"It's not that simple," she said. But of course it was. It was simply a question of breaking another man's heart. "We've been together for two years. It's not something I can just throw away. He needs me. I'm sorry I didn't tell you about him before."

"That's OK," Joe said. *I have lied to you, so it's only fair that you should have lied to me.* "What's his name?"

"Anthony."

"Is he married?"

This was just a shot in the dark, but by coincidence he had stumbled on the truth. Isabella looked amazed.

"How did you know?"

"Instinct," he said.

"Yes, he is married. Or was." Involuntarily she touched her face, covering her mouth as if ashamed by the role she had played in this. "He's separated now. With two teenage children . . ."

". . . who hate you."

She laughed. "Who hate me."

In the wake of this, a look passed between them which told Joe everything that he needed to know. So much of life happens in the space between words. She will leave London, he thought. She's going to follow me to the East. He ran his fingers across Isabella's wrists and she closed her eyes.

That night, drunk and wrapped in each other's bodies in the Christmas chill of Kentish Town, she whispered: "I want to be with you, Joe. I want to come with you to Hong Kong," and it was all he could do to say, "Then be with me, then come with me," before the gift of her skin silenced him. Then he thought of Anthony and imagined what she would say to him, how things would end between them, and Joe was surprised because he felt pity for a man he had never known. Perhaps he realized, even then, that to lose a woman like Isabella Aubert, to be cast aside by her, would be something from which a man might never recover.

5 | THE HOUSE OF A THOUSAND ARSEHOLES

Waterfield wasn't happy about it.

Closing the door of his office, eight floors above Joe's in Jardine House, he turned to Kenneth Lenan and began to shout.

"Who the fuck is Isabella Aubert and what the fuck is she doing flying eight thousand miles to play house with RUN?"

"RUN" was the cryptonym the Office used for Joe to safeguard against Chinese eyes and ears. The House of a Thousand Arseholes was swept every fourteen days, but in a crowded little colony of over six million people you never knew who might be listening in.

"The surname is French," Lenan replied, "but the passport is British."

"Is that right? Well, my mother had a cat once. Siamese, but it looked like Clive James. I want her checked out. I want to make sure one of our best men in Hong Kong isn't about to chuck in his entire career because some agent of the DGSE flashed her knickers at him."

The ever-dependable Lenan had anticipated such a reaction. As a young SIS officer in the sixties, David Waterfield had seen careers crippled by Blake and Philby. His point of vulnerability was the mole at the heart of the Service. Lenan consoled him.

"I've already taken care of it."

"What do you mean, you've already taken care of it?" He frowned. "Is she not coming? Have they split up?"

"No, she's coming, sir. But London have vetted. Not to the level of EPV, but the girl looks fine."

Lenan removed a piece of paper from the inside pocket of his jacket, unfolded it and began to improvise from the text: "Isabella Aubert. Born Marseilles, February 1973. Roman Catholic. Father Eduard Aubert, French national, insurance broker in Kensington for most of his working life. Womanizer, inherited wealth, died of cancer ten years ago, aged sixty-eight. Mother English, Antonia Chapman. 'Good stock,' I think they call it. Worked as a model before marrying Aubert in 1971. Part-time artist now, never re-married, lives in Dorset, large house, two Labradors, Aga, etcetera. Isabella has a brother, Gavin, both of them privately educated, Gavin at Radley, Isabella at Downe House. The former lives in Seattle, gay, works in computer technology. Isabella spent a year between school and university volunteering at a Romanian or-phanage. According to one friend the experience 'completely changed her.' We don't exactly know how or why at this stage. She didn't adopt one of the children, if that's the point the friend was getting at. Then she matriculates at Trinity Dublin in the au-tumn of '92, hates it, drops out after six weeks. According to the same friend she now goes 'off the rails for a bit,' heads out to Ibiza, works on the door at a nightclub for two summers, then meets Anthony Charles Ellroy, advertising creative, at a dinner party in London. Ellroy is forty-two, mid-life crisis, married with two kids. Leaves his wife for Isabella, who by now is working for a friend of her mother's at an art gallery in Green Park. Would you like me to keep going?"

"Ibiza," Waterfield muttered. "What's that? Ecstasy? Rave scene? Have you checked if she's run up a criminal record with the Guardia Civil?"

"Clean as a whistle. A few parking tickets. Overdraft. That's it."

"Nothing at all suspicious?" Waterfield looked out of the window at the half-finished shell of IFC, the vast skyscraper, almost twice the height of the Bank of China, which would soon dominate the Hong Kong skyline. He held a particular affection for Joe and was concerned that, for all his undoubted qualities, he was still a young man possibly prone to making a young man's mistakes. "No contact with liaison during this stint in Romania, for instance?" he said. "No particular reason why she chucks in the degree?"

"I could certainly have those things looked at in greater detail."

"Fine. Good." Waterfield waved a hand in the air. "And I'll have a word with him when the dust has settled. Arrange to meet her in person. What does she look like?"

"Pretty," Lenan said, with his typical gift for understatement. "Dark, French looks, splash of the English countryside. Good skin. Bit of mystery there, bit of poise. Pretty."

6 | COUSIN MILES

It wasn't a bad description, although it didn't capture Isabella's smile, which was often wry and mischievous, as if she had set herself from a young age to enjoy life, for fear that any alternative approach would leave her contemplating the source of the melancholy that ebbed in her soul like a tide. Nor did it suggest the enthusiasm with which she embraced life in those first few weeks in Hong Kong, aware that she could captivate both men and women as much with her personality as with her remarkable physical beauty. For such a young woman, Isabella was very sure of herself, perhaps overly so, and I certainly heard enough catty remarks down the years to suggest that her particular brand of self-confidence wasn't to everyone's taste. Lenan, for example, came to feel that she was "vain" and "colossally pleased with herself," although, like most of the stitched-up Brits in the colony, given half a chance he would have happily whisked her off to Thailand for a dirty weekend in Phuket.

At the restaurant that night I thought she looked a little tired and Joe and I did most of the talking until Miles arrived at about half-past eight. He was wearing chinos and flip-flops and carrying an umbrella; from a distance it looked as though his white linen shirt was soaked through with sweat. On closer inspection, once he'd shaken our hands and sat himself down next to Joe, it became clear that he had recently taken a shower and I laid a private bet with myself that he'd come direct from Lily's, his favourite massage parlour on Jaffe Road.

"So how's everybody doing this evening?"

The presence of this tanned, skull-shaved Yank with his deep, imposing voice lifted our easygoing mood into something more dynamic. We were no longer three Brits enjoying a quiet beer before dinner, but acolytes at the court of Miles Coolidge of the CIA, waiting to see where he was going to take us.

"Everybody is fine, Miles," Joe said. "Been swimming?"

"You're smelling that?" he said, looking down at his shirt as a waft of shower gel made its way across the table. Isabella leaned over and did a comic sniff of his armpits. "Just came from the gym," he said. "Hot outside tonight."

Joe stole a glance at me. He knew as well as I did of Miles's biweekly predilection for hand jobs, although it was something that we kept from Isabella. None of us, where girls were concerned, wanted to say too much about the venality of male sexual behaviour in the fleshpots of Hong Kong. Even if you were innocent, you were guilty by association of gender.

Did it matter that Miles regarded Asia as his own personal playground? I have never known a man so rigorous in the satisfaction of his appetites, so comfortable in the brazenness of his behaviour and so contemptuous of the moral censure of others. He was the living, breathing antithesis of the Puritan streak in the American character. Miles Coolidge was thirty-seven, single, answerable to very few, the only child of divorced Irish-American parents, a brilliant student who had worked two jobs while studying at the Georgetown School of Foreign Service, graduating *summa cum laude* in 1982 and applying almost immediately for a position with the Central Intelligence Agency. Most of his close friends in Hong Kong—including myself, Joe and Isabella—knew what he did for a living, though we were, of course, sworn to secrecy. He had worked, very hard and very effectively, in Angola, Berlin and Singapore before being posted to Hong Kong at almost the exact same time as Joe. He spoke fluent Mandarin, workable Cantonese, a dreadful, Americanized Spanish and decent German. He was tall and imposing and possessed that indefinable quality of self-assurance which draws beautiful women like moths to a flame. A steady procession of jaw-dropping girls—AP journalists, human rights lawyers, UN conference attendees—passed through the revolving door of his apartment in the Mid-Levels and I would be lying if I said that his success with women didn't occasionally fill me with envy. Miles Coolidge was the Yank of your dreams and nightmares: he could be electrifying company; he could be obnoxious and vain. He could be subtle and perceptive; he could be crass and dumb. He was a friend and an enemy, an asset and a problem. He was an American.

"You know what really pisses me off?" The waitress had brought him a vodka and tonic and handed out four menus and a wine list. Joe was the only person to start looking at them while Miles began to vent his spleen.

"Your guy Patten. I talked to some of his people today. You know what's going on down there at Government House? Nothing. You've got three months left before this whole place gets passed over to the Chinese and all anybody can think about is removals trucks and air tickets home and how they can get to kiss ass with Prince Charles at the handover before he boards the good ship *Rule Britannia*."

This was vintage Coolidge: a blend of conjecture, hard facts and nonsense, all designed to wind up the Brits. Dinner was never going to be a sedate affair. Miles lived for conflict and its resolution in his favour and took a particular joy in Joe's inability fully to argue issues of state in the presence of Isabella. She knew absolutely nothing about his work as a spy. At the same time, Waterfield had made Miles conscious of RUN back in 1996 as a result of blowback on a joint SIS/CIA bugging operation into the four candidates who were standing for the post of Chief Executive of the Hong Kong Special Administrative Region. That had created a nasty vacuum in the relationship between the four of us, and Miles was constantly probing at the edges of Joe's cover in a way that was both childish and very dangerous.

It is worth saying something more about the relationship between the two of them, which became so central to events over the course of the next eight years. In spite of all that he had achieved, there is no question in my mind that Miles was jealous of Joe: jealous of his youth, his background as a privileged son of England, of the apparent ease with which he had earned a reputation as a first-rate undercover officer after just two years in the job. Everything that was appealing about Joe—his decency, his intelligence, his loyalty and charm—was taken as a personal affront by the always competitive Coolidge, who saw himself as a working-class boy made good whose progress through life had been stymied at every turn by an Ivy League/WASP conspiracy of which Joe would one day almost certainly become a part. This was nonsense, of course—Miles had risen far and fast, in many cases further and faster than Agency graduates of Princeton, Yale and Harvard—but it suited him to bear a grudge and the prejudice gave his relationship with Joe a precariousness which ultimately proved destructive.

Of course there was also Isabella. In cities awash with gorgeous, ego-flattering local girls, it is difficult to overstate the impact that a beautiful Caucasian woman can have on the hearts and souls of Western men in Asia. In her case, however, it was more than just rarity value; all of us, I think, were a little in love with Isabella Aubert. Miles concealed his obsession for a long time, in aggression towards her as well as wild promiscuity, but he was always, in one way or another, pursuing her. Joe's possession of Isabella was the perpetual insult of Miles's time in Hong Kong. That she was Joe's girl, the lover of an Englishman whom he admired and despised in almost equal measure, only made the situation worse.

"When you say 'Patten's people,'" I asked, "who exactly do you mean?"

Miles rubbed his neck and ignored my question. He was usually wary of me. He knew that I was smart and independent-minded but he needed my connections as a journalist and therefore kept me at the sort of length which hacks find irresistible: expensive lunches, covered bar bills, tidbits of sensitive information exchanged in the usual quid pro quo. We were, at best, very good professional friends, but I suspected—wrongly, as it turned out—that the minute I left Hong Kong I would probably never hear another word from Miles Coolidge ever again.

"I mean, what exactly has that guy done in five years as governor?"

"You're talking about Patten now?" Joe's head was still in the menu, his voice uninflected to the point of seeming bored.

"Yeah, I'm talking about Patten. Here's my theory. He comes here in '92, failed politician, can't even hold down a job as a member of parliament; his ego must be going crazy. He thinks, 'I have to *do* something, I have to make my mark. The mansion and the private yacht and the gubernatorial Rolls-Royce aren't doing it for me. I have to be The Man.'"

Isabella was laughing.

"What's funny?" Joe asked her, but he was smiling too.

"Guber *what*?" she said.

"'Gubernatorial.' It means 'of the government.' A gift of office. Jesus. I thought your parents gave you guys an expensive education?"

"Anyway . . ." Joe said, encouraging Miles to continue.

"Anyway, so Chris is sitting there in Government House watching TV, maybe he's arguing with Lavender over the remote control, Whisky and Soda are licking their balls"—Lavender was Patten's wife, Whisky and Soda their dogs. Miles got a good laugh for this—"and he says to himself, 'How can I *really* mess this thing up? How can I make the British government's handover of Hong Kong to the People's Republic of China the biggest political and diplomatic shitstorm of modern times? *I know.* I'll introduce *democracy*. After ninety years of colonial rule in which none of my predecessors have given a monkey's ass about the six million people who live here, I'm gonna make sure China gives them a vote.'"

"Haven't we heard this before?" I said.

"I'm not finished." There was just enough time for us to order some food and wine before Miles started up again. "What's always really riled me about that guy is the hypocrisy, you know? He's presented himself as this Man of the People, a stand-up guy from the sole remaining civilized nation on the face of the earth, but you really think he wanted democracy for humanitarian reasons?"

"Yes I do." The firmness of Joe's interjection took us all by surprise. To be honest, I had assumed he wasn't listening. "And not because he enjoyed making waves, not because he enjoyed thumbing his nose at Beijing, but because he was doing his job. Nobody is saying that Chris Patten is a saint, Miles. He has his vanities, he has his ego, we all do. But in this instance he was brave and true to his principles. In fact it amazes me that people still question what he tried to do. Making sure that the people of Hong Kong enjoy the same quality of life under the Chinese government that they've enjoyed under British rule for the past ninety-nine years wasn't a particularly bold strategy. It was just common sense. It wasn't just the *right* thing to do morally; it was the *only* thing to do, politically and economically. Imagine the alternative."

Isabella did a comic beam of pride and grabbed Joe's hand, muttering, "Join us after this break, when Joe Lennox tackles world poverty . . ."

"Oh come on." Miles drained his vodka and tonic as if it were a glass of water. "I love you, man, but you're so fucking naïve. Chris Patten is a politician. No politician ever did anything except for his own personal gain."

"Are all Americans this cynical?" Isabella asked. "This deranged?"

"Only the stupid ones," I replied, and Miles threw a chewed olive stone at me. Then Joe came back at him.

"You know what, Miles?" He lit a cigarette and pointed it like a dart across the table. "Ever since I've known you you've been delivering this same old monologue about Patten and the Brits and how we're all in it for the money or the personal gain or whatever argument you've concocted to make yourself feel better about the compromises you make every day down at the American embassy. Well call me naïve, but I believe there is such a thing as a decent man and Patten is the closest thing you're going to get to it in public life." The arrival of our starters did nothing to deflect Joe from the task he had set himself. Miles pretended to be enthralled by his grilled prawns, but all of us knew he was about to get pummelled. "It's time I put you out of your misery. I don't want to come off sounding like a PR man for Chris Patten, but pretty much all of the commitments made to the people of Hong Kong five years ago have been fulfilled by his administration. There are more teachers in schools, more doctors and nurses in hospitals, thousands of new beds for the elderly. When Patten got here in '92 there were sixty-five thousand Cantonese living in slum housing. Now there are something like fifteen thousand. You should read the papers, Miles, it's all in there. Crime is down, pollution is down, economic growth up. In fact the only thing that hasn't changed is people like you bitching about Patten because he got in the way of you making a lot of money. I mean isn't that the argument? Appeasement? Isn't that the standard Sinologist line on China? Don't upset the suits in Beijing. In the next twenty years they'll be in charge of the second biggest economy in the world. We need them onside so we can build General Motors factories in Guangdong, investment banks in Shenzhen, sell Coca-Cola and cigarettes to the biggest market the world has ever known. What's a few votes in Hong Kong or a guy getting his fingernails ripped out by the PLA if we can get rich in the process? Isn't that the problem? Patten has given you a *conscience*."

Joe gave this last word real spit and venom and all of us were a little taken aback. It wasn't the first time that I had seen him really go at Miles for the lack of support towards Patten shown by Washington, but he had never done so in front of Isabella and it felt as though two or three tables were listening in. For a while we just picked at our food until the argument regained its momentum.

"Spoken like a true patriot," Miles said. "Maybe you're too good for freight forwarding, Joe. Ever thought about applying for a job with the Foreign Office?"

This was water off a duck's back. "What are you trying to say, Miles?" Joe said. "What's that chip telling you on your shoulder?"

This was one of the reasons Miles liked Joe: because he took him on; because he bullied the bully. He was smart enough to pick apart his arguments and not be daunted by the fact that Miles's age and experience vastly outweighed his own.

"I'll tell you what it's telling me. It's telling me that you're confusing a lot of different issues." Things were a little calmer now and we were able to eat while Miles held forth. "Patten pissed off a lot of people in the business community, here and on both sides of the Atlantic. This is not just an American phenomenon, Joe, and you know it. Everybody wants to take advantage of the Chinese market—the British, the French, the Germans, the fuckin' Eskimos—because, guess what, we're all capitalists and that's what capitalists *do*. Capitalism drove you here in your cab tonight. Capitalism is going to pay for your dinner. Christ, Hong Kong is the last outpost of the British Empire, an empire whose sole purpose was to spread capitalism around the globe. And having a governor of Hong Kong with no experience of the Orient parachuting in at the last minute trying to lecture a country of 1.3 billion people about democracy and human rights—a country, don't forget, that could have had this colony shut down in a *weekend* at any point over the past hundred years—well, that isn't the ideal way of doing business. If you want to promote democracy, the best way is to open up markets and engage with politically repressed countries at first hand so that they have the opportunity to see how Western societies operate. What you *don't* do is lock the stable door after the horse has not only bolted, but found itself *another* stable, redecorated, and settled down with a really fuckin' hot filly in a meaningful relationship." Joe shook his head but we were all laughing. "And to answer your accusation that my government didn't have a conscience until Chris Patten came along, all I can say is last time I checked we weren't the ones willingly handing over six million of our own citizens to a repressive communist regime twenty miles away."

It wasn't a bad retort and Isabella looked across at Joe, as if concerned that he was going to let her down. I tried to intervene.

"Confucius has been through all of this before," I said. " 'The superior man understands what is right; the inferior man understands what will sell.' "

Isabella smiled. "He also said, 'Life is very simple. It's men who insist on making it complicated.' "

"Yeah," said Miles. "Probably while getting jerked off by a nine-year-old boy."

Isabella screwed up her face. "If you ask my opinion—which I notice none of you are doing—both sides are as bad as each other." Joe turned to face her. "The British often act as though they were doing the world a favour for the last three hundred years, as if it was a privilege to be colonized. What everybody always seems to forget is that the empire was a money-making enterprise. Nobody came to Hong Kong to save the natives from the Chinese. Nobody colonized India because they thought they needed railways. It was all about making money." Miles had a gleeful look on his face. Seeing this, Isabella turned to him. "You Yanks are no better. The only difference, probably, is that you're more honest about it. You're not trying to pretend that you care about human rights. You just get on with doing whatever the hell you want."

All of us tried to jump in, but Miles got there first. "Look. I remember Tiananmen. I've seen the reports on torture in mainland China. I realize what these guys are capable of and the compromises we're making in the West in order to—"

Joe was pulled out of the conversation by the pulse of his mobile phone. He removed it from his jacket pocket, muttered a frustrated: "Sorry, hang on a minute," and consulted the screen. The read-out said: "Percy Craddock is on the radio," which was agreed code for contacting Waterfield and Lenan.

Isabella said, "Who is it, sweetheart?"

I noticed that Joe avoided looking at her when he replied. "Some kind of problem at Heppner's. I have to call Ted. Give me two minutes, will you?"

Rather than speak on a cellphone, which could be hoovered by one of the Chinese listening stations in Shenzhen, Joe made his way to the back of the restaurant where there was a payphone bolted to the wall. He knew the number of the secure line by heart and was speaking to Lenan within a couple of minutes.

"That was quick." Waterfield's *éminence grise* sounded uncharacteristically chirpy.

"Kenneth. Hello. What's up?"

"Are you having dinner?"

"It's OK."

"Alone?"

"No. Isabella is here with Will Lasker. Miles, too."

"And how is our American friend this evening?"

"Sweaty. Belligerent. What can I do for you?"

"Unusual request, actually. Might be nothing in it. We need you to have a word with an eye-eye who came over this morning. Not blind flow. Claims he's a professor of economics." "Blind flow" was a term for an illegal immigrant coming south from China in the hope of finding work. "Everybody else is stuck at a black-tie do down at Stonecutters so the baton has passed to you. I won't say any more on the phone, but there might be some decent product in it. Can you get to the flat in TST by ten-thirty?"

Lenan was referring to a safe house near the Hong Kong Science Museum in Tsim Sha Tsui East, on the Kowloon side. Joe had been there once before. It was small, poorly ventilated and the buzzer on the door had been burned by a cigarette. Depending on traffic, a taxi would have him there in about three-quarters of an hour. He said, "Sure."

"Good. Lee's looking after him for now, but he's refusing to speak to anyone not directly connected to Patten. Get Lee to fill you in when you get there. Apparently there's already a file of some sort."

Back in the dining area, Joe didn't bother sitting down. He stood behind Isabella—almost certainly deliberately, so that he didn't have to look at her—and put his hands on her shoulders as he explained that the bill of lading from a freight consignment heading to Central America had been lost in transit. It would have to be retyped and couriered to Panama before 2 a.m. Neither Miles nor myself, of course, believed this story for a minute, but we made a decent fist of saying, "Poor you, mate, what a nightmare," and "You'll be hungry" as Isabella kissed him and promised to be awake when he came home.

Once Joe had gone, Miles felt it necessary to polish off the lie and began a sustained diatribe against the phantom clients of Heppner Logistics.

"I mean, what's the matter with these people in freight? Bunch of fuckin' amateurs. Some asshole on a ship can't keep hold of a piece of paper? How tough is that?"

"They work him so hard," Isabella muttered. "That's the third time this month he's been called back to the office."

I was trying to think of ways of changing the subject when Miles chimed in again.

"You're right. You gotta guy there working hard, trying to climb the ladder from the bottom rung up, they're always the ones who get treated badly." He was enjoying having Isabella more or less to himself. "But it can't last. Joe is way too smart not to move onto bigger and better things. You have to stay positive, Izzy. *Mah jiu paau, mouh jiu tiuh.*"

"What the hell does that mean?"

It was Cantonese. Miles was showing off.

"Deng Xiaoping, honey. 'The horses will go on running, the dancing will continue.' Anybody join me in another bottle of wine?"

7 | WANG

Joe hailed a cab on the corner of Man Yee Lane and was grateful for the cooling chill of air conditioning as he climbed into the back. A humid three-minute walk from the restaurant had left his body encased in the damp, fever sweat which was the curse of living in Hong Kong: one minute you were in a shopping mall or restaurant as cool as iced tea, the next on humid streets that punched you with the packed heat of Asia. Joe's shirt glued itself to the plastic upholstery of the cab as he leaned back and said, "Granville Road, please," with sweat condensing on his forehead and sliding in drops down the back of his neck. Five feet from the cab, a group of Chinese men were seated on stools around a tiny television set drinking cans of Jinwei and watching a movie. Joe made out the squat, spike-haired features of Jean-Claude van Damme as the taxi pulled away.

Traffic on Des Voeux Road, coming both ways: buses, bicycles, trucks, cabs, all of the multi-dimensional crush of Hong Kong. The journey took forty minutes, under the cross-hatch of neon signs in Central, past the mamasans loitering in the doorways of Wan Chai, then dropping into the congested mid-harbour tunnel at North Point and surfacing, ten minutes later, into downtown

Kowloon. Joe directed the driver to within two blocks of the safe house and covered the last 200 metres on foot. He stopped at a street café for a bowl of noodles and ate them at a low plastic table in the heat of the night, sweat coagulating against his clothes. His shirt and the trousers of his suit seemed to absorb all of the dust and the grease and the slick fried stench of the neighbourhood. He finished his food and bought a packet of counterfeit cigarettes from a passing vendor, offering one to an elderly man jammed up at the table beside him; his smile of gratitude was a broken piano of blackened teeth. Joe drank stewed green tea and settled the bill and walked to the door of the safe house at the southern end of Yuk Choi Road.

The burned buzzer had been replaced with a blue plastic bell. Joe pushed it quickly, twice, paused for three seconds, then pushed it again in four short bursts to establish his identity. Lee came to the intercom, said, "Hello, fourth floor please," in his awkward, halting English, and allowed Joe to pass into a foyer which smelled, as all such foyers did in the colony, of fried onions and soy sauce.

Lee was thirty-two, very short, with neat clipped hair, smooth skin and eyes that constantly asked for your approbation. He said, "Hello, Mr. Richards," because that was the name by which he knew Joe.

"Hi, Lee. How are things?"

The stale air in the light-starved apartment had been breathed too many times. Joe could hear the high-frequency whine of a muted television in the sitting room as he laid his jacket on a chair in the hall. No air-con, no breeze. His only previous visit to the safe house had taken place on a cool autumnal day six months earlier, when Miles had done most of the talking, pretending to comfort a cash-strapped translator from a French trade delegation while three CIA stooges took advantage of his absence from the Hilton to ransack his room for documents. To the right of the hall was a cramped bathroom where Joe splashed water on his face before joining Lee in the kitchen.

"Where is he?"

Lee nodded across the hall towards a red plastic strip-curtain which functioned as the sitting-room door. The sound had come back on the television. Joe heard Peter O'Toole saying, "We want two glasses of lemonade," and thought he recognized both the film and the scene. "He watch *Lawrence of Arabia*," Lee confirmed. "With Sadha. Come with me into the back."

Joe followed the slap-and-drag of Lee's flip-flops as he walked through to the bedroom. Once inside, with the door closed, the two men stood in front of one another, like strangers at a cocktail party.

"Who is he?" Joe asked. "Mr. Lodge wasn't able to tell me very much on the phone."

Mr. Lodge was the name by which Kenneth Lenan was known to those former employees of the Hong Kong police force, Lee among them, who occasionally assisted SIS with their operations.

"The man's name is given as Wang Kaixuan. He claims to be a professor of economics at the University of Xinjiang in Urumqi City."

"So he's not a Uighur?"

Uighurs are the Turkic peoples of Xinjiang—pronounced "Shin-jang"—a once predominantly Muslim province in the far north-west of China which has been fought over, and colonized, by its many neighbours for centuries. Rich in natural resources, Xinjiang is China's other Tibet, the province the world forgot.

"No, Han Chinese, forty-eight years old. This morning at dawn he swam from the mainland to the east of Sha Tau Kok, where he became involved in a struggle with a soldier from Black Watch." Lee picked up the file that Lenan had mentioned and studied it for some time. Joe watched him flick nervously through the pages. "The soldier's name was Lance Corporal Angus Anderson, patrolling a beach on Dapeng Bay. Mr. Wang try to present himself as Hong Kong citizen, a birdwatcher, says he is a professor at the university here in Western District. Lance Corporal Anderson does not believe this story and they get into a struggle."

"Birdwatcher," Joe muttered. "What kind of struggle?"

Outside on the street a young man was trading insults in Cantonese with a woman who yelled at him as he gunned off on a motorbike.

"Nothing. No injury. But something about the situation makes

Anderson uneasy. Most blind flow in his experience do not speak fluent English, do not, for example, know much about the history of the Black Watch regiment. But Mr. Wang seems well informed about this, very different to what Anderson has been trained to look for. Then he begs him not to be handed over to immigration."

"Isn't that what you'd expect someone in his situation to do?"

"Of course. Only then he claims that he is in possession of sensitive information relating to the possible defection of a high-level Chinese government official."

"And Anderson swallowed this?"

"He take a risk." Lee sounded defensive. For the first time he was beginning to doubt the authenticity of the man who had spent the last three hours beguiling him with stories of China's terrible past, its awkward present, its limitless future. "The soldier walks him back to Black Watch base and tells his company commander what has happened."

"Barber was the company commander?" Joe was starting to put the pieces together.

"Yes, Mr. Richards. Major Barber."

Major Malcolm Barber, an ambitious, physically imposing Black Watch officer with impeccable contacts in the local military, was known to SIS as DICTION. He had been feeding regular gobbets of information to Waterfield and Lenan for three years on the tacit understanding that he would be offered a position within MI6 when he resigned his commission in 1998. To my knowledge he was last seen wandering around the Green Zone in Baghdad, trying to hatch plots against the local insurgency.

"And he believed the story? Got on the phone to Mr. Lodge and had him brought south for questioning?"

"That is correct. Mr. Lodge send a car to Sha Tau Kok. Had to make sure police and immigration know nothing about it. Every detail is in the report."

Joe thought the whole thing sounded ludicrous and briefly considered the possibility that he was being wound up. Professor of economics? Dawn swims across Dapeng Bay? A defection? It was the stuff of fantasy. Why would Lenan or Waterfield take it seriously? And why would they consider RUN for such a job? Surely by presenting himself to an unidentified eye-eye Joe was running the risk of breaking his cover. If most of his colleagues were up to their eyeballs in port and Stilton at a Stonecutters function, why not keep Wang overnight and have them tackle him in the morning? What was the hurry?

Lee handed the file to Joe, let out an exhausted breath and took a respectful step backwards. It was like marking a change of shift. Joe said, "Thank you," and sat on the bed. Barber had typed a covering letter, written in a tone which suggested that he shared the broad thrust of Anderson's conviction. Nevertheless, he had been wise enough to cover his back:

> I would be very surprised if Professor Wang turns out to be bona fide, but he is natural defector material, highly intelligent, immense charm and perfect English, clearly knows his way around the Chinese political structure, claims to have been tortured at Prison No. 3 in Urumqi sometime between 1995 and 1996. Has the scars to prove it. At the very least he may have the sort of local information in which HMG might be interested. Suggest you hold him for 24 hours, then we can spit him back to Shenzhen with no awkward questions asked. No harm in finding out what he has to say, etc. Of course always the danger that he might be a double, but that's your area of expertise. As far as the central claim regarding defection is concerned, I'm afraid I can't be much help. Wang is a sealed vault on that. Insists on speaking to CP in person. But he hasn't been difficult about it. In fact, rather grateful to us for "taking him seriously," etc. Best of luck.

"Has he said anything to you?"

Lee was sipping a glass of tea. Joe's question caught him off guard.

"About what, Mr. Richards?"

"About anything? About SIS setting up the defection? About swimming to Cambodia?"

"Nothing, sir. We talk about general Chinese political situation, but very little connected to the report. The conversations have been recorded in accordance with instructions from Mr. Lodge."

"And is that tape still running?"

"The tape is still running."

Joe gathered his thoughts. He had no experience of this sort of interrogation, only those particular skills of human empathy and intuition which had been recognized, and then nurtured so successfully, by SIS. He had left Isabella alone in a restaurant with two close friends whose good intentions towards his girlfriend he could not guarantee. He was very hot and craved a shower and a fresh set of clothes. It was going to be a long night. He followed Lee into the sitting room.

"Professor Wang, this is Mr. John Richards from Government House. The man I tell you about. He has come to see you."

Wang had not slept for twenty-four hours and it was beginning to show. The spring had gone out of his step. Rather than leap to his feet with the effervescence that Anderson would have recognized, he lifted himself slowly from an armchair in the corner, took two steps forward and shook Joe Lennox firmly by the hand.

"Mr. Richards. I am very glad to make your acquaintance. Thank you for coming to see me so late at night. I hope I have not been any inconvenience to you or to your organization."

What can you tell about a person right away? What can you take on trust? That Wang had the face of a man who was decent and courageous? That he looked both sharp and sly? Joe studied the broad, Han features, absorbed the power of the squat, surprisingly fit body and considered that last phrase: "*Your organization.*" Did Wang already suspect that he was British intelligence?

"It's no trouble at all," he said. "I've very much been looking forward to meeting you."

Wang was wearing the same blue jeans and black shirt into which he had changed on the beach. His tennis shoes were resting on the floor beside the armchair, a pair of grey socks balled into the heels. He looked to have made himself at home. Sadha, the burly Sikh charged with guarding Wang, nodded at Joe and excused himself, following Lee into the kitchen. In time Joe heard the bedroom door clunk shut. The sweat and the humidity of the hot Asian night had combined in the sitting room to leave a stench of work and men and waiting.

"What do you say we get some fresh air in here?"

Wang nodded and turned to open the window. Joe made his way across the room and parted the curtains to help him. It was as if they understood one another. Outside, the still night air remained stubbornly unmoved: no breeze ventured into the room, only the permanent cacophony of traffic and horns. To preserve the take quality of the microphones installed in the safe house, Joe decided to close the window and to begin again. The return of the heat and the silence seemed to act as an ice breaker.

"You are hot," Wang said. It was a statement more than a question.

"I am hot," Joe replied. Wang had the sort of face in which a man would willingly confide: eyes without malice, a smile of seductive benevolence. "Are you comfortable? Have you eaten? Is there anything that I can get you before we begin?"

"Nothing, Mr. Richards." Wang pronounced the name pointedly, as if he knew that it was not Joe's true identity and wished that they could dispense with the masquerade. "Your colleagues have looked after me far better than I could ever have anticipated. I have nothing but good things to say about British hospitality."

"Well that's wonderful." Joe gestured Wang back into his chair. There was a bottle of Watson's water resting on a low coffee table between them and he filled two white plastic cups to the rim. Wang leaned forward and accepted the drink with a nod of thanks. Joe settled back into Sadha's fake leather sofa and wondered how to kick things off. It seemed to be even hotter in the room at this lower level. Why couldn't Waterfield stretch to a fan? Who was running the safe house? Us or the Americans?

"So I would say that you are a very lucky man, Mr. Wang."

The professor frowned and a squint of confusion appeared in his eyes.

"How so?"

"You survive a very dangerous swim. You are surprised on the beach not by Hong Kong immigration, who would almost certainly have turned you back to China, but by a British soldier. You claim to have information about a possible defection. The army believes your story, contacts Government House, we send a nice, air-conditioned car to pick you up and less than twenty-four hours after leaving China here you are sitting in a furnished apartment in Tsim Sha Tsui watching *Lawrence of Arabia*. I'd say that qualifies as luck."

Wang looked across the room at the small black-and-white television set, now switched off, and his face elasticated into a broad, wise smile. He sipped his water and looked over the cup at Joe. "Seen from that point of view, I of course share your opinion, Mr. Richards. May I ask, what position do you hold within Government House?"

"I am an assistant to Mr. Patten's senior political adviser."

"But you are still very young, no? Young enough to have been one of my students, I think."

"Perhaps," Joe said. "And you are old enough to have been one of my professors."

Wang liked that one. The professor's delighted expression suggested the intense relief of a cultured man who, after a long hiatus, has finally encountered evidence of intelligent conversation.

"I see, I see," he laughed. "And where did you study, Mr. Richards?"

"Call me John," Joe said, and felt that there was no harm in adding, "Oxford."

"Ah, Oxford." A Super 8 of dreamy spires and pretty girls on bicycles seemed to play behind Wang's eyes. "Which college, please?"

"I studied Mandarin at Wadham."

"With Professor Douglas?"

That impressed him. There was no getting round it. For some reason Wang knew the identity of Oxford's leading authority on imperial Chinese history. "No. Professor Vernon," he said.

"Oh. I do not know him."

They paused. Joe shifted his weight on the sofa and his hand slid into a dent the size of a beach ball created by Sadha's substantial girth. Wang was watching him all the time, trying to assess the hierarchical importance of his interlocutor and wondering whether to reveal something of his terrible secret to a probable agent of the British SIS.

"And you, Professor Wang? What's your story? Why does a highly educated Chinese intellectual with a position at a prestigious university wish to flee his homeland? Why didn't you go through the normal channels? Why not just apply for a visa? Surely you have friends in Hong Kong, family you could visit? Why risk your life swimming across Starling Inlet?"

"Because I had no choice."

"No choice?"

"This was no longer an option for a man like me. I had lost my job. I was no longer permitted to leave China."

"You've lost your job? That's not what you told Major Barber."

Wang tilted his head to one side and the poor light in the room momentarily lent his face the granite stillness of a sculpture. "I was concerned that the British army would not take my situation seriously. I had already been very lucky to be captured by a soldier with the Black Watch. I lied in order to increase my chances of remaining in Hong Kong. For this I apologize."

"Well at least you're honest," Joe said, with more candour than he had intended. He felt an odd, almost filial sympathy for Wang, and found his position of power over him oddly disconcerting. "Tell me, why are you no longer permitted to leave China?"

"Because I am regarded as a political undesirable, a threat to the Motherland. My actions as an academic drew me to the attention of the authorities in Xinjiang, who jailed me along with many of my students."

"What kind of actions?" Joe remembered the line in Barber's letter—*Has the scars to prove it*—and wondered why a man like Wang would be tipping the British off about a high-level defection. From the start he had doubted this element of the professor's story: ten-to-one it was just another ruse to win his way past Anderson. More likely, the professor was simply a radicalized intellectual who had fostered anti-Beijing sentiment on campus. That was the sort of thing for which you were flung in jail in China. It happened all the time. "Why was it necessary for you to leave China?" he asked.

"As I have told you and your colleagues many times, I am holding information for the British government which will be of vital importance to the relationship between our two countries. That is why I have to see Governor Patten immediately."

Joe smiled. He knew now that he was being lied to, in the way that you know when a person is bored by your company. "And where do you want to meet him?" he asked. "Surely not in Government House? Aren't the Chinese disdainful of our *feng shui*?"

This was intended as a joke, but Wang did not find it funny. Speaking in Mandarin for the first time, he said, "Do not make fun of me, young man."

"Then tell me the truth." Joe wasn't about to be patronized and snapped back his response. He was struck by the sudden fierceness in Wang's gaze, not because it unsettled him, but because for the first time he could see the force of the professor's will.

"I am telling you the truth."

"Well, then I'm sorry to have to inform you that a meeting of that kind is highly unlikely. I am as close to Governor Patten as you are likely to get. And unless I leave here tonight with some firm answers, the Black Watch are under instructions to return you to China without delay. Your presence here contravenes political understandings between our two countries."

Wang breathed very deeply so that his chin lifted to the ceiling. Joe's sudden shift in mood had forced his hand and he was now at the edge of his luck. He would have to confide in this Mr. John Richards, whoever he was, and run the risk that his revelation would simply be ignored by an indifferent British spy.

"Why don't . . ."

Both men had started speaking at the same time. Joe said, "Go ahead."

"You first, please."

"Fine." Joe wanted to light a cigarette but decided against it. The air in the tiny room was already stale and unpleasant enough. "When you were first interrogated by Lance Corporal Anderson, you mentioned an apartment here in Kowloon." He thought back to Barber's report and recalled the address from memory. "Number 19, 71 Hoi Wang Road. What was the significance of that?"

"There was no significance. I made it up."

"Just like that?"

Wang did not understand the idiom and asked for a translation in Mandarin. Joe provided it and the conversation briefly continued in Chinese.

"So Hoi Wang Road is not the address of someone you know here in Hong Kong? It's not an apartment at which you have stayed on any previous visit to the colony?"

"I have never been to Hong Kong before."

Joe made a mental note to have the address investigated before reverting to English. "And why now?" he said. "Why do you have to see Governor Patten in person?"

Wang stood up. When he turned towards the window and leaned against the curtains, Joe had a sudden mental image of the popular professor organizing his notes in a packed Urumqi lecture hall, preparing to address a room full of eager students. "Because he is the only man in any Western government who has demonstrated an interest in the preservation of our basic human rights. Because he is the only man who might have the power to do something about this."

"About what? We're talking about human rights now? I thought you wanted to talk about a defection?"

Wang turned round and stepped closer to Joe. He looked angry, as if finally exasperated by a long day of pressure and lies. "Mr. Richards, you are clearly an intelligent man. You know as well as I do that I know nothing about any plans for any member of the Chinese state apparatus to defect. You know as well as I do that this was a story I invented to assist my journey to Hong Kong."

"So what *do* you know?" Joe wasn't surprised by the sudden confession. It had been coming for some time. "What is this pressing story you want to share with us? What makes you think that the British government is in any sort of position to grant political asylum to a man like you? What makes Professor Wang Kaixuan so special?"

And Wang fixed him hard in the eyes and said, "I will tell you."

8 | XINJIANG

"My father's name was Wang Jin Song." On the surveillance recording you can hear an eerie silence in that cramped, air-starved safe house, as if all of Hong Kong were suddenly listening in. "He was born in Shanghai and worked as a schoolteacher in the Luwan district, close to People's Square. He married my mother, Liu Dong Mei, in 1948. She was the daughter of a Kuomintang soldier killed during the Japanese invasion. I was born in 1949, Mr. Richards, so at least I share a birthday with the People's Republic of China, if nothing else. When I was five years old, my parents were obliged to relocate to Xinjiang province as part of Mao's policy of mass Han immigration. Perhaps you have heard of this? Perhaps it was mentioned in one of your lectures at Oxford? *Sinicization*, I think they call it in English. I apologize if I am not correct in my pronunciation. Based on a Soviet model, the Stalinist idea of diluting a native people with the dominant imperial race, so that this native population is gradually destroyed. My parents were two of perhaps half a million Han who settled in Xinjiang during this period. My father was given a job as a schoolteacher in Kashgar and we lived in a house that had been owned by a Uighur landowner whom my father believed had been executed by the communists. This was part of Mao's gradual purging of the Muslim elite, the execution of imams and noblemen, the confiscation of Uighur properties and the seizure of lands. All of this is a matter of historical record."

"Let a hundred flowers bloom," Joe said, trying to sound clever, but Wang produced a look of reproach which corrected him.

"That came later." There was an edge of disappointment in the professor's voice, as if a favourite student had let him down. "Of course, when my family had been living in Kashgar for two or three years, they became aware of the policy that we now know as the hundred flowers bloom. The Party's seemingly admirable desire to listen to the opinions of its people, of Party members, in this case the Uighur population. But Mao did not like what he heard. He did not like it, for example, that Turkic Muslims resented the presence of millions of Han in their country. He did not like it that Uighurs complained that they were given only nominal positions of power, while their Han deputies were the ones who were trusted and rewarded by Beijing. In short, the people demanded independence from communist China. They demanded the creation of an Eastern Turkestan."

"So what happened?"

"What happened is what always happens in China when the people confront the government. What happened was a purge." Wang helped himself to another glass of water. Joe had the feeling that the story had been told many times before, and that it was perhaps best to avoid any further interruptions. "A Party conference was called in Urumqi, but rather than listen to their complaints, the provincial government took the opportunity to arrest hundreds of Uighur officials. Fifty were executed. Without trial, of course. Trials do not exist in my country. This is what became of the flowers that bloomed, this is what became of Mao's promise to create an independent Uighur republic. Instead, Xinjiang became an 'autonomous region,' which it remains to this day, much as Tibet is 'autonomous,' and I surely do not need to educate you about that."

"We are aware of the parallels with Tibet," Joe said, a statement as empty, as devoid of meaning, as any he had uttered all night. What did he mean by "we?" In three years as an SIS officer he had heard Xinjiang mentioned—what?—two or three times at official level, and then only in connection to oil supplies or gas fields. Xinjiang was just too far away. Xinjiang was somebody else's problem. Xinjiang was one of those places, like Somalia or Rwanda, where it was better that you just didn't get involved.

"Let me continue my little history lesson," Wang suggested, "because it is important in the context of what I will tell you later. In 1962, driven by hunger and loss of their land and property, many Uighur families crossed the border into the Soviet Union, into areas that we now know as Kazakhstan and Kyrgyzstan. This was a shaming moment for Beijing, a terrible loss of face in the eyes of their sworn enemy in Moscow, and it created problems for any Uighur family who remained in Xinjiang with relatives in the Soviet Union. In the madness of the Cultural Revolution, for example, a man could be imprisoned simply for having a brother living in Alma-Ata. I was by now a teenager, a diligent student, and it was in this period that I began to understand something of these historical injustices and to see my father for the man he was. You see, it is difficult to be brave in China, Mr. Richards. It is difficult to speak out, to have what you in the West would call 'principles.' To do these things is to risk annihilation." Wang rolled his neck theatrically. "But my father believed in small gestures. It is these gestures which kept him sane. When he saw examples of disrespect, for example of racism, of the typical Han contempt for Uighur or Kazakh people, he would admonish the guilty, in the street if necessary. I once witnessed my father punch a man who had insulted a Uighur woman as she queued to buy bread. He made presents of food and clothing for impoverished native families, he listened to their ills. All of these things were dangerous at that time. All of these things could have led to my father's imprisonment, to a life in the gulag for our family. But he taught me the most valuable lesson of my life, Mr. Richards. Respect for your fellow man."

"That *is* a valuable lesson," Joe said, and the remark again sounded like a platitude, although in his defence he was growing restless. In Chinese storytelling there is a tradition of long-windedness of which Wang was taking full advantage.

"But gradually things improved after the death of Mao. When I was a student, studying at the university in Urumqi, it seemed that the Party developed a more sympathetic attitude to the native peoples. During the previous decade, mosques had been shut down or converted into barracks, even into stables for pigs and cattle. Mullahs had been tortured, some ordered to clean the streets and the sewers. Loyalty to a communist system was demanded of these men of God. But the bad times briefly passed. For once I was not ashamed to be Han, and it was a source of deep regret to me that my parents had not lived to see this period for themselves. For the first time under communism, China officially acknowledged that the Uighurs of Xinjiang were a Turkic people. Nomads who had roamed the region for centuries were allowed to continue their traditional way of life as the Marxist ideologues realized that these men of the land would never be loyal state workers, could never alter their lives to suit a political system. At the same time, the Arabic language was restored to the Uighurs, their history once again studied in schools. Koranic literature was circulated without fear of arrest or punishment and many of those who had had land or property confiscated by the state were compensated. It was a better time, Mr. Richards. A better time."

Joe was conflicted. As a student of China, a Sinophile, to hear the history of the region related so intimately by one who had lived through it was a rare and valuable experience: the scholar in him was enthralled. The spy, on the other hand, was frustrated: RUN was failing in his Lenan-appointed task to squeeze the truth out of a man who had risked his life in the waters of Dapeng Bay to bear a potentially priceless secret into the arms of British intelligence. But Wang seemed no closer to revealing it.

"And what was your role at this time?" he asked, in an attempt to push the conversation along.

"I was in my thirties. I was teaching and lecturing at the university. I had completed postgraduate work at Fudan University and was determined only to succeed in my career as an academic. In other words, I was a moral coward. I did nothing for the separatist movement, even as Uighur students protested the barbarism of nuclear testing, even as they took to the streets to demand the reinstatement of the Uighur governor of Xinjiang who had been forcibly and unfairly removed from power."

"And then came Tiananmen Square. Is that what changed you?"

The question had been no more than an instinctive lunge for information, but Wang reacted as though Joe had unlocked a code. "Yes, Mr. Richards," he said, nodding his head. "You are correct." He looked almost startled. As Wang cast his mind back to the events of 1989, recalling all of the horror and the shock of that fateful summer, his face assumed a dark, contemplative mask of grief. "Yes," he said. "The massacre in Tiananmen changed everything."

9 | CLUB 64

By coincidence, Miles, Isabella and I were drinking at Club 64 in Wing Wah Lane, a Hong Kong institution named after the date of the Tiananmen massacre, which took place on the fourth day of the sixth month of 1989. Shortly after midnight, in the middle of a conversation about Isabella's new job—she was working for a French television company in the run-up to the handover—Miles excused himself from our table and went downstairs to make a phone call.

On the consulate recording of the conversation, the official who picks up sounds startled and sleepy.

"I wake you?"

"Hey, Mr. Coolidge. What's happening?"

Miles was using the bar landline, feeding coins into the slot. "Just a question. You guys have any idea where Joe Lennox went tonight? He got a call at dinner and took off pretty quick."

"Heppner Joe?"

"That's him."

"Let me check."

There was a long pause. I walked downstairs on my way to the gents just as Miles was taking the opportunity to check his reflection in a nearby mirror. He wiped a sheen of sweat from his fore-head, then ducked his nose into his armpits to check for BO. He saw me looking at him and we exchanged a nod as I passed.

"Mr. Coolidge?"

"Still here."

"We're not getting anything from the computer, but Sarah says somebody's using Yuk Choi Road."

"The safe house?"

"Looks that way."

"Who's in there?"

"Hold on."

Another lengthy delay. Miles had another look in the mirror.

"Mr. Coolidge?"

"Yup."

"From the audio it sounds like just Joe and one other guy."

"British or Chinese?"

"Chinese. But they're speaking English. You know anything about this?"

"No," Miles said. "But I know somebody who will."

10 | ABLIMIT CELIL

The Uighur, Ablimit Celil, drove the maintenance truck though the gates of the People's Liberation Army barracks at Turpan at approximately 6:15 a.m. A soldier, not much older than nineteen or twenty, stepped out of his hutch and waved the truck to a stop.

"What is your business?"

"To clean," Celil replied. He did not make eye contact with the soldier. The uniform was the embodiment of Han oppression and control and Celil always tried to maintain his dignity when confronted by it. "Please direct me to the kitchens."

Asleep on the seats beside him were two other Uighur men, both well-known faces around the barracks. The young soldier shone a torch into their eyes.

"Wake up!"

The order was a shrill, authoritarian bark. The men stirred, shielding their faces from the light. It was a cold morning in eastern Xinjiang and the open window of the truck had quickly robbed the cabin of heat and comfort. The soldier appeared to recognize both men before returning his gaze to Celil.

"Who are you?" he said. He shone the torch into Celil's face, then down into his lap.

"He's the new cleaner," one of the men replied. Celil had been pestering them for months to find him a job. "It's all been cleared with your superiors."

"*Shen fen zheng!*"

Another barked command, this time a request for identification. There was distrust and mutual suspicion in almost every encounter between the PLA and members of the local Uighur population who worked on the barracks. Celil reached into the back pocket of his trousers and produced the fake ID prepared for him in the back streets of Hami. There followed the obligatory ten-minute delay while the soldier returned to his hutch to record the details of the *shen fen zheng* in a logbook. He then walked back to the truck, returned the papers to Celil and instructed one of his comrades, who operated the security barrier separating the barracks from the main road, to allow the vehicle to pass. A minute later, Celil had parked the truck beneath the first-floor window of the catering block.

For the rest of the day, the three men went about their business. They cleaned toilets, urinals, ovens. They polished floors, windows, pictures. The soldiers of the People's Liberation Army ignored them as they went about their business.

Celil, a more devout Muslim than the two men with whom he had travelled to work, was prevented from praying during the day. There was, of course, no mosque at the barracks, nor any area set aside for the *salaah*. For half an hour at lunch the three men were allowed to return to their truck, where they ate bread and sheep's cheese, washed down with tea kindly provided by a Han woman who prepared soup in the kitchens.

At approximately 1:30 p.m., when his Uighur colleagues had returned to work in the dormitory building on the western edge of the barracks, Celil opened the rear doors of the truck and stepped inside. He picked up a large cardboard box and carried it into the kitchens. Bottles of sprays and cream cleaners protruded from the top; old rags, stained and torn, had been wedged between them. Nobody paid any attention as he walked into the hall which separated the kitchens from the main dining area and walked downstairs towards the basement. The floors still smelled of cleaning fluid; he had washed them just an hour earlier.

Celil knew that there was a store cupboard located on the landing between the basement and the ground floor. It contained overalls, brooms and various cleaning products. He unlocked the door, placed the cardboard box at the back of the cupboard and concealed it with a screen of buckets and mops. The timer had been set for 8 p.m. He then switched off the light, locked the door behind him and returned to the second floor, where he spent the next three hours cleaning windows.

Ablimit Celil's first and last day at the barracks ended at dusk. He had wanted to check the device at least once to ensure that the timer was running, but could not risk being seen by a passing soldier. Instead he climbed into the truck with his colleagues at seven o'clock and drove towards the gates.

There were two new soldiers on duty at the barrier. As Celil approached, the Uighurs beside him said that they had not seen either man before.

"*Shen fen zheng!*"

"We are going home," Celil replied. "Your colleague checked our IDs this morning."

"*Shen fen zheng!*"

It was part of the game. Wearily the three men produced their papers and passed them through the open window. The soldier, more experienced and intelligent than the colleague who had allowed them through at dawn, flicked through the documents with a lazy ruthlessness.

"Name?" he said to Celil. He was looking directly into his eyes.

"Tunyaz," Celil replied. It was the fake name on the *shen fen zheng.*

"Where were you born?"

"Qorak."

Very slowly, he turned his gaze to the two men beside Celil and asked them the same questions. Name? Where were you born?

He asked to be shown into the rear of the truck, with the clear implication that the men might have stolen items from the barracks. Celil duly stepped down and opened the rear door of the vehicle. The soldier stepped inside. The truck was full of boxes, blankets, empty plastic bottles and discarded packets of cigarettes. It was soon twenty-past seven. No other vehicles had pulled up behind the truck, so there was no need for the soldier to hurry.

Just after half-past seven, a blacked-out Oldsmobile, driven by a uniformed chauffeur, was waved through the barrier ahead of them. The soldier went into his hutch. Celil knew now that he should have set the timer for half-past eight or even nine o'clock. He had learned, by listening carefully to the conversations of his friends, that dinner was served in the catering block at precisely eight o'clock. He had wanted to ensure maximum carnage in the dining area, but now he feared that the truck would still be parked outside at the gate when the bomb exploded.

Finally, with only fifteen minutes remaining, the soldier emerged from the hutch and opened the barrier. Celil had switched off the engine, and he waited to be instructed to turn it back on. You could never be too careful. The game was humiliation. The game was threat and this might be a trap. The soldier was just waiting for him to make the wrong move. Finally, a gesture towards the road. They were waved through.

"Have a good night," Celil told him as he pulled out into the evening traffic. "See you again in the morning."

The bomb tore through the thin prefabricated walls of the storeroom, the force of the detonation driven upwards and collapsing a large central section of the catering building. Eight Han soldiers and four staff—among them a young Uighur woman— were killed instantly by the blast. Dozens more were injured and several nearby buildings wrecked.

Ablimit Celil dropped his Uighur colleagues at their homes at 8:05 p.m. Later that night, they were arrested. Celil himself drove to the prearranged point at Toksun, where he abandoned the truck and boarded a night bus for Hami.

"**May I ask** you something, Mr. Richards?"

Wang had broken off the conversation in order to use the bathroom and he posed the question as he came back into the room, rubbing his eyes before settling down in his chair. Joe noticed that he betrayed no signs of physical injury or discomfort.

"Of course."

"At what point were you recruited as a spy by British intelligence?"

Joe had been trained to deflect accusations of this kind but he was momentarily stunned. It was the first time in his career that anybody had directly questioned his cover. Wang seemed to detect his disquiet and looked pleased, as if he had gained face at Joe's expense.

"I can assure you, professor, I am no more a spy than Lance Corporal Anderson. Believe me, when you talk to me you are talking directly to Government House. What is it that you want to tell us?"

The lie was met with a blank, indifferent stare. "Fine." Wang rubbed the palm of his left hand vigorously across the near-stubble of his close-cropped hair and leaned forward. Joe, rolling up the sleeves of his shirt, finally capitulated to his desire for a cigarette.

"You spoke of Tiananmen," Wang said. "You asked me to explain what has happened in my country since the massacre of 1989, what has happened while the world's back has been turned. I will tell you. While America and France and Germany and England have fixated on the Chinese economic boom, dreaming of their yachts and profits, young men have had their fingernails torn out in Chinese prisons, their testicles burned by electric pipes, their bodies broken by torture."

Joe did not light his cigarette.

"Two months before the Tiananmen massacre there was a demonstration in Urumqi. A sit-in by students, partly in support of their comrades in Beijing, but also as a religious protest at the depiction of Muslim sexual customs in a book circulated throughout the country. This demonstration became a riot, Mr. Richards, a riot in which Communist Party headquarters in the capital was attacked and more than two hundred police injured. We now look back on it as a mistake, because it confirmed in Beijing their worst fears about the separatist movement." Joe noted the "we" here, the inference that Wang had been directly involved. "As the Soviet Union broke up, as the Islamic border nations began to assert their authority once more after years of oppression under communism, the Chinese government reverted to its hardline stance on Xinjiang. Islam was once again viewed as a threat to the Republic. Mosques that had only recently been rebuilt were destroyed. Those who attended study meetings to learn more about the Koran were arrested and thrown into prison. The Arabic language was once again banned. Matters became so serious that one of my students, Yasin, told me that his father, who worked in a government office in Karamay, had been warned that he would lose his job if he attended daily prayers. During Ramadan, the police actually *spied* on certain individuals in the Uighur community to ensure that they were prevented from observing the fast. Can you *imagine* such a humiliation? How would the good citizens of Iowa, or of Liverpool, feel if they were forbidden to practise their faith? In some areas, women were punished for wearing headscarves. Even devout Muslims who denied themselves alcohol in observance of sacred custom were forced to drink *maotai* by Communist Party officials. This has been the reality of China in the last decade, Mr. Richards. This has been the reality of the country to which you will soon hand over your precious Hong Kong."

"And what has been your role during this period?" Joe was still trying to do his job, still trying to suck out the secret.

"Do you know what a *meshrep* is?" Wang asked, apparently evading the question. Joe said that he did not. "A *meshrep* is a traditional form of gathering for young people in Xinjiang. These youth groups existed for positive reasons. To revive Islamic traditions, for young men to recite poems, to sing music and so on. You would think of them in the West perhaps as a community or social project, where problems of alcohol or drug abuse within the population are openly discussed with a view to improving the lifestyles and conditions of all young Muslims throughout the region. The first of these *meshreps* was revived in the city of Gulja, in Ili Prefecture, a city known to the Han as Yining. Within a few years there were dozens of them throughout Xinjiang, perhaps as many as four hundred, and all established with the strict agreement of the provincial government. Because what could be wrong with this? Young Uighur people trying to solve their own problems and, at the same time, revive their traditions in a sensible fashion."

"But the authorities cracked down?"

"Absolutely." A sheen of sweat had appeared on Wang's forehead, which glistened in the low light of the room. "In 1995 it was declared that the *meshreps* were cover organizations for separatist radicals seeking to undermine the Motherland. They must be closed down, their leaders arrested. This was the paranoid state of our government in Beijing, who cannot sleep in their beds for fear of an uprising, for fear of an Eastern Turkestan. Four students from a *meshrep* in Kashgar were subsequently arrested in that year for allegedly discussing political and human rights issues at a birthday picnic. A *picnic*. Beijing has informers at every level of Chinese society and they had mistakenly trusted one of their own friends, who had reported them. These young men were then accused of being counter-revolutionaries and sentenced to fifteen years in prison. When one of them appealed to the People's High Court, his sentence was actually *increased* by the judge, who accused him of wasting the court's time. It is a situation that Kafka would recognize, no?"

Joe remained still.

"All of these many issues have come to a head in the last two years. The Uighur people were tired of racial abuse, tired of discrimination from the state, tired of sending their children to schools where they were obliged to write sitting on the floor because of a lack of desks and chairs. Unemployment is running so high among Uighurs in Xinjiang that the sons and daughters of proud Muslims have been obliged to turn to crime, even to prostitution, in order to provide for their families. Of course this only deteriorates their image in the eyes of the Han men who use up these women for sex and then discard them like old bones." Joe noticed that Wang's voice was gradually growing louder, his rhetoric increasing to a politician's intensity. "Let me now tell you that when thousands of Uighurs gathered in Yining in February of this year to make a peaceful protest, to demand better jobs, better working conditions, they were gunned down by armed police."

Joe started forward. "Gunned down? What do you mean?"

"I mean what I say." Wang looked angry, as if Joe had questioned his integrity. "I mean that the police beat them with sticks, they used tear gas, they attacked them with dogs. Those with cameras or recording equipment who attempted to witness what was happening had these items confiscated. And as the people saw what was happening, the riot exploded."

"And this is when the shooting began? This was in Yining two months ago?" Finally Joe had sight of the product, another Tiananmen that all of his veteran colleagues appeared to have missed.

"That is correct. We estimate that four hundred people were killed, thousands more arrested. The jails became so full that prisoners were taken to a sports stadium on the outskirts of the city, where they were obliged to live for days without shelter in the snow. The police hosed them with water cannons to make their situation worse. Some froze as a result. Many lost hands and fingers through frostbite."

"None of this has been reported in the West," Joe said, a statement which he believed to be true. Had they all been so wrapped up in the handover, in Patten's democratic reforms, that they had ignored mass slaughter in China? He was witnessing, more or less for the first time in his career, the operational limitations of Western intelligence. With all their money, all their resources and know-how, SIS and the CIA had been blindsided by a massacre in China. Joe thought that he should be seen to write something down, to give Wang the impression, however false, that the safe house was not wired for sound. But the professor was in the sweat of a sustained revelation, apparently paying little attention to how Joe was behaving.

"A curfew was imposed," he said. "You must have learned of this. All airports and railway stations in Xinjiang were shut down for weeks. All foreign journalists were expelled from the region. The entire area was sealed. This is what they do in China when they have a problem. Nobody comes in, nobody gets out. In the wake of the Yining riot, house-to-house searches were conducted and another five thousand arrests made. *Five thousand.* And at the end of this, thirty-five of the so-called ringleaders were sentenced to death. They were taken to the outskirts of the city and simply shot through the back of the head." Wang joined two fingers on his right hand and stabbed them into the base of his neck. Bang. "Of course these bodies were never returned to their families, just as the parents and relatives of the thousands of Uighur men and women who have been illegally imprisoned on false charges in the past several years have no idea where their loved ones are being held. And after the executions, as if to taunt the other prisoners, to make a spectacle of them, other so-called ringleaders were then paraded through the streets of Yining at a mass sentencing rally, already so drugged and physically damaged by their brief experience of prison that many of them, exposed in open trucks, were unable to stand or even to communicate with the crowd. I saw this with my own eyes, Mr. Richards, because I happened to be in

Yining for a conference. I saw that their hands and feet were bound by wire as they knelt in the trucks. Many of the prisoners had been forced to wear placards around their necks, proclaiming their crimes, their sins, like something from medieval times. When one of the prisoners found his strength and shouted a slogan against the Communist Party, in full view of the crowd he was forced to the ground and beaten around the head by two police-men. I saw this with my own eyes." Wang's voice briefly tight-ened to an enraged pitch. "A gag was then forced into his mouth to prevent him from shouting further. When certain supporters in the crowd complained about this, they too were arrested by plain-clothes officials who had surrounded them."

"And you were among these people?"

"No." The professor looked exhausted. "I was first held after a different disturbance, in 1995. I was accused of discussing a riot in Xinjiang in class. One of my students was a spy and he reported me. I know who this was. Luckily I had said very little. Luckily my activities have never properly been exposed. I was treated badly in captivity, I was beaten and kicked, but as nothing com-pared to others. I am, after all, a Han." Joe experienced a strange, sadistic desire to see the scars on Wang's body and hid his shame in a cigarette. He offered one to Wang, who refused. "I also have influential colleagues who were able to pay for my release and clear my name. I was soon back at work. Others were not so lucky. One Han doctor was arrested recently for treating the wounds of an alleged separatist following a riot in Kashgar. Three Yining shopkeepers who discussed the demonstration I have described with a foreign journalist were sentenced to fifteen years in the gulag. For a single conversation. In Xinjiang now, even to think about separatism is to be jailed."

"You mentioned a second riot in Kashgar," Joe said, and real-ized that either Lee or Sadha was moving around in the kitchen. How long had they been there? He heard a pan being filled with water, then the closing of the bedroom door as privacy was re-stored.

"Mr. Richards, there are riots all the time in China. Surely you are aware of this? They simply go unreported. What I am here to tell you today is the intensity, the *frequency* of these riots in Xin-jiang. The people are ready for revolution."

"And that's why you've come?"

"That is one reason I have come, yes." Creases appeared at the edge of Wang's eyes. "Perhaps Governor Patten's staff will be interested in the political implications of revolution in north-western China, yes?" The tone of the question seemed deliberately to mock Joe's denials that he was involved in intelligence work. Wang now took the cigarette he had been offered and drew out the silence as he lit it with Sadha's plastic lighter. "But it is of course primarily because of what has happened in the prisons that I have come to see Governor Patten."

"What has happened in the prisons?"

Wang inhaled very deeply. He was now entering the final phase of his long exhortation. "Two men were released," he replied. "They came to me, because I am known in the underground as a safe outlet, a haven. Once I see Governor Patten I can explain more about this."

Joe was aware of contradictions emerging in Wang's story. He had earlier said that he was a political undesirable, that he had been jailed alongside his fellow students for inciting revolution, then stripped of his chair at the university. But where was the evidence of this? "Who are these men?" he asked.

"Their names are Ansary Tursun and Abdul Bary. Ansary had been arrested for 'reading a newspaper,' Abdul for swearing at his Chinese boss."

"That's all?"

"That is all. And like the others they received no trial, no *habeas corpus*, no lawyer. Instead they were sent to the Lucaogu prison in Urumqi by a judge who presided over—what do you call it in English?—a kangaroo court. Before his escape, Ansary was locked up in a cell with eight other men, Abdul with seven. The cell was so crowded that the prisoners had to take it in turns sleeping. You see there was not enough space for everybody to lie down. All of the men told Ansary that they had been beaten and kicked by the guards, just as I was two years before. At some point Ansary was taken into what he believes was the basement of the prison. His left arm and his left leg were handcuffed to a bar in a room of solitary confinement. He was left to hang like this for more than twenty-four hours. He had no food, no water. Remember that his crime was only to read a newspaper. Perhaps you look at me and think that this is not so bad, that these sorts of violations are acceptable. Perhaps your own government abuses human rights and tortures prisoners from time to time. When they have problems with the Irish, for example."

Joe wondered what had caused Wang to become more aggressive. Had he failed to look suitably distraught? "Let me reassure you," he said, "that the British government takes the greatest possible—"

The professor held up his hand to stall his predictable rebuttal.

"Fine, fine," he said. "But let me reassure *you* about what happened to my friends. Then you can decide if the treatment of prisoners in China is compatible with Western values. Because Abdul Bary was also taken into solitary confinement, and the largest toenail of his right foot removed by a pair of pliers held in the grip of a guard who laughed as he did this, who was so drunk on the power and the humiliation of what he was doing that he found it *funny.*"

"I am so sorry," Joe said.

"Other prisoners, we later learned, had been attacked by dogs, burned with electric batons." Wang's cigarette was shaking as he spoke. "Another had horse's hair, that is the hard, brittle hair of an animal, inserted into his penis. And through all this, do you know what they were forced to wear on their heads, Mr. Richards? Metal helmets. Helmets that covered their eyes. And why? To create disorientation? To weigh them down? No. Ansary later learned from another prisoner that there had been an instance when an inmate had been so badly tortured, had been in so much pain, that he had actually beaten his own head against a radiator in an attempt to take his own life. This is the extent of what they had done to him. This is the extent of human rights abuses in so-called reformist, capitalist China. When I had finished protecting these two men, I knew that I had to come to Hong Kong. When I heard this I knew that our only salvation lay in England."

Joe allowed a silence to develop in which he gathered his thoughts. It was almost two o'clock in the morning. The streets outside were quiet now and he heard only the occasional barking of a neighbourhood dog, the distant sound of a police siren. So much information had been spilled over the course of the interview that he was finding it difficult to pick his way through it. Joe knew that it was his job to report the uprising in Yining, and the extent of separatist fervour across Xinjiang was certainly valuable intelligence. But he could not piece together Wang's role in the struggle and felt that there were holes in his story. And what of the human rights issues? To Joe's shame, he was surprised by how little impact the news of the torture had had on him. The suffering of these jailed men was somehow an inchoate thing, a nebulous concept around which he could not assemble sympathy. Only when Wang had spoken of the man beating his head against the radiator had he felt even the faintest tremor of discomfort. What was wrong with him? Had he grown immune to human suffering already? Had three years in SIS turned him into a machine? How was it possible to sit in a room with a man like Wang Kaixuan and not weep for the state of his country?

There were two sudden bursts on the doorbell. Joe noticed that Wang did not flinch. After a short pause the bell was rung again, four times. The agreed signal. Either Lenan or Waterfield was waiting outside. Lee emerged from the bedroom, rubbed his eyes as if he had been asleep and picked up the intercom. Joe heard him say, "Yes, Mr. Lodge," with an air of tense servility and a minute later there was a knock at the door. Joe left Wang in the sitting room and went into the hall.

"Sorry to have taken so long." Kenneth Lenan was wearing a white dress shirt tucked into formal black trousers, but no jacket and no bow tie. The function at Stonecutters appeared otherwise to have left no other visible impression upon him. He was neither drunk nor sober, neither particularly relaxed nor tense. He was the way that Kenneth Lenan always was. Unreadable. "Is everything OK?"

"Everything's fine. I wasn't expecting to see you."

"You look tired, Joe. Why don't I give you a break? We might give Mr. Wang a few hours' sleep then tackle him first thing in the morning."

The act of standing up and walking out into the hall caused Joe to realize the extent of his own mental and physical exhaustion. Without thinking, he told Lenan that, yes, he would appreciate a few hours of sleep. Following him into the bedroom, he added that Isabella might be wondering why it had taken him more than five hours to fix a simple paperwork problem at Heppner's, and that it would be wise to return home to protect his cover. This detail seemed to settle it.

"Do you want me to run through what's been said?" Joe asked, picking up his jacket on the way out.

"In the morning," Lenan replied. "Go home, grab a few hours' sleep, be back here around eight. We'll go through all of it then."

It only remained for Joe to bid Wang farewell. Returning to the sitting room, he explained that a second official from Government House, a Mr. Lodge, would be staying at the apartment overnight and that Wang could now rest until morning. The interview was concluded. They would see one another again in a few hours.

"I thank you for listening," Wang told him, standing and shaking Joe's hand.

It would be another eight years before the two men would meet again.

Three months earlier, a little more than 8,000 miles away on a sun-kissed Virginian golf course, former United States Assistant Secretary of Defense William "Bill" Marston had stood over his Titleist Pro V1 and intoned a favourite golfing mantra.

"The ball is my friend," he whispered, "the ball is my friend," and as he shook out his fattened hips and gripped the shaft of his gleaming five iron, Marston pictured the arc of the shot—just as he had been taught to do by the Turnberry professional who had charged him more than $75 an hour on a summer vacation to Scotland three years earlier—and truly believed, in the depths of his reactionary soul, that he was going to land the ball on the green.

He steadied his head. He drew back the club. He was one up with one to play. The five iron whistled through the warm spring air and connected with the Titleist in a way that felt powerful and true, but on this occasion, as on so many others throughout the course of his long, frustrating golfing life, the ball was not Bill Marston's friend, the ball was not soaring gracefully towards the stiff red flag at the crown of the seventeenth green; the ball was his enemy, hooking violently towards the trees at the edge of the vast Raspberry Falls golf course and ending its days approximately 120 metres away in a camouflage of earth and leaves from which it would never be returned.

"Fuck it," Marston spat, but managed to maintain his composure in the presence of his personal assistant, the Minnesota-born Sally-Ann McNeil who, for reasons which she was never properly able to explain, had been impelled to caddy for her boss. Sally-Ann, who was twenty-eight and college-educated, was somewhat wary of William "Bill" Marston. Nevertheless, when he lost his temper like this, she knew exactly what to say.

"Oh that's so *unfair*, sir." The boss was already telling her to pick him out another ball and indicating to his opponent that he would be happy to drop a shot.

"You sure about that, Bill?" CIA deputy director Richard Jenson had sliced his own drive into the deep rough on the opposite side of the fairway. He was wearing moleskin plus-fours and preparing to attack the green. "You sure you don't just wanna concede and call it all-square going up eighteen?"

"I'm sure." Marston's reply was so quiet that even Sally-Ann had difficulty making it out. Handing him a replacement Titleist— his fourth of the round—she took a step backwards, caught the eye of Jenson's caddy, Josh, who was thirtysomething and tanned and kept looking at her, and shuddered as the man from Langley struck a faultless six iron slap-bang into the middle of the green.

"Great shot, Dick," Marston shouted out, muttering "Asshole" under his breath as soon as he had turned round. Sally-Ann struggled to disguise a smile. It was just after one o'clock in the afternoon. Lunch at the clubhouse was booked for two. Standing over the ball, Marston glanced quickly at his PA, as if the sight of a beautiful woman might calm him in his hour of need. Then he drew back the graphite shaft a second time and prayed for a golfing miracle.

It was the worst kind of shot. The Titleist lifted itself no more than three inches from the ground before shooting in a plumbline across the immaculate Virginia fairway for about eighty metres, finally bobbling to rest at the edge of the green. Marston sniffed the air.

"I can still take a five," he muttered. "Dick can three-putt," offering just a glimpse of his ferocious competitive spirit. You didn't get to be one of Reagan's favourite sons, you didn't get to be chairman and director of Macklinson Corporation, you didn't get to sit on the Defense Policy Board Advisory Committee by quitting when the going gets tough. Bill Marston was a winner. Bill Marston was a fighter. Bill Marston let his five iron drop to the ground so that Sally-Ann could pick it up.

He had been playing most of the round in a bad mood. In the trunk of his armour-plated Mercedes, secured under lock and key and watched over by a 250-pound former Navy SEAL chauffeur, was a leaked, top-secret copy of the Report of the Select Committee on US National Security and Military/Commercial Concerns With the People's Republic of China—now commonly referred to as the Cox Report. Cox was a classified document until a few years ago and, strictly speaking, Marston shouldn't have been anywhere near it. However, a disgruntled staffer in the House of Representatives had suggested to one of Marston's senior employees that he might be able to obtain a draft copy in return for a position as a Macklinson executive in Berlin earning low six-figures after tax. Marston had agreed to the deal and had spent most of the previous evening reading the report at his home in Georgetown. The process had left him incensed to the point of insomnia.

These were the edited highlights, digested over a bowl of his wife's notoriously insipid clam chowder:

> The People's Republic of China (hereafter the PRC) has stolen classified design information on the United States' most advanced thermonuclear weapons. These thefts of nuclear secrets from our national weapons laboratories have enabled the PRC to design, develop, and successfully test modern strategic nuclear weapons sooner than would otherwise have been possible.

"Fuckers," Marston muttered.

> The stolen information includes classified information on seven US thermonuclear warheads, including every cur-

rently deployed thermonuclear warhead in the US ballistic missile arsenal. The stolen information also includes classified design information for an enhanced radiation weapon (commonly known as the "neutron bomb") which neither the United States, nor any other nation, has yet deployed.

"Jesus."

The Select Committee judges that the PRC will exploit elements of the stolen design information on the PRC's next generation of thermonuclear weapons. The PRC has three mobile ICBM programs currently underway, all of which will be able to strike the United States.

Since the joyful, Cold War-ending events of 1991, Bill Marston had been looking around for a new global enemy. Finally he had found one.

Jenson won the seventeenth hole with a nerveless putt from eight feet, but Marston produced a second shot onto the eighteenth green which effectively won the match when his opponent failed to escape a fairway bunker at the third attempt. Afterwards, while Josh explained to Sally-Ann that he worked in an office "about forty feet" from CIA director John Deutch and wondered if she was by any chance free for dinner, the two old friends showered and met at the bar for a pre-prandial Scotch and soda. After polite exchanges with several fellow club members they got down to business.

"What are you guys working on with China?" Marston enquired.

"You mean Cox?" The Deputy Director was initially reluctant to play Marston's game. "You know I can't talk about that, Bill."

As far as Marston was concerned, this was just standard-issue bluff. One more glass of Highland Park, a decent bottle of Californian Merlot over lunch and Jenson would be more inclined to talk.

"What if I told you I'd heard some things on the grapevine?"

"What kind of things?"

"That one of our most prestigious satellite communications companies provided some much-needed technical assistance on rocket propulsion to the Chinese without obtaining the correct licences from the federal government. That this prestigious satellite communications company is now facing a multi-million dollar fine for consorting with the enemy."

It was the one part of the Cox Report that Marston had enjoyed. While thousands of Chinese spies had been busy ripping off American nuclear secrets for the best part of two decades, Canyon Enterprises, one of Macklinson's fiercest rivals in the field of satellite communications, had colluded with the PRC on sensitive technologies. Play their cards right and Macklinson stood to benefit from Canyon's fall from grace, scooping up defence, electronics and system integration businesses worth billions of dollars.

"That story is already in the public domain, right?" Jenson said. "I can understand why you might be interested."

A waiter who had worked in the clubhouse for almost seventeen years, and whose name Marston had never successfully committed to memory, approached the two men and ushered them through to the dining room. They ordered seafood cocktails and broiled Porterhouse steaks and the conversation continued.

"What if I also told you that I'd heard about the extent of Chinese infiltration of our nuclear fraternity?" Jenson was looking through the wine list. "What if I knew that thanks to American tax dollars and American scientific breakthroughs and American hard work, Beijing now has dozens of fully functioning, effectively US-made ICBMs pointed at New York, Washington and Los Angeles?"

"Well then I'd say that nothing has changed. I'd say that Bill Marston still has great sources of information."

"I'm *pissed*, Dick." Marston hissed the words into a flower arrangement in the centre of the table. He had a history of heart trouble and had to watch himself when he became angry. "These guys have infiltrated our business environments, our scientific communities, our colleges. They're selling American military technology to rogue states, to regimes hostile to the United States. China has sold guidance components and telemetry equipment to the *Iranians*, for Christ's sakes. They're proliferating to the Syrians, North Korea, fuckin' Gaddafi. Are you guys on top of this? What's happening at Langley these days? Ever since Clinton came in, everything's gotten so goddam *soft*."

"We're on top of it," Jenson assured him, though this was far from what he believed. He wanted to hit the gooks just as much as Marston did, but his hands were tied. He resorted to a flimsy soundbite. "Sure, we've been the victims of a highly successful campaign of industrial and political espionage, but let me assure you that the United States still maintains an overwhelming military and commercial advantage over the People's Republic—"

"I don't give a shit about that. I know we can still kick their ass in a straight fight. I just don't like the way they do business. I don't like the way highly qualified Macklinson executives come to me every day complaining about the impossibility of making a decent buck in Beijing. My people in China have to get to know their clients' families, remember birthdays, take their wives to health clubs. What are we? A fucking charity? Off the record, Dick, Macklinson is paying for six Chinese kids to go to Stanford. You have any idea what that costs? And just so some board of directors in Wuhan will guarantee the legitimacy of a telecoms contract. And these guys have the nerve to steal our technology at the same time. Who the hell do they think they are? You know, not so long ago American soldiers were fighting in Manchuria trying to stop the entire region speaking Japanese." Jenson felt the historical argument was somewhat strained. "That's right. American boys putting their lives on the line for China's future. And this is how they repay us."

"So what are you suggesting?"

Marston paused. His glass from the clubhouse bar was a pale yellow meltdown of ice and whisky.

"What I'm suggesting is an *idea*." He had lowered his voice. Jenson was obliged to push forward in his chair and felt a muscle twitch in his lower back. "Off the books, if it has to be. A clandestine operation looking into ways of destabilizing Beijing. Just the same way we gave the Poles a little push. Just the same way the

Agency funded Walesa and Havel. Now I know you guys already have operations out there, but this would be in conjunction with Macklinson, using our infrastructure and our people on the ground in China. Come up with something and we'll help you." Jenson produced a low, enigmatic whistle. "Communism is a dying art, Dick, and communist China has been around too long. You've seen what happened in the Soviet bloc. All we're lookin' at is giving these guys a helping hand. Call it a push to a delayed domino effect. And when Beijing falls, I want America there picking up the pieces."

13 | THE DOUBLE

When Joe returned home he found Isabella asleep, a white cotton sheet pushed down below her feet, her face turned towards the bedroom wall so that in the darkness he could make out the lovely cello curvature of her back and legs. He drank a small glass of single malt in their cluttered kitchen, showered in a stuttering stream of vaguely sulphurous Hong Kong water and slipped into bed beside her. He wanted to wake her with kisses that laddered down her spine, to encourage her body to turn towards his, to place his hand in the blissful envelope created by her closed thighs, but he could not do so for fear that she would wake up, look at the clock and ask where he had been, ask why it had taken him so long to resolve a simple problem at Heppner's, and why it was now almost four o'clock in the morning when he had left the restaurant before ten? Best just to set his alarm for six and to slip out before the questions started. Best just to leave her a note.

Despite his exhaustion, Joe found it difficult to sleep. Unable to shut down his mind he lay motionless on his back as the clock on the bedside table thrummed towards five, turning over the details of the long conversation with Wang and plotting the possible trajectory of their imminent second meeting. Shortly before dawn he fell into a deep sleep from which he was woken by dreams of prisons and pliers and Urumqi. At six he gave up on sleep, rolled out of bed, kissed Isabella gently on the shoulder and went into the kitchen. From the fridge he removed a mango, some bananas and a pineapple and prepared a fruit salad for when she woke up. He then laid out a breakfast tray, wrote her a short note, placed a sheet around her body to keep her warm in the cool air of the morning, dressed and slipped outside in search of a cab.

Twenty minutes later he boarded a half-empty Star ferry which chugged across Victoria Harbour like a faithful dog. Junks and cargo ships assumed silhouettes in the gradually improving light. Joe stood at the stern railings like a departing dignitary, looking back at the coat-hanger lights of the Hong Kong and Shanghai Bank, at the fading neon outlines of Central and Causeway Bay, at the great massed lump of the Peak behind them. As the sun grew brighter he picked out workmen buzzing in the bamboo scaffolding of the Convention and Exhibition Centre, working day and night to finish the building before the handover. Inside the ferry, businessmen and cleaning ladies and ageing shopkeepers, most of whom had known the same view every morning of their working lives, snoozed on cramped plastic chairs, undisturbed by the day's first aeroplanes which roared in low overhead.

On the Kowloon side Joe shuffled out of the terminal through a crush of rush-hour workers and walked east along Salisbury Road. There was still an hour to go before he was expected at the safe house and he gave in to a sudden, imperial urge to eat breakfast at the Peninsula Hotel. A waiter in late middle age guided him through the marble splendour of the ancient lobby and found him a quiet table with a view onto the bustling streets outside. Joe ordered eggs Benedict and orange juice and read the *International Herald Tribune* from cover to cover while thinking of Isabella eating breakfast alone in their apartment. Towards eight o'clock he paid the bill, which came to almost HK$300, and took a cab to within a block of Yuk Choi Road.

Only when he was at the door, waiting for Lee to respond to his four short bursts on the buzzer, did Joe remember that he had switched off his phone the night before. As he waited on the steps of the building, the machine burst into life. The read-out said: "FORGET ABOUT TOMORROW. CHANGE OF PLAN. GO TO WORK AS NORMAL. KL" and Joe felt all the tiredness of a night without sleep catching up with him. It was too early in the morning for an anti-climax.

Lee's surprised, groggy voice crackled on the intercom.

"Who is this please?"

"It's John."

It took some time before Lee finally buzzed Joe inside. He looked unusually anxious when he opened the door to greet him. His forehead was creased with worry lines and he was breathing quickly, as if he, and not Mr. Richards, had just climbed four flights of humid stairs.

"You forget something?" he asked. Nor was this Lee's typical greeting. He was usually more deferential, keen to smile and make a good first impression. There were windows open throughout the flat and Joe sensed immediately that Wang, Sadha and Lenan had all left. He briefly entertained the wild notion that he had caught Lee with a girl in the back bedroom. He certainly looked not to have slept.

"No, I didn't forget anything," he said. "Is everything all right, Lee?"

"Everything fine."

Joe moved past him into the kitchen and saw that the bedroom was empty. "I just got the message," he said. "I've made a wasted journey. Mr. Lodge told me not to come. Where the hell is everybody?"

"They went home," Lee replied uneasily.

"What do you mean, they went home?"

"Leave at five. Mr. Wang go with them."

"Mr. Wang doesn't have a home."

This remark seemed to confuse Lee, who looked like an actor struggling to remember his lines. For want of something to say, he muttered, "I really don't know," an evasion which irritated Joe. He was beginning to suspect that he was being lied to.

"You don't know *what*?"

"What, Mr. Richards? I think they take Mr. Wang somewhere else. I think they leave at five o'clock."

"You *think*?"

Lee looked ever more sheepish. He clearly didn't know whether to tell Joe what had happened or to obey orders and keep his mouth shut.

"What about Sadha?" he asked. "What happened to Sadha?"

"Sadha go with them."

"With who?"

"With Mr. Lodge and Mr. Coleman. They take the professor north."

Joe had been passing through the red plastic strip curtains on his way into the sitting room but the shock of this information spun him round. Malcolm Coleman was one of Miles's cover names.

"The Americans were here?"

Lee looked embarrassed, because he had uttered a secret which it was now too late to retract. His head shook very quickly, like a shiver passing through him, but his decent eyes betrayed the truth. Joe felt pity for him as Lee said, "You did not know this, Mr. Richards?"

"No, Lee, I did not know this. How long was Coleman here for?"

Lee sat down on the chair in the hall and disclosed that Miles had arrived shortly after 3 a.m. Only moments, in other words, after Joe had left the building himself. Had he been waiting outside?

"Why didn't Coleman come up with Mr. Lodge?" he asked. "Why didn't they say something to me?"

Lee shrugged his shoulders. It was a mystery as much to him as it was to Joe. "We were in the bedroom," he said, as if that absolved him of all responsibility. "I was in the bedroom with Sadha."

Joe had known moments like this before, moments when he, as the junior spook, had been kept out of the loop by his professional masters. It was as if Waterfield and Lenan, in spite of everything that he had already achieved in his short career, still did not trust him to sit at the top table with older and wiser souls. Why were they so cautious? Everything in SIS was a club; everything was "need to know," "expediency" and "restricted access." But what were they concealing from him? Why would Lenan send a message to Joe telling him to "forget about" Wang and then conspire with the CIA to have him moved to a new location?

"Have you got a number where I can reach Lodge?" he asked.

Lee immediately stood up and produced a card from the pocket of his shirt. He smiled as he handed it over, relieved of his duty to lie on Lenan's behalf. It was a cellphone with a Taiwanese prefix. Joe didn't recognize the rest of the number but dialled it anyway, using the phone by the door.

A message system clicked in and he was aware of the need to speak carefully on what might be an open line.

"Hi. It's me. I'm at the flat. I only got your text this morning, when I was already here. Just wondering what the story is. Just wondering what's going on. Any chance you could call me?"

Lee looked intently at Joe as he hung up, like a relative in a hospital anticipating bad news. Lenan rang back within a minute.

"Joe?"

"Speaking."

"You say you're at the flat?"

It was impossible to tell where Lenan was calling from. The tone of his voice suggested that he was both annoyed and slightly disconcerted.

"Yes, I'm here with Lee. I didn't get your page until–"

"No, obviously you didn't." Lenan was not known for outbursts of temper; rather, he preferred to imply his displeasure with a gesture or carefully chosen phrase. "Why did you switch it off?" he asked, with the clear suggestion that Joe had acted unprofessionally.

"I'm sorry. I wasn't thinking at the time. I didn't want to wake Isabella."

"I see."

That was a mistake. He shouldn't have mentioned Isabella. The Office still weren't happy about their relationship. They wanted it put on a more formal footing.

"Anyway, I'm here now and Lee says you took off with Wang at five o'clock. He also said that Malcolm Coleman was here." Lee, listening in, took a deep, chest-inflating breath.

"Lee said that?"

"Yes, sir."

Why had Joe bothered to call him "sir?" He never called anyone "sir." In his relationship with Waterfield, whom he regarded as something of a father figure, there was respect and understanding, but also a quality of candour which allowed Joe to relax and speak his mind. The more guarded, watchful Lenan, on the other hand, was a different proposition: he brought out something deferential in Joe, who could never escape a feeling of slight nervousness, even of intellectual inferiority, in his company.

"Well, as you know, the Cousins have ears on the safe house." Joe sensed that this was already more information than Lenan had been prepared to divulge. Restricted access. Expediency. Need to know. "Somebody at the consulate was listening in. They contacted Miles. Reckoned they'd run into Wang before."

"Run into him before?"

"That's right."

"And had they?"

Lenan reacted as if Joe was asking dull, obvious questions to which there were dull, obvious answers. "Yes." Then it sounded as if the line had gone dead.

"Hello?"

"I'm still here."

"I'm sorry, you said Wang had been to Hong Kong before? You're saying the Cousins had a file on him?"

"That is what I am saying, Joe, yes."

Don't patronize me, you prick. Why should I have to keep pressing you for information? Why is one of my own colleagues blatantly lying to me?

"And?"

Lenan dropped the bad news. "Well, the conclusion that Miles and I arrived at pretty quickly is that Professor Wang was MSS. So we spat him back this morning."

Joe was stunned. It simply didn't make sense that the man he

had interrogated less than eight hours earlier was a Chinese double. Wang Kaixuan may have been many things—a smooth-talker,
a liar, a sentimentalist—but he was surely not an *agent provocateur*.

"Well, I have to say that I'm amazed by that. It certainly wasn't
my instinct when I spoke to him."

"No. It wasn't. We might have to chalk that one up to experience."

The implied criticism was clear: Joe had fallen for a basic Chinese deception. All of which would reflect badly on his reputation
within the Office. It was a body blow.

"So he's already back in China?"

"Dropped him off in Lo Wu this morning."

14 | SAMBA'S

When Miles Coolidge wanted to avoid awkward conversations he adopted a number of different tactics: meetings cancelled at the last minute; phone calls ignored for days on end; letters and emails left stubbornly unanswered. If it wasn't in his best interests to tackle a problem, he would leave that problem unresolved. So when Joe walked into Samba's at nine o'clock that evening and spotted Miles at the crowded bar surrounded by a seven-strong group of his American consulate co-workers, he saw it not as a happy accident of the diplomatic life in Hong Kong, but as a deliberate delaying tactic to prevent any serious discussion of Wang. They had agreed to meet alone. Miles was playing games.

"Joe!"

One of the girls from the consulate—Sharon from the Commercial Section—had spotted Joe coming through the door. Her greeting had a ripple effect on the rest of the party and those who knew him broke off from their conversations to acknowledge his arrival.

"Hey, man, great to see you again."

"It's Joe, right?"

"How's the shipping business?"

Miles was the last to turn round. Resplendent in a lime-green Hawaiian shirt, he removed a tanned, muscular arm from the shoulder of a Chinese woman at the bar and moved a couple of steps forward to shake Joe by the hand. His impassive eyes said nothing about their broken arrangement; there was no apology in them, no embarrassment or regret. If anything, Joe sensed a certain triumph in Miles's expression, as if he was actually glad to be wasting his time. Joe knew that it was useless to complain. Any formal expression of his frustration would simply play into Miles's hands. The trick was to stay the course, to act as though nothing had happened, then to corner him at the end of the evening when everyone else had gone home.

To that end Joe ordered a round of drinks—eight bottles of beer, eights shots of tequila—and went to work on the crowd. He was a genius with names and faces. He remembered that Sharon had a brother in the US navy who was currently serving in Singapore. He reminded Chris, a gay African-American who worked in the Culture Section, that he still owed him a hundred dollars for a bet they'd had about Chelsea Clinton. When Barbara and Dave Boyle from Visas came over and complained that Joe was a "bad influence" for plying them with drink, he bought them two more tequilas and asked fascinated questions about their recent wedding in North Carolina. Meanwhile Miles, who was attempting to seduce an Australian backpacker near the cigarette machine, occasionally looked over in Joe's direction as if surprised to see him still there. The clincher was the backpacker's departure at eleven o'clock. Claiming the sudden onset of a migraine headache, she climbed into a cab with Barbara and Dave and took off down Lockhart Road. With a belly full of alcohol and a wounded ego, Miles was left with nobody to play with. Joe was the obvious target.

"So how's Isabella?" he asked. He had eaten garlic for dinner and the smell of it on his breath cut through the smoke and the sweat of the bar.

"You tell me."

Miles seemed to take this as a compliment. "What's that supposed to mean?"

"You were the last person to talk to her. When I got home last night she was asleep. When I left this morning she was asleep."

"And where is she now?"

Joe looked at his watch. "Asleep."

One by one, the consulate crowd departed until Chris was the last of them. At around half-past eleven he spotted a vacant table at the window overlooking Lockhart Road and ordered another round of drinks. Joe was keen to get Miles alone but could see that Chris was gearing up for a long night out on the tiles. Realizing that he would have to resort to a lie, he waited for Miles to go to the bathroom, then slumped down at the table with deliberate exaggeration and played what was, in the circumstances, his only viable card.

"Thank God for that."

"What do you mean?" Chris asked.

"I've been trying to have a serious conversation with Miles all night. It was impossible to pin him down with everybody here."

Chris was a sensitive soul and would soon pick up on the signals. "Talk to him about what?"

Joe opened a packet of cigarettes. He made a point of crushing the cellophane wrapper nervously in his hand and let out a stagey sigh.

"Can I tell you something in confidence?"

"Sure." Chris's gentle, attentive face was quickly filled with concern. "What's up, man?"

"I've got a bit of a problem at Heppner's. A serious problem. I called Miles about it earlier today and he said he'd be able to help. We arranged to meet for this drink but with everything that's been going on I haven't been able to talk to him."

"Shit." Chris looked genuinely crestfallen. "Anything I can do to help?"

"That's really good of you, but I'm afraid Miles is the only person who can do anything at this stage. Apparently he knows somebody in logistics in San Diego who's the one guy that might be able to solve things. But I have to catch a flight to Seoul at eight tomorrow morning and this needs to be sorted before then."

Joe looked up at a clock on the wall, then at his watch. "It's still the late afternoon in California . . ."

Chris interrupted him. "Listen, man, if you need some privacy to talk things over with Miles . . ."

"No, no, that wasn't what I meant. Sorry, I didn't mean to imply . . ."

"You didn't imply anything." Chris was in his late thirties, a decent, obliging "soul," and he adopted an expression of infinite wisdom and understanding in the presence of the younger man. "You got a tough job, Joe, and—"

"No, no, please don't worry. We can do it later."

"—and I'd like to help you out." Chris laid a firm, understanding hand on Joe's arm and gave it a meaningful squeeze. "You don't wanna be sitting here listening to me all night when you've got this shit preying on your mind. And you're right. Miles is *exactly* the guy you should be talking to. That man is *unbelievable*." He stalled a little here, as if unsure whether Joe was aware that Miles was CIA. "I can see how frustrated you are and I totally understand. In any case, I could do with an early night. When he gets back I'll finish my beer and slip away."

Joe, who was certainly not above using his looks to gain an advantage in such a situation, whispered, "That is very kind of you, Chris, thank you so much," and offered up what might have been construed as a flirtatious smile. Then they both spotted Miles returning from the bathroom. Joe calculated that Chris would be gone in under fifteen minutes.

It took ten. He smoked one of Joe's cigarettes, drained his Michelob, then stood up from the table and announced that he was heading for home.

"You sure, man?" Miles asked. There was neither concern nor particular surprise in the question.

"I'm sure. I've got an early start tomorrow. You guys be good. Take care now."

Joe rose to his feet.

"Thanks," he mouthed as Miles bent down to pick up a fallen beer mat. Chris gave a second airing to his expression of infinite wisdom and understanding and whispered the word "Pleasure" back. After handshakes all round, Chris left a hundred-dollar tip on the table and disappeared into the crowds of Wan Chai.

"What got into him?" Miles was fingering the hundred-dollar note, as if weighing up whether or not to steal it. "I go to the bathroom, I come back, suddenly he wants to leave."

"Search me."

"Did you arrange for him to take off, Joe? Did you want me all to yourself?"

Joe smiled as the chorus of "With or Without You" played loud on the Samba's sound system. They were sitting opposite one another at the table, drunk blondes from England singing at the bar. "If you play games with me," he said, "I'm obliged to play games with you."

Miles looked away. "Noisy in here," he said. Their relationship was frequently a sparring match in which neither side was prepared to concede ground or admit to weakness. Isabella once compared them to a couple of alpha-male gorillas grappling it out in the eastern Congo, which may have been hard on Joe, but was certainly a compliment as far as Miles was concerned. Their mutual bravado concealed a deep affection, but it saddens me to look back and realize that any loyalty between them was strictly one-way traffic.

"So you wanted to know about Wang?" Miles said finally.

"Yes. I want to know about Wang."

"Why didn't you just ask Kenneth?"

"I did. And now I'm asking you."

Samba's is the sort of place where expats gather to drink in the evening before moving on to dinner or a nightclub in Lan Kwai Fong. It is always packed and always noisy and, with the music as a constant smothering background, there is little danger of conversations being overheard. Nevertheless Miles lowered his voice as he said, "I'm prepared to tell you anything you want." The lime-green Hawaiian shirt glowed against the dull red upholstery of his chair, sculpting gym-toughened shoulders into slabs of power. Very few men in Hong Kong could have worn that shirt and not looked ridiculous. "You look a little pissed, Joe," he said. "Everything OK?"

Joe hadn't meant to look angry but he was aware that thirty-six hours without meaningful sleep, combined with an evening of beer and tequila, had scrambled his senses. He tried to appear more relaxed.

"What's the situation between you and Kenneth? Why did you wait outside last night instead of coming in?"

Miles leaped forward at the accusation. "Why did I *what*?"

There were customers all around them, standing at the bar, between tables, sitting on chairs near the window. Joe warned Miles with his eyes and began to repeat the question. "I said, why did you–"

"I heard what you said. Is that what you *think*? Is that what you think I'd do to you?"

"That's what it looked like." Joe ordered two more beers from a passing waitress and felt a tremor of guilt for doubting Miles's story. Then he remembered that he was speaking to one of the colony's most accomplished liars, a man whose characteristic response when cornered was to become confrontational and aggressive. "Is that not what happened?"

"No, it's not." Miles shot back the reply with apparent disbelief. "What *happened* is that you left because it was three o'clock in the morning and Kenneth thought you looked wiped out. I was on my way over and must have missed you by less than five minutes."

"Why didn't Kenneth mention to me that you were coming over?"

"How the hell am I supposed to know? Isn't that something you should be asking *him*?"

At the next table a Chinese girl turned round and scowled at them, as if to make it clear that their argument was proving detrimental to her enjoyment of the evening. Miles saw her off with a flare-eyed stare.

"What time did you leave Isabella?" Joe was determined to check every inch of Miles's story.

"I have no idea. I got a call around midnight saying Wang was using one of our houses. I told her I had to get going and left her in Club 64."

"You left my girlfriend on her own in Club 64?"

Miles shook his head. "Oh come on, Joe. She's a big girl. Why do British guys always act like that around women?"

"Act like what?"

"Like the fucking knight in shining fucking armour. She's a tough lady. She can take care of herself."

"At around midnight?" Joe repeated.

"Sure. At around midnight."

Was there a slight hesitation here, a gap in the story?

"And you're saying that your people had already heard of Wang Kaixuan?"

Miles swallowed a mouthful of Michelob and emerged with a look of disgust on his face. "'My people?' Are you OK, Joe? Aren't we supposed to be fighting the same war? Aren't we supposed to be working on the same side?"

"Apparently."

"What's that supposed to mean?"

Joe wondered whether to back off. They were both drunk, both tired, both ambitious, fractious spies talking around a subject which would be better discussed in the sober light of a new day. "It means I'm confused," he said. "It means I've not been given the full picture . . ."

"So you've spent most of your day moping around feeling sorry for yourself, wondering whether Kenneth and Miles, and probably David, too, have got their own little conspiracy going that you aren't a part of?"

Joe didn't bother denying this. "The thought had occurred to me."

"Oh come on." Miles raised his hands in the air, finally pushed too far. It looked for a moment as though he might leave.

"It surprises you that I would ask that?" Joe offered him a cigarette. "You don't think there's anything strange in what's happened over the last twenty-four hours?"

"Frankly, no." Miles's eyes were on the Chinese girl's back and the worst of his anger seemed to have passed. "Look. Wang draws a lot of water on the mainland. He was involved in an operation in Beijing three years ago which exposed two of our agents. Led to deportations. That's how we already knew him."

Joe frowned. "What kind of operation?"

"The kind I'm not allowed to talk about."

When a spook says that to another spook, you know you're in trouble.

"So all anyone has to do is hear Wang's voice on a safe-house microphone and they immediately know it's him?"

It was the obvious flaw in Miles's version of events, but the American had it covered.

"We got lucky," he said.

"How?"

"You know Steve Mackay?"

Joe knew Steve Mackay. "Yes."

"He was involved in what happened in Beijing. Got a routine call from Kenneth yesterday asking if it was cool for you guys to use Yuk Choi Road. Said they had a Xinjiang walk-in who'd rafted over from Shenzhen. Bill asked for a description, got a hold of the audio, called me in when he put two and two together."

"Hence Kenneth's presence this morning."

"Hence." Miles made a face at the word. "He was your man, Joe, he was your walk-in. You had a duty to share."

Joe leaned back and caught the eye of a girl at the bar. She smiled through the crush of bodies, dark, interested eyes. For some reason "With or Without You" was playing a second time on the sound system and he felt as though he were trapped in a loop of persistent evasions.

"What happened when you got there?"

"Like Kenneth told you. We already knew who he was and took him back up to the border."

Joe seized on this. "You've spoken to Kenneth about me today?"

"Sure." Miles took a drag on his cigarette, like a tell in poker. "You think that's odd?"

"I don't think it's normal." Miles produced a look of bewilderment which invited Joe to continue. "Try to see it from my perspective. I get to the apartment this morning, Lee acts like I'm a priest about to walk in on an orgy. It was as if he'd been instructed to keep me in the dark."

"That's the nature of the business we're in." Miles illustrated his point with hard, staccato chops of his hand, as if stating the obvious to a junior officer still learning the ropes. "That's how Lee has been trained to operate. When a Chinese double gets turned back to the mainland, the less people that know about it, the better. Right?"

"So I can't be trusted with that information? I spend three hours interviewing this guy, uncover intel about riots in Yining, revolutionary fervour across north-west China, as well as what appear to be astonishing human rights abuses in Xinjiang prisons, but his whereabouts are to remain a complete mystery to me."

Miles was about to say "What mystery?" when two things happened. First, the Chinese girl stood up, along with the other four members of her table, and left the bar. Second, a troupe of five stewardesses passed her on their way into Samba's wearing the bright red uniforms of Virgin Airways. It was Christmas Day for Miles Coolidge. He forgot all about the Wang situation and produced a low, involuntary hum like the mating call of a sperm whale.

"Sweet Mary mother of all that is good and sacred. Look at what we have here."

Joe could follow their progress in a mirror hung on the opposite wall, a moving tapestry of hair and make-up laughing all the way to the bar. He watched as Miles's tanned, shaved head rotated through a hundred and eighty degrees.

"Don't even think about it."

"Oh come on." The American was already on his feet. "Isabella's all tucked up in bed. Let's go get some before it gets cold."

But Joe was lucky. As Miles walked towards the bar, taking with him all hope of their conversation continuing, the stewardesses were enveloped in a ring of freshly showered pilots and cabin crew, never to be seen again. Miles turned on his heels.

"Fuckers," he said, returning to his seat. "Fuckers."

15 | UNDERGROUND

They lasted another ten minutes before Miles announced that he wanted to go "someplace else." Joe should have been wise to the implication—it was one o'clock in the morning, after all—but he allowed Miles to lead him through the stifling, humid streets to a basement nightclub on Luard Road where there was a bouncer on the door, a dimly lit staircase and no entry fee. In Wan Chai, that usually meant only one thing: the club would be full of hookers.

"Been here before?" Joe asked as he pushed through a warped double door at the foot of the stairs to be hit by a wall of cigarette smoke and house music. Miles said, "Coupla' times," and followed close behind him. To their left was a darkened, open-plan seating area where groups of expat men, varying in age from perhaps eighteen up to sixty-five, sat at tables talking to girls from the Philippines, Vietnam and Thailand. The bar was directly ahead of them, a high-countered rectangle surrounded on all sides by customers and girls on stools. A sweat-oozing dance floor heaved to their right. Miles walked past Joe, found a table in the far corner of the club and brought over two vodka and tonics.

"Why not Neptune's? Why not Big Apple?" Joe asked, tilting

the question towards sarcasm. Big Apple and Neptune's were Miles's favoured knocking shops on the island, ports of call for a certain type of *gweilo* looking for easy sex after a night out in Hong Kong. Both were awash with women from South-east Asia who would accompany you home for less than the price of a three-course dinner at Rico's. Joe had been to Neptune's on several occasions and had hated everything about the experience, not least the barely disguised contempt the trafficked girls held for their cash-rich clientele. But sex for sale was part of everyday life in Hong Kong and Joe wasn't the type to sit in judgment. If Miles wanted to pay an eighteen-year-old girl from Haiphong who spoke no English to spend the night with him at his apartment in the Mid-Levels, that was his problem.

"I'm not here to get laid, man," Miles said, as if reading his mind. "I just like the atmosphere. It's smaller than those other places, right? More intimate. You rather be someplace else?"

Joe knew that Miles had probably brought him to the club as a means of testing the boundaries of his fidelity to Isabella, but he was not about to give a drunk, randy, belligerent American the pleasure of his moral indignation.

"I really don't care," he said. "I just want to find out what happened to Wang."

Miles rolled his eyes and curled a grin at a passing girl wearing a short pink skirt. "Jesus. Can't you let that go? You fucked up, Joe. You thought Wang was going to make your career and you fell for it. It's nobody's fault but your own. Deal with it."

It took a lot to trigger Joe Lennox's temper, and this was as close as anyone had come in a long time. He looked across at the dance floor, at the unchosen girls dancing in solemn pairs, at a pot-bellied businessman draping his heavy, sweat-stained arms over the shoulders of a micro-skirted hooker, at a Thai girl laughing as she ground her arse into the crotch of a man whose face was a rictus of consternation, and wondered why the hell he spent so much time in the company of this craven spy whose behaviour was a constant affront to his sensibilities. Was it just a sense of professional responsibility which kept them together? Isabella seemed to like Miles; perhaps that had something to do with it. Or was it simply that Joe had always preferred the company of mavericks and nonconformists, if only because they offered an antidote to the mostly strait-laced sons and daughters of middle England around whom he had grown up?

"I don't think I fucked up," he replied, controlling his anger. "I just think you're lying to me."

Miles shook his head. "Jesus." A girl in tottering heels approached their table and he waved her away as if she were little more than a fly in his face. Joe felt a thump of despair. "Let's put this argument out of its misery, OK?" Miles took one of Joe's cigarettes and moved his vodka to one side of the table, as if clearing space in which he could make his point. "I've listened to last night's tapes. I've listened to what Wang told you. And none of it is news to us. None of it is in the slightest bit of any fucking interest whatsoever."

Joe caught a wave of garlic breath and pitched away, his eyes going back to the dance floor. He thought of Isabella asleep in bed and wanted to be beside her, entwined in her, away from this. It occurred to him that he had no idea how she had spent her day and this depressed him. "None of it?" he said.

"None of it. The Agency has known about Yining since day one. Christ, we had informants who took part in the riots. Everybody knows what's going on up there. I'm surprised Wang had the nerve to show up with such an old story."

Joe had spent the afternoon in the House of a Thousand Arseholes shuttling around the SIS computer system looking for recent reports on Xinjiang. Suffice to say, the Brits had nothing on record about a February uprising in Yining. It was the extent of Joe's distrust that he suspected Lenan of having wiped the files that morning.

"What about the torture?" he said. "What about the human rights abuses?"

"What about them? Last time I checked I didn't work for Amnesty International." Miles was scoping girls, barely seeming to listen to him. At a nearby table, two of them, possibly sisters, slid in next to an American with a thick beard and a deep Texan accent. The low boom of his voice carried to where Joe was sitting and he could hear the man asking if they wanted drinks. "Look, do you know about Baren?"

Joe shook his head.

"Baren is a township in Aktu, near Kashgar." Miles turned back to the table and now adopted a more serious expression. He had a near-encyclopaedic memory and enjoyed reeling off chunks of history. "Back in April 1990, the Chinese police broke up a public prayer meeting outside some government offices in Baren. Accused the worshippers of inciting *jihad*, of getting funding from the Afghan *muj*. Caused a riot involving about two thousand local Muslims. The cops and the Public Security Bureau, probably the Bin Tuan as well, brought in helicopters, riot troops, shot about fifty of them, including the ones who were running away. Surely you know about this?" Joe ignored the effortless condescension. "Baren was just about the biggest ethnic separatist uprising in Xinjiang in the last seven years. Out of a Muslim community of ten thousand, every man between the age of thirteen and sixty was arrested in connection with what happened. That's how serious the Chinese take the situation up there. Then you got bombs going off right across Xinjiang. One on a bus in Urumqi killed about thirty people in early '92. This shit is happening all the time."

"What about Yining?" Joe asked.

"What about it?"

"Is what Wang told me true?"

Miles drained his vodka and frowned. "Forget about Wang," he said. "Wang Kaixuan is a myth, a spook story. Nothing that old fuck told you has any meaning."

Joe was not an aficionado of American movies and did not realize that Miles was lazily quoting dialogue from *The Usual Suspects*. *Myth. Spook story*. For ten seconds in a Hong Kong nightclub, Wang Kaixuan was Keyser Söze. "So there was no uprising in Yining?" he asked. "No riots? No mass imprisonments? No torture?"

"Of course there was." Miles was shrugging his shoulders but seemed equally interested in the fact that his drink was now finished and that it was Joe's turn to buy a round. He looked down at his glass, rattling the ice. "Nobody's denying that Yining was a shitstorm. Nobody's saying that. But you gotta ask yourself a bunch of serious questions about the kind of guy you thought you were dealing with last night. Professor of economics? A Han Chinese who somehow speaks perfect English? Nobody north of Guangdong speaks English like that unless they're MSS. For Christ's sake, Joe, Wang spent a year at Oxford University in the seventies pretending to study law." Miles saw Joe's look of astonishment and added, "What? He didn't tell you that?"

"Not in so many words . . ."

"Then he suddenly develops a conscience about Uighurs getting butt-fucked in Liu Daowan? Give me a break. What do you have here? An entirely new concept? The self-hating Han?" Miles laughed at his own joke and then narrowed his eyes. "How come he just *happens* to be in Yining when the riot takes place? He was a fucking government agent. You think a Chinese academic from northern Xinjiang is going to risk his life to save a few hundred Muslims? Don't you have any understanding of the national character? All the Chinese care about is themselves. It's me, myself and I—then me again if you've still got some time left over afterwards. I can't believe how naïve you are." Miles lifted his glass, waved it at the barman and indicated that he wanted two further vodka and tonics. "You're paying for these, by the way."

Joe was at a dead end. Experience had taught him to doubt the word of those who argued their case with a mixture of hostility and impatience; it usually meant that they were concealing something. He believed very little of what Miles was telling him, but had to tread carefully. Miles clearly enjoyed a much closer working relationship with Lenan than Joe had previously realized. As a result, everything that he said about the Wang situation would certainly be reported back to his SIS masters, with potential consequences for his career. So it was better to act dumb, to appear to accept Miles's version of events and then to check the veracity of his story at a later date. Joe had a hunch that Lenan had handed Wang to the Americans. If that was the case, there was very little he could do about it. There was certainly no future in making waves. He just resented the fact that he was being treated like an idiot.

"Fine," he said. "I'll go and pay for the drinks."

At the bar he handed a five-hundred-dollar note to a middle-aged Chinese cashier who looked as though she had been living underground for the best part of ten years. Her eyes were black pools of fatigue, her light-starved complexion a sickly yellow glow beneath the cruel lights of the neon bar. He put the drinks down on the table, told Miles he was "off to buy cigarettes" and walked to the entrance of the club, splashing water on his face in a toilet that stank of sex and piss. *Go home*, he told himself, though he was wired and hot and still angry that Wang had slipped from his grasp. Joe thought of Ansary Tursun and Abdul Bary, two Uighur men whose faces he had not yet seen, the one handcuffed to a basement wall in wretched solitary confinement, the other held down by laughing guards as his toenails were extracted by pliers. What was the true character of this country to the north, this ancient land to which Joe had committed so much of his young life? What would become of Hong Kong when the PLA goose-stepped over the border at midnight on 30 June? Joe felt drunk and melancholy. The thud of music in the club reverberated through the toilet walls and he walked outside onto the street to buy cigarettes from a 7–Eleven.

Returning to the club ten minutes later he was struck by a sight so extraordinary that it took him several seconds to realize what was going on. As Joe passed the dance floor, pushing through a crush of men and bored hookers, he saw Isabella straddling Miles at the table, her legs squeezing his hips as she rocked and writhed in his lap. Of course it was not her, yet the shape of the woman, her long dark hair, her sinuous body encased in a dark blue *qipao* dress, was an uncanny double. Joe felt a surge of desire and jealousy. He sat down and stared at her back in a brief drunken trance.

"Joe, man! You're back!" The girl turned. She was Chinese, exquisitely pretty, but with flat, wide features that seemed almost Turkic. Joe felt that he was hallucinating. Was this a Xinjiang prostitute in the act of selling herself to the CIA? He was by now so drunk and exhausted that little was making sense. "You gotta meet Kitty. Fuckin' gorgeous. Kitty, meet Joe."

The girl stretched out a long, slender arm which looked tanned in the low light of the club. Her touch was cold and Joe saw that there was no life behind her painted eyes, only the sad routine of seducing strangers and laughing at *gweilo* jokes. He wondered how Miles, or any of the other men in the club, could fail to see through the artifice as the girl smiled and tipped her head provocatively. Then he realized that they probably didn't care.

"Hello, handsome," Kitty said.

"Hello."

She reached for a narrow champagne flute on the table and took a sip while holding Joe's gaze. "Fuck wine," they called it, a mixture of cold tea and flat Coca-Cola which sold for twice the price of a vodka and tonic. At the end of the evening the girl and the bar would split fifty per cent of the cost of the drink, with the rest going to the Triads. Kitty's aim would be to draw another girl to the table, to see to it that Joe also bought her a drink, and then to replenish their glasses as often as possible before leaving the club towards dawn.

Sure enough, more or less as soon as Joe had sat down, a second, less attractive girl, with the paler skin and slightly finer features particular to northern China, dropped herself into Joe's lap and began stroking his neck.

"My name Mandy," she said.

"Hello, Mandy. Let me find you somewhere to sit."

Miles grinned as Joe gently tipped the girl onto her feet, walked past the Texan and found a chair at a vacant table. He had a good deal of difficulty returning it through the crowds and was obliged to lift the chair over the heads of several people at the bar. Joe heard Miles stage whisper "Jesus" but did not mind being the central player in a brief comedy of British incompetence. If anything, he wanted to show by his actions that he was unsuited to this environment, that his presence in the club was by accident, rather than design. He sat down beside her, looked at his watch and tried to make conversation.

"Where are you from?"

He never used Mandarin unless it was necessary. There was always an advantage to being regarded as an outsider, even in a place like this.

"Mongolia. You know it?"

"I know it."

Mandy was perhaps twenty or twenty-one and dressed so casually that she might have been at home, watching television in a Shatin apartment, doing some ironing or washing-up. Most of the girls in the club wore skirts or dresses, but Mandy was wearing faded denim jeans and a plain white T-shirt. Oddly, this made her more difficult to talk to. She was real. She broke the careful spell of the club. Joe could see in her expression that she did not regard him as a potential customer, nor that she particularly resented him for this. Perhaps she had given up on herself. Perhaps she was just grateful for the company.

"How long have you been here?"

"One month," she said.

"Have you had a chance to see much of Hong Kong?"

"Not really." Melancholy crept into Mandy's exhausted eyes and he wondered how she had ended up working in such a place. Had she been tricked, or travelled willingly? Most of the women came because they had no choice. "No time for sightseeing," she said. "All day sleep."

He thought of her, crammed into a tiny, ten-bed Triad dormitory, probably just a few blocks away in Wan Chai, sleeping fitfully on a damp fleabitten mattress alongside other girls just like her who had left their families, their happiness, their self-esteem, thousands of miles away.

"How long will you stay here?" he asked. They were talking over a dance track in which a man was cackling like a jackal. Mandy could not seem to come up with an answer. Part of Joe's work on snakehead gangs involved preventing the trafficking of Chinese girls to brothels in the UK, but he knew that somebody like Mandy would simply be rotated from club to club in the local area, west to Macau, north to Shenzhen, until age or illness finished her. Kitty, with her looks, might be a bit different. The lucky ones sometimes found husbands. It was the way of things.

"You guys OK?"

Miles had emerged from another cloying embrace with Kitty, whose *qipao* rode up briefly above her knees.

"Fine," Joe told him.

"Didn't you buy your chick a drink?"

Joe had deliberately not done so because he had resented handing over HK$200 to the cashier for their vodka and tonics. SIS was meant to be fighting these arseholes, not supporting them. But a glass of fuck wine for Mandy would at least earn her fifty or sixty bucks. Thirty pieces of silver to salve his conscience. Joe made a gesture of sincere apology and was on the point of going to the bar when Miles waved at one of the barmen and indicated that he would pay for another round.

"You gotta forgive my friend," he said to Mandy, shouting over the music. "Englishmen. They got no manners."

Joe ducked the insult and lit a cigarette. He was suddenly tired again and regretted allowing Miles to order him another drink. No good could come from staying in the club any longer. He was going home.

"This is my last one. Then I'm off."

"Oh relax."

"Seriously. It's time for me to go."

"Seriously," Miles repeated, imitating him as the music shifted from house to a slow, corny ballad that Joe recognized from his days at Oxford. "I Believe I Can Fly." Miles began mouthing the words while his right hand slid around the taut silk waist of Kitty's *qipao*, her mouth once again nuzzling into his neck. They both started giggling. As if she was feeling left out, Mandy now reached across and put her hand tentatively on Joe's leg.

"I'm OK," he said, though she failed to understand. He felt that it would be rude physically to lift her hand from his leg so instead shifted backwards in his chair, dropping it like a rag doll.

"You like R Kelly?" she asked, oblivious to this. It was some time before Joe realized that she was talking about the song.

"Not really," he replied. Miles emerged from his embrace and shouted "Relax" across the table, as if he had been watching and listening all the time.

"I am relaxed," he said. "I'm just tired. It's two o'clock in the morning."

"So what? You're twenty-six years old. Enjoy yourself, man. You got someplace else you'd rather be?"

The question coincided with the arrival of their drinks. Miles reached into his back pocket and retrieved a silver money clip from which he peeled off a series of hundred-dollar notes, a process that Kitty and Mandy watched in a state of near-hypnosis.

"Tell me," he said, as the cashier walked away. "Do you even know what it's like to fuck a Chinese girl?"

Joe could only laugh, bewildered at his tactlessness. He looked across at the girls, wondering if they had understood the question, although neither of them seemed to be paying much attention. "On second thoughts," he said, "I'm taking off now."

"Why?"

"Because I—"

But Miles did not let him finish. For a second time he said, "Tell me, have you ever fucked a Chinese girl?" and Joe tried to kill the exchange with a look. "Have you?"

"You're drunk," he said.

"What is it? You don't like Asian pussy?"

"Let it go, Miles."

The American took a first sip of his drink and rested his hand in the small of Kitty's back. *I believe I can fly.* A prince in his domain. "You want me to tell you about it? Is that it? You can really *move* them, you know?"

"Miles . . ."

"And they *love* it, don't ever lose sight of that. Chinese chicks *love* Western guys. When I take Kitty home tonight, she's gonna have herself a great time. I'm paying her, I'm supporting her family, where's the harm? People like you need to take your Christian moral heads out of your ass and start to see what's really going on."

"If you say so, Miles."

"Why if I say so? Do you feel sorry for them?"

"I don't feel *happy* for them."

"Do you feel sorry for *me*?"

This last question carried a sting. The tone of the conversation had abruptly shifted. It appeared as though Miles expected a serious answer.

"You're gone," Joe said, but it was not enough.

"Answer me."

"I'm going home."

"No, you're not." Lifting his hand from Kitty's back, Miles leaned forward and pinned Joe's forearm to the table, preventing him from standing up. His grip was strong and purposeful. "You do, don't you?"

"Do what?"

"You do feel sorry for me." Joe instructed him to let go but Miles wasn't hearing. The music returned to thumping house and the American had to shout above it to be heard. Joe could see in his eyes that he was obliterated by alcohol. He had witnessed this in Miles only once before. "You think you're better than me and better than these girls." He was swaying slightly in his seat. "You've been brought up in that typical fucking British way to believe that sex is wrong, that desire is guilt, that the best thing you can do in a situation like this is just patronize everybody and slip out the back. You're a fucking coward."

"No Miles, I'm just not you."

Joe again tried to release his grip but Miles only squeezed harder. Finally Joe lost his temper. "Let it go," he said.

"Why? What are you going to do?"

What he did was very simple. In a single abrupt movement, Joe pulled his entire body away from the table, taking Miles and Kitty and four glasses of fuck wine and vodka and tonic with him. Kitty screeched in Chinese like a scalded cat as Miles, realizing that they would both fall, quickly released his grip. The commotion silenced a small section of the club as Joe turned from the toppled table and walked directly through a parted sea of bewildered customers, stunned that he had so quickly lost his temper. Behind him he could hear Miles saying, "Let him go, just let him go," in Mandarin and he felt a sickness in his gut. It was as if twenty-four hours of frustration and resentment had exploded inside him like an ulcer.

He expected to be stopped by bouncers on his way out but nobody stepped into his path. He climbed the steep stairs and emerged onto the street. On the corner of Jaffe Road he stopped and spun slowly through an almost complete circle searching for a cab, the fresh Hong Kong air, the diesel and the dust and the salt of the South China Sea sobering him up until he felt almost calm. He looked at his arm and saw the sunburn imprints of Miles's hands beneath the hairs on his wrist. A taxi stopped at the lights and he stepped into it, travelling home without a word to the driver. When his mobile phone rang after five minutes, he ignored it, assuming that Miles was calling to make peace. Talk to him tomorrow, he told himself. Sort it all out in the morning.

Isabella was dreaming about Miles Coolidge. This is the entry in her diary:

> Very weird. We were at a beach house, possibly New England? I was standing next to Miles on a curved staircase while Joe went swimming in a pool outside with about four Chinese businessmen, all of them wearing white-collared shirts. It was hot and everyone's drunk. In full view of the other guests, Miles suddenly leans towards me and kisses me.
>
> Then we walked up the stairs into a room where someone had laid out multi-coloured pills and lines of blue (?!) coke on a huge white sheet. There were lots of people in the room but Miles was kissing my neck and my back all the time. Either the shock of him doing this, the pleasure and surprise of what was happening, or the noise of Joe coming home woke me up.

Isabella was sitting up in bed when Joe walked into the room.

"You're up," he said.

"I've just had the weirdest dream."

"What about?"

"Can't remember." It was easier to lie.

"You all right?"

"I'm fine."

Joe picked up a bottle of mineral water from the floor and stumbled as he passed it to her.

"You're pissed," she said.

"Very."

She looked at the clock. "Where have you been?"

"Miles. I'm finished with him. Last time we go out."

"Did you have an argument?" Isabella stood up and padded past him into the bathroom. She was wearing a blue silk pyjama top and a pair of white cotton knickers. "You really stink, Joe."

He checked this by inhaling a mouthful of stale tobacco from his shirt and jacket, taking both of them off so that he was standing bare-chested in the centre of the room. "Yeah. A fight. I lost my temper in a club."

"Which club?" Isabella was sitting on the loo.

"In Wan Chai."

She knew what that meant. "What kind of place?"

"The kind of place Miles likes. The kind where he can feel up girls from Ulan Bator." It was a cheap shot. He had never before betrayed Miles's confidence, but wanted Isabella to think better of him for not being part of his world. The tactic didn't work.

"God," he heard her say, running water at the basin. "He's so lonely. He must be so unhappy if he's doing stuff like that."

The remark was like a prophetic indication of Isabella's desire to change Miles, to save him from himself. Joe couldn't think how to reply.

"What about you?" she asked.

"What about me?"

"Did *you* feel up any girls from Ulan Bator?"

"What?" She was drying her hands. The tone of the question had been mischievous rather than disapproving. "Of course not," he said.

"Really?" Isabella came back into the room and saw that Joe

was now standing in his boxer shorts, hanging his suit near the window. Her pyjamas were unbuttoned almost to the waist and she came up behind him, her hands touching his stomach. "Did you want to fuck one of the girls? Were you jealous of Miles? Is that why you had a fight?"

He turned and his eyes went to the dark brown freckles at the crown of her breasts. He kissed them, saying nothing, falling to his knees and pushing her onto the bed. The scent of Isabella's skin was a paradise which he breathed and tasted, as if it would free him from all of the stress and the madness of Wang and Lenan and Miles. But in the half-light of their bedroom, as he moved inside her, Isabella suddenly became Kitty and Kitty became Isabella and Joe's head swarmed with guilt. For the first time between them he lost all trace of her as they made love, and he could sense that she knew this. Adrift in the warmth of the woman he adored he went through the motions of a drunken, head-spinning fuck before collapsing in a funk of guilt and booze.

The diary entry continues:

> It was as if he wasn't with me. For the first time it felt ordinary and boring and I just wanted it over. Then I started thinking about what had happened with Miles. I started thinking about the dream.

17 | QUID PRO QUO

Miles woke the next morning at 8 a.m., pitched out of an all-too brief sleep by the same Sanyo radio alarm clock which had served him well for the previous thirteen years. Purchased in a West Berlin shopping mall in the winter of 1984, it had survived a three-year posting to Germany, a one-year stint back at Langley, four post–Cold War summers in Luanda and a period in Singapore during which he had contracted dengue fever and been nursed back to health by an Indonesian beauty therapist named Kim. Miles was a heavy sleeper and needed to maximize the volume control on the alarm clock in order to be sure of waking up. Today, RTHK Radio 3 was playing The Verve's "Lucky Man," a song Miles enjoyed, but the suddenness of the opening bars acted upon him like an electric shock. He rolled out of bed and moved to a sitting position, turning down the volume on the radio and holding his head in his hands. Through open curtains Miles Coolidge could see fog enshrouding the Peak. Kitty, he recalled, had left at 5 a.m. There was an empty highball glass on the floor at his feet, a discarded condom, an ashtray full of half-smoked cigarettes and an unopened bottle of warm white wine on the bedside table. When Miles drank heavily, he made sure to consume at least a litre of water before going to bed, the only effective preventative measure against a hangover that he had ever encountered. He made his way slowly to the shower, adjusted the nozzle setting to "Massage" and blasted his scalp in a shuddering jet of scalding water. Afterwards, naked and dripping water on the spiral staircase, he walked slowly downstairs to the open-plan kitchen and sitting room, where he retrieved three Panadol Extra from a drawer in his desk, juiced four oranges and made a mug of instant coffee which he drank while scrambling eggs. Americans, he had been repeatedly told, drank filthy coffee, and Miles was oddly proud of this, regularly importing vast cans of Folger's Instant into Hong Kong after trips back home to the States.

By midday he had cleared his in-tray at the consulate, jogged along Bowen Road and sat in the steam room at his local gym expunging the poisons of the previous evening: the tequilas of Samba's, the vodkas of Luard Road, the lines of coke aggressively snorted from Kitty's flat, soft belly at 3 a.m. Yet the fight with Joe preyed on his mind. Miles realized that he had behaved unpleasantly in the club. He knew that Joe would be angry. Their friendship was a delicate web into which the American frequently pushed a fat, obnoxious finger, but he cared enough about Isabella to make amends. Joe, after all, was the link to the woman he craved.

With this in mind, Miles called Joe's cellphone at around one o'clock, adopting a tone of contrition which might almost have been heartfelt.

"Joe, man. Listen, buddy, I'm sorry for what happened last night. I was being a dick."

Joe was coming down the steps of the MTR station at Yau Ma Tei having discovered that there were only twelve apartments—not nineteen—at number 71 Hoi Wang Road, and that nobody in the building had ever heard of Professor Wang Kaixuan. He had shown an elderly Chinese lady, who informed him that she had lived on the ground floor since 1950, a photograph of Wang taken by one of Barber's men in the early hours of 10 April. The woman, who was widowed and smelled strongly of White Flower oil, shook her head, insisted that she had never seen such a person, then invited Joe inside and fed him green tea and Khong Guan biscuits for half an hour while recalling, in vivid detail, stories of the Japanese occupation of Hong Kong.

Joe walked back up the stairs to street level, absorbed Miles's apology, and placed his hand over the receiver so that his reply could be heard above the noise of Nathan Road.

"Don't worry about it," he said. The polite, conciliatory part of his nature had already kicked in. "It's me who should be apologizing to you."

"You think?"

"Did the club ask questions? I didn't mean to make a scene."

"We were both shit-faced, man. They were cool about it."

"Did you take Kitty home?"

Joe had been crass to ask the question, but was nevertheless interested in the reply.

"No. We called it a night." Miles sniffed involuntarily as he uttered the lie. "Had to get an early start." He began flicking a ball of paper around his desk and said: "Look, I shouldn't be encouraging you to go with Chinese girls. You got a great thing with Isabella. It's obviously not right and it's obviously not what you want."

"Oh, I *want* to fuck a Chinese girl."

"You do?"

Joe was surprised at himself. "Sure. I'm just not *going* to fuck a Chinese girl."

"Why?" Miles was genuinely confused.

"You don't understand?" A bicyclist mounted the pavement beside him and sped past, ringing her bell. "Because then I would have to tell Isabella and that would mean I couldn't fuck *her* any more. Do you get it?"

"I get it." Miles flicked the paper into the bin and put his feet on the desk. "So where are you?"

"Having a suit fitted." The lie was instantaneous. "Kowloon."

Joe wondered whether Miles would mention Wang again. If he did, it would imply that he and Lenan were still concerned about his attitude. But the subject did not come up and when it began to rain, he rang off.

"Listen, I'm going inside," he said. "No umbrella."

"Sure. I'll see you around, Joe."

"See you around."

Several hours later, long after the majority of consulate staff had returned home for the evening, Miles passed through three sets of security doors in the basement of 26 Garden Road and made another phone call, this time on a secure line to a townhouse in Washington DC where Bill Marston, his assistant, Sally-Ann McNeil, Richard Jenson and Josh Pinnegar of the Central Intelligence Agency, and Mr. Michael T. Lambert, Chief Financial Officer of Macklinson Corporation, had gathered for a daylong conference on TYPHOON, the CIA's nascent plan for the political and economic destabilization of the People's Republic of China.

The six-bedroom house, which was located a block north of Pennsylvania Avenue, within spitting distance of Capitol Hill, was used by Macklinson as a venue for lobbying congressmen, hosting fund-raising dinners and as a place for out-of-town executives to hang their hats, saving the expense of a downtown hotel. If one or two of them had girlfriends to stay overnight, well, that was one of the perks of the job.

"Nice place you got here, Bill," Jenson had said as he walked in shortly after ten o'clock. "Party much?"

But Marston had not been in the mood for jokes. Instructing Sally-Ann to make coffee for six, he watched two former technicians with the NSA, now employed by Macklinson's security division, sweep the house for bugs, jam UHF and VHF frequencies within a 200-metre radius and ensure that all cellphones, pagers and personal computers in the building were switched off. The younger of the two men then walked into the kitchen, where he set a small portable compact-disc player on the windowsill and put a Beethoven piano concerto on loop. Towards eleven o'clock, the technicians were joined by a third man, from the CIA's Directorate of Science and Technology, who set up an encrypted link to the US Consulate General in Hong Kong before escorting the technicians from the building to a mocked-up FedEx van parked on 5th Street.

"Mr. Coolidge? You there?"

Marston was chairing the meeting from a central position in the main lounge. All doors and curtains were closed. Sally-Ann was sitting on a sofa to his right with Josh directly beside her. Josh would shortly be making a presentation to the group using notes hastily assembled from the Historical Intelligence section of the library at Langley. The prospect had made him intensely nervous and he was eager to make a good impression. Jenson, who was relying on Josh to put the case for the CIA, was seated to Marston's left at a small wooden table beside a door leading into the kitchen. He could hear the piano concerto as a faint background melody and wondered whether the Agency should have employed a man to mow the lawn outside, just to add an extra layer of noise. Probably not worth the effort. Michael Lambert was still on his feet, pacing the room like a senator on election night.

"I'm here, sir."

Miles's voice was clearly audible through a set of conference-call speakers positioned on a large dining-room table in the centre of the room. Marston liked it that Miles had called him "sir." It set the tone.

"We're all ready to go here," he said. "You getting a clear line through to Hong Kong?"

"Crystal."

Josh reached for his notes. Shuttling his eyes between Jenson and a reproduction of Thomas LeClear's portrait of Ulysses S. Grant, he began to speak.

"Well, thank you all for coming here today. We'd like to thank Macklinson Corporation for making their townhouse available for our discussions. As you know, Richard Jenson has called this meeting to bring everybody up to date on certain developments with TYPHOON. Miles Coolidge, one of our officers in Hong Kong, is joining us by secure telephone from the US consulate. On behalf of Mr. Jenson, I'd also like to welcome Michael Lambert, CFO of Macklinson, whose long experience and expertise we predict will be crucial in the effective running of the project on the Chinese mainland."

Nobody said a word. Lambert came to a halt in front of the

largest of three bay windows, ignored the compliment and placed his hands behind his back. Feeling that he needed to be on his feet, Josh stood up, stepped away from the sofa, unwittingly brushing Sally-Ann's leg as he did so, and walked to the other side of the dining-room table so that he was facing an expectant semi-circle of all-powerful Americans. He placed his notes on the varnished wooden surface, reached to straighten a tie that wasn't there, and continued speaking.

"So, uh, to begin, it is the Agency's position that we believe a primary point of weakness for any destabilizing effort in China is going to be the Xinjiang Autonomous Region in the far northwest."

"Where?" Marston said.

"Xinjiang, sir." Josh hadn't expected an interruption so soon. He spelled out the name and pronounced it slowly—"*Shin-jang.*" "If you look on the map we've provided you, you'll find the region nestled between Mongolia and Russia to the north, Kazakhstan, Kyrgyzstan and Tajikistan to the west, India and Pakistan in the south. Roughly speaking."

"And it's a part of China?" Marston didn't seem to mind going public with his ignorance.

"Yes, sir, it is a part of China. As you are all no doubt aware, the government in Beijing has been under constant threat from Muslim separatists in the region for the past ten years."

"And what do these guys want?" Marston was in a bullish mood. The coffee had kicked in. It was as if he wanted to topple Beijing by lunchtime. "You're saying they're Muslims?"

"That's right, sir." Sally-Ann dropped her pen on the floor and picked it up, a distracting movement which caused Josh momentarily to lose his concentration.

"I said what do they want?"

"Uh, an independent Eastern Turkestan, sir. They're Turkic Muslims."

"What's that? Like a Muslim from Turkey?"

Sally-Ann inwardly groaned.

"Not exactly, Bill." Jenson had moved forward to help out. He tapped a pen on the small table in front of him while Josh stole a glance at his notes. Jenson was sitting with his back to a closed set of curtains. A bright desk light shining in his face gave his expression a spectral quality. "There are many millions of Turkics in Turkey itself, but they're also spread out right across Central Asia, Russia, the Caucasus . . ."

"Exactly," Josh interjected. "The Turkic regions include Azerbaijan, Turkmenistan, Iran, Kazakhstan—"

"All right, all right, I get it." Marston scrawled a note on the clipboard in his lap and muttered something under his breath. In the second uncomfortable silence of the morning, Lambert finally chose to sit in an armchair next to the sofa and emitted a bored, arthritic gasp as he did so. Josh felt slightly dizzy.

"Anyway, just a few weeks ago we got reports of three separate bomb attacks carried out by Uighur separatists in Beijing." He had assumed that it was time to continue but, still chastened by Marston's rebuke, aimed his remarks roughly in the direction of Lambert's midriff.

"Uighurs?" Marston said. He pronounced the word like "Niggers." Jenson coughed.

"Yessir. There are several different ways of saying 'Uighur,' usually with a kind of blowing sound on the first syllable, but 'Wiggers' works. 'Wiggers' is good." Sally-Ann hid a smile.

"And these are the guys we're concentrating on today? A bunch of Muslims? I didn't think there were any Muslims in China."

"At the last count, there were about twenty million."

From the echo chamber of the long-distance line to Hong Kong, Miles Coolidge saved Marston's blushes. "If I could just come in here," he said. His voice emerged crisp and true from the speakers on the dining-room table. "Josh is correct in stating that Uighur revolutionaries have been orchestrating low-level bombing and assassination campaigns in mainland China, but this phenomenon has only recently spread to Beijing. Formerly the separatists tended to operate solely in urban centres in Xinjiang, targeting Chinese soldiers and officials. This expansion of a campaign of violence into the Han heartlands is, we feel, significant."

There are moments in intelligence briefings, indeed in business meetings of all kinds, when it becomes clear to those taking part that a single individual knows a great deal more about the subject under discussion than anybody else. This was one of those moments. The disembodied voice speaking fluently and informatively from the impossibly distant reaches of East Asia confirmed both Marston and Lambert's vivid first impressions of the CIA structure on TYPHOON: that Jenson had delegated Josh Pinnegar to run the operation as a test of his worth, but that Pinnegar was just a kid. Miles Coolidge was the one driving the strategy.

He continued. "It's a generally accepted view that separatists seeking to create an Eastern Turkestan were inspired by the defeat of the Soviet occupying force in Afghanistan and, more recently, by the post-Soviet independence of their neighbouring Muslim republics. However, there's nothing like the same level of understanding or support for the Uighur cause on an international basis as there is for, say, Tibet." Coolidge's expert pronunciation of the word "Uighur" here—capturing the whistled "Ui" at the start, the swallowed "ghur" at the back—contrasted vividly with Pinnegar's lazy Americanization. It was another mark against him. "In fact, there are probably only a handful of people in North America who really understand or care what's going on up there." If this was a dig at Marston, it had no effect. Reagan's favourite son was nodding slowly whilst enthusiastically taking notes. "That said, there's now every indication that the separatist movement is becoming increasingly coherent and well organized. Beijing is also worried about a possible domino effect if Urumqi falls, with Tibet and Taiwan following suit."

"Urumqi being the capital of Xinjiang," Marston said. He had taken the time to look at his map.

"That is correct, sir, yes." Miles shook his head quietly in the booth, wondering who the hell Jenson and Pinnegar had got themselves involved with. "Probably I should make it clear at this stage that there are also significant oil reserves in the Tarim basin."

The single word "oil" acted upon Michael Lambert like a shot of espresso. Oil was profit. Oil was power. A grey-haired executive in late middle age was suddenly lifted from his armchair slumber by visions of construction contracts, pipeline deals, Macklinson refineries and chemical plants.

"The Tarim basin?" he said, eyes squinting like knives.

Miles asked who was speaking and Lambert told him. "Call me Mike," he said.

"Well, Mike, the Tarim basin is essentially the western section of Xinjiang province. It's mostly sand. The Taklamakan. Locals call it the Desert of Death, the Place of No Return. The literal translation is 'Go in, and you won't come out.' Either way, it's a great spot for a vacation."

It was the first joke of the meeting. Sally-Ann smiled into her lap, Josh and Jenson dutifully smirked, while Lambert and Marston dwelled with regret on the cruel indifference of Chinese geography. Getting oil out of a desert made life infinitely more complicated.

"However, regardless of what goes on there, if the economy accelerates in China over the next fifteen years in the way most analysts are predicting, Beijing is going to need to import a further twenty million tons of oil in that period just to maintain current growth trends." A car alarm triggered on 5th Street and Miles was asked to repeat what he had said. Josh picked up the baton.

"So the communist government is obviously keen to keep a hold of Xinjiang," he said. Sally-Ann gave him an encouraging smile. "In case there's something down there. In case there's oil or gas."

"It's not definitely there?" Lambert looked confused. He hadn't been expecting a qualifier. Did Xinjiang possess significant oil reserves or not? Marston was staring at the speakers. He seemed to be wondering the same thing.

"Not definitely." Josh picked through his notes until he arrived at a Canadian SIS report on oil exploration in Central Asia. "The situation is not dissimilar to what's going on in the Caspian Sea right now. Nobody knows how much oil, how much gas they've got down there."

Miles eased back in. "I might have to disagree with that analysis, Josh." Prior to the meeting, the three men from the CIA had taken part in a telephone conversation in which Jenson had stressed the importance of presenting a united front at all times to Macklinson executives. Miles was aware that his contradiction would reflect badly on Josh, but knew that it was essential to point out the error. "It's a common misconception that China doesn't have any oil," he said. Josh did what he always did when he felt uncomfortable and patted down his hair. "In fact, quite the opposite. The Chinese authorities have known about the oil and gas potential in Xinjiang for decades. The China National Petroleum Corporation began exploration and production activity in the early 1950s. We don't really know too much about this in the West because foreign involvement has been limited. That, coupled with the difficulty of operating in what is an extremely hostile and remote region, has also thwarted investment."

Lambert looked crushed.

"Nevertheless, Xinjiang is going to remain of huge strategic importance to Beijing as a conduit for any oil coming in by pipeline from, say, Kazakhstan. This is the point I think Mr. Pinnegar was about to make when he referenced the Caspian basin." It was a skilful redressing of the balance and Josh made sure to catch Marston's eye. "The question everybody out here wants an answer to is how that oil travels to markets in China, Korea and Japan if Urumqi falls. There isn't any alternative route unless you detour through Russia."

Marston looked down at his map. With his fingernail he traced an imaginary pipeline from Baku which passed through Taliban-controlled Afghanistan, the tribal areas of northern Pakistan, east via disputed Kashmir and finally into Tibet. An impossible journey. He felt a strange surge of empathy for his political brethren in Beijing and realized, with a fizz of satisfaction, that Xinjiang was the key. TYPHOON had its target.

"Could I also add a note on China's nuclear capabilities?" Josh asked.

Nobody seemed particularly interested in this. Marston was gazing at the speakers again. Eventually, when nobody responded to the question, Jenson said, "Go ahead, Josh."

"Well, largely as a relic of the Cold War era, China still maintains a huge military presence, both ground and air, in Xinjiang. Most of its nuclear ballistic missiles are also housed there and we've seen up to fifty nuclear tests conducted in the Taklamakan desert since the mid-1960s. Those tests have further fuelled separatist violence in the region. Muslim groups ask, with some justification, why Turkic peoples are being subjected to fallout, groundwater contamination and birth defects while the Han population to the east sleeps soundly in their beds."

Marston stirred. "So you're saying these guys are ripe for revolution?"

Josh risked a gentle put-down. "Well I wouldn't want us to get too ahead of ourselves, but you would certainly have to look at the Uighur population and conclude that the notion of separation from the state wouldn't be a particularly hard sell."

"Does somebody want to put that in plain English?"

Jenson defended his man against yet another Marston attack. The former Assistant Secretary of Defense was incapable of conducting himself in a professional environment without finding at least one individual to pick on. Usually it was Sally-Ann, but in the late twentieth century's rampant climate of political correctness, he didn't want to appear sexist. "What Josh is saying, Bill, is that the Uighurs are sick of being treated as third-class citizens." Sally-Ann looked up at Josh and did something with her eyes which he interpreted as sympathetic. "Fifty years ago, Xinjiang was their country. When Mao came to power in '49, Uighurs made up— what?—about eighty per cent of the population. Today that figure stands at somewhere nearer fifty. There's been a deliberate policy of Han immigration to dilute the ethnic group."

"Stalin had the same routine," Lambert muttered. "Latvia, Estonia, Lithuania. Same routine." Marston, a fellow Cold Warrior, made a noise which confirmed this. He liked to be reminded of the good old days.

"Stalin had nothing on these guys," Josh replied. If his voice had assumed a tone of mild insolence it was because he no longer cared what Marston thought of him. He just wanted to get to the nub of the issue and then break for lunch. "The Communist Party hands out financial rewards to Han who intermarry with Uighur Muslims. They've also waived the one-child policy for their offspring."

"Offspring who are registered as Chinese," Jenson added, continuing to support his boy.

"What you're talking about is a systematic attack on Uighur religion, Uighur resources, Uighur freedom of expression." Josh paused briefly to gather his thoughts. "Most senior officials and all of the military commanders in Xinjiang are Han stooges appointed by Beijing. The Han control almost every element of the local economy, an economy geared exclusively to the needs of China. This builds a huge amount of resentment, a resentment not solely confined to the Turkic population."

"What do you mean by that?" Lambert asked.

"Don't forget that we're talking about Sufi Muslims here. The examples of fundamentalism seen across the Islamic world in recent years, most notably in Algeria with Hezbollah and in Taliban-controlled Afghanistan, have thus far failed to manifest themselves in Xinjiang. The Uighur people are not by nature extremist. That said, some of them fought with the mujahaddin and Beijing has long been concerned about cross-pollination between the Taliban and the Uighur minority. Any kind of trade in weapons across the Afghan–Chinese border, for example, would be virtually unpoliceable. And, of course, those same Taliban have strategic knowledge of fighting the Soviets, knowledge which they might be only too happy to pass on to their Muslim brothers in China. Allow me to finish."

Marston had begun to speak, but such was the force and confidence of Josh's request that he was silenced. The CEO of one of the largest corporations in the United States of America, a man who had supped with Kissinger and Gorbachev, was briefly humbled.

"I also wanted to add something here about Saudi Arabia." Josh cleared his throat and saw that Sally-Ann was looking at him. "We believe that the more the Chinese repress the Muslims of Xinjiang, the more the Saudis will be inclined to give financial assistance to their cause. Again, you only have to look at their support for the Afghan resistance between '80 and '89 for evidence of what they're prepared to do. Now this is vitally important as far as China is concerned. Saudi Arabia is a source of oil for China, and China needs to keep that oil flowing in order to facilitate its rapid economic growth. In short, Beijing cannot afford to upset the House of Saud."

"I know the feeling," Marston muttered.

It was an impressive monologue, produced in its latter stages entirely without notes. Sally-Ann found a more explicit look of admiration for Josh and the young man from the CIA felt buoyed. Then Miles's voice came thumping out of the speakers.

"So what does all this add up to?" he asked.

Josh and Jenson caught each other's eye. The question was rhetorical and they knew that Miles had every intention of answering it. He was about to make the CIA's case for TYPHOON.

"What it adds up to is an opportunity for the American government to run a clandestine operation in mainland China aimed at bringing about the restoration of democracy in an independent Eastern Turkestan. And, as I understand it, you gentlemen have kindly offered us the full co-operation of your organization in pursuit of that goal."

Miles's words substantially shifted the tone of the meeting. Everything was now political. Lambert and Marston leaned forward in their chairs and tried to look like patriots.

"We're here to help," Marston said.

"And that's great. But why do we need your help, sir? Why is this meeting today necessary?" Again, the questions were self-evidently rhetorical. "Well, I guess on one level it's pretty obvious." He took a sip of water. "If organizations such as the National Endowment for Democracy, or Freedom House, want to help run fair elections in, say, Central Africa, maybe try to bring democracy to eastern Europe, then that's something that the Company has always been able to help them with." Miles's mouth was dry and he went for more water. Maybe last night's hangover was finally kicking in. "But trying to pull that kind of thing off in China is infinitely more complex. Beijing has always been suspicious of non-profit organizations operating within its borders. Fact is, they don't get in. You might find a few Christian missionaries operating in major cities, some of them even on our books, but as far as China is concerned, the Agency's hands are tied. There are just too many obstacles to running effective campaigns. So we have to resort to other methods. We've had to think out of the box."

Both Lambert and Marston looked at Jenson as if they were now expected to speak. Instead, aware of the gathering silence in Washington, Miles carried on.

"What we want to suggest to you today, gentlemen, is a strategy on several fronts. Dick, Josh, you OK if I go ahead?"

"Absolutely."

Miles glanced at a sheet of paper on the desk in front of him on which he had scrawled some bullet-pointed notes. "Now it's my understanding that Macklinson has offices outside of Beijing in Shenzhen, Shanghai, Harbin, Golmud, Xining and Chengdu. Is that correct?"

"That is correct," Lambert told him.

"Well then here's what we would like to suggest."

Sally-Ann McNeil is nowadays a mother of three children—
two boys, one girl—living in a quiet suburb of Maryland, married
to a balding, wealthy, not exactly charismatic tax attorney named
Gerry. Their house, with its low white roof and its sprinkler on
the lawn, is no more than an hour's drive from the airport and
resembles every other house on the anonymous residential street on
which they have chosen to make their home. Sally-Ann works
part-time at a local real estate office, offers private tuition to dys-
lexic schoolchildren and plays golf with her friend Mary up to three
times a week.

"Bill Marston got me into it," she says. "If he was still alive today, I could kick his ass."

It took a while to track Sally-Ann down. Her name has changed
through marriage and, in the wake of TYPHOON, she was understandably reluctant to stick her head above the parapet. We
spoke one weekday afternoon in 2006 in a warm, plant-filled
conservatory at the back of her house when Gerry was away at
work and the eldest of their children at school. If she was nervous
about talking to a nosey writer, she did not betray it, although the

breaking of her long silence was something for which she had clearly been preparing herself for some time.

"To be honest, it was all so long ago. I thought nobody would ever ask," she said, letting the two-week-old baby she was holding in her arms suckle on a manicured finger. "It was part of my job to be anonymous, to be the note taker, the assistant who fixed coffee. Nobody even seemed to notice I was there." She looked sideways out of the window and her gaze seemed regretful. "I knew right away that I was carrying a pretty burdensome secret. I've never told Gerry a thing, you know? I figured the day that I did would be the day that they came looking for me."

Sally-Ann now began to relate what Miles had said on the long-distance line as the Washington meeting developed either side of lunch. Her voice was low and steady and I was impressed both by her memory and by her grasp of the political ramifications of the discussion. In common with most Europeans over the previous five or six years, I had tended to underestimate the intelligence of the average Bush-voting American, but Sally-Ann was as lucid and as perceptive as I could have wished.

"What you have to remember is that Bill Marston was a politician first and a businessman second," she said. "With Mike Lambert it was the other way around." I was taking notes and my pen ran out of ink. She was still talking as I swapped it for a biro in my jacket pocket. "Both of them had this image of themselves as patriots, when in fact they were just ignorant, ambitious neocons. I guess you've seen it a lot in the past few years. Throwbacks from a different era with little or no understanding of how anybody east of New York really behaves. Men of money and power whose sole objective is to make America richer and more powerful than she already is. So when this articulate, seemingly well-informed spy from Hong Kong started to suggest using Macklinson hardware and know-how to get access into mainland China, they both just started to glow. The plan was so crazy, but it was perfect. They were going to conceal explosives, weapons, cellphones, laptop computers, printers, photocopiers, even Korans, in Macklinson freight shipments coming in by air or sea from the United States.

Coolidge knew we had contracts running in dozens of Chinese cities, including four, I think, in Xinjiang itself, and others just over the border in Gansu and Qinghai. He proposed funding the setting up of English-language schools on site, nominally for teaching Chinese-speaking employees how to communicate with their American bosses, but in reality as cover for CIA teachers in Xinjiang and surrounding provinces to recruit disaffected laborers for the creation of civil strife."

"Some of those teachers got caught," I muttered.

"Sure," she replied, as if this wasn't news to her. "Then they sent out literally hundreds of video cameras for distribution among the peasant underclass so they could record the riots when they took place, with the idea of exerting extra pressure on Beijing through the subsequent outrage of the international community. I think maybe that was one idea that actually worked, right, because I saw a news report on CNN." I nodded, unsure whether CNN had covered the same riot story as the one picked up by the *Washington Post* in the summer of 2003, when video footage of a pitched battle between disgruntled peasants and gangs employed by a Chinese electricity company was leaked to the *Post* by a farmer. The film showed a small group of peasants who had refused to abandon their land being attacked by a gang armed with pipes and shovels. "And then of course they were going to fill Macklinson with deep-cover CIA guys who would nominally be working on road or rail construction projects but would in fact be running agents across the entirety of north-west China. It was all on an unbelievable scale. Coolidge talked about encouraging Saudi funding using 'well-established channels,' about the need to identify and fund a Uighur leader at the head of an Eastern Turkestan government-in-exile. They even talked, at that early stage, about recruiting Uighur pilgrims when they travelled to Mecca. It was very imaginative, very persuasive. Yet even as I was listening to it all, with everybody going into detail and new ideas springing up all the time, I remember thinking, How can it be that this morning neither Bill Marston nor Mike Lambert could point to Xinjiang on a map? Yet here they are signing up a publicly listed company to a top-secret CIA project which nearly bankrupted its operations in Asia."

"Oil," I said, because, when it came to TYPHOON, oil was the answer to almost everything.

"I guess you're right." Sally-Ann's middle child, a blond-haired toddler called Karl who was watching television in the next room, suddenly waddled in and asked for some fruit juice. She fetched it for him and then returned to the conservatory carrying a plate of apparently home-baked cookies. As if she had been turning the idea over in her mind, she said, "I think Mike was always a lot smarter than Bill, y'know? The top guys at Macklinson were almost always figureheads, former government officials who lent a certain kind of gravitas and credibility to the boardroom. Men like Mike Lambert were the ones making the decisions. He'd been with the company from the age of twenty-two. Now he's worked his way to the top. And I definitely think you're right when you say that it was the prospect of the oil and gas in Xinjiang that made him go along with it. That was the quid pro quo with the CIA as far as he was concerned. You scratch our back now and we'll scratch yours later. You could actually see him envisaging an independent Xinjiang run by a puppet government of the United States. That was how delusional they were. Macklinson sweeping up contracts to build pipelines, refineries, road networks, hotels in the desert . . ."

Sally-Ann suddenly looked tired and I realized that she had probably been up most of the night feeding her baby. She laid the child in a crib on the floor and I wondered whether this was my cue to leave. We had been talking for several hours.

"What time is Gerry due back?" I asked.

She looked at her watch. "In about a half-hour."

"Is there anything else you can tell me? Anything else you can remember?"

She looked directly at me, as if she knew what I was angling for. The best journalists already know the answers to half the questions they want to ask. A contact had placed Kenneth Lenan in Garden Road on the night of the conference call and I needed that information confirmed.

"Well, there was one last thing," she said. I picked up one of the cookies and took a bite out of it in an effort not to appear too eager. "Towards about four o'clock, a second man joined Coolidge in the booth and started to take part in the conversation."

"An Englishman?" I asked, just to help her along.

"Sure, an Englishman. How did you know that?"

"Go on."

"I can't remember his name. Only that he had one of those typical British accents, you know? A little bit superior, a little bit upper class."

"Could his name have been Kenneth Lenan?"

"That's right." Sally-Ann's voice leaped to such an extent that the carefully swaddled baby stirred and moaned. "Kenneth Lenan. Sounded like a member of the British Royal family. Real snooty."

"That's the one." I was smiling to myself. "Lenan was Coolidge's contact in MI6, the British end of TYPHOON. What happened?"

"Well, he just kind of showed up. Miles was in the middle of talking about some of the terrorist activities that had been happening on Urumqi public transportation and he suddenly announces that somebody else was going to be joining us."

"Did that surprise Jenson? How did Josh react?"

Sally-Ann appeared to struggle for the memory here, which suggested to me that Lenan's appearance had been preordained. "No, I think they kind of just ran with it," she said. "We'd all been there so long it didn't seem weird that someone should be coming in at that point. I guess we'd lost sight of the fact that it was maybe three or four o'clock in the morning over in Hong Kong and that for somebody from MI6 to be sitting in with Miles was not unusual."

"So Miles acknowledged that he was from British intelligence?"

"Yup."

"And what did Lenan say?"

"Far as I can remember, the tone of the conversation became a little bit—how can I put it?—triumphalist. I guess the point was to show Macklinson how serious the Agency was about TYPHOON and how far down the line they already were in terms of planning. Coolidge introduced Lenan and said they were about to run a particular agent into Xinjiang, a professor of something or other who'd just come over from China. It sounded kind of far-fetched to me but Bill was real impressed."

This astonished me. "They were talking about Wang already, even at that stage?"

"Who?"

"Wang Kaixuan. A Han academic from Urumqi. He was recruited by Lenan and sent back into Xinjiang to organize a network of separatist radicals."

"*He* was the one?" Sally-Ann was frowning. It was all starting to fall into place. She looked down at the baby and said, "Well it certainly sounds like the same person. Coolidge was real excited by it. Said this guy had just fallen into their laps."

"What about Lenan? What did he say?"

From the front of the house I could hear what sounded like a car pulling up in the drive. It might have been on one of the neighbouring properties, or somebody turning around in the road, but I was concerned that Gerry had returned home early and would now interrupt this last vital stage of our conversation. I had a flight to catch to Beijing the next day and this would be my last chance to talk to Sally-Ann for several weeks.

"He was more measured," she said, "like he was too superior to get excited about it. You know how a certain type of English person can be like that? A little condescending, like everything is beneath their dignity?" I smiled. "From what I remember Lenan kind of picked up where Coolidge left off. Said he had just gotten back from Taiwan where he'd debriefed the agent and that it 'was indeed very encouraging news,' or some shit like that. Said that Wang represented the new China, was a forward-thinking democrat, a man of hope. Kind of thing that made Bill Marston drool. Maybe my memory is playing tricks on me, but in some ways it sounded as though the British guy would have preferred not to be there." Sally-Ann pushed a twist of hair behind her ear. "Makes me wonder why Miles called him in."

"Me too," I said.

"Unless . . ."

"Unless what?"

I heard the boot of the car slam outside and knew that Gerry would soon be at the front door. Sally-Ann appeared not to have noticed.

"Unless Miles didn't know about Wang Bin."

"Who's Wang Bin?"

"Wang's son."

I stopped taking notes. At first, Sally-Ann didn't seem to notice my surprise. "Maybe Lenan had been to Taiwan and found out what had happened to him," she said. "When he told us over the conference phone it certainly sounded like it was fresh information."

"What information? What the hell happened to Wang's son?"

"You didn't know?"

"Tell me, Sally."

"Wang Bin was killed," she said. "Shot by the Chinese PLA. During some riot in Xinjiang. I guess that was his justification for what he did. I guess that was Wang's justification for everything."

19 | THE ENGAGEMENT

Do spies believe in God?

During one of our many conversations in the flat in Brook Green that Joe rented in 2004, he brought up the subject of religion. It was not something that I had ever expected to discuss with him, and his attitude took me by surprise.

"I've always believed in God," he said. "I don't really know why. How does something like that begin?"

Certainly not with his father. Peter Lennox was what might loosely be described as an agnostic moralist, a man of science whose experience with organized religion was limited to making occasional appearances at a wedding or funeral. On Christmas mornings, for example, he preferred to remain behind in the house to "watch the turkey" while the rest of his family went to church. At the same time, he maintained that he lived his life "by Christian principles," a nebulous claim that very few people—Joe included—could be bothered to argue with. Joe's mother, Catherine, was a more recognizable type, an old-fashioned, lapsed Anglican whose face was known to her local vicar. Though not ostentatiously spiritual, Catherine occasionally appeared at church fêtes and, as a child, Joe vividly remembers sitting beside her at the start of an

Easter Sunday service when a ladder appeared in her tights as she knelt down to pray.

At the age of eight, Joe was sent away to the same top-of-the-range preparatory school in Wiltshire where his father, his uncles and his paternal grandfather (as well as an heir to the throne of Nepal) had all been pupils at one time or another. It was a Christian school. There was a small private chapel on site and, every evening, shortly before packing the boys off to their windy dormitories, the headmaster would call for silence in the cavernous dining room and read from the Book of Common Prayer.

"I can still picture it," Joe told me. "I can still hear his voice: *Lighten our darkness, we beseech thee, O Lord, and by thy great mercy defend us from all the perils and the dangers of this night.* What perils? What dangers? We were a hundred and sixty boys wearing Aertex shirts, miles from home, living in an old monastery in the middle of the English countryside. Who the hell was coming to get us?"

At thirteen Joe went on to a larger, though still all-male, public school where the students were obliged to attend a fifteen-minute church service every weekday morning, with a longer version on Sundays. By and large it was more of the same: long, humourless sermons, eight-verse hymns which never seemed to end, older boys flicking spit and hard stares across the nave. For most teenagers, such an experience would have put them off religion for life, but somehow Joe maintained his faith.

"But you don't go to church," I said to him. "I didn't exactly see you down at St. John's Cathedral every Sunday when we were living in Causeway Bay."

He looked at me as though I was being naïve. Joe would no more have wasted a Hong Kong Sunday in church than he would have broken cover.

"Why was that?" I asked. "Was Isabella an atheist?"

It was the first time I had mentioned her name for weeks. Joe looked down at the glass of wine he was drinking and ran his thumb along the stem.

"No. She wasn't." He stood up and walked away from the table, ostensibly to fetch me another can of Guinness, but doubtless as a means of preventing me from seeing the expression on his face.

"She was Catholic, although I think probably we had a pretty similar attitude to religion. It wasn't something that we talked about very much. Both of us hated the paraphernalia, the *interference*, that you get with religion, at least in its British incarnation. Wide-eyed vicars and half-empty pews. Bankrupt businessmen reading the lesson, trying to pass themselves off as pillars of the community. Going to church is at best a social occasion, isn't it? A place where people can go and not feel lonely or devoid of hope."

"Maybe," I said, suspecting that this cynicism was a little forced. Then Joe surprised me again.

"When it came to Isabella," he said, "I had this extraordinary feeling that she was a gift from God. That was the extent of the spell she cast over me." I made to interrupt him but he looked at me with a fierce intensity. Both of us knew that what he was about to say was not something that a man like Joe might ordinarily disclose. "As our relationship developed, I felt that God was saying to me, 'Here, this is the person that I want you to be with. This is the opportunity I am giving you to lead a happy and fulfilled life. Don't mess it up.' It was extraordinary. It was as if I had no choice."

"And that's why you wanted her to marry you?"

"Sure. That's why I wanted her to marry me."

So Joe went to Waterfield, because Waterfield was his mentor in Hong Kong, his priest and father figure. When he had first arrived in the colony, their relationship had even formed part of Joe's cover. SIS created what is known as a Backstop, verifying a fiction that Waterfield had done National Service with one of Joe's tutors at SOAS by doctoring a few military records and even airbrushing an old black-and-white photo from Sandhurst. He had therefore "looked him up" as a useful contact a few days after landing at Kai Tak and attended a dinner party at the Waterfield's apartment where, for the benefit of any gossips or Chinese bugs, the two of them had engaged in a forty-minute conversation about Brian Lara and the difficulty of obtaining decent red wine in Asia. So it was not remarkable for both men to be seen together one Saturday afternoon at the bird market in Mongkok. Even if a Chinese spook had developed suspicions about Joe, he would have encountered an impenetrable wall of deep cover should he have chosen to investigate.

"You wanted to ask me about something." Waterfield had brought his wife with him, but she was busy buying orchids on Flower Market Road.

"It's about Isabella."

"I see."

It is difficult to exaggerate the extent to which SIS was a male-dominated culture among Waterfield's generation. Talk of wives and girlfriends generally made them suspicious and bored. Women were like children in the era of Victorian parenting: to be seen and not heard.

"I think I'd like to ask her to marry me."

"Really. Well, congratulations."

They were walking side by side down a cramped alleyway that was lined with bird cages, the smarter ones fashioned from varnished bamboo. Rainwater from a recent storm dripped from corrugated-iron roofs and made a thin mud of the dirt and straw at their feet. If anybody had been attempting to record the conversation, the take quality would have been severely compromised by a perpetual, tuneless squawk of mynah birds and parakeets.

"Does that present any difficulties as far as the Office is concerned?"

More than a month had passed since Joe had interviewed Wang and he was still wary of putting his foot wrong. Waterfield glanced down at a table covered in sealed transparent bags and stopped walking.

"Crickets," he said, prodding one of the bags so that the insects inside them leaped out of a camouflage of leaves and dried grass. "They feed them to the birds. With chopsticks." Waterfield appeared to remember that Joe had asked him a question and looked up into his eyes. "It presents a difficulty, of course, only if you're going to want to have everything out in the open."

"I will want that," Joe replied without hesitation.

"Then we'd better sit down and have a proper chat."

They walked a further three hundred metres until the head-ache din of the birds had largely died away and they were alone in a small market stall selling noodles, simple Cantonese dishes and cheap Peking duck. There was a half-empty bottle of soy sauce on the table. When Joe moved it to one side the neck left a dry, sticky glue on his hands.

"I'm going to be patronizing," Waterfield said, ordering a pot of green tea. It was one of the things that Joe liked about him: he had the confidence to be self-effacing. "You're very young to be think-ing about getting married."

"I realize that."

"Do you? One of the things that's most difficult for men of your age to grasp is the enormous span of time left to you on the planet. That may sound grandiose, but so many years lie ahead, do you see? I'm not talking here about careers. I mean in a strictly personal sense. It's extremely hard for a human being to have any notion of the extraordinary changes that they will undergo in their future lives, particularly between the ages of twenty-five and thirty-five. Changes in approach. Changes in personality."

Joe didn't know what to say. He wondered if Waterfield, in a roundabout kind of way, was telling him that he was immature.

"Let me divulge something about getting older." The tea came and the SIS Head of Station poured it quickly into two white bowls. "Life *contracts*. Less room for manoeuvre, if you follow me. One acquires responsibilities that are perhaps unimaginable to someone of twenty-six. Responsibilities towards one's children, of course, but also the added burden of work, of longer hours, of scrambling up the greasy pole. In a very real sense one must put away childish things." Waterfield saw the look in Joe's eyes and must have felt obliged to defend himself. "I can see what you're thinking: 'The old man is full of regrets, didn't have enough fun in his youth. Insists the younger generation sow a few wild oats.'"

"Isn't that partly what you're saying?" Joe asked.

"Well I suppose it is, yes." Waterfield laughed at himself and plucked a toothpick out of a small plastic canister on the table. Rather than put it in his mouth, he tapped one of the sharp points into the ball of his thumb. "Look, I think you are a very remarkable

young man, Joe, and I say that both as a colleague and as a friend."
Joe had to remind himself that he was talking to a spy, but it was
difficult not to extract a pulse of satisfaction from the compliment.
"What you've achieved out here in such a short time is very impressive. But you are still *young*. You are still at the very beginning
of what should be an extremely interesting and eventful life."

Joe knew that he was expected to speak, but took his time before responding. Two elderly women passed the table carrying
plastic bags stuffed with *bok choi* and washing detergent. Joe took
out a cigarette, lit it, and blew the first smoke up into a flapping
tarpaulin canopy that functioned as a roof over the stall. The gesture may have looked self-conscious.

"The thing is, David, I can only deal with what's in front of
me. I can only deal with the reality that I'm at this point in my life
and that I'm in love with Isabella Aubert."

Silence.

"What that means is that I want to spend the rest of my life
with her. What that means is that I don't think I'll ever meet anybody like her ever again, whether I'm twenty-six, thirty-six or a
dying man of ninety-one."

Waterfield produced a rueful smile as Joe thought of God's instruction to him. *Marry this woman. She is the best thing that will ever
happen to you.* He knew that such thoughts were absurd, yet he
could not shake them.

"You see that's just it, Joe, that's just it. One feels that way now,
but will one feel that way in the future?"

Irritated by a creeping formality in Waterfield's tone, Joe again
paused for thought. It occurred to him—not for the first time—
that Isabella was deeply unpopular within the walls of SIS. Why
should that be? Whom had she offended? Was it simply that she
was beautiful and charming and kind, and therefore coveted by
dozens of unhappily married spooks who wished that they could
live their lives all over again, preferably in her company? Why else
had she not been accepted by them?

Then it became very plain to him, very quickly. Waterfield
wanted to prevent the marriage in order to protect the integrity of
RUN. He wanted to interfere with Joe's private life in order to

give SIS one less thing to worry about in the run-up to the handover. His advice and good counsel were simply political.

"I think I'm an old soul," Joe said, trying to find a way round this. Waterfield's encouraging smile convinced him to keep going. "I've always been decisive, I've always known what I want. And I want to take care of Isabella. I want us to be husband and wife. Maybe I'm being naïve, maybe I'm too young to be thinking like this, maybe I'm just a lovestruck teenager who'll learn a hard lesson. But I want to stop lying to her. I want my girlfriend to know what I do for a living. I'm sorry, I can see that that is going to present problems for you. I can see that you'll be concerned about my cover and whether it'll affect the quality of my work. But I've made my decision and I need the Office's support. I love her."

"Then you must marry her," Waterfield said. "It's as simple as that."

"But why *did* you want to marry her?" I asked. "What was the fucking hurry?"

We are back in 2004 again, on the eve of his departure for Shanghai. I was opening my can of Guinness and Joe's subsequent laughter smothered the hiss of the widget. He produced another one of those looks that appeared to question my innate common sense and shook his head.

"Isn't it obvious?" he said. "Isn't it straightforward?"

It was obvious, to a certain extent. They were perfect for each other. Where Joe was often concealed and emotionally withdrawn, Isabella was open and honest. On those rare occasions when she became anxious or depressed, he knew how to listen to her and to soothe her worries. Isabella could be unpredictable, but not in a way that was threatening or unkind, and I think Joe fed off her impulsiveness and volatility. They made each other laugh, they had similar interests, they were both naturally inquisitive and adventurous people. Above all, there was an innate understanding between the two of them which made you jealous that there was not some sort of similar chemistry in your own life.

Nevertheless, in answer to Joe's question, and in an effort to find out exactly what was going through his mind back in 1997, I said: "No, it's not obvious. To be honest, it doesn't make any sense to me at all."

So Joe tried to explain himself. He had drunk the better part of a bottle of wine by then, which had loosened up his natural reticence.

"I had a drink the other day with a friend from university," he began. "A guy called Jason. He'd only been married about six weeks and already had the shortest recorded incidence of the seven-year itch. He said to me, 'Joe, in an ideal world no man would ever have conceived of the institution of marriage. It's counter-intuitive. Why would we limit our options like that? Marriage is a feminist conspiracy designed to exercise control over men.'"

"Your friend's got a point," I said.

"My friend is an idiot," Joe replied. "What would you have done in my place? Isabella and I had been together for more than two years. There were no other circumstances in which the Office would have tolerated me telling her about RUN. Waterfield would have handed me a P45 and told me to swim back to London."

"So that was the reason?" I seized on this. "You did it just to ease your conscience? You felt so guilty about lying to Isabella that your only way out of it was to *propose*?"

I have already written about Joe's temper, about the extent to which he had to be pushed before the lid came off, and for a split second here I wondered whether he was going to launch at me. My words were ill-chosen and his face tightened in anger. In an instant, all of the easygoing, wine-fuelled bonhomie of our conversation evaporated.

"Isn't that reason enough?" he said. "Do you have any concept of what it's like to grow up through your twenties living a lie to all but four or five people in the world?"

"Joe, I . . ."

Just as quickly, his anger abated and his face regained its tranquillity, as if he had subjected himself to a private admonition. "Forget I said that," he insisted, waving a hand at me. "That's not what I meant." It was only the second time that Joe had ever voiced a complaint in my company about working under deep cover. On both occasions he had immediately retracted the grievance. After all, nobody had forced him to work for MI6; it was nobody's fault but his own if he occasionally found the demands of the secret life overwhelming. The last thing Joe Lennox ever wanted was for people to feel sorry for him. "Everything about her was intoxicating to me," he said, trying to return to the original subject. "Every day she said or did something that took my breath away. We were *connected*." He stopped momentarily, as if trying to remember something. "There are some lines in T. S. Eliot. 'We think the same thoughts without need of speech. And babble the same speech without need of meaning.' Does that make sense? When I think back to it, there was a kind of perfect relaxation between us, an effortless timing. It's very hard to explain. And I knew that I would never meet anybody who made me feel that way again." He gestured at the walls of the kitchen in the Brook Green flat, as if they contained actual physical evidence of this theory. "So far that's proved true," he said.

"I guess what interests me is the timing," I said. "You had the meeting with Waterfield about a month before the handover, right? Isabella wasn't planning to leave Hong Kong. She had the job with the French television company, but there was no risk of her going to Paris or elsewhere. You were living together, you were getting on. Why the hurry?"

Joe picked up on the subtext of the question. "What's relevant about the job?" he asked. "What are you getting at?"

I hesitated, because once again I was venturing into treacherous waters. Both of us reached for a packet of cigarettes that Joe had placed on the table in front of him. He got there first, offered one to me, and repeated the question.

"What do you mean?"

I poured the Guinness into a pint glass and waited for it to settle. "My theory about marriage is this," I said.

Joe shuffled back in his chair, folded his arms and smiled. "I can't wait to hear this one."

I struggled on. "I think part of the reason why men finally

decide to cash in their chips and settle down, apart from love and convention and pressure, is proprietorial."

"Proprietorial in what sense?" He was frowning.

"In the sense that you want to take your girlfriend off the market. You want to make sure, once and for all, that nobody else can fuck her."

This produced a deservedly contemptuous laugh. "Are you serious? *Ownership*? Isn't that a bit passé, Will?" Then Joe saw my expression and realized what I was getting at.

"I suppose I am serious." I looked at the clean white stripe at the head of my Guinness and risked it. "It always struck me that you must have been worried about Miles, even if it was only in an intuitive way. Deep in your heart, you must have known that your relationship with Isabella was doomed."

This is how rumours get around, on a small island, among spies.

David Waterfield held a meeting with Kenneth Lenan in his office in the House of a Thousand Arseholes five days after talking with Joe in the Mongkok bird market. Lenan had been in Thailand on a week-long holiday and was sporting one of his characteristically deep suntans. Waterfield was running a light tropical fever and looked as though he needed to spend three days in bed.

"So we not only have eight thousand journalists showing up on June the 30th, Prince Charles, the all-new, all-smiling British Prime Minister, the US Secretary of State, the right-on, Right Honourable Mr. Robin Cook, most of the outgoing Tory cabinet, half of the Chinese Politburo and probably Sir Cliff Richard as well. We now have the added problem that RUN wants to propose to his bloody girlfriend."

"At the handover ceremony?" Lenan asked.

"How the hell am I supposed to know?"

"Is that a good idea?"

"I refer the honourable gentleman to my previous answer."

Lenan didn't smile much but he smiled at that one. "He wants her to know he's a NOC?"

"Absolutely."

Lenan frowned. "He wants her to know that for the past two years he's been lying to her morning, noon and night?"

"That would appear to be the scenario, yes." In the corridor outside Waterfield's office, one of the secretaries sneezed. "Joe and I had a chat in Mongkok. He actually said he wanted the Office's help in making it happen."

"Our *help*?"

"Mmmm." Waterfield began coughing and spat something into his handkerchief. "Not exactly sure what he meant by that." He looked out across Victoria Harbour, following the progress of a distant junk. "Does he want us to tell her we *made* him do it? That he was perfectly happy in the shipping business until SIS came along?" The joke went nowhere so he became more serious. "This is a tough life we have chosen, Kenneth. Hard on marriages. Even harder when you bring children into the frame. You've been sensible. Kept yourself unattached. I just hope to God Joe knows what he's doing."

Forty-eight hours later Lenan had dinner with Miles Coolidge in a quiet corner of his favourite Indian restaurant in Hong Kong, situated a few blocks south of Kowloon Park on the third floor of the Ashley Centre. Both men had ordered chicken dhansak and several plates of unnecessary vegetable dishes. Above their heads, an ageing air-conditioning unit hummed, threatening to drip water onto the carpet. Towards ten o'clock, when most of their fellow diners had left for the evening, Miles ordered a bowl of ice cream and instigated a conversation about TYPHOON.

"Any word from your buddy?"

"Back in Urumqi," Lenan replied flatly. "Classes begin on Monday morning."

"And there were no problems? Nobody asked where he'd been to?"

SIS had developed a support agent in Urumqi, a salesman with a British passport who worked for a large German car manufacturer. Codenamed TRABANT, he was initially the first point of contact between Wang and Lenan, and would in due course be replaced by Lenan himself.

"No. Nobody asked. He told them he'd been on holiday in Guangdong and that was that."

Miles was halfway through a glass of iced Sprite. It was an idiosyncrasy of his relationship with Lenan that he rarely drank alcohol in his presence. "This whole thing has happened pretty fast," he said.

Lenan reacted to the doubt implicit in Miles's comment by taking his napkin off his lap and balling it up on the table. "Meaning?"

"Meaning it's still not clear to some of my guys back home, even after everything that's gone down, why he risked the swim."

"Is it at least clear to you?"

Miles rotated the Sprite on the tablecloth and lifted a shard of poppadom into his mouth. He had spun the lie so confidently to Joe in Samba's and the Wan Chai nightclub partly because he had always possessed private doubts about Wang's credentials. "Sure. It's totally clear to me. But I had Josh Pinnegar on the phone for an hour and a half earlier this week wanting to go over every detail of the initial interrogations one more time, the transfer to Taiwan, the means by which you were able to get him back into Xinjiang. He told me there's a feeling back home that this whole thing might have been played by the MSS."

"A *feeling*?" Lenan became impatient. "What does that mean? Who is experiencing these *feelings*? Isn't it a bit late in the day for all this? Is a plug about to be pulled, Miles?"

"Shit no. It's just background. The professor's a fifty-year-old guy, for Chrissakes. He could have drowned. You can see why people might ask questions."

Kenneth Lenan panned his narrow, impassive eyes around the room, settling them on a distant waiter. As always, he looked enormously bored and enormously frustrated by the intellectual limitations of inferior men. "Well, the next time anybody brings the subject up, it's quite simple. You tell them to see it from a Chinese perspective. If Beijing wanted to play one of their top agents into Hong Kong and drop him into the lap of British intelligence so that we all broke out the bubbly, they'd hardly risk putting him on a makeshift raft at three o'clock in the morning on the off-chance he might wash up on a beach in Dapeng Bay. Far more likely they'd give him papers to come across from Shenzhen and allow him to present himself as a walk-in."

Miles's customary mood in the presence of Lenan was not dissimilar to Joe's. He felt generally inferior and second rate in his company, a consequence of the older man's nerveless self-confidence. "You're right, Kenneth," he said, crunching another poppadom. "Of course you're right." He decided, right then and there, to go for a hand job at Lily's after dinner. Miles always wanted sex when he was put under pressure; it was a way of reasserting his authority.

"What about Macklinson's end of things?" Lenan asked. Miles's pudding arrived, a bright red cocktail cherry perched on the summit of four enormous balls of vanilla ice cream. "Are they having doubts as well?"

"None," Miles told him, though he had spoken to neither Michael Lambert nor Bill Marston for several days. "Nobody is having any doubts, Ken. Everything at Macklinson is under control. Shipments are being arranged, personnel prepared. All you have responsibility for is Professor Wang."

Lenan shuddered, both at the explicit mention of Wang's name and at Miles's curt dismissal of his responsibilities. His involvement in TYPHOON was, of course, a closely guarded secret. Nobody on the British side knew that the CIA was, in effect, employing one of their best men on a subcontractual basis. Why was Lenan doing it? Why did he risk everything to go off-piste with Miles Coolidge? He was being paid, certainly, and may have believed that there would be long-term benefits in cosying up to the Cousins. But I think his desire to play a central role in TYPHOON was born chiefly out of frustration.

"Let me tell you something about the British mindset," he had told Miles when the American had first suggested using British know-how and infrastructure to spirit Wang out of Hong Kong and to return him as an agent to Urumqi. "If I go to David Waterfield with what you're proposing, the answer is going to be 'No.' The Office will want him back in Sha Tau Kok by sunset. Why?

Because as a nation we're *small*, risk averse. We lack the imagination to do anything that might actually *change* things. If there's a reason not to do something, you can guarantee that the British will find it. Added to that is the small problem of the handover. Nobody wants to ruffle any Chinese feathers just at present."

Miles had performed a quick calculation. As TYPHOON accelerated over the next few years, his own responsibilities would also quicken and multiply. Lenan would be a useful ally, both as an experienced hand and as a window onto secret British thinking. They were standing in the bedroom of the safe house where Joe, just a few hours earlier, had been exhaustively interrogating Wang. Right there and then, with a wild decisiveness born of instinct and pressure, Miles agreed to Lenan's request "to keep SIS out of it" and to pay him as an asset of the CIA. For the next four years, $50,000 a month made its way into a Luxembourg bank account that Vauxhall Cross couldn't have traced to one of their own if they'd spent fifty years looking. Lenan was therefore nominally answerable to Miles, although a fellow diner at the Indian restaurant, observing the manner and body language of both men, would have assumed that Coolidge was very much the junior partner.

"So I have something else I need to tell you, Ken."

"You do? What's that?"

"Our people need somebody on the mainland to co-ordinate things. A focal point. A leader. The task force we're putting together is ultimately going to stretch to maybe twenty or thirty agents, the majority of whom are currently stationed all over the Far East. When Bill's shipments start rolling in, somebody is going to have to pull all those disparate elements together."

Lenan reacted as though Miles were being unnecessarily oblique. "You're telling me that you've been promoted," he said. "You'll shortly be leaving Hong Kong for bigger and better things."

It was characteristic of Lenan that he should manage to puncture any sense of pride that Miles might have felt in his achievement. To control an operation on the scale of TYPHOON at this stage in his career was a significant feather in his cap.

"You got it," he replied flatly. He wanted to fling a neat white ball of vanilla ice cream across the table into Lenan's smug, tanned face. Yet he also craved the Englishman's respect. Miles spent the next seven years of his life trying to reconcile these two conflicting positions. "Langley wants me to pack my bags and settle there by Christmas," he said. "That means I'll be leaving Hong Kong in the fall."

So many consequences flowed from this statement that Lenan's initial response might have been construed as flippant.

"You'll miss the wedding, then," he said.

Miles's head jerked up. "What wedding?"

"Oh, haven't you heard?"

"Heard what?"

"Joe and Isabella are getting engaged."

Miles Coolidge possessed many attributes as a spy—tenacity, self-confidence, a bold if sometimes reckless imagination—but a poker face was not chief among them. All of the tautness and the colour in his expression slipped down like a collapsing building. It was a sight that filled Kenneth Lenan with a profound if childish satisfaction, for he had long suspected Miles of harbouring a secret desire for Isabella. He took a sip of water from a glass on the table and watched the American scramble for answers.

"They're *what*? Engaged? Since when? Who told you that?"

"It's common knowledge." It wasn't, of course, but it was the sort of thing Lenan said when he was needling people.

Miles looked down at the table and tried to assemble some dignity. "Jesus. So how did he pop the question?"

"Oh it's not popped." Lenan seemed to enjoy the playful language.

"I don't understand."

"Rumour has it he's going to do it at the handover."

"On June 30th?"

"That is the day that has been outlined for the transfer of Hong Kong's sovereignty back to the People's Republic of China, yes."

Miles said "Jesus" one more time.

"You seem shocked, Miles."

"I'm pretty surprised, sure." He was thinking, calculating, his mind turning over, like the low hum of the air-conditioning unit above their heads. "Does David know?"

"David is the one who found out."

"What? Joe asked his permission?"

"Apparently."

A sniff of laughter from both men. Colleagues on both sides of the Atlantic liked to console themselves with the theory that Joe was still young and inexperienced in the ways of the world. It made them feel better about their own shortcomings.

"So he wants her to know all about RUN? He's prepared to break cover?"

Lenan nodded.

Which gave Miles an idea.

21 | C H E N

Twenty minutes later—no time for coffee, for *digestifs*—
Miles was making a phone call on the corner of Haiphong Road
and Kowloon Park Drive having put Lenan into a cab.

"Billy? I got a problem. What are you doing for *wui gwai*?"

Billy Chen was an American asset in the Triads whom Joe
distrusted as a faithless opportunist, a drug-running hoodlum
whose lust for the trappings of wealth and power was matched
only by his colossal vanity and self-importance. Chen must have
been about twenty or twenty-one in 1997, and had been taking
Miles's dollar for three years in return for information about
criminal activity in Guangdong province, Macau and Hong
Kong. Joe had had the chance to recruit him as an agent of SIS
shortly after he arrived in 1995, but had turned it down flat on
the basis that Chen was clearly unreliable. The Yanks, he quickly
discovered, were less discerning; they tended to throw money at
anybody who was willing to tell them what they wanted to
hear.

"*Wui gwai*?" Chen replied, pronouncing the Cantonese phrase
for "handover" with a native finesse denied to Miles. "Maybe I'm

in Hong Kong, maybe I'm not. How come you don't call me so long?"

"Listen, Billy. I need you to do me a favor."

"What kind of favour?"

Chen was sitting in the front seat of his favourite BMW with one hand on his mobile phone and the other sliding up the leg of a teenage girl plucked from a KTV bar in Shenzhen.

"Nothing serious, nothing special," Miles told him. "Just involves a couple of friends of mine in the run-up to June 30th."

"The run-up?" It was as if Chen didn't understand the expression.

"That's right, the run-up." Miles couldn't be bothered to explain it. He was in a panic over Isabella and had made a lightning quick decision to undermine Joe's proposal with a simple if somewhat clumsy strategy of his own. For the time being, all thoughts of going to Lily's had been postponed.

"Everybody take five days off," Chen said, referring to the common assumption that Hong Kong would grind to a halt in the week of *wui gwai*, as offices closed and the colony's residents waved their final farewells to British rule.

"Yeah, everybody's taking five days off. But on one of those days you'll be helping me, Billy. You'll be at the end of the phone and you'll be doing me a favor. Like I said, it's nothing special. Just make sure you're in Hong Kong."

It felt good to be bullying someone after two hours of Kenneth Lenan. Miles had the leverage to make demands of Billy Chen because, for all his suits and his cars and his blank-eyed girls, the gangster was just another creature of American power, a small fish in a great sea whose elevated position within the Teochiu could be ended with a single phone call.

"OK, Miles. OK. So tell me what you want to do. Tell me why you need me around."

"You remember my friend Joe?"

"Who?"

"The English guy. Tall. You met him a couple of years back at the Lisboa."

A memory of meeting Joe in a hotel room at Macau's largest casino assembled itself in Chen's mind. Hesitatingly, he said, "Sure."

"Well that's who you'll be dealing with," he said. "That's the guy I'm after."

In the final weeks of British rule—that strange, chaotic period of excitement and regret and uncertainty over the colony's future—many people commented on the change that came over Miles Coolidge. Several of his consulate colleagues at Garden Road, for example, noticed that he was less brash and self-assured around the office, while Joe was struck by a sudden courteousness in Miles's behaviour, bordering on humility. Unaware of what was going on behind the scenes, we all assumed that he was simply putting his house in order before making the big move to Chengdu, and didn't want his final months in Hong Kong to be obscured by a fog of conflicts and hedonism. There were parties almost every night in June, yet Miles kept his head down and worked hard, laying further foundations for TYPHOON and popping up socially only for the occasional beer at Club 1911, or a bowl of pasta at Grappa's.

The primary motivation for this uncharacteristic behaviour was undoubtedly Isabella's imminent engagement. Miles wanted to present himself as a viable alternative to Joe and must have believed, in his strange, corrupted pathology, that he had a chance of breaking them up if he appeared to be the sort of man who could put his life back on track at the flick of a switch. As a strategy, it was ambitious to the point of lunacy, yet it had the effect of creating a sense of confusion within Miles's circle of friends. What had come over him? Why was the celebrated Lothario suddenly cleaning up his act? And, of course, this confusion fed its way down to Isabella.

At the same time, she had begun to tell her close friends that her relationship with Joe was in a dip. They were seeing less of one another. They were constantly working. Habits of his that had once been charming and idiosyncratic now seemed commonplace, even annoying.

"He's never around when I need him to be," she told me. "There's always an excuse or an apology. We can't ever plan anything because he's always at the beck and call of his job. Yet he has this fixed way of seeing the world which somehow prevents us being spontaneous."

Their sex life, which had been dizzying in its initial intensity, had now moved into a second, more predictable phase. It had been the same story with Anthony, her married lover who had left his wife for her after the summers in Ibiza; two years of bliss, then the power cut of over-familiarity. Yet a part of Isabella was determined to make this latest relationship last, to go through the wall of her momentary indifference and to build something constructive and lasting with Joe. She knew that he adored her. She knew that if she left him it would break his heart. If he proposed, she would find it very difficult to turn him down, yet she knew that she was not quite ready, at twenty-six, to take the plunge into marriage.

Every snake needs his bit of luck and, against this background, Miles experienced a further slice of good fortune. The French television company for whom Isabella had been working decided to remain in Hong Kong after the handover and to shoot two supplementary films: a documentary about the first few months of Chinese rule, and a factual programme about the history of the Triads. I was in Hong Kong when Isabella was first approached to act as a researcher on the second film, so it was perhaps telling that she turned to Miles as her primary source of information. There was an additional irony, of course. Isabella had a man sharing her bed who knew just as much about Chinese organized crime as anyone in the Hong Kong CIA. But Joe was just a freight forwarder at Heppner Logistics. Joe didn't know anything.

Miles played the whole thing very cleverly. He was keyed in to Joe's itinerary because of the crossover between both services and suggested to Isabella that she come to his apartment to discuss the documentary on a night when he knew that Joe would be tied up until the small hours discussing handover security issues with David Waterfield. It was necessary to meet at his flat, he explained, because he was expecting delivery of a painting at some point after six o'clock.

Miles left the consulate at five in order to be home in good time to prepare supper, have a shower and put on a clean set of clothes. An enormous amount of time and thought had gone into every element of the evening. Should he shave or leave a stubble? Should he cook a three-course dinner, or would that look ostentatious? Was it better to have the apartment looking lived-in and scruffy, or reasonably clean and organized? Miles had been to the best supermarket in town—Oliver's in the Prince's building—to pick up the ingredients for a decent meal: a rack of lamb, some expensive French cheese, a homemade apple pie and a tub of Ben and Jerry's vanilla. He then blew HK$150 on a bottle of Sancerre at Berry Bros & Rudd and a further HK$230 on a Robert Mondavi Pinot Noir. At about seven o'clock he began scattering CD cases on the floor near his hi-fi and placed a stack of old *New Yorkers* and well-thumbed paperbacks on the coffee table in the sitting room. If Isabella sat on the sofa at any point in the evening, she would see that Miles was reading Graham Greene's *Brighton Rock*, Jacques Gernet's *Daily Life in China on the Eve of the Mongol Invasion*, Mikhail Lermontov's *A Hero of Our Time*, and a brace of novels—*Ladder of Years* and *The Accidental Tourist*—by Anne Tyler. No harm, after all, in being seen to read fiction by women. (The book that Miles was actually reading—and was quite gripped by—was *The Firm*, momentarily stashed in a cupboard in the spare bedroom next to Michael Crichton's *Disclosure* and a hygienically unreliable copy of *Playboy*.)

Isabella arrived at eight o'clock. She was wearing a dark blue Agnes B dress and a pair of wedge-heeled espadrilles. It was a hot night, muggy in the Mid-Levels, and she had wanted to dress in a way that was striking without seeming provocative. Miles buzzed her in and came to the door of his apartment wearing a pair of blue jeans and a white linen shirt. He had taken a shower an hour earlier and the fresh warm smell of his skin tugged in Isabella's stomach in a way that surprised her. She thought back to her dream and felt oddly embarrassed. Music was playing in the sitting room ahead of them—The Fugees' *The Score*—and a smell of garlic and rosemary wafted through from the kitchen.

"Wow. Something smells good."

"You eat meat, right?"

Miles knew very well that Isabella ate meat. He had just wanted to appear casual.

"Of course."

"Great, because I bought us some lamb. Is that gonna be OK?" He was not wearing socks or shoes, and the sight of his tanned feet padding down the corridor ahead of her added to the entirely artificial sense of homeliness and relaxation that Miles had hoped to create.

"Lamb's wonderful. You're very sweet to have cooked anything. I should have taken you out." She paused at the edge of the sitting room. "Great flat, Miles."

"You never been here before?" Another question to which he already knew the answer. "The American taxpayer can be pretty generous. You should check out the view."

They now walked in different directions: Miles towards the open-plan kitchen, where he popped the cork on the Sancerre; Isabella towards the vast rectangular window at the northern end of the apartment. Spread out beneath her was the city at night, a brilliant wide shot of Hong Kong light and colour, every building from Sheung Wan to Causeway Bay illuminating the sky with a phosphorescent glow that framed the distant neon blur of Kowloon. She thought about all the girls that Miles must have lured to this place, the one-liners and seductions, and watched her own grin reflected in the glass.

"Pretty, huh?"

"It's amazing. Did your painting arrive, by the way?"

"Sure," he lied. "I've already got it hanging upstairs."

The Sancerre was corked, which broke the ice. Miles swore and made a joke at the expense of the French which Isabella found funny, in spite of herself. It flattered her that he seemed slightly nervous and hesitant in these early moments, a side of his usually supremely confident personality that she had not experienced before. Was this just loyalty to Joe, or the uncertainty of a serial philanderer who did not know how to behave in the presence of a younger woman not visiting his flat solely for sex? Miles poured the wine down the sink—he didn't want to appear cheap by corking it for a refund—and Isabella asked instead for a vodka and tonic. She was intrigued to watch him operate in his home environment, a domesticated male fetching ice from the freezer, switching CDs on the hi-fi, filling pans with water to boil vegetables on the stove. It somehow made him more human, more intriguing.

"I brought a notebook," she said, because there was a danger that the atmosphere between them might quickly become flirtatious.

"Do you need me to ask you questions or can I just listen to you talk?" she asked.

"You want to listen to me talk, Izzy?" Miles seized on the opportunity to make another joke. "Works for me. Nothing I like more than the sound of my own voice."

He sat beside her on the sofa, the weight of him, and they spoke in general terms about the film. What did she need to know? What was the purpose of the documentary? Isabella's eyes wandered to *Ladder of Years* and *The Accidental Tourist* and she knew that Miles had placed them there to impress her. She mentioned that she had studied *Brighton Rock* at school. When Miles began to talk about the book, however, she found it difficult to concentrate on what he was saying. Her mind was suddenly scrambled by a nervous apprehension, the source of which she could not trace. Was it that she had long suspected Miles of harbouring feelings for her, feelings which he had been forced to suppress because of his responsibilities towards her boyfriend? Or was it possible that

Miles felt nothing for her, that his soul had been so corrupted by a life of lies and easy sex that he was no longer capable of loving a woman? This last possibility made Isabella intensely sad, but it also intrigued her. She had had a glass of wine while getting dressed at home and wondered if she was already slightly drunk.

"So the triangle of that relationship is very interesting."

"What?"

She had not been listening.

"Pinkie, Rose and Ida. The triangle. I thought that was incredibly powerful. It's what really stuck with me about the book. The heat between them."

Isabella took a sip of her vodka. It was already half finished. That was the danger of living in a humid climate; you drank alcohol like water. She looked at the window again because she needed somewhere to settle her eyes. An aeroplane was flying low over Victoria Harbour, piercing a vertical searchlight that shot up from the top of the Bank of China building like a column of fire.

"I should read it again," she said, desperate to move away from talk of Catholic guilt and love triangles. She hoped, somehow, that Miles's observations on *Brighton Rock* might move them seamlessly from a discussion of organized crime on the south coast of England to the Triads of Hong Kong. Instead, operating from a pre-rehearsed list of topics, he asked her endless questions about her life in Hong Kong, her past relationships, her jobs, a discussion that took them through a second vodka and tonic, into dinner, then three-quarters of the way down the bottle of Pinot Noir until they were eating pudding.

"So tell me about life at English boarding schools," he said.

"What do you want to know?"

"Do the girls all sleep in the same dormitory?"

It was a typically flirtatious question. Miles had been grinning as he asked it and Isabella, by now drunk and relaxed, enjoyed playing the role of gatekeeper to his fantasies.

"Oh sure," she told him. "And when it was hot we all slept naked and had pillow fights at the weekends."

"Gardeners?" Miles asked immediately.

"Gardeners?" She was starting to laugh. "What do you mean?"

"Isn't that what upper-class English girls do? Hump the gardener? Please don't tell me that's a lie, Izzy. I always had this image of you—what do you call it?—'rogering in the undergrowth.'"

Other stretches of the conversation were more sedate; Miles was careful to maintain a balance. How, for example, did Isabella find working for a French company? Were they respectful towards her? Did they seem to know what they were doing? Had television, he asked, pouring her another glass of wine, always been something that she had wanted to become involved in, or was it just an accident of her life in Hong Kong? For every joke or anecdote there was a subtle, intuitive observation about Isabella's life. It must have been difficult, he said, to be separated from her mother in Dorset who, if he remembered correctly, had never remarried. Didn't she also have a brother who lived in the States? Isabella was flattered that Miles should have remembered so much about her background. The only subject which remained uncovered was Joe himself; instead, he hovered over the evening like an invisible chaperon, determined to ruin their fun. Isabella concluded that Miles had not mentioned his name out of a deliberate sense of mischief, yet as the evening wore on and the wine began to take effect, she longed to speak about the frustrations of their relationship and even to open herself up to the possibility of desire. For all Miles's bravado and roguery, he was a thoughtful, perceptive man and she thrilled to the energy of their flirtation. It was harmless, she told herself, but it had been bound to happen. In some strange way, they had been dancing around one another for years, even during the period when Isabella had been blissfully happy with Joe.

"Listen, we should talk about my documentary," she said, suddenly aware that she was risking everything on their increasing closeness.

"Sure. Just tell me what you want to know."

Miles was pouring boiling water into a cafetière that he had used only once before.

"Anything," Isabella said, taking out her notebook and pen. "There are only six people in Hong Kong who know less about Triads than I do and four of them are still in kindergarten. If you tell me that the average Triad is five foot six, listens to Barbra Streisand records and spends his weekends in Wolverhampton, I'll believe you. The gaps in my knowledge are shaming."

Miles was too busy moving to a mental lecture he had prepared to laugh at her joke. "Well, the term 'Triad' was coined by the British authorities here in Hong Kong to refer to a disparate group of secret societies that originally sprang up during the Qing dynasty to overthrow the emperor." Isabella put her glass down and started writing. "Just about the only thing you can credit Chairman Mao with achieving in China is the eradication of opium abuse after 1949. Thirty million peasants may have died from starvation under communist rule, but at least they weren't high." Miles plunged the coffee. "That opium trade had been controlled by the Triads, who were forced to move their operations to Hong Kong. I guess you could say we're living in the spiritual home of the Chinese mafia."

Miles poured the coffee into two bottle-green espresso cups, sat opposite Isabella at the table and lit a cigarette. They smiled at one another in an attempt to lighten the suddenly didactic mood but, for the next twenty minutes, he swamped her in information about the various societies that controlled Hong Kong life in the post-war years, "Each of them," he said, "responsible for a particular geographical area or sector of the economy." It was exactly what Isabella needed in terms of her research, but she remained nostalgic for the earlier part of the evening and tried frequently to catch Miles's eye, to make him revert to his earlier mood of playfulness. At the same time she enjoyed the process of watching Miles's mind open up, his expertise, the confidence he clearly felt in his own intellectual abilities.

"This is great stuff," she told him, scribbling onto a third sheet of paper, like a journalist on the scent of a good story. "So they operate in the same way as the Sicilian mafia? It's about protection money, drug-running, prostitution?"

"They operate like the Sicilians, sure. And the Turks, and the Russians, and the Albanians. All wiseguys are basically the same. But Chinese criminal activity has its own particular characteristics."

"What kind of characteristics?"

"Different societies use different hand signals to communicate secretly with other members. But your average French camera-man is gonna find it pretty difficult to capture those gestures on tape. He'd need to be like those David Attenborough guys making a nature documentary, sitting around in a hut on Lantau Island for eight months waiting for Mr. Chan to give the thumbs up." Isabella laughed and curled a thick handful of hair behind her neck. "These guys are masters of concealment. The way they might offer a cigarette, sign a credit card transaction, even pick up a set of chopsticks, all those gestures are sending signals to other Triads. I know a guy in the 14K who has this way of accepting a bowl of tea with his thumb and two of his fingers extended so it forms a kind of tripod."

Miles picked up his coffee cup in the manner he had described to illustrate the gesture more clearly. Isabella wanted to take a photograph to show her boss, but thought better of asking.

"One of the prejudices you should maybe think about parking is the idea that all Triad activity is inherently violent and anti-social." Miles finished the coffee and set it down on the table. "Making that clear to the audience would probably make your programme a lot more interesting. Sure, there's drug-running, people smuggling, violence. But Triad societies also pay for schooling in their local communities, find jobs for the unemployed, help out families who might have fallen on hard times. It's not all protection money. It's not all turf wars and assassinations."

"They run the construction industry here."

"That's right." Miles didn't patronize Isabella by seeming surprised that she should know this. "Part of the reason why Patten has had so much trouble with the airport out at Chek Lap Kok isn't because of threats from the Chinese government, but because the building contractors have had to pay millions of dollars in kickbacks to the Triads. You want land reclaimed from the sea? Call the Teo-chiu. You want your runway built in record time? Have words with the Sun Yee On. If you don't pay these guys, your scaffolding doesn't go up, your illegal coolies don't make it across the border,

your concrete gets mixed with salt. It's the same story on the mainland, in Indonesia, Singapore, Thailand. Triad groups control most
things in South-east Asia."

Miles took the opportunity to stand up and walk across to the
sofa. He sat down and put his bare feet on the low coffee table,
leaning back with a sigh. He was convinced that he had won her
round. There was a haughtiness that went out of Western girls
when they had finally succumbed to him. Their pride was replaced by a sort of desperate, manic energy and he knew that it
would only be a matter of time before he could possess her. Across
the room he could see the lower part of Isabella's legs as she sat
drinking coffee and scribbling notes. As if sensing this, Isabella
looked at him, her eyebrows giving a little knowing bounce over
the rim of her espresso cup, and she stood up from the table. He
watched as she picked up their glasses, filled them from a bottle
of wine that he had found to replace the empty Pinot Noir, and
walked over to join him.

"What about kidnappings?" she said.

"What about them?"

Isabella discarded her shoes and sat at the opposite end of the
sofa to Miles, her body twisted towards him so that the lower part
of her dress lifted up over her knees. But Miles had drunk heavily all evening and some of the finesse now started to go out of his
performance. Carelessly, he stole glances at her calves and thighs
and allowed his eyes to drift along the length of her body. He was
annoyed when Isabella responded to this by covering her legs
completely, tucking her feet beneath her thighs.

"Well, are things like that common?" she asked. A little of the
haughtiness had returned to her voice. It angered him. "Do you
come across them at the consulate?"

"Oh sure." A nonchalant response. He stood up to convey a
sense that he was indifferent to her physical proximity and crossed
to the hi-fi, shuffling through randomly scattered CDs until he
found a bootleg copy of Cannonball Adderley's *Nippon Soul*.

"Go on," she said, because he was stalling. Rudeness was always a failsafe option and Miles built a level of deliberate condescension into his response.

"Well, if you want stories for your film, as opposed to just a bunch of facts about Triad history, you could tell your guys what happened to Leung Tin-wai."

"Leung Tin-wai?"

"I think it was June of last year." Miles now sat at the table where they had eaten, as if oblivious to the tensions racing between them. He was just a teacher with a bothersome student, a man of the world making time for a girl. "The story was all over the TV. Leung owns a tabloid magazine which ran a piece about the Triads. Next thing he knows, two guys are in his office slicing his arm off with a meat cleaver. Took seventeen hours of surgery to reattach it."

"Jesus."

"Yeah." Miles feigned a profound concern for his fellow man. "A bunch of Hong Kong journalists put up about a four-million-dollar reward for information leading to the arrest of the guys who did it."

"And nobody's come forward."

"I guess not."

Isabella looked at her watch. Seeing that it was almost twelve o'clock, she closed her notebook.

"I should be going."

Miles had expected this. To stay any later than midnight would look suspicious to Joe, and the last thing Isabella would want would be to create the wrong impression. He watched her spring decisively to her feet. "Can I order a cab?"

"Sure." It was important to look nonchalant. "They usually take about twenty minutes."

Which left them with what turned out to be another half an hour, time filled only with further talk about the Triads. It was as if the documentary had broken the spell between them. Isabella continued to take notes, Miles continued to impress her with the depth of his knowledge. But their shared intimacies, the excitement they had both felt at dinner as they began to unravel one another's lives, had passed. The long day, the food and booze, had rendered Isabella exhausted. Miles, who would usually at this stage have made a bid for sex, realized that his best hope now lay in waiting for the intrusion of Billy Chen.

Nevertheless, as they made their way downstairs towards the waiting cab, he tried to revive some of the attraction they had felt for one another with a carefully constructed compliment.

"Make sure Joe sees you in that dress. You look amazing."

It wasn't too late. Isabella felt the buzz of flattery again. All her life she had been subjected to the advances—both charming and insidious—of older men. Under normal circumstances, her response was to ignore what had been said. Yet she knew there was an underlying meaning in Miles's choice of words, a code which needed to be cracked. She turned towards him at the entrance of the apartment building and took a chance.

"What a funny way of telling me that you think I look nice."

Cicadas were clacking in the humid night. She stared directly into Miles's eyes. If there had been less at stake, if he could have been completely sure of how she would respond, he would have placed his hands around her waist and pulled her body towards his.

"How else do you like being told that you're beautiful?"

This was too much. Isabella felt the force of Miles's desire and it flooded her, but knew that she had no choice but to stop him overstepping the mark. Their time would come. "It was lovely to see you, Miles," she said, and in an instant she was poised and elegant and British. "Thank you so much for all your help." Every word closed him out. They stumbled, off-balance, into a brief cheek kiss. "I've got amazing notes," she said. "The guys are going to love me."

The driver of the cab opened the back door of the vehicle using the automatic lever beside his seat. It swung open quickly on its hinge, almost knocking Isabella over.

"Hey, buddy!"

"It's all right." Isabella defused the situation by leaning into the taxi and showing the driver that she was unhurt. Then she climbed inside and wound down the window.

"What are you doing for the handover?"

"Parties all over town," he said.

"Want to get together?" Isabella did not want to leave him with the feeling that she had rejected him, but the invitation was intended to imply that she would be with Joe. What other choice did she have?

"Sure. It'd be great to hook up with you guys." Miles recognized that wherever Joe and Isabella ended up for *wui gwai*, Billy Chen would have to follow. It was useful to know their plans. "I have to go to a dinner at the American Chamber of Commerce on the 28th. Otherwise I'm pretty much free."

"Well, there's a big party in Lan Kwai Fong on the night of the 29th. Let's go to that."

"Good."

The cab was sliding down the hill as Isabella leaned out of the window, smiling as she looked up at the low night sky. "It'll probably rain," she said, leaving Miles with a memory of her curled dark hair, those eyes that tricked and lured him. "It'll probably rain."

Which, of course, famously, it did.

And not just any old rain. A monsoon that made the red dye in Lance Corporal Angus Anderson's Black Watch hackle run pink like a child's watercolour as he marched in the gala parade. Rain that soaked the crisp white tunic of the lone bugler who played the "Last Post" as the standard was lowered over Government House for the final time. Rain that tried to drown out every solemn, stubborn word of Prince Charles's speech to the "appalling old Chinese waxworks" at HMS *Tamar.* And rain that stained the shoulders of Governor Christopher Francis Patten's already crumpled blue suit as he aimed one final shot across China's bows.

"As British administration ends, we are, I believe, entitled to say that our own nation's contribution here was to provide the scaffolding that enabled the people of Hong Kong to ascend," he said. Huddled under complimentary umbrellas beneath a lightless, granite sky, 9,000 Chinese and expatriate spectators looked on. "This is a Chinese city, a *very* Chinese city, with British characteristics. No dependent territory has been left more prosperous, none with such a rich texture and fabric of civil society. Now

Hong Kong people are to run Hong Kong. That is the promise. And that is the unshakeable destiny."

Watching the live broadcast on television from a suite in the American consulate, Miles Coolidge turned to Dave Boyle of the Visa Section and said, "In other words, Beijing can go fuck itself."

"One country, two systems," Boyle replied.

"Exactly."

Miles watched as Patten reluctantly returned to the dais to accept the thunderous applause of his most loyal subjects.

"You know that can't be easy," he said.

"What can't?"

"Clapping. Most of the people out there are holding umbrellas. You gotta really commit if you want to clap while you're holding an umbrella."

In common with about three-quarters of the international community in Hong Kong, Boyle had been drunk for the better part of five days. Yet the character of Patten's conduct in these moments triggered something in his melancholy soul. When the governor returned to his seat and briefly bowed his head, as if holding back tears and searching for renewed strength within himself to cope with the magnitude of the occasion, the man from the Visa Section choked up.

"When a great man leaves, the heavens open," he said, as the pitiless rain sliced across the parade ground. A boozy sleeplessness formed a knot in his Adam's apple.

"What's that?"

"A Chinese proverb," Boyle replied.

In different circumstances, Miles would have poured scorn on this. *You wanna hear another Chinese proverb? It takes many days of rain to wash away 150 years of shame.* But he thought better of it. Guys in the Visa Section weren't worth the trouble. Instead he said, "So you're a fan of Fat Pang, are you?"

"Fat Pang" was the affectionate nickname that Patten had been given by the people of Hong Kong who, over a period of five years, had noted his fondness for Cantonese food, and for custard tarts in particular.

"He did his best," Boyle replied.

Less than a kilometre away, David Waterfield raised his own silent toast to the waterlogged sunset of the British Empire and squeezed his wife's hand. They had gathered at the Hong Kong Club on Chater Road to see out the final hours of colonial rule at a black-tie event attended by several hundred of the island's business and diplomatic elite. When the post-*Tamar* fireworks began to explode over Victoria Harbour at around 8:30 p.m. there was a brief moment of panic when the glass walls of the club became so thick with condensation that a waiter had to be dispatched to the top of a ladder to wipe them clean. Thereafter, as the night sky erupted in umbrellas of light and fire, the assembled guests were afforded a clear view of proceedings.

"Beautiful," Waterfield muttered. "Beautiful. God we do this sort of thing well." Then he realized that somebody was missing. "Have you seen Joe Lennox at all this evening?" he asked his wife.

"No, darling" she replied. "Have you?"

The Waterfields had turned down the most sought-after and pres-tigious invitation of 30 June, the official handover dinner at the newly completed Hong Kong Convention and Exhibition Centre. Kenneth Lenan, on the other hand, had lobbied long and hard for his place at table. Waterfield's number two believed that it was his right to break bread with the great and the good, to exchange knowing glances with Douglas Hurd and Sir Geoffrey Howe, to get a decent look at the all-new, all-smiling Tony Blair, and to witness Baroness Thatcher in the misery of her perpetual retire-ment. For some reason the menu for the event had been one of the most closely guarded secrets in the colony, but as Lenan chewed on his flavourless smoked salmon and sawed into a stuffed breast of chicken, he reflected that he could have eaten better at the airport. His suit was wet through from the celebrations at HMS *Tamar* and he was intensely bored by the property developer making conversation to his left. All anybody could talk about was the weather. Wasn't it *symbolic*? Wasn't it just a *disaster*? The only disaster, he reckoned, was that he had been forced to stand for over an hour in the shivering, air-conditioned hall while an international array of bored, exhausted VIPs had gradually made their way into dinner. The champagne had been over-chilled and, several times, the recently completed roof had dripped water onto his head.

Sovereignty was officially transferred at midnight in a ceremony at the Convention Centre which felt sterile and anti-climactic. The Union Jack came down, the flag of China went up, and then the international array of bored, exhausted VIPs made their way back to their $10,000-a-night suites at the Mandarin Oriental. Twelve hundred miles away, in Tiananmen Square, a specially invited crowd of the Party faithful consigned 150 years of shame and humiliation at the hands of the British to the dustbin of history, celebrating the safe return of their beloved Hong Kong with a fireworks display that shook the foundations of the Forbidden City. Meanwhile, the Royal Yacht *Britannia* slipped her moorings in Central and embarked on a final journey home, heading eastward through the Lei Yue Mun gap bearing a heavy cargo of grieving royals and weeping Patten daughters. The governor himself gave a triumphant, neo-Nixonian wave on the port-side railing and then was gone, disappearing into the bowels of the ship.

It was a chaotic night to be a journalist, fighting against deadlines and rain. Whenever I had a spare moment I tried—unsuccessfully—to reach Joe on his mobile, but neither he nor Isabella were taking calls. As Tung Chee Hwa was being sworn in as the first elected Chief Executive of the Hong Kong Special Administrative Region, I went down to the democracy rally in Central Square which had begun at about 10:30 p.m. and which straddled the midnight handover. Most of those taking part relished the irony that by the time the gathering had dispersed, at around 1:30 a.m., their right to public protest had effectively been stripped away by Beijing. They could now be arrested and locked up for promoting, say, an independent Eastern Turkestan, or for criticizing elements of Chinese government policy. Twenty-one armoured personnel carriers and 4,000 PLA troops had rolled over the border into the New Territories at midnight to be welcomed by stage-managed villagers waving flags and throwing flowers, smiles decorating their faces in spite of the wind and incessant rain. Hong Kong's police officers had already removed their colonial insignias and replaced them with the gold star of China. British coats of arms had been taken down from government buildings and the royal emblem quietly detached from the governor's Rolls-Royce. As Martin Lee, the founding chairman of the Hong Kong Democratic Party, finished a speech in front of the Legislative Council building in which he had called on Chinese President Jiang Zemin to respect the rights of the people of Hong Kong, a dry-witted wag from the *Daily Telegraph*, standing directly behind me, muttered, "That'll be the last we see of him for a while. See you in the gulag, Marty," and a bevy of hacks duly laughed in unison. It was depressing stuff. All of us were tired and wet and hot, and it felt as though something decent and hopeful had come to an end.

As a sworn enemy of the Communist Party, Ansary Tursun took little interest in the handover celebrations. At around nine o'clock, on what was a typically warm summer evening in Urumqi, he left his parents' apartment on Tuan Jie Lu and made his way to the bazaar at Shanxi Hangzi. He walked through the narrow channels of the market, past stalls selling vegetables, sweaters, nuts and dried fruit, occasionally stopping to sift through a table of cassettes or to make brief conversation with Uighur friends from the neighbourhood. The market was crowded and noisy: Uighur songs competed with the new popular music from India and combined with the shouts and arguments of the stallholders to create a discordant yet somehow innocuous din. Large crowds were gathered around television screens showing highlights of the fireworks display over Victoria Harbour.

At the western edge of the market, Ansary became aware of a

smell that he loved—pieces of lamb being grilled on a *kavabtan*. As it always did, the odour of cumin and meat and slow-burning charcoal triggered his appetite and he ordered *kavab* and *nan* from a young man who took his responsibilities as a chef so seriously that he barely spoke a word in conversation. As a treat, Ansary also purchased a bottle of *musdek piva*, opening it with his teeth and taking a first, thirst-quenching slug of lager before his lamb had finished cooking.

In order to eat, he was obliged to sit at one of the small wooden tables beside the *kavabtan*, because his left arm had still not recovered sufficiently from the period of solitary confinement at Lucaogu prison. Ansary had been hung from a wall by his left arm and leg for more than twenty-four hours; as a result, he could not stand up while holding both the *kavab* and the bottle of beer. Ansary had adjusted quickly to the constraints of a temporary injury and rarely reflected on the injustice of his physical condition; his scars were purely psychological. As he ate, placing his food on the table in order to drink the ice-cold beer, he made conversation with the mother of the young man who had served him, a middle-aged woman who wore a black skirt, a headscarf, a bright red jacket and a pair of thick, knee-length socks in which she kept the stall's money. When she was not threading chunks of marinated lamb onto metal skewers with practised efficiency, she was scrabbling around inside the socks trying to find change for a customer.

It was only when Ansary turned to observe an argument between two cloth tradesmen at a neighbouring stall that he realized he was sitting no more than a stone's throw from Abdul Bary. Abdul had been one of Ansary's fellow prisoners at Lucaogu. A former student of Professor Wang Kaixuan at the University of Xinjiang, Abdul had spoken passionately in prison of his desire to topple the provincial government in Xinjiang. The two men had been released on the same day and had recovered from their ordeal at Wang's apartment, under pretence of paying their respects for the death of his son, Wang Bin.

Aware that Abdul might be under surveillance, Ansary made no attempt to communicate with him, but calculated that his appearance was more than coincidence. He tried to watch him as carefully as possible. He was buying fruit at a nearby stall. Was he trying to tell him something with his body language? Did he want Ansary to follow him to a new location, or even to pretend that they had accidentally bumped into one another? It was not clear. Yet it would be extremely dangerous for them to be observed—or, worse, photographed—by Chinese surveillance officers or by informers within the Uighur community. The authorities needed only the slightest provocation, backed up by scant evidence, to prosecute Uighur men for treasonable activities.

Ansary finished his *kavab* and wiped his fingers on a small piece of cloth which he kept in the hip pocket of his trousers. He drank the rest of the beer and watched Abdul pay for a melon and a bag of apples. At no point did his fellow prisoner turn round and attempt to make eye contact. Perhaps his appearance in the market was just coincidence after all. Finally, he walked away from the stall. Ansary noted that he was not limping. The injury to his leg, inflicted by a laughing guard who had torn out the largest toenail of Abdul's right foot, must have healed. A few metres away, Ansary noticed a Han trying on a *doppa*, the coloured hats worn by Uighur men throughout the year. It was an incongruous sight: they were at the minority end of town, in an area where Han were rarely seen. As Abdul passed him, disappearing into the narrow alleyways of the bazaar, the man returned the hat to its table and began to follow him. It was as obvious to Ansary as it would have been to Abdul that he was a plain-clothes surveillance officer with the PLA. Ansary turned towards the *kavabtan* and indicated that he wished to drink some tea.

The note was hidden between the base of the dirty metal pot in which the middle-aged woman had brewed the tea and the tray on which she carried it to Ansary's table.

"Your friend left this for you," she said. "Do not come here again."

Ansary saw the crumpled piece of paper, folded once in half, and looked around to see if he was being watched. When he was sure that there were no eyes upon him, he lifted the pot, poured the tea, and opened the note. His heart was racing, but he was intrigued by Abdul's sleight of hand. How had he given the note to the woman without being observed?

The words had been written quickly, in black ink:

Our teacher has a new friend who will provide for us. The friend is rich and has our best interests at heart. We are not to meet or to communicate until the teacher instructs us to do so. You have a class with him at dawn on the first morning of August at the place we both know. Tell as many of our brothers as you can. The teacher's friend has a great and wonderful plan. I am glad to see you. Burn this.

Professor Wang Kaixuan claimed that he watched the Hong Kong celebrations on a small black-and-white television set at his apartment in Urumqi, although I later discovered that this, like so many of his utterings, was a lie. TRABANT had calculated—correctly as it turned out—that the eyes of Chinese Intelligence would be momentarily averted by the handover celebrations and that it would therefore be a good opportunity to hold a meeting in a room at the Holiday Inn to discuss developments with TYPHOON. Wang must have watched highlights of the broadcast when he returned home at about two o'clock in the morning. His wife was ill in bed next door, which gave him the opportunity to mutter insults under his breath whenever Chinese triumphalism threatened to get out of hand. Drinking a beer on the very couch where his slain son had slept for almost every night of his twenty-five-year life, Wang marvelled at the stoicism of the magnificent British soldiers as they paraded in the rain, and raised his glass of beer to Patten as tears fell from the governor's eyes. How many other Han Chinese, he wondered, on this night of triumph for the Motherland, would be toasting the health of the "Triple Violator" and his "capitalist running dogs" in London?

One thing, in particular, provoked Wang's ire. In Jiang Zemin's speech, delivered in the Convention Centre just a few minutes after midnight, the British were accused of having subjected Hong Kong to more than a century of "vicissitudes." I remember the

Mandarin word he used—*cangsang*—because it provoked considerable argument among the press corps at the time, not least because nobody was entirely sure of its precise meaning. Had Jiang meant "difficulties" or "problems?" Was "vicissitudes" the correct translation? Had he really intended to insult the British at such a delicate and sensitive moment in their history? But Professor Wang Kaixuan was in no doubt, and the childish slur appalled him. What problems, after all, had Hong Kong suffered under colonial rule? A few riots in the fifties and sixties, all of them engineered by agents of Chairman Mao. By comparison, China in the same period had been decimated by communist rule: millions dead from famine; families torn apart by the insanity of the Cultural Revolution; minority ethnic groups tortured and flung into prison. The hypocrisy was breathtaking.

Towards dawn Wang shut off the television and lay awake on his son's bed, dreaming of Dapeng Bay as the tune of "Land of Hope and Glory" formed a loop in his mind. He thought of all the lies he had told, and all the truths he had uttered in his extraordinary journey to meet the now departed Patten. What had come over him in those long, crazy weeks? Why had he believed that he had even the slightest chance of fulfilling his quest? He might have drowned. He could have been shot or imprisoned. And yet he had succeeded, in a fashion that he could never have imagined. Western intelligence now given him the opportunity to make sense of his loss and rage. Lenan and Coolidge had allowed Wang Kaixuan the chance to avenge his son's murder.

One question, however, continued to puzzle him. What had happened to the first of them, the spy from Government House? Wang had warmed to the young graduate of Wadham College Oxford, who had seen through his lies and reacted with genuine horror to the brutalities of Yining and Baren. Why had he never seen him again? What on earth had become of Mr. John Richards?

Young couples break up all the time. It's an old story. It's a new story. This one was a little different.

I sensed there was trouble brewing the moment I saw Billy Chen forcing his way through the sweat- and rain-soaked crowds of Lan Kwai Fong. It was about eleven o'clock on the night of the 29th. Imagine a Mardi Gras or New Year's Eve in a sticky, tropical climate, with thousands of over-excited, emotionally exhausted, inebriated Westerners puking and kissing and laughing and dancing and you'll have some idea of what it was like to be out in Hong Kong that night. Joe, Isabella, Miles and myself—along with about a dozen other colleagues and hangers-on—were drinking in F-Stop, a long-established bar halfway up Lan Kwai Fong. Joe had left the bar momentarily to buy cigarettes at a nearby convenience store and had been gone about five minutes. The bar was popular with Chinese yuppies but Chen still looked out of place squeezing himself through the bottleneck of customers at the entrance, wearing a pair of cheap jeans, trainers and a dirty white T-shirt. He was sweating profusely and his eyes had a kind of wild, narcotic stare that I can still picture vividly to this day.

At first I couldn't place him, but when he was about ten feet away I had a vivid recollection that I had met Billy in either Macau or Shenzhen about eighteen months earlier while researching an article for the *Sunday Times*. What the hell was a Teochiu Triad doing in F-Stop the night before the handover? I had done a line of coke and must confess that my first, somewhat hysterical reaction was that Chen was going to pull out a knife or gun and start slaying random expats as a symbolic act of violence on the eve of *wui gwai*. He certainly looked capable of causing a serious disturbance. Then I saw that he was looking around for somebody and assumed that he was meeting a girl, or perhaps wanting to have words with the management. Yet that didn't properly explain the look of urgency on his face, the near-panic which characterized his every gesture. Miles was standing beside me talking to a couple of women from Credit Suisse and I pulled him out of his conversation to let him know what was going on.

"What's that?" he said.

It was difficult to be heard above the noise of the bar and I had to shout as I repeated myself. "Billy Chen has just walked in."

"Who the fuck is Billy Chen?"

Looking back, that was the first clue. It didn't make sense that Miles would forget the name of one of his prize assets. I was about to reply when Chen looked directly at Miles through the ruck of heaving bodies and produced an expression that was as malevolent as any I have ever seen. It was as if the two of them were engaged in a blood feud. I heard Miles mutter: "Oh Jesus Christ" under his breath and then he tried to start a staged conversation with me, as if we were two extras standing at the back of a crowd scene attempting to look normal. "Just act natural, man, just act natural," he said. "Talk to me, keep talking." Of course the whole set-up was an elaborate piece of theatre; it was just that Miles and Billy were the only actors among us who knew their lines. Taking hold of my shoulder, Miles twisted me towards the bar, so that we both had had our backs to the room.

"What the fuck is going on?" I asked, and instinctively looked to my right to see what was happening to Isabella. She was standing twenty feet away, squeezed against a wall by a pincer movement of three drunken expats, all of whom seemed to be taking advantage of Joe's absence from the bar to try to chat her up. To my astonishment, Chen burst through all three of them and grabbed her by the arm. She looked visibly, understandably shocked, but the men must have clocked Chen's physique and seen the possibility of violence in his vivid, fevered eyes because they made no attempt to intervene, nor to protect Isabella from what was happening. Seeing this, I broke clear of Miles and tried to make my way through the crowd to help her. On a normal night this would have taken no time at all, but with so many people dancing and talking and oblivious to anything but their own enjoyment of the party, it was some time before I could reach her.

"What's on your mind?" I said to Chen when I got there, and he immediately released his grip. Isabella no longer looked so frightened, and she was clearly relieved that one of her friends had shown up to help her.

"He says he knows Joe," she said, trying to smile and sound relaxed, but obviously unsettled by what was happening. "He says that Joe has to help him with something."

I realized immediately that there was a danger of Joe's cover being blown. I also assumed—as Miles had surely hoped I would—that something had happened between the CIA and the Triads and that Billy was coming to the Brits to help him out.

"This guy doesn't know Joe," I replied, intent on salvaging the situation. "Believe me, this guy does not know Joe."

There was a kind of drunken deliriousness about what was happening, as if the conversation was taking place in a parallel dimension. "You stay out of it," Chen countered, pointing a finger at me. He had obviously recognized my face. Either that, or Miles had briefed him that I would be in the bar. "I'm looking for her boyfriend," he said, pointing the same finger at Isabella. "Her boyfriend have to help me. Otherwise we all in trouble."

"But how *can* he help you?" Isabella asked. I was relieved to see that she was beginning to act as if the whole thing was a case of mistaken identity.

"He help me because he work for British government," Chen replied.

I produced a hopeless fake laugh, on the off-chance that it would make a nonsense of the accusation and, at first, Isabella seemed amused. "Joe doesn't work for the British government," she said. "You've got him confused with someone else."

"Don't trick me," Chen replied, a clever answer, because it kept the conversation going. "I need to talk him urgent. He only man I can trust. I have seen you with him many times. You tell me where I find him."

We were standing directly beneath a speaker which was blaring out music at a near-deafening volume. I simply couldn't believe that what was unfolding was happening tonight, of all nights, when there was so much in the way of distraction and chaos around us. I was too drunk and high, not sharp enough to make decent, accurate decisions. I should have written Chen off as a lunatic, but I became obsessed by the idea of protecting Joe's cover and the simplest solution did not present itself. I was also starting to wonder what the hell had happened to Miles.

"Let's go outside, Billy," I said, calculating that it was best to get Chen out of the bar and away from Isabella. "Let's talk where there aren't so many people and we can actually hear what's being said."

"You *know* this guy?" Isabella asked.

I felt like I had no choice but to answer truthfully and said, "We've met before." But of course this was a mistake, because it added an entirely new layer of confusion to the crisis unravelling before my eyes. Isabella looked unsettled again. She frowned and slowly shook her head, as if she knew that she was being lied to.

"*When* have you met?" she said. The noise of the music was annoying her and she ducked under the speaker to make it easier for her to hear. "Does Joe know him as well?"

"Let's go onto the street," I shouted, and that's when Chen just came out with it.

"Of course Joe know me," he said. "Why you pretend he work for Heppner's when everybody know he is a British spy?" He rattled the words out and added something about being "betrayed by the CIA." I never did discover what tall story Miles had concocted to justify Chen's intrusion, but the quality of his acting could not be faulted. Under the deafening assault of the speakers, Isabella seemed to fold in on herself, as if all of her elegance and poise and that lovely, open self-confidence in her face was being sucked out of her like a cancer. Was it just my imagination, or had Chen confirmed some dark suspicion that she had long held about Joe's true identity? Right on cue, Miles now came up behind her—he had watched the whole thing being played out—and grabbed Chen by the arm, frog-marching him from the bar like a bouncer. It was an impressive physical sight, her knight in shining armour, and several of the revellers in F-Stop, as well as a couple of bar staff, stepped aside to absorb what was going on, as if it were all part of the handover fun. God knows what Miles did with him afterwards. Probably slapped him on the back and slipped him a thousand dollars for his trouble. I was more concerned about Isabella, who was looking at me as if I myself had betrayed her.

"What's going on?" she said.

"I have no idea," I replied. "I really have absolutely no idea." Wearily, I tried to lay the blame at the door of the CIA, saying, "He's a Triad who must have got Joe confused with Miles. Believe me, your boyfriend does not work for MI6."

But we were too far down the line and Isabella was too smart and too shocked to be deceived. However drunk she had been, what had happened had sobered her up to an absolute clarity. I can only compare the look on her face to the impact that sudden loss can have on a grieving friend or relative. Either to get some air, or to follow Miles and Chen outside in the search for further answers, she now pushed past me and made her way out of the bar onto Lan Kwai Fong. It was extraordinarily humid on the street and the contrast with the air-conditioned bar was enervating. It felt as if you were drowning in a wet, suffocating heat. The pavements and the road itself were rammed with Westerners, and Billy Chen was nowhere to be seen. Isabella, moving with that certain force and determination which obliges people to step out of your way, began walking downhill, perhaps because she had seen Miles heading in that direction, perhaps because she was simply confused and wanted to go somewhere she could think and move more freely. I was quickly swallowed up by the crowd and found myself walking several metres behind her when I noticed Joe coming up the hill. He was smoking a cigarette and must have seen the confusion on Isabella's face because a plume of uninhaled smoke emerged from his mouth and he started to run towards her.

"What's the matter?" he said when he was close enough to be heard. "What's happened? Why are you crying?"

I wasn't thinking straight and barged in on this, trying to warn Joe with my eyes while placing a hand on Isabella's shoulder. Sensing me behind her, she spun round and shouted, "Just fuck off, Will" and spittle landed in my eyes and on my cheeks. Joe looked stunned. But she was right to have said it. I had no place intervening. Joe was either going to convince her that Billy Chen had been a madman, or it was all over between them. I couldn't see how he was going to salvage things, but I had to leave him to work it out. There was still no sign of Miles and people in the crowd were beginning to stare at me as I backed off.

"What's going on?" Joe said again. I noticed he had dropped his cigarette on the street.

"I need to go home," Isabella told him. "I want you to take me home." So he immediately put his arm round her and started walking down the street. They looked like survivors stumbling away from a plane crash. Seconds earlier, Joe Lennox had been a young man in the prime of life, less than twenty-four hours away from proposing to a woman he loved as he would never love again. Now he was on the brink of fighting to save that relationship because of an incident engineered by a jealous friend and colleague. It was bewildering. I stared at them walking down the hill and knew in my heart that Joe was doomed. I also knew that things between the four of us would never be the same again.

PART TWO | London
2004

25 | NOT QUITE THE DIPLOMAT

After the handover, Joe remained in Hong Kong for six months, but Isabella left him for Miles almost immediately. Certain women, I suppose, might have been thrilled to discover that their boyfriend was not a run-of-the-mill shipping clerk, but instead a spy doing work of unimaginable importance on behalf of the secret state. But not Isabella. She felt utterly betrayed. It was as if Joe had been deliberately toying with her emotions; she would not listen to any of his protestations of innocence nor expressions of regret. As far as I know, he never mentioned the fact that he was on the point of proposing. Miles, ever the opportunist, sided with Isabella in the ensuing days and I am convinced that she turned to him so quickly as a means of wounding Joe for the intense pain that his deception had caused her.

"At least Miles is honest about what he does for a living," she told me. "At least he doesn't manipulate me and hide behind a wall of lies. It's not the spying that I object to. It's the treachery. Every day for three years Joe was deceiving me. *I'm going to the bank. I'll be late home from work. I can't make dinner.* How could I trust a single thing he said to me ever again?"

Miles left Hong Kong for Chengdu in September of that year,

and he took Isabella with him. All of us were stunned that she was prepared to take such a gamble, but there was no doubt that the two of them had forged an extraordinary bond in the short time that they had been seeing one another. It didn't surprise me, for example, to run into Isabella at a wedding in Paris two years later and discover that she and Miles were engaged.

"He's very romantic, you know," she said, almost as if apologizing for falling in love with him. "He's always surprising me, taking me away for little breaks and weekends." I tried to summon up a picture of Miles presenting Isabella with boxes of chocolates, perfumed candles or flowers, but the images wouldn't compute. After dinner, we spoke at length about the years in Hong Kong and she was a good deal less brittle on the subject of Joe. There were underlying reasons for her decision to end their relationship which Isabella seemed to have accepted. She admitted, for example, that she had perceived Miles as a challenge. He had a reputation as a ladies' man; he was almost feral in his refusal to conform to people's expectations of how a man in his position should behave. When he wanted to, Miles Coolidge could make a woman feel as though she was the only person in the room. Life with such a man was never going to be dull. Perhaps Isabella had been prepared to overlook his myriad faults for this reason. She doubtless started out in the naïve belief that she could change him.

For Joe, however, the knowledge that his girlfriend was making a new life in an anonymous Chinese city with a man he despised corroded something elemental in his soul. For a long time after '97 he was utterly withdrawn and focused only on work, recruiting and running as many as a dozen new Chinese political and military targets, to the delight of London but to his own almost total personal indifference. Just after the East Asian stock market crash in October, Joe gave serious consideration to quitting SIS but was persuaded to stay on by David Waterfield, who offered him a plum job in Kuala Lumpur.

"Get away," he said. "Make a fresh start. Find out why you got into this business in the first place." Joe packed his bags that Christmas.

His postings to Malaysia and, latterly, Singapore, are not particularly relevant to the story I am here to tell. People I have spoken to who knew Joe during this period refer to him as "quiet" and "reliable," lively only when drunk but respected by everyone with whom he came into contact. He remained in South-east Asia, without seeing or speaking to either Miles or Isabella, for four years. I flew in to Singapore for his thirtieth birthday in the summer of 2001 and discovered that Joe had been seeing an Italian medical doctor named Carla for about three months. This seemed a positive step, but the two of them had soon gone their separate ways. "It just didn't feel right," he told me in an email. "It wasn't going anywhere." These were phrases Joe would often employ when discussing his relationships with women. In final analysis, none of them matched up to the Isabella template. It was as if he was walking around with a ghost of the perfect woman and would not rest until Isabella had come to her senses. Of course, with each new relationship there was the added complication that Joe was repeating the same mistake he had made with Isabella; that is to say, he was bound by duty and could not come clean about his work for SIS. As far as he was concerned, he was entering a pointless cycle of deception and hurt. Why bother? Why put another woman through the same agony?

What gave the situation an added complexity was the shame Joe felt at having been outmanoeuvred and humiliated by Miles. The resentment he harboured towards his former friend and colleague was almost as strong as the love he continued to feel for Isabella. Even seven years later, when the two of us were walking in west London on a wet night during the turbulent summer of 2004, I could sense that his memories were still as detailed and vivid as if his break-up with Isabella had taken place only days earlier.

"So do you think they've made it work?" I asked.

"Made what work?"

"The marriage. China. Do you think she made the right decision?"

We were heading towards Al-Abbas, the famous Arab supermarket on Uxbridge Road. Joe turned to cross the street outside a branch of Blockbuster Video and gave me an impatient, quizzical look.

"Who knows?" he replied flatly.

"But you're still holding out, aren't you? You still believe there's a chance of the two of you getting back together?"

"Will," he said, "when people make decisions of any kind, they do so in the belief that what they're doing is right. Now that decision may prove to be self-destructive, it may turn out to be the worst decision they ever made. But at the time it didn't feel that way. At the time it felt like they had no choice."

He jaywalked across the road. A light drizzle was falling and I watched him weave between an oncoming bus and a beaten-up Fiat Punto. There was something about Joe living in London that didn't make sense. He didn't seem to belong in England; he wasn't settled or happy. Much of this had to do with the circumstances under which he was working for SIS; 2004 had been a wretched year for MI6. The Butler Report had been published in July, castigating the quality of the intelligence that Six had passed on to government ministers and officials in the run-up to the war in Iraq. SIS officers had been criticized for the manner in which they had gathered intelligence on WMD and, in particular, for their readiness to believe dissident Iraqi sources who later proved unreliable. As a requirements officer for the Far East Controllerate, Joe was not directly involved in any of this, but he felt the slump in Office morale none the less and questioned, on several occasions, the good sense of continuing to work for an organization which was being constantly undermined by the government and relentlessly criticized in the media. At the tender age of twenty-three, Joe Lennox had signed up to a life in the secret world partly out of a belief that British values were worth fighting for, that it was admirable to dedicate one's working life to the security and prosperity of the British people. One of the organizing principles of any intelligence agency is patriotism of this kind, but to be patriotic in the age of Blair and Bush, of Guantanamo and Abu Ghraib, was a task of Herculean proportions. Everything from Alastair Campbell's "sexed-up dossier" to the death of Dr. David Kelly ate away at Joe's faith in the system. What was he fighting for? What would be the price of his own professional complicity in the invasion of

Iraq? To work for British intelligence in this period was to work on behalf of the American government; there was no other way of spinning it. Yet Joe would switch off the television in his flat rather than suffer the grinning, adolescent rictus of President George W. Bush. He abhorred Cheney and Rumsfeld, whom he regarded as borderline sociopaths, and even joked about asking Sky TV to remove Fox News from his satellite television package. I once asked him, in a similar spirit of jocularity, whether this newfound anti-Americanism was connected to what had happened with Miles. To my surprise, Joe became very angry.

"I am not anti-American," he said. "I just despise the current American administration. I despair that Bush has made ordinary, decent people all over the world think twice about what was once, and still could be again, a great country, when what happened on September 11th should have made ordinary, decent people all over the world embrace America as never before. I don't like it that neo-conservative politicians bully their so-called allies while playing to the worst, racist instincts of their own bewildered electorate. I don't like it that we live in an era where to be anti-war is to be anti-American, to be pro-Palestine is to be anti-Semitic, to be critical of Blair is somehow to be supportive of Putin and Chirac. All anybody is asking for in this so-called age of terror is some leadership. Yet everywhere you look in public life there is no truth, no courage, no dignity to speak of."

Such sentiments inevitably caught the attention of the SIS personnel department, a shifty, cynical lot who often seem to me to be more interested in undermining the confidence of their employees than in ensuring that staff are in the correct frame of mind to do their jobs properly. There were dark mutterings that Joe had "gone soft": he had been observed reading a copy of *No Logo* on the District Line and had even recommended articles by Robert Fisk and John Pilger to an Arabic translator in the Vauxhall Cross canteen. Luckily, calmer heads prevailed. Lennox wasn't a proto-lefty; his record demonstrated that he was prepared to take tough decisions and to condone some fairly unsavoury operational practices in order to secure a long-term advantage for the Service.

Any misgivings he felt about the direction of government policy in Iraq were merely reflective of wider public opinion and, for that matter, of about seventy-five per cent of SIS personnel.

One additional characteristic of Joe's three-year posting to London was that he was bored. Travelling by Tube to Vauxhall station every morning doesn't really compare to the eye-popping spectacle of taking the Star Ferry across Victoria Harbour. Nor does liaising with Whitehall on intelligence requirements compare to the excitement and challenge of obtaining that intelligence oneself. A night owl by nature, Joe missed the bars and restaurants of Kuala Lumpur, the crush and sweat of Asian streets. Going out in Singapore was a case of picking up the phone, arranging to meet a friend two hours later, and of staying out until five or six in the morning. Going out in London involved making an arrangement two weeks in advance, securing names on a guest list, queuing for half an hour for entry into an overpriced, crowded nightclub, and then dodging piles of vomit on the way home. In any case, by 2004 most of Joe's friends from the old days had settled down. He felt increasingly disconnected from their world of nappies and marriage. Joe was fond of quoting Goethe's maxim—"A man can stand anything except a succession of ordinary days"—and longed to be posted back to Asia. "That's where I'm most at home," he said. "That's where I'm happiest."

Matters came to a head in the autumn of 2004. At a dinner party in Tufnell Park, Joe ran into an old university friend named Guy Coates who was looking to recruit a fluent Mandarin speaker to set up a representative office in Beijing for Quayler, a niche pharmaceutical company which was hoping to expand into China. Offices of this kind need be no more than a desk and a fax machine, but they allow Western companies to promote and market their products on a limited scale in advance of being registered as a fully fledged business by the Chinese government. At a lunch in the City three days later, Coates offered Joe a five-year contract worth about £90,000 a year, with an apartment in Sanlitun and a small amount of equity thrown in. Joe was tempted, not least by the salary, which was more than twice what he was earning at SIS. I also played a part in trying to lure him back to the East. By coincidence, SIS had just pulled some strings to secure me a job in Beijing with an American news organization and I reckoned my social life would be greatly enhanced if Joe was on the scene. "It'll be just like the old days," I told him on the phone. "Besides, you need to get the hell out of London."

Joe was in a dilemma. Stay with SIS and risk a three-year posting to an Asian backwater, or jump ship to work in the Chinese capital during a period which would coincide with the run-up to the 2008 Olympics? Joe had never been motivated by money, and the Far East Controllerate might have more interesting options than, say, North Korea, but he felt compelled to discuss the situation with his line manager at Vauxhall Cross. Disheartened that Joe might pull the plug at a difficult time for the Service, and anxious not to lose one of their best and most experienced officers, SIS dispatched David Waterfield in a last-ditch effort to talk him round. After all, the interventions of Joe's mentor had succeeded before. There was no reason to suppose that they could not succeed again.

Nobody really knows what happened to Josh Pinnegar. Nobody knows if it was accident or design. The incident is still talked about in the bars and restaurants of San Francisco, although in Chinatown itself enquiries are met with a wall of silence. More than a year after his murder, no witnesses from the local community have come forward to describe Pinnegar's assailants, nor to confirm specific details of the attack. FBI efforts to prove that the Triad gang responsible were hired by the MSS have fallen on predictably fallow ground. Pro-Chinese newspapers in the San Francisco area—the *Singtao Daily*, *China Press*, *Ming Pao*—blame a simple case of mistaken identity. Others argue that the tentacles of the Chinese Communist Party extend across the Pacific Ocean into every facet of Chinese life in the United States of America. The government in Beijing, they claim, uses Triad gangs to intimidate ethnic Chinese overtly critical of the regime back home. It follows, therefore, that they would find it all too easy to bankroll an assassination of this kind.

These are the facts.

In the early winter of 2004 Josh Pinnegar received a coded message at Langley from a dormant source in the Chinese military

who had briefly provided information to the CIA during TY-
PHOON. The source arranged for Pinnegar to meet him at a
well-known bar on Grant Avenue, in the Chinatown district of
San Francisco. Further investigations revealed that the source was
scheduled to fly into LAX on 10 November in order to attend a
wedding in Sacramento on the 13th. He never boarded the plane.

On the night in question, Pinnegar made his way to the bar and
waited at a table by the window for two hours. The bar was popular with students and tourists and it was a busy Friday night. One
member of staff recalls that Pinnegar looked somewhat out of place
as "a thirtysomething male reading a novel and drinking soda,"
while all around him young Americans were "sinking beers and
playing pool."

Towards 10 p.m. Josh became convinced that his contact was
not going to show up. He asked for his cheque and left a ten-
dollar tip. He went to the bathroom, collected his coat, and then
left the bar by the main entrance on Grant Avenue.

The two members of the Triad gang approached on foot from
across the street wielding meat cleavers that had been dipped in
excrement to cause immediate septicaemia. The first strike severed Pinnegar's right arm at the shoulder. A second hit a cellphone
in the pocket of his trousers, causing a shallow cut to his upper
thigh. There were at least seven eyewitnesses, six of whom were
Chinese. A passing law student from Yale, who spoke to the police on condition of complete anonymity, heard a woman scream
and somebody else shout out "Call the police!" as the attack continued. As far as she could recall, Pinnegar made no sound whatsoever as the blows rained down upon him.

Within seconds, he had lost at least two pints of blood. The
wounds to his head and torso are too hideous to describe. Josh
Pinnegar was pronounced dead on arrival at San Francisco General. The assailants fled on motorbikes which were later found
abandoned, and torched, in Redwood Park.

Well spoken, patrician, reluctant to suffer fools, David Waterfield was a British spy of the old school. When working in London he invariably wore a suit cut by Hawkes of Savile Row, brogues from John Lobb, a tailored shirt by Turnbull and Asser and socks from New and Lingwood. He would lunch frequently at his club on Pall Mall, spend every third weekend at a cottage in Dorset and occasionally attend meetings of the Countryside Alliance. In the summer, for three weeks, he and his wife holidayed at a luxurious farmhouse in the Portuguese Alentejo, courtesy of a former SIS colleague who had made it big at Cazenove's. Retirement, when it came, would probably involve a brief stint working for the National Trust, with the odd lecture at IONEC thrown in. Indeed, David Waterfield conformed so readily to a certain Foreign Office stereotype that as he emerged from platform 16 at Waterloo to make his way across the crowded station concourse, it occurred to the waiting Joe that he was exactly the sort of upper-class gentleman spook who had given MI6 a bad name. They were too easy to lampoon, a cinch to satirize. Yet Joe also knew that the image was completely misleading: beneath Waterfield's public-school bonhomie lurked an intellect as sharp and as persuasive as any in the

Service. Joe was fascinated to discover how he was going to try to talk him round.

From Waterloo they made their way north towards the river, discussing the broad impact of Butler and reflecting on the old days in East Asia. Waterfield had stayed in the newly minted Hong Kong SAR until 2000, before a three-year stint in Beijing. Their paths had crossed only twice while Joe had been based in Malaysia and Singapore, but the two men had renewed their professional friendship while working together at Vauxhall Cross.

"Tell me," Waterfield said as they descended, side by side, a spiral staircase attached to the Festival Hall. "What do you re-member about Kenneth Lenan?"

Of all the questions Joe had been expecting, that wasn't one of them. As far as he was aware, Lenan had quit the Office in early 1998 to work for an American construction company in China. What relevance would his story have to Joe's uncertain future with SIS?

"He left shortly after I moved to KL, didn't he?" he said. "Got a big offer from Halliburton or Bechtel to work in Gansu prov-ince."

Perhaps there was a cautionary tale in Lenan's subsequent be-haviour.

"The job was with the Macklinson Corporation," Waterfield corrected. They had emerged onto the wide, pedestrianized path which runs from the London Eye to Tate Modern, heading east in the direction of Blackfriars Bridge. "He did six weeks in Lanzhou, then moved to Urumqi on a more or less permanent basis."

A teenage boy on a skateboard rattled past, ducking under the concrete overhang of the Queen Elizabeth Hall. Hearing the word "Urumqi," Joe was beginning to forge a vague, uncertain link in his mind between Lenan and Professor Wang Kaixuan when Wa-terfield said, "And what do you remember about Kenneth's rela-tionship with Miles Coolidge?"

Gulls were swooping low over the slate-grey waters of the Thames. Joe felt the past rushing up behind him like a flood tide.

"I remember that I didn't trust him," he said. "I remember that there was some trouble over Professor Wang."

"Now why was that?"

"It's a long story." Joe sensed that Waterfield already knew most of it.

"We've got lots of time."

A set of railings near by looked out over the Thames. Joe walked towards them. It was a crisp September morning, not a cloud in the sky. As if it would help to trigger his memory, Joe lit a cigarette and began to relate, as best he could recall, the events of that frustrating week seven years earlier: Lenan's sudden appearance in the small hours; Lee's fumbling lies at the safe house; Miles's inexpert denials of a CIA conspiracy, uttered in the depths of a Wan Chai nightclub. Waterfield listened as his eyes followed the boats on the river, the trains on Hungerford Bridge.

"And that was the last you heard of it?" he asked, when Joe had finished. "Neither Miles nor Kenneth ever mentioned Wang again?"

"Never."

They turned and began walking east. Another skateboarder rumbled past and Waterfield cursed under his breath. "Let's go inside," he said. "Coffee."

The café of the National Film Theatre is spacious, glass-fronted. Waterfield and Joe might have been father and son ordering cappuccinos and cakes at the counter. Joe found them a table in the window looking out over the booksellers who ply their trade under Waterloo Bridge. As crowds of passers-by hovered around the stalls of old maps and paperbacks, Waterfield removed his heavy winter coat and settled down to business.

"Have you ever, at any stage in your career, come across the name TYPHOON?"

Joe said that he had not.

"TYPHOON was the cryptonym for a CIA operation to destabilize the Xinjiang Autonomous Region which was abandoned after 9/11. Miles Coolidge ran it with assistance from, among others, Kenneth Lenan." Joe was eating the milk and powdered chocolate from the surface of his cappuccino. He was astonished by the revelation, but force of habit concealed his reaction. "During the early stages of your interview with Professor Wang, Miles telephoned Garden Road and discovered that you were using a shared safe house. Kenneth Lenan confirmed in a subsequent phone call that you were involved in an interrogation of a Han national from Urumqi who was antagonistic towards Beijing. Miles began listening to a live feed at the consulate and moved on it immediately. He and Kenneth had been involved in several little schemes before, some of which I knew about, some of which I didn't. You might call it a mutually beneficial relationship, particularly for Kenneth, who managed to squirrel away enough American money for ten retirements. To cut a long story short, Miles had been looking round for ways of developing operations in Xinjiang. Wang looked just the ticket. Miles convinced Kenneth to hand him over to the Cousins and to use SIS channels to spirit the professor out of Hong Kong and back to mainland China. Wang was subsequently recruited and trained in Taiwan as an agent of the CIA with instructions to put together a network of radicalized Uighur youth who would cause chaos on the streets through bombings, riots and anti-communist demonstrations."

"Jesus Christ," Joe said. "And you say you knew nothing about it? I spent six weeks worrying that I'd failed to identify Wang as MSS."

"That's what Miles told you?"

"They both did. Insisted he was a Chinese intelligence officer known to the Cousins who had been involved in an operation that had led to CIA expulsions."

"And you believed this?"

"Not exactly. But I was young. I was inexperienced. I was too far down the food chain to make a fuss."

Waterfield's body language suggested that he accepted the broad logic of this. He took a bite of his cake and spent the next ten minutes outlining Macklinson's role in TYPHOON. Joe was still reeling from the revelation that Wang Kaixuan, the benign, idealistic intellectual he had interviewed in Tsim Sha Tsui, had somehow been transformed, almost overnight, into a patriarch of terror. For seven years Joe Lennox had been privy to intelligence

reports coming out of China about terrorist incidents in Xinjiang
and beyond. It was hard to believe that Wang, with American help,
might have been responsible for orchestrating some of them.

"How big was TYPHOON? What sort of scale are we talking
about?"

"Initially limitless. Of course Langley kept the sharp end of
things to a minimum. Any weapons and explosives found their way
to a small group of extremists—some of them under Wang's control, some of them not—who continued to blow up buses and super-
markets in places like Lanzhou and Kashgar. But the softer
propaganda tools—video cameras, pro-democracy documents,
briefcases of cash—went to a much wider circle of student intel-
lectuals and fledgling democracy types. TYPHOON began as an
operation aimed at bringing about independence for Eastern
Turkestan, but very quickly spread into a generalized, American-
sponsored pro-democracy movement all across Han China."

"How did the Yanks think they were going to get away with
this?"

"God knows. And the short answer is that they didn't." Waterfield scratched the side of his neck, producing a raw red mark
above the collar of his shirt. "The one thing the Cousins understood only too well was Beijing's fear of massed, organized rebellion in the provinces. That's what they were trying to catalyse. *Da
luan.* 'Big chaos.' But at the same time they had very little understanding of the situation on the ground. You don't just walk into a
country like China and start fomenting peasant rebellion. By all
means fund and supervise a small network of pseudo-Islamist radicals, but don't get ideas above your station. Informants operate at
every level of Chinese society. You're going to get caught. You're
going to get found out."

"And that's what happened?"

"Of course it is." If Waterfield sounded frustrated, it was only
because he was still flabbergasted by the naïvety of TYPHOON's
conception. "In the spring of 2000, one of the Macklinson shipments was intercepted by Chinese customs in Dalian. A barn stuffed
with copying machines and anti-communist literature was discovered shortly afterwards about fifty miles outside Shihezi. At

least three cells with TYPHOON fingerprints were penetrated by the MSS between 1999 and the spring of 2001, with as many as nineteen Uighur separatists subsequently tortured and executed for splittist activities. Four so-called Macklinson employees, all of them in reality CIA, were expelled from China for 'undermining the security of the Socialist Motherland through acts of subversion and sabotage.' It was a total bloody disaster."

"How come we didn't get to hear about it?"

"Good question. Essentially because the Chinese and the Yanks came to an arrangement."

"What sort of an arrangement?"

"The sort that got people killed."

For a strange and exhilarating moment, about which Joe would later feel ashamed, he wondered if Waterfield was about to tell him that Miles Coolidge had been executed by the PLA. A waitress approached and cleared away their plates and cups.

"Here's the situation," Waterfield said. He flicked a speck of dust from the sleeve of his suit. "Three weeks ago, Kenneth Lenan's body was pulled out of the Huangpu River. His tongue had been cut out. Every tendon in his body had been sliced open. The Chinese authorities claim that they have no idea who did this to him. We don't exactly believe that."

28 | RETREAD

Murders are a rare occurrence in the secret world. SIS prides itself on the fact that no officer has been killed on active duty since World War II. Kenneth Lenan may have been a traitor to the Service, a cast-off in the private sector, but it still took Joe a while to process what Waterfield had told him. They left the café and walked past the entrance to the National Theatre.

"The manner of his death," he said. "It's a signature of the Green Gang. Do people realize that?"

"People realize that," Waterfield replied.

The Green Gang were the infamous criminal fraternity who operated in Shanghai until the communists took over in 1949. Lenan had been the victim of a specific form of revenge killing, whereby traitors had every tendon in their body severed with a fruit knife before being left to bleed to death on the street. Unable to move because of their injuries, they were often placed in a sack weighed down by rocks and thrown into the Huangpu River.

"So who did he betray?"

Waterfield looked up at the sky and smiled. He had done his grieving.

"Whom," he corrected.

Joe wasn't in the mood to play games. "All right then. *Whom?*"

"Could have been anybody."

"Someone on our side?"

Waterfield suggested with a tightening of the eyes that he found that idea both distasteful and preposterous.

"What, then? You think his murder was connected to TYPHOON?"

"I would have said almost certainly."

They walked in silence for about a hundred metres. It was as if Waterfield was anticipating a particular line of questioning that Joe had not yet produced. The sun was warm on Joe's face. A young, dreadlocked juggler was unpacking a suitcase on the path in front of them.

"You said that TYPHOON was wound up after 9/11."

"Yes." Waterfield scratched his neck again. Joe assumed that he had been bitten by an insect of some kind, just behind the left ear. "After that, all bets were off. Langley was under instruction to withdraw support for any Muslim group within five thousand miles of Kabul."

"But TYPHOON kept going?"

"Not really. By the summer of that year the operation had been so severely compromised it was all but dead in the water."

"Was Wang arrested?" For a reason that he could not precisely explain, Joe hoped that the professor was still alive.

"No. He was one of the lucky ones. Last I heard, Wang was living in Tianjin."

They turned a corner and it occurred to Joe that the professor was the source of Waterfield's information. How else did he know so much about TYPHOON?

"Did we turn Wang?" he asked. "Did you recruit him when you were stationed in Beijing? How come you know where he is?"

Waterfield seemed amused by the idea. "Everything that I've told you this morning has come from two separate sources, neither of whom is Professor Wang Kaixuan." He blew his nose aggressively on a freshly laundered handkerchief. "The Controllerate has a new, highly placed official in the MSS recruited by Station in Beijing in the last twelve months. We also have an older, established contact on the American side with whom I formed a relationship long ago in Hong Kong."

"You had a Cousin on the books in '97?"

Waterfield allowed himself to feel flattered. "I had all sorts of things going on that RUN wasn't privy to. As you said, Joe, you were very low down on the food chain."

It sounded like an insult but Waterfield decorated his quip with a knowing grin. The slightly tense atmosphere which had existed between them since the café had now eased away.

"And what have your sources told you about Lenan's death?"

"It's still largely a mystery." Waterfield offered a fatalistic glance at the sky. "I can hazard an educated guess."

Joe stepped aside to allow an undernourished jogger to limp past them.

"It involves Macklinson. According to my Cousin, as a consequence of his relationship with the CIA, Kenneth developed a close personal friendship with the company's chief financial officer, an individual by the name of Michael Lambert. Played golf together, that sort of thing. Lambert is now Macklinson CEO, because the lovely Bill Marston dropped dead of a heart attack a couple of years ago. With TYPHOON in full flight in the late 1990s, Lambert had become very excited by the oil and gas potential in Xinjiang and invested the company, for strategic reasons, with Petrosina."

"The Chinese state oil producer? But they don't allow foreign investment on any kind of scale."

"That's not strictly true. Macklinson bought a controlling stake in a specialist oil services company called Devon Chataway which had been sold a two point four per cent holding in Petrosina by the Chinese government. The way Lambert saw things panning out, if TYPHOON failed, Macklinson would still have a significant claim on fossil fuels in Xinjiang. If it was successful, the corporation would be well placed to become a major player in an independent Eastern Turkestan. He explained all this to Kenneth, who remortgaged his house in Richmond, wrote his stockbroker a cheque for £950,000 and told him to sink it in Chinese oil."

Joe shook his head.

"The one thing neither man anticipated was a clusterfuck on

the scale of TYPHOON. As the operation began to unravel, the MSS applied intense pressure on Macklinson, and on Lambert in particular. 'Tell us what you know about your operations in China and you can continue to do business here. Give us the names of the CIA operatives with whom you have an association and we will continue to allow Devon Chataway to benefit from their investments in Petrosina. Refuse to co-operate and Beijing will turn TYPHOON into an international scandal which will humiliate the American government.'"

Joe swore and looked out at the river. Here was the limitless cynicism of greed and power, the curse of the age. Every man for his bank balance and screw the consequences. It was a quiet, blameless morning on the Thames and he felt a sense of helpless anger close to the impotent frustration of watching the day-to-day horrors in Iraq.

"So Lenan gave them up?" he asked. It was the only possible outcome. "He and Lambert sold out the CIA to protect their investments?"

Waterfield nodded. "That's just my personal opinion," he said. "That's just a David Waterfield theory."

The two men had known one another for almost ten years and yet the characteristics of their relationship had not changed a great deal in that time. Although Joe was now in his mid-thirties, he still looked upon Waterfield in the same way that he had done back in Hong Kong: as a surrogate father and mentor, as an old hand of far greater experience than his own, whose wisdom and intuition was almost sacred. With no other senior colleague at SIS did Joe experience feelings of this kind. It was as if he had been programmed never to question Waterfield's judgment.

"What about Miles?" Joe asked. "What's happened to him?"

The question was loaded and both of them knew it. Miles meant Isabella, and Isabella was Joe's past. Wherever the two of them might be, he was surely going to follow. That was the purpose of the meeting. That was what Waterfield was going to ask him. It was now just a question of how he was going to articulate his offer.

"Miles appears to have remained below the Chinese radar.

Whatever information Macklinson and Lenan gave the MSS, we don't think it included anything about Coolidge's networks."

"Unless the Chinese are deliberately giving him enough rope to hang himself."

Waterfield conceded the possibility of this but flicked the notion to one side, like the dust off the immaculate sleeve of his jacket. "Given that Wang is also walking the streets as a free man, we might assume some sort of connection between the two of them."

"But you said earlier that Lenan was living in Urumqi. Wouldn't that imply that he, rather than Miles, was running Wang, and that Wang would therefore be the first person he would have given up?"

Waterfield seemed briefly caught out. Sometimes he allowed himself to forget the sharpness of Joe's memory, the speed with which he made operational calculations.

"That wasn't how things worked. As far as we know, the Cousins tried to put as much water between themselves and the cell structures as possible. For example, Miles ran Wang from Chengdu. They met only twice a year in locations that we still haven't been able to identify. Lenan's people were in Gansu and Qinghai, which is where most of the post-TYPHOON arrests were made. Two of the three CIA officers who worked undercover at Macklinson were based in Shenzhen, but were observed meeting contacts as far afield as Taiyuan, Harbin and Jilin. The third was operating out of a Macklinson office in Golmud but was tenuously linked to Uighur groups in Yining and Kashgar. TYPHOON criss-crossed China. Anyway, it's all water under the bridge. That has nothing to do with what I'm proposing."

"And what are you proposing, David?"

"Let's go to the Tate."

A silent quarter-mile later, David Waterfield and Joe Lennox were queuing for sandwiches in the near-deserted Members Room at Tate Modern. Waterfield paid while Joe found a couple of facing seats with a view across the river to St. Paul's. He had so many questions running through his mind that he had been glad of the brief time alone to compose himself. Had Isabella been introduced to Lenan? Had Miles made her conscious of TYPHOON? He thought of all the weeks and months she must have spent alone in Chengdu while Miles shuttled around the country running his network of subversives. What a life. That she was prepared to exchange their future together for a thankless existence in Sichuan province had always struck him as the final, debilitating irony of their separation. To swap one spy, one set of lies, for another. Wasted love.

"You look deep in thought," Waterfield said, bearing a plastic tray on which he had balanced two bottles of mineral water and a brace of pre-packaged sandwiches. "Is everything all right?"

He sat opposite Joe, looking down at the Millennium Bridge.

"Where was Isabella through all of this?" Joe asked.

Waterfield was surprised by his candour. Isabella Aubert was the name you didn't mention around RUN.

"They're still together," he said, answering the question that he felt Joe had wanted to ask. "She's been living in Shanghai with Miles for the past two years."

Joe's heart did its usual thing: the thump of loss, then the bile of jealousy and regret. Nothing had changed in seven years. He said, "So they were friends with Lenan?"

"Kenneth was visiting Shanghai when he was killed. We don't know if he had meetings with Coolidge during that period. If he had sold out the CIA, and if Miles had found out about that, you can imagine that he might have felt somewhat aggrieved."

"This has something to do with Isabella, doesn't it?" Joe had not thought through the question, which betrayed the true direction of his feelings. Waterfield buried his reaction in a sip of water.

"Do you want it to have something to do with Isabella?"

Joe had made a mistake. An officer made privy to the information that Waterfield had disclosed should not be dwelling on an aspect of his private life. He should be thinking about blowback, about murder, about the implications of TYPHOON for the Special Relationship.

"I'm sorry," he said. "It just sounded as though . . ."

Waterfield put him out of his misery. "Look, from what I can gather, it hasn't all been plain sailing between them. Let's leave it at that. She got a job working with underprivileged children in Chengdu and might have chucked the whole thing in had it not been for that."

Joe felt his spirit quicken. "Where are you getting your information?"

"Grapevine." Waterfield stared at a point beyond Joe's shoulder. "Wasn't Isabella Catholic?"

Joe nodded.

"That might explain a few things. Marriage vows. No release in the eyes of God from a lifetime of commitment. Graham Greene country. Never underestimate the obstinacy of the Catholic bride. How else do you explain a woman like Isabella spending the rest of her life with Miles Coolidge?"

Joe was beginning to feel a curious and not entirely enjoyable sense of disorientation. Why was Waterfield telling him all this? To get his hopes up? Was it all just a pack of lies? Two elderly women settled at the next-door table and Waterfield quickly generalized the conversation.

"Tell me," he said, "how serious is all this anti-war stuff?"

Joe was glad for the change of subject and tore open the plastic packaging of his sandwich. "What do you mean?"

"I mean, how much has the Iraq fiasco contributed to your decision to work for Guy Coates?"

Joe had two reactions to this. The first noted that Waterfield had referred to Iraq as a "fiasco." It was the first time that he had heard him utter such a direct criticism of the war. The second was that David knew about Quayler. Joe had not disclosed the name of his prospective employer to anyone at SIS.

"How did you find out about that?"

Waterfield returned his gaze to the river. There is an unwritten rule among spies that you do not question a colleague on the nature of his sources unless it is absolutely necessary. Joe had broken that rule at least twice in one morning.

"Grapevine," he replied again. "Look." Waterfield leaned towards him. He wanted to reassure Joe about something. "I know that you have misgivings about rendition. I know that you have concerns about using product possibly gained from the torture chambers of Cairo and Damascus. We all do." He lowered his voice as the two elderly ladies stirred sachets of sugar into cups of tea. "But what's the alternative? We all resign in protest and leave the Office in the hands of a bunch of Blairite careerists? Go off and write our memoirs? Come off it. In any case, the current lot"—he nodded across the river in the general direction of Whitehall—"will be out of a job in a few years" time. Politics is cyclical, Joe. All one has to do is bide one's time and the right people will come round again. Then things can go back to the way things were." Joe was looking down at the floor. "What I want to tell you is this." Waterfield was now almost whispering. "You could go all the way in this business. People are keeping an eye on you, Joe." He tried a joke to ice the compliment. "You can't leave us at the mercy of the love children of Percy Craddock and Deng Xiaoping. We've already got too many Sinologists on the books in thrall to the Middle Kingdom. You were always tougher than that. You see the Politburo for what they are. The next ten to fifteen years are going to be vital in terms of Anglo-Chinese relations and we can't afford to roll over and run up the white flag. You could play an absolutely critical role in that."

It was a decent enough pitch, accurate in places, too. Ever since the days of Patten and Wang, Joe had been profoundly suspicious and distrustful of communist China, an attitude not always shared by his colleagues in the Foreign Office, most of whom had both eyes on the country's vast market potential for British business. But Waterfield could see that he still wasn't quite getting through. He put his bottle of water on the table and tried a different approach.

"It strikes me that you're bored," he said. "It strikes me that you would prefer to be out in the field, making a difference. Nobody wants to be kicking their heels behind a desk in London."

"But what can you offer me?" Joe said, not as a bargaining position, but rather as a statement of his belief that all the best jobs in China had been taken. Nowadays it was all Iraq and Afghanistan. The Far East Controllerate had been filleted down to its bare bones. "If it's a choice between carving out a decent career in the private sector or being posted to some shithole like Manila or Ulan Bator, I know where my instincts lie."

"Your instincts, yes. But what about your loyalties?"

Waterfield knew Joe well enough to gamble on playing the guilt card. In spite of all of his misgivings about the direction of British policy since 9/11, Joe Lennox was at heart a patriot. Scratch the liberal humanist who railed against Bush and Blair and you would reveal an old-fashioned servant of the state who still believed in the mirage of Queen and Country, in the primacy of Western values. It was like Joe's faith in the concept of a Christian God, a strange, institutionalized consequence of his privileged upbringing. Yet still he said, "Oh come on. Is that what this comes down to? Both of us know which way to pass the port so I have to keep the British end up?"

"The Pentagon may be trying to reactivate TYPHOON," Waterfield replied, sabotaging Joe's argument with the clean, flat timing of his revelation.

"Says who?"

"Says a watertight source in Washington." Before Joe could interrupt, Waterfield was pitching him again.

"The details we have are sketchy. Of course the formal Bush position is that the East Turkestan Islamic Movement is a terrorist organization with links to al-Qaeda. Best guess is that Miles used to fund some of the ETIM boys pre-9/11 and has now gone off piste. We think he's running a clandestine operation on CIA time without the knowledge of his masters at Langley. Somebody at the Pentagon, almost certainly an individual adjacent to Donald Rumsfeld, has given him carte blanche to make merry in China."

"Even after everything that's happened?"

"Even after everything that's happened."

Joe was bewildered. This was in direct contradiction of the Bush administration's position on Xinjiang. "Surely someone at Langley knows what's happening? Why don't they bring him home?"

"Search me." It was common knowledge in the intelligence fraternity that the CIA had been turned inside-out in the wake of 9/11. "Earn the wrath of Dick and Donald these days and you might as well start clearing your desk. Best to keep your mouth shut, right? Best just to sit down and stop rocking the boat." Waterfield took a sip of his water. "Look. We need somebody who already knows Miles to go out there and find out exactly what's going on. To put a stop to it, if necessary. Is the Office vulnerable? Was Coolidge responsible for what happened to Kenneth and will the trail lead back to London? We can't afford to have British fingerprints on a new TYPHOON. If the Chinese know that Lenan was once one of ours, we need to do something about it."

The Members Room was a ripple of crockery and small talk as Joe's mind spun through the deal. When Waterfield saw that he was not going to respond, he added, "Come on, Joe. Are you really telling me that you want to spend the next five years of your life living in a soulless apartment in Beijing, flogging around China trying to secure patents for a tiny pharmaceutical company that in five years' time probably won't be worth the paper they're written on?"

But Joe didn't need any more persuading. The offer was too enticing to resist. It was Miles, it was China, and it was Isabella. Adopting a more playful tone of voice he said, "What's wrong with Beijing, David?" and, in that instant, Waterfield knew that he had finally hooked his man. Matching Joe's grin with one of his own, he leaned back in the sofa and stretched out his arms.

"Oh, everything's wrong with Beijing," he said. "Freezing half the year, baking hot the other. Anybody with any taste prefers Shanghai."

29 | THE BACKSTOP

It was getting Joe to Shanghai that posed the problem.

First, Waterfield had to go to Guy Coates with a proposition. Did he want to help Her Majesty's Government fight the good fight against Chinese tyranny and oppression? He did? Oh good. In that case, would Quayler be prepared to open up a second representative office, this one in Shanghai, staffed by Joe and two local Chinese, all of whom would be on the books with the Secret Intelligence Service? The British government would pay, of course, but Quayler would have to find somebody else to man their operation in Beijing. Joe's done this sort of thing before, so there's nothing to worry about. No, he wasn't working for the Ministry of Defence in London. That was just his cover. I'm sure you are a bit surprised. You'll have to clear the idea with your board of directors? Fine. But Guy Coates must be the only member of staff privy to what's going on. You want an extra sixty grand? Not a problem. Least we can do in the circumstances. Just sign here where we've printed your name at the bottom.

After that, it was just a question of Joe handing in his notice, citing "ethical problems with the so-called War on Terror," and serving out his final three months at Vauxhall Cross. To anyone who would listen, he complained about the "iniquity" of Sir John Scarlett's appointment as "C" and suggested that the former head of the Joint Intelligence Committee had struck a deal with No. 10 whereby he would be handed the top job in SIS in return for massaging the dossier on Iraqi WMD. After that, most of Joe's colleagues became convinced that he had lost his marbles. Which was precisely Joe's intention.

"We'll have to throw a leaving party for you," Waterfield said.

"Really? Isn't that taking things a bit far?"

"Not at all. Make sure to invite a few Yanks along from Grosvenor Square. That way, word might slip back to Langley. The more people that get to hear about Joe Lennox's crisis of conscience, the better."

PART THREE | Shanghai
2005

China had dominated Joe's life. When he was a small boy, his parents had read him stories about the vast, populous country to the east of the Himalayas, a fantastical land of fearless warlords and sumptuous pagodas which had seemed as remote and as mysterious to his childhood imagination as the galaxies of science fiction or the menacing peaks of Mordor. In his early teens he had read the great doorstop novels of James Clavell, *Tai-Pan* and *Noble House*, steamy sagas of corporate greed set in colonial-era Hong Kong. With adolescence came *Empire of the Sun*, both the book—which Joe devoured in a single weekend during the Easter holidays of 1986—and the Spielberg film, released a year later. Spotting this affinity for the East, Joe's godfather had presented him with a first edition of Edgar Snow's *Red Star Over China* as a present for his eighteenth birthday and Joe had given serious thought to spending a gap year in Beijing before the massacre at Tiananmen obliged him to go straight up to Oxford. For the next three years he had been drenched in Chinese history and literature, reading the novels of Lao She, Luo Guanzhong and Mo Yan in the original Mandarin and poring over scholarly articles about the Qing dynasty. His gradual mastery of the language—honed by an undergraduate year spent in Taiwan—had opened up new under-standings of Chinese history and culture and Joe might have spent a further three years as a postgraduate at SOAS had it not been for the timely intervention of SIS.

In all that time, however, including more than a decade work-ing in the Far East Controllerate, he had never visited Shanghai. As a result, China's most famous city remained a place of his imag-ination, the Paris of Asia, a teeming commercial port where sto-ries of violence and excess, of vengeance and sin, of fortunes won and fortunes lost, formed a lavish narrative in his mind. Shanghai was Big-Eared Du, the fearsome godfather of the Green Gang who had ruled the city in tandem with Chiang Kai-shek in the era before communist rule. Shanghai was the Bund, the most fa-mous thoroughfare in all Asia, a gorgeous, quarter-mile curve of colonial architecture on the western bank of the Huangpu River. Shanghai was the Cathay, the great art deco hotel on the Bund built by Sir Victor Sassoon where, legend has it, opium could be ordered on room service and Noël Coward wrote *Private Lives* after succumbing to a bout of flu. The city's history was as vivid and engrossing as it was surely unique. Where else, in the age of imperialism, had British, French, American and Japanese citizens lived side by side with a native population in foreign concessions governed by their own laws and policed by their own armed forces? Before Mao, Shanghai was less a Chinese city than an in-ternational sorting office for the world's ravaged minorities. It was to Shanghai that Europe's Jews had fled the pogroms. It was in Shanghai that 20,000 White Russian émigrés had found refuge from the revolution of 1917. As Joe flew in over the East China Sea on a damp January afternoon in 2005, he felt as though he was travelling into a dream of history.

Did he know what he was letting himself in for? The purpose of Joe's operation in Shanghai was to get as close to Miles Coo-lidge as possible. But getting close to Miles meant getting close to Isabella.

"If you come to China, it's only going to be a matter of time before you see her," I had said to him. "If you move to Shanghai, you will bump into Isabella and rake up everything from the past."

He had that one covered. "That's the whole point," he said. "Don't you get it? That's the whole idea."

Joe's history with Miles was the key to the operation. It would only be a matter of time before word reached the American that his old sparring partner had settled in town. As soon as that happened, Miles wouldn't be able to resist the challenge of renewing their acquaintance.

"Look at it this way," Waterfield had told his colleagues in one of several pre-departure brainstorms at Vauxhall Cross. "If Miles thinks Joe's come to Shanghai to try to win back Isabella, he'll see that as a challenge. If he thinks he's working undercover at Quayler, he'll want a piece of that action."

"Exactly," Joe added, warming to the theme. "And if he really believes that I've suffered a crisis of conscience over Iraq, he'll enjoy trying to shred my arguments. If there's one thing Miles Coolidge hates, it's smug Limeys."

They were right, of course. Their reading of Miles's psychology was spot-on. No other British spy had the potential to get as close to Coolidge as quickly and as effectively as Joe. Nevertheless, it concerned me that Joe seemed to be in denial both about the implications of what he was doing and the nature of his own feelings. However hard he tried to make it look as though he was going to Shanghai purely out of loyalty to the firm, it was obvious that a far deeper, more personal impulse was in play.

31 | TOURISM

The key to his approach was the deliberate absence of subter-
fuge. From the moment he passed through customs at Pudong
International Airport, travelling on his own passport and a thirty-
day tourist visa, Joe Lennox was just another Western businessman dipping his toes in the waters of China's most vibrant city.
His cover was to assume the behaviour of a wide-eyed European,
a role which required little or no effort on Joe's part because he
was only too keen to visit every nook and cranny of the city. In the
airport terminal, for example, he did what most inquisitive Brits
would have done and bought a ticket for the Maglev, the German-
engineered electromagnetic train which hums between the airport and downtown Pudong at over 300mph. As the flat, humid
marshlands ripped past, Joe's first glimpse of Shanghai was a forest
of distant skyscrapers obscured by smog. He had left London less
than fifteen hours earlier, yet already he felt the thrilling anonymity of being at large in Asia.

Under different circumstances, an undercover SIS officer might
have booked himself into one of the smaller hotels in Shanghai, in
order to keep a low profile. But Joe had reasoned that a businessman in his thirties on an expense account, recently released from

a decade in the Civil Service, might want to splash out on some high living. To that end he had arranged for Quayler to book him into the Portman Ritz-Carlton on Nanjing Lu, a five-star high rise with a spa roughly the size of Kowloon, where Joe's room set the bean-counters at Vauxhall Cross back more than $300 a night. The other luxury hotel which had caught his eye was the Grand Hyatt, situated on the top thirty-four floors of the Jin Mao Tower in Pudong, but Joe had been reliably informed that it was a mistake to be based on the eastern side of the Huangpu: all of the action in Shanghai took place to the west of the river, in the area known as Puxi. There was also an added operational advantage to being registered at one of the city's top hotels. Every night a list of foreign residents was obtained by the PLA. If Joe was "Beijing Red"—that is to say, if his identity as an MI6 officer had ever been uncovered by Chinese intelligence—his presence as a guest at the Ritz-Carlton would be flagged up. Thereafter he would be subjected to round-the-clock surveillance which would not let up for the duration of his stay in China. In the event of that happening, Joe would be obliged to leave the country and to abandon the operation against Miles.

Joe's first few days in Shanghai were a magical release from what he described as "the straitjacket of London." Armed only with a small rucksack containing his wallet, a camera and the *Rough Guide to China*, he set out to familiarize himself with the geography of the city and to visit the dozen or so places he had longed to see following a lifetime of movies and reading. Having checked in and showered, he headed first for the Bund, not least because it felt like the spiritual centre of Shanghai, a place where the Chinese and European experiences collided with the force of history. Strolling along the broad walkway that looks out over the skyscrapers of downtown Pudong, he watched young Chinese couples with frozen smiles pose for photographs against a background of stilled ships and neon. Dominating the eastern shore was the bizarre, bulbous rocket of the Oriental Pearl TV Tower while, behind it, the Jin Mao soared into the late-afternoon sky like a jagged, glinting dagger. These astonishing buildings were the visible symbols of the Chinese economic miracle and it seemed apt that they should look out across the Huangpu at the great neoclassical edifices on the Bund, which themselves bore architectural witness to an earlier era of rampant prosperity and growth.

The next day, having woken at five with jet lag, Joe took a morning boat trip to the mouth of the Yangtze, realizing, to his gradual disappointment, that the Huangpu was not the river of his romantic imagination—a Seine or a Danube of the East—but instead a churning sea lane as grey and as polluted as the bloated corpse of Kenneth Lenan. That afternoon, to maintain basic cover, he held the first of several meetings with a consultant who advised overseas companies on the logistics of setting up a business in China. The meeting, which had been arranged from Quayler headquarters in London, lasted two hours and took place in the lobby of the Ritz-Carlton, for maximum public exposure. Joe continued to make work-related telephone calls from his room, and was regularly seen using the email and fax facilities in the hotel's business lounge. Back in tourist mode, he lunched on dumplings at Nanxiang Mantou Dian, took the obligatory tea at Yu Yuan Gardens and made an excursion to the nineteenth-century basilica built by Catholic missionaries out at She Shan. For anyone who happened to be watching, Joe Lennox was just as he appeared to be: a single man of independent means, gradually finding his feet in Shanghai.

In these early stages my new SIS handler had calculated that I would be a useful support agent for Joe from my base in Beijing. My first task was to put him in touch with one of the most popular and well-connected expats in Shanghai, an old friend of mine named Tom Harper. I had no idea that the two of them would go on to hit it off as resoundingly as they did, although Joe's natural affinity for flawed mavericks should have tipped me off.

Educated in England, Tom had inherited a small fortune at the age of twenty when his parents had died within six months of each other. He had spent the next fifteen years bouncing around the globe, earning an undergraduate degree at Berkeley, an MBA from INSEAD, marrying—briefly—a French television actress and bewildering a long line of expensive psychoanalysts. He was a man of almost limitless good humour and generosity, about whom one rarely heard an unkind word spoken. He also knew everything there was to know about having a good time in Shanghai. In three years living in the city, Tom had been a male model, a nightclub impresario, a yacht broker and a restaurateur. He was at every dinner party, every movie première and every bar and club launch worth mentioning. He didn't seem to sleep more than four or five hours a night and survived on a diet of caffeine, alcohol and illegal recreational drugs. He did not know Miles Coolidge personally, but that hardly mattered; the way things worked in Shanghai, there would be a maximum of two or three degrees of separation between them. On that basis, it would only be a matter of time before Tom led Joe to his quarry.

Sunday brunch at the Westin seemed an ideal place for the two of them to meet. The Westin is the Indonesian-owned hotel on the junction of Henan Road and Guangdong Road that spoils a certain view of the Bund: look behind the old HSBC building and it's the fat high-rise, two blocks back, with an illuminated metal crown sprouting from its roof. On Sunday mornings the hotel lays on an opulent buffet attended by wealthy Western families and twenty-something rich kids keen to impress their latest girlfriends. For around 400 renminbi—the equivalent of £25 in 2005, or a week's wage to the average Shanghai Chinese—guests can help themselves to limitless quantities of sushi, Parma and Serrano ham, Russian caviar, roast rib of beef, freshly made tortellini and as much Veuve Clicquot champagne as they can swallow. The Westin brunch has become an institution in the city, not least as a place where people can catch up on the latest gossip, a commodity—both social and commercial—on which the overseas community thrives.

I had given Joe Tom's number and they had arranged to meet in the lobby at midday on Sunday 30 January. Rather than describe the brunch in detail, I'll quote from a couple of letters that Tom sent to me, both of which help to paint a picture of Joe's first few weeks in Shanghai.

Will—

One of the things I like about China, and about Shanghai in particular, is that it's completely meritocratic. That may

sound like a strange thing to say about a city where obscene wealth and obscene poverty exist side by side, but it
always seemed to me, at least from a foreigner's point of
view, that you get nowhere in China on the basis of reputation alone. Ex-Yale, ex-Sorbonne, a double-starred First
from Cambridge—none of that really matters here. This
place is immune to class or background. If you can't do
what you promised to do, you'll get found out. It's not like,
say, Hong Kong or Singapore, where a lot of really average
people have been making a lot of really easy money for decades. If you come to China expecting the locals to roll
over and say how grateful they are, you're in for a big
shock. Only the best people succeed here. It's completely
ruthless.

So whenever I meet the latest Jardine Johnnie fresh off
the plane who wants to "try his luck in Shanghai," I'm
always a bit suspicious. Do they think China owes them a
living? Have they got the slightest idea what they're getting themselves into?

All of this is a roundabout way of thanking you for
putting me in touch with Joe, who I've been seeing a lot
of over the past few weeks. For a start, he didn't arrive with
any illusions about China, which always helps. He also
seems to know a hell of a lot more about China and the
Chinese than most people who've been living here for five
or ten years. Where did you say you knew him from?

We met at the Westin, as you'd recommended. There
was the usual scene there: guilty investment bankers finding a three-hour slot between meetings and hookers to
spend "family time" with their wife and kids; underage
Chinese gymnasts turning themselves inside out in the
lobby while a live band played the best of Carly Simon; a
guy dressed up in a Spiderman outfit, attached to the roof
by a harness, cleaning the glass windows 100ft over our
heads. I'd been out clubbing all night and hadn't been to
bed. At about 10 in the morning I was sitting in Dragon
with two girls from Barcelona, one of whom was coming

down off a bad pill, when I looked at my watch and saw the time. Gave serious thought to cancelling the whole thing but because Joe was a friend of yours—and because I'm an extremely decent, upstanding person—I grabbed my jacket, had a shower and took a cab down to the Westin. Was at least twenty minutes late, knackered, etc, but Joe couldn't have been nicer about it. He was in the lobby making conversation (in fluent, very old-school Mandarin) with an octogenarian cleaning woman who had bags under her eyes like Huan Huan the Panda. She looked as though nobody had bothered to speak to her since the Cultural Revolution and was busy telling Joe stories about all the old buildings in her neighbourhood which had been knocked down by developers. He took one look at me and must have realized what a mess I was in because he did most of the talking for the first twenty minutes. He also paid the bill for both of us as we went in and before long we were three-quarters of the way through a bottle of champagne, I'd forgotten all about my hangover, and it was as if we'd known one another for years.

This is the second of them. Tom Harper is one of the world's last great letter writers, but the first half of the following email was mostly a 1,500-word account of a trip to Thailand. The section which was relevant to Joe began about halfway through:

What's funny about Shanghai is how quickly word gets round that there's an interesting new face in town. The other day I took Joe down to Babyface (that's a nightclub, Will, just in case you're too old) and introduced him to a few people I knew there, told them he used to work in the Foreign Office, etc. For some reason, this piece of information spread around town like the clap. I'm not exaggerating when I say that at least a dozen random people subsequently asked me about Joe in the space of a few weeks. "How did you meet him?" "Is he single?" "Did he really leave the Foreign Office as a protest against the war?" One (predictable) rumour going round is that he used to be a spy, but I'm not sure about that. I can't picture him doing the dirty. Also, he spends most of his time sleeping off hangovers at the Ritz-Carlton. Aren't Foreign Office types supposed to behave themselves?

On the phone the other day you were asking about Quayler, which seems to be up and running. When he first arrived I put Joe in touch with a letting agency contact of mine from restaurant days who had an office free in a building looking out over Xintiandi. Joe's found himself two Chinese staff and I think they moved in there last week. I also introduced him to an Australian girl who has an apartment to rent in the French Concession. If things work out, he should be in there by the end of March, and might be able to sublet for a year or even 18 months because the girl is going home to look after her mother who has cancer or something. So don't say I don't look after my friends, OK? My performance has been nothing short of heroic.

One small complaint: he has a habit of droning on about his job, but I suppose he's new here and that's what we all did when we first arrived, so I can't really blame him. And he certainly seems to know what he's talking about. You'd warned me that he could be a bit intellectual and withdrawn, but he hasn't seemed that way to me. The guy can drink like Sue Ellen. I don't know what his story is as far as women are concerned, but I've found him very open and funny and easy to hang out with. There's obviously a big brain whirring away back there and I'd like to know more about his story. He says he's lived in Hong Kong, Singapore, Malaysia, but always seems to change the subject whenever you try to delve too deeply into his past. (Christ, maybe he WAS a spy . . .)

Anyway, give me a call and fill me in. Better still, tell your newspaper you have to come down to do a story. We all want to know the truth about Joe Lennox . . .

Love Tom

Tom probably won't thank me for reproducing his private correspondence, but I'm fascinated by these letters for what they reveal about Joe's tradecraft. "Droning on" about Quayler, for example, would have been a deliberate tactic that he employed to prevent people digging around in his cover. The purpose behind it was simple: to bore anyone who happened to be listening to the edge of coma. Believe me, once you'd heard Joe's ten-minute monologue about the future of niche pharmaceuticals—*China has twenty per cent of the world's population but only one point five per cent of the global pharmaceuticals market . . . The sector is growing by sixteen per cent a year, largely because drug use is rising among the Chinese middle classes . . .* – you never wanted to ask him about his work ever again.

There are other details from the Westin letter that interest me: offering to pick up the bill; taking the time to talk to the elderly cleaning lady in the lobby; demonstrating a fluency in Mandarin. All of these things would have been premeditated tactics designed to impress upon Tom the idea that Joe Lennox was a generous, intelligent man, experienced in Chinese affairs, but without airs and graces, who would be worth cultivating as a friend. It's also interesting that Joe was "three-quarters of the way through a bottle of champagne" not long after sitting down for brunch. Joe rarely drank alcohol during the day, but he must have intuited that Tom was the sort of person for whom booze was a semi-religion, and acted accordingly. Sipping mineral water wouldn't have conveyed the right image. You can also guarantee that when Joe was supposedly "sleeping off a hangover at the Ritz-Carlton" he was in reality investigating the police and media reports into Kenneth Lenan's murder and further waterproofing his cover. His decision to reveal that he had quit the Foreign Office on moral grounds would also have been intentional. If anything was designed to set off a firestorm of rumour and half-truth, it was that. I had told Joe that Tom Harper was one of the epicentres of Shanghai gossip, but I had no idea that he was going to give him so much to work with.

Then, of course, there is that mysterious line in the second letter: "I don't know what his story is as far as women are concerned." For some reason, Joe wasn't telling anybody about his relationship with Isabella. This may have been tactical—he didn't

mention Miles by name to any of Tom's friends, either—but neither was he responding to the myriad sexual opportunities which
are part and parcel of life in Shanghai. The slight possibility of
reconciliation with Isabella was one of the principal catalysts which
drove Joe's work in China. He told me later that summer that he
had dreaded what he described as "the Zhivago moment," when,
passing in a bus or taxi, he might catch sight of Isabella on a busy
Shanghai street or, worse, find himself standing in front of her at
a party and seeing only vague recollection in her eyes. Despite all
this, the hold she exerted over him continued to be unhealthy. I
told him as much, of course, but he wouldn't listen. When it came
to Isabella Aubert, Joe was closed and distant, seemingly hell-bent
on a collision between the two of them which I was convinced
would end in tragedy.

All that remained of TYPHOON was four Uighur men living 2,000 miles apart, on opposite sides of China. A terrorist cell. A time bomb.

Ansary Tursun and Abdul Bary lived and worked in Shanghai, but were never seen together in public. Abdul was married with a son and worked fourteen-hour days packaging parts for children's toys at a factory in Putuo district.

Ansary had no girlfriend, nor any blood family to speak of. He had a part-time job as a waiter at a Uighur restaurant on Yishan Lu. Both men, under the guidance and tutelage of Professor Wang Kaixuan, had been responsible for carrying out low-level terrorist attacks against Han targets between October 1997 and late 2001. On Wang's advice, they had curtailed their activities as TYPHOON disintegrated in 2002. Miles Coolidge had recruited them back two years later.

The third member of the cell was a twenty-nine-year-old Kazakh named Memet Almas who had bombed four Beijing taxis in successive weeks in 2000 using explosives shipped into China by the Macklinson Corporation. In January 2001, to the CIA's dismay, Almas was arrested on unrelated charges of petty theft and sent to Beijing Second Prison for two years. In the circumstances, it was the best thing that could have happened to him. While he languished in jail, nine Uighur radicals, with whom he would almost certainly have been linked, were arrested and executed by the Chinese authorities. Upon his release in 2004, Memet met Miles Coolidge during a football match at the Workers' Stadium in Beijing and was instructed to move to Xinjiang and await further instructions. The cell, Miles told him, would perform only one or two large-scale terrorist attacks in China over the course of the next five years. Those attacks, he said, would draw unprecedented attention to the Uighur cause. Memet bided his time working on a clothing stall at a market in Kashgar. He was regarded as a quiet, hard-working man with little interest in religion or politics. His wife, Niyasam, was a schoolteacher who knew nothing about his revolutionary past. They did not have children. Ansary, Abdul and Memet were all practising Muslims, but Miles had forbidden them to attend mosque for fear of drawing the attention of the authorities. They were also ordered to shave off their beards.

The leader of the cell, and its oldest member, was Ablimit Celil. As a teenager in the 1980s, Ablimit had been arrested and imprisoned for stealing a Kalashnikov rifle from police headquarters in his home town of Hotan. In prison, he came under the influence of a Uighur imam who developed both his Islamic faith and his hatred of the ruling Han. Later Ablimit joined an underground group which bombed train lines, office blocks and other "soft" targets in Xinjiang. He took part in the Baren riot of April 1990 and fled into the Kunlun mountains alongside hundreds of other activists as Chinese troops poured in. Many of these activists, as well as villagers sympathetic to the separatist cause, were subsequently rounded up and imprisoned. However, Ablimit evaded capture and, two years later, planted a bomb on an Urumqi bus packed with Han revellers celebrating the Chinese New Year. Six people were killed when the device exploded. In 1997 he had been responsible for the deaths of eight soldiers and four catering staff at an army barracks in Turpan when a bomb he had planted in a store cupboard blew up during the evening meal.

Shortly before 9/11, Ablimit Celil made the first of two journeys to an al-Qaeda training camp in the Pamir mountains of Tajikistan. A more devout Muslim than the other members of the cell, he managed to obtain permission to undertake the Haj, and it was at Mecca that he was recruited as an agent of the CIA by Josh Pinnegar, who was posing as an American newspaper reporter.

The cell was unusual in that its four members were deliberately kept apart. Ablimit, a widower, lived in Urumqi where he worked as a doorman at a five-star hotel catering to foreigners and rich Chinese businessmen. Whenever he visited the city, Miles always stayed at the hotel and was able to communicate with Ablimit simply by passing him messages in the form of tips. Typically, these would be written on Chinese and American banknotes using inks visible only under ultra-violet light. Shortly after the Madrid bombings of March 2004, Ablimit informed Miles that he was keen to move with Memet to Shanghai and to team up with Abdul Bary and Ansary Tursun. The atmosphere between Hans and Uighurs in Urumqi, he said, had deteriorated dramatically. September 11th had handed the Chinese authorities carte blanche to clamp down on the minority Muslim population and to treat them with a previously unimaginable contempt. Informers now operated at every level of society. Black-clad anti-terrorist police roamed the streets. Where once Han and Uighur had lived contentedly side by side, the two ethnic groups were now divided by fear and mutual suspicion. Passports belonging to thousands of Muslim citizens had been confiscated by the authorities. All travel now had to be approved by a Chinese government paranoid that its oppressed minorities would join militant groups in Chechnya and Pakistan and return to the Motherland, planning to wreak havoc. Only a Madrid-style incident in either Shanghai or Beijing would be sufficient, Celil said, to accelerate the cause of an independent Eastern Turkestan.

Ablimit's theory chimed with Miles, who had concluded that small-scale mainland attacks, most of which went unreported in the West, were of no strategic value to the United States. He had learned this lesson from TYPHOON's earlier incarnation. The ultimate goal of the group of individuals in Washington with tactical control of Miles's operation was an American-sponsored catastrophe at the Beijing Olympics. Yet that event was so far off that Miles had not disclosed the objective to any member of the cell. Instead, he told Ablimit that he would begin to consider targets in Shanghai for a possible operation in the summer of 2005. Memet told his wife that he was going to Shanghai to look for work in the construction industry. Ablimit found himself a job in the kitchens of a hotel belonging to the same chain for which he had worked in Urumqi.

There was one complication. The cell had briefly had a fifth member. Enver Semed had fought alongside the Taliban at Tora-Bora and had been captured by American soldiers in December 2001. He was taken to Guantanamo Bay where he was held alongside twenty-two other Uighur fighters with alleged links to al-Qaeda. In early 2004 Semed had his detention analysed by the Combatant Status Review Tribunal, which determined that he was no longer an "enemy" of the United States. There was a simple reason for this: the CIA had recruited Semed as a double agent. Repatriated to China on false documentation, he reported to Josh Pinnegar, who passed control for Semed to Kenneth Lenan. Lenan, under pressure from the MSS because of his links to Macklinson, gave him up almost immediately. Two months later Semed was arrested on charges of belonging to ETIM and executed at a gulag in Qinghai. It was the news of Semed's demise that Lenan was bringing to Coolidge on his final visit to Shanghai.

33 | STARBUCKS

After almost seven weeks in China, Joe was ready to accelerate the operation. Every one of his counter-surveillance exercises—carried out with metronomic regularity, whether he was working at the office, travelling by cab to a restaurant, walking around the French Concession or using the gym at the Ritz-Carlton—convinced him that he was being neither bugged nor followed. In an encrypted email to Vauxhall Cross, sent from a randomly selected internet café on Shanxi Road, he told Waterfield that, in his opinion, RUN was clean. Neither the Americans, nor Chinese liaison, had the first clue what Joe Lennox was up to.

London responded a day later with the text message that Joe had been waiting for: "Tony wants to meet for drinks at six on Monday. Bring your book about Spain." This was simple, prearranged code. "Tony" was the operational name for Zhao Jian, a Han Chinese SIS asset who lived and worked in Shanghai. Jian and his two younger brothers were secretly on the British embassy payroll and had been following Miles since Christmas, documenting his movements in preparation for Joe's arrival. "Meet for drinks" meant that Joe should make contact with Jian at the branch of Starbucks on the north side of Renmin Park. "Six on Monday" meant simply five o'clock on the following Sunday afternoon. The "book about Spain" was a hardback copy of Arturo Pérez-Reverte's novel *The Queen of the South*, which Joe was to make visible at an out-door table as a signal that the meeting could proceed. Joe had committed half a dozen similarly innocuous phrases to memory. "Ring your sister," for example, meant that we were to contact one another immediately, using clean mobile phones. "Dad has found your stolen car" was an emergency instruction to abort the operation and to return to London on a pseudonymous passport.

On the late Sunday afternoon of his first meeting with Zhao Jian, Joe made his way down to the lobby of the Ritz-Carlton, shared a joke with the doorman—after almost two months at the hotel, he was on friendly terms with most of the staff—and stepped into a cab. The driver was overweight and overtired and did not bother to acknowledge Joe until he was instructed, in impeccable Mandarin, to head for the Park Hotel, whereupon he asked where Joe was from and embarked on an animated discussion of the circumstances surrounding the death of Diana, Princess of Wales. Joe, sitting in the back of the cab, pressed himself against the perspex separator in which the driver was encased and reassured him that, to the best of his knowledge, the People's Princess had not been murdered by MI6.

The air conditioning in the cab was broken and Joe wound down the window, breathing hot, polluted air that tasted of sulphur. He was wearing a white linen shirt, cotton trousers and a pair of worn Campers, because it was a humid day and he knew that Jian would want to walk some distance prior to their meeting to ensure that neither of them had picked up a tail.

Approaching the park, the driver indicated to pull over and Joe turned in the baking back seat to check for unusual movements in the vehicles behind them. Having paid the fare, he handed his Quayler card to the driver—"Look out for our products!"—and went into the lobby of the hotel to draw any possible surveillance off the street. A minute later he left by an obscure side exit which he had discovered three days earlier. Joe continued to observe the exit from a phone booth on Fenyang Road for about ninety seconds. When only a kitchen porter emerged to empty a bin during that period, Joe was satisfied that he was not being followed.

The branch of Starbucks which is situated across Nanjing Road from the park is one of dozens of franchised outlets which have opened up across China in recent years, selling lattes and muffins and cinnamon teas indistinguishable from those available in Sydney and Paris and Washington. Joe later wrote in his report that he entered the café using the Nanjing Road entrance at approximately 4:40 p.m. With a mug of cappuccino, he headed for the back and found an outdoor table looking south over Renmin Park. Joe's fellow customers were mainly Western tourists and a few wealthier Chinese, and he smoked a cigarette while the smog-screened sun warmed his face. A previous occupant of the table had left a copy of *That's Shanghai*, the weekly English-language listings magazine, on the chair beside him. Joe opened it, flicked his way backwards through the contents and read a review of a new lounge bar which had opened up in Pudong. Shortly before five o'clock he removed *The Queen of the South* from his rucksack and placed it on the table. He was neither nervous nor particularly apprehensive. He had done his preparation and this sort of work was second nature to him.

At approximately 5:05 p.m. Joe became aware of a man standing close to the table, about two metres away, talking in Mandarin into a mobile phone. He was a middle-aged Han wearing cheap leather slip-on shoes, high-waisted black trousers and a white short-sleeved shirt. His demeanour roughly fitted the cheerful, portly description of Jian which Waterfield had provided in London. To be certain, Joe glanced at the man's right hand and saw a thick scar running from the top of his wrist to the knuckle of his middle finger. ("Fishing accident," Waterfield had explained.) In the same hand, Jian was carrying a slim, black attaché case. Joe finished his coffee, placed the book in the rucksack and pushed his chair back from the table. As a formal signal, he bent down to tighten the laces on his shoes, and by the time he had stood up, Jian was already twenty metres away, heading into the park.

Joe's task was simple: to follow his contact and to ensure that he was not being tailed. In due course, it had been arranged that Jian would stop at a clearing beside a small lotus-covered pond where local men and women played cards and *majiang*. At this point their roles would be reversed: Joe would continue ahead while Jian followed at a discreet distance, ensuring that he too was clean. The chances of either man having been compromised were minimal, but it was partly because they had exercised caution of this kind in the past that they had survived so long undetected in their respective careers.

Jian was walking in a westerly direction towards the new Grand Theatre and, very quickly, the noise of Shanghai became no more than a distant hum. To scout the location, Joe had visited Renmin Park on four previous occasions and he always enjoyed this sudden, miraculous tranquillity. It was as if the narrow paths and the branches of the trees around him somehow closed up to absorb the city's perpetual din. Even the usually choking, polluted air seemed, for once, blessedly clean. After about three minutes Jian stopped and made a call on his mobile phone from the centre of the path in a standing position. This allowed Joe to observe the men and women around him for any matching behaviour. If they also stopped suddenly, or attempted to conceal themselves, Joe would abandon the meeting by walking directly out of the park. Jian would then be obliged to make emergency contact with his embassy handler and the operation against TYPHOON would almost certainly be shelved. Yet there was nothing unusual to report. During the conversation, a pair of young lovers, walking shyly, hand-in-hand, moved off the path and laid out a rug on the grass. An elderly Chinese lady, catching sight of a friend sitting on a nearby bench, waved and walked across to join her. Having closed his phone, Jian continued on his way. After about four minutes he came to a halt beside the lotus-covered pond and joined a small group of standing spectators who had gathered to watch a game of *chudadi*. Joe saw a movement in the trees beyond them, but it was just an elderly man practising tai-chi in the shade of a gingko. Joe moved past their group and was obliged to walk around an old wooden cart into which a gardener was throwing litter and weeds. The atmosphere was peaceful and he could hear only the murmur of talk, the slap of playing cards on the hard concrete tables, the plastic click of tiles. He then continued in a counter-clockwise direction towards the Shanghai Museum, sipping from a bottle of Evian and listening to the sound of singing birds. Joe knew that Jian was following him, that his experienced Chinese eyes had not detected a problem, because twice he used the reflective metal surface of the park bins to locate Jian's position behind him. He had the easy, loose-hipped walk characteristic of Chinese men of a certain build and moved at a steady pace. When Joe had reached the south-eastern corner of the park, he waited at the circle of secluded benches where the meeting was scheduled to take place.

Joe saw that two of the four benches were occupied, but he was not concerned by this. The principal advantage of the location was the presence of a number of public address speakers in the vicinity which piped classical music into the surrounding area. Conversation was therefore almost completely smothered, negating any concerns about audio surveillance. Looking up from the path, Jian made eye contact with Joe for the first time and moved towards the furthest of the four benches, a broad smile on his cheerful face.

"Mr. Joe," he called out. "Very good to see you again."

The benches were situated in a small clearing, about half the size of a tennis court, and surrounded on three sides by a thick screen of acacia trees and peony bushes. Joe and Jian could be observed from the main path that runs along the southern perimeter of Renmin Park, but the sight of a middle-class Han conversing with a Westerner in this part of town was not at all incongruous. Their body language suggested that they knew one another reasonably well and had probably chosen to conduct an informal business meeting out of doors, taking advantage of the warm weekend weather. Jian shook Joe's hand, pointed out a couple of half-finished skyscrapers and mentioned that Renmin Park had once been a racecourse. He then extracted a slim laptop computer from his attaché case and settled down to business.

"What have you got for me today?" Joe asked.

A Chinese student, seated at the closest of the three benches, was listening to rock music at high volume on an mp3 player. A tinny, synthetic din of drums and guitars emerged from the moulded white earpieces. The second occupied bench was more than ten feet away and situated directly beneath one of the speakers. Samuel Barber's "Adagio for Strings" had just replaced the aria from the Goldberg Variations and Joe tried to remember the name of the film in which the music had featured.

"Your American friend goes out of town a lot," Jian began. It had been decided that they would speak in English. "We have followed his car to the airport seven times."

"Destinations?" Joe asked. It felt liberating finally to be discussing Miles Coolidge's movements in the city where the American had made his home. After weeks of careful planning, the operation was finally under way.

"I have found it best in my years of long association with your company to be honest about my shortcomings," Jian said. He was smiling, but his round eyes were plain and serious. "So I must say that we are only absolutely certain of his destination on two occasions. Our resources are small, you see."

Joe appreciated his honesty and knew that he would enjoy working with Jian. It was the ones who had all the answers that you had to be wary of. "Of course," he said.

"On both those occasions your friend flew to Urumqi."

Joe concealed his surprised reaction by offering Jian a cigarette. The older man declined and Joe replaced the packet in the pocket of his trousers, having lit one of his own.

"And the other five? Were they all domestic flights out of Hongqiao?"

"No." Jian shook his head. He was about fifty-five, with smooth, pouchy cheeks which reminded Joe of a squirrel storing up nuts for winter. "Twice he was collected by car from his apartment very early in the morning and driven to the airport at Pudong. If I was to speculate on the nature of these journeys, I would say that he was travelling to the United States."

"Why would you think that?"

"Because both times he did not return for over a week, because there were flights to Washington that fitted with his schedule on those mornings, and because he did not take his wife."

Isabella. The thought of her name was melodramatized by the soaring violins of Barber's "Adagio." Joe wanted to ask Jian how she was, what he thought of her, whether she seemed happy or sad. He found himself reflecting, not for the first time during his short stay in Shanghai, that he was breathing the same air as the woman he loved. This was the quiet madness in which his heart resided.

"But the other three were internal flights within China?"

"Yes. And one of these could have been to Urumqi, because the timings were also similar. But this is just speculation on my part. The others we are almost certain were to separate destinations."

"As part of his job?"

Jian nodded. Miles's cover involved posing as an employee of Microsoft, investigating incidents of copyright theft in China. It was a clever ruse, not least because it allowed a senior CIA man the freedom to move around the country without arousing suspicion.

"What else can you tell me about his movements?"

Jian exhaled through puffed-out cheeks and tilted his head to one side. His eyebrows hooked in a comic expression of exhausted bewilderment and it was obvious to Joe that Miles hadn't changed. No other man could produce a reaction like that in an asset of Jian's experience.

"He is quite a character, the American." Jian booted up the laptop, clicked through various folders and passed it across to Joe. It was a small Lenovo, light and state-of-the-art. There was a photograph on the screen, about the size of a holiday snap, and Joe adjusted the tilt of the lid so that he was able to see the image more clearly.

"If we are disturbed," Jian told him quietly, looking out at the grass in front of them, "if anybody should approach us and request to see the information on this computer, you only have to hold down the key marked F8, which has been programmed to delete all relevant files." A more theatrical personality might have paused here for dramatic effect, but Jian moved swiftly on. "The first picture shows you an individual who will probably interest you a great deal." The photograph was a close-up shot of a beautiful Chinese woman, taken on a busy street in bright sunlight. "We think your friend is conducting a sexual relationship with this woman. Her English name is Linda, with the Chinese name Ling Shu. He is not in Shanghai at the present time and we believe they are together in Hainan. I have written a more detailed account of their meetings in the main research file contained on the desktop." Joe felt a strange, conflicting surge of relief and anger: relief because Miles was undermining his marriage through infidelity; anger because he was hurting Isabella by doing so. Jian reached across and pushed the right arrow key on the laptop. The photograph of Linda was replaced with another picture, this time of a different woman. "This second image also shows a girl, as you can see, who is Chinese and of approximately the same age as the first."

Jian withdrew his hand and leaned back on the bench. Was there a slight undercurrent of moral disgust here? Joe knew nothing of Jian's private life, but the brisk manner in which he had described the second woman led him to suspect that he was himself the father of a girl.

"Miles is seeing both these women at once?"

Jian produced a curious glottal noise in the base of his throat which might have been the laughter of male camaraderie, but might equally have been the sound of an older man's disapproval. "Yes. Again, we believe so." A bird settled on the grass in front of them before quickly flying away. "This one lives in an apartment not far from here and has a number of different boyfriends."

"You mean she's a prostitute?"

Jian shrugged. Western men preyed on Chinese girls; Chinese girls preyed on Western men. Sometimes money changed hands; sometimes it didn't. It was the way of things. The music emerging from the speakers had changed to the waltz from *Sleeping Beauty*. The sun had disappeared behind a bank of yellowed clouds but the temperature in the clearing was still warm. Joe remembered that the "Adagio" had featured in the film *Platoon* and found that the tune had stuck in his mind.

"There are many more photographs," Jian told him. Joe was surprised when the next picture showed Miles himself standing at what appeared to be the bar of a smart hotel. It had been so long since Joe had seen a contemporary shot of his face that he found himself squinting at the image in near-disbelief. Miles's weight had ballooned to fourteen or fifteen stone and, perhaps to compensate for the commensurate swelling in his face, he had grown a wild black beard which somehow amplified his natural charisma. Miles was surrounded at the bar by three Caucasians—a man and two women—all of whom were younger than he was and laughing uproariously at something he had said. It was both reassuring and debilitating to see this. Joe stubbed out his cigarette.

"Click through these," Jian said, pointing at the keyboard. As Joe moved through a slide show, Jian produced a detailed running commentary. *These are your friend's colleagues from work. This is an American lawyer who he meets at least twice a week. This is his gym. This is his car. This is where he goes to the movies.* Like the bullet in Russian roulette, Joe was waiting for his first glimpse of Isabella, but it was the bullet that never comes.

After perhaps thirty or forty photographs, he said, "What about his wife?"

"What about her, please?"

"Well, where is she?"

It was the only moment of awkwardness between them. Jian reacted as though SIS were questioning the quality of his work. Joe felt obliged to reassure him.

"Don't misunderstand me," he said. "It's just that they don't seem to be spending much time together."

"They don't," Jian replied flatly. "She is hardly ever with him."

This, Joe supposed, was good news, but he could feel no elation. He had always known that Isabella's marriage to Miles would be a sham, that the American would betray her, that she would be unhappy. To see it played out as he had predicted was grim and dispiriting. "Hardly ever?" he asked. "They don't go out?"

"Hardly ever."

There were a great many photographs of Miles at night. In a sequence of backlit images taken inside what Jian described, somewhat mysteriously, as "a Mexican nightclub," Miles could be seen in heated conversation with a young man, no older than twenty-six or twenty-seven, who looked of Pakistani or north Indian origin. It was quite rare in Shanghai to see Asians from the subcontinent, and Joe began to speculate on a possible link with TYPHOON.

"Who's this guy?" he asked, pressing the screen so that his fingertip blurred the man's face.

"We don't know," Jian replied quickly. "These images were very difficult for us, because the light was so low. My brother could only use his telephone."

"He's not a diplomat? Is he resident here?" Joe was thinking about the Pamir mountains which separate Xinjiang from India and Pakistan. Waterfield's source in Beijing had told him that explosives which were later used by TYPHOON cells in terrorist incidents had been smuggled through the Khunjerab Pass in the summer of 1999.

"We know nothing. I am sorry. This photograph you are looking at was taken only one week ago, maybe ten days. But I have seen him with your friend several times and he is always in this place. We call him 'Sammy' because he reminds us of somebody in our family."

"Sammy?"

"Yes. He is part of your friend's group who go out at night to the bars and clubs. He is younger than most of them. That is all I can tell you."

By coincidence, the next photograph was a medium close-up of a mustachioed Uighur man, slightly out of focus and taken from waist height, possibly from below a table in a restaurant. He was wearing a traditional embroidered yellow shirt and a *doppa*.

"Who's this?" Joe asked immediately. "Is there any connection between them?"

"No, this man is just a waiter." Jian sensed Joe's quickening interest.

"If he's just a waiter, why did you take his photograph?"

"Your friend goes to Urumqi," Jian replied quietly. "He also eats at the Kala Kuer restaurant where he speaks to this man a great deal. I have seen them together. And I have been in this business long enough to know that when foreigners take an interest in Xinjiang, it is not always because of the food."

Joe smiled. There was a nice curl of irony at the perimeter of Jian's grin. Perhaps he knew why Joe had come to Shanghai, after all. A man with Jian's contacts—his *guanxi*—had probably caught a whiff of TYPHOON long ago.

"So do you know the waiter's name?" he asked.

"Of course." Jian seemed pleased finally to have a correct answer. The slide show was over and he reached across to retrieve his laptop. "The waiter's name is Ansary Tursun."

All the way back to the hotel, in the lift to his room, down to the spa and through twenty laps of the Ritz-Carlton's outdoor pool, Joe Lennox tried to remember where he had heard the name Ansary Tursun. Switching on CNN at eight o'clock, he watched a news report about a car bomb in Iraq and contemplated sending a message to Vauxhall Cross asking them to comb the files for mention of Tursun's name. But Joe was a stubborn man and it became a point of operational pride that he should remember where he had heard the name before London woke in the morning. If he could not come up with an answer, he would admit defeat and contact Waterfield. Yet he had retrieved *Platoon* from his memory, and the violins of Barber's "Adagio" still soared in his mind. What was the difference? It was just a question of locating the melody of Ansary Tursun.

The phone rang beside his bed. Joe muted the television and picked up.

"Joe? It's Tom. What are you doing for dinner?"

He had seen Tom Harper three times in the previous week. In other contexts, this might have been considered excessive, but it was quite normal in Shanghai, where groups of Western expats met up sometimes three or four nights a week. The alternative was bleak: to stay at home watching cheap, pirated DVDs of the latest Hollywood blockbusters with a takeaway from Sherpa's for company. Most of the interesting overseas radio stations were banned by the Chinese internet censor and state television consisted largely of game shows, military parades and historical soap operas. When Joe had lived in Hong Kong, Malaysia and Singapore, expats had also clung together in gangs, and life was lived to an excess which would have been unthinkable back home. It was one of the things he had found most frustrating about returning to London: his social life had somehow seemed stale and predictable by comparison.

"I hadn't got any plans," he replied.

Tom explained that half a dozen of his friends were going to Paradise Gardens, a Thai restaurant on Fumin Lu. Joe was pleased to be invited, and not simply because of the operational advantage to being seen out in Shanghai. He had also begun to feel the restrictions of life in the hotel. He had no desire for women, but neither did he want to spend every waking moment thinking about Miles and Isabella. Although it was in the nature of his profession to exist in what might be described as a perpetual artificial state, Joe was no different from most people in that he required the escape valve of an occasional night out.

They arranged to meet at the restaurant at nine. Joe took the lift down to the first-floor bar, where he sank a vodka and tonic and nodded at the band, a New Orleans jazz trio who had been playing at the hotel for the previous fortnight and knew Joe on sight. He bought the pianist a Coke ("I'm AA," he had disclosed during their one and only conversation), malt whiskies for the vocalist and drummer, and signed the bill to his room. There was a long queue for cabs downstairs, so he walked a block east along Nanjing Lu and hailed one off the street.

By the time Joe arrived at the restaurant, Tom's friends—three men, two women—were already sitting down. He knew all of them except for one, a striking woman in her mid-twenties who looked lively and possibly Malaysian. The others—Ricky, a Scouser who managed a factory on the outskirts of Shanghai making ladies' underwear; Mike, a physics teacher at the American School in Pudong; Jeff, a Canadian ex-lawyer who now hawked teeth-whitening products to the Chinese; and Sandrine, a senior French employee of Estée Lauder—were familiar faces. They were all of a similar age and had lived in Shanghai for several years.

"Watch out, here comes the spy," Ricky called out as Joe walked in. "You're looking very handsome tonight, mate."

"That's because I'm wearing one of your bras, Ricky," Joe replied, and everybody laughed. He apologized for being late and sat at the vacant seat between Tom and the Malaysian girl, who introduced herself as Megan. Her voice was confident and international and Joe suspected that she had been educated, at some point, in America. He scoped her ring finger and saw that she was not married.

"So how's the Ritz-Carlton?" Jeff asked. Jeff always asked about the Ritz-Carlton.

"Expensive. I had my company accounts director on the phone this morning asking why I'd sent her a bill for fifteen thousand dollars."

"Fifteen thousand dollars? Why so much?"

"Because spies watch lots of porn," said Ricky.

Joe was shown a menu from which he ordered a beer and a green chicken curry. It didn't bother him that Ricky made jokes of this sort: on the one hand, they added to the Lennox legend, which was helpful in terms of rumours filtering down to Miles; on the other, Ricky's sheer effrontery suggested that he did not take the idea that Joe might once have been a spy particularly seriously. Had he done so, he would almost certainly have kept his mouth shut. Popping a napkin and placing it in his lap, Joe felt the momentary apprehension that comes from being seated next to an attractive woman and was glad when Tom engaged him directly in conversation. They spoke about a building which was being torn down in Tom's neighbourhood to make way for a shopping mall, but Ansary Tursun was still on Joe's mind and he set about trying to trigger his memory.

"Have you ever eaten in a restaurant called Kala Kuer?"

"Xinjiang food?"

Joe nodded.

"Sure. It's on Yishan Lu. Probably the best *la mian* noodles in town. Why? You getting bored of Chinese?"

"Very," Joe replied. "We should go there sometime."

Joe's beer arrived and he decided to keep pressing. Tom was a walking *Yellow Pages* of Shanghai bars and restaurants and it saved time to pick his brain.

"What about Mexican nightclubs?"

"What about them?" Megan had leaned across to interrupt, bringing with her an invisible mist of scent and shampoo. She looked at Joe and smiled a smile that told him she was a test. *I'm single, you're single. These guys are setting us up.*

"One of the musicians at the bar in my hotel told me what a good time he'd had at this Mexican nightclub." He took his beer from the waiter and said "Thank you" in Mandarin. "Said I should go down there but couldn't remember the name of the place."

Megan and Tom shared a look that Joe could not quite interpret. After a beat, she said, "That's where we were going to go afterwards."

"Seriously?"

"He must have been talking about Zapata's," Tom explained. "That's the only Mexican bar between here and Tijuana."

"It's a bar, not a nightclub?"

"It's everything," Megan whispered. "You'll see."

A two-storey building on the corner of Hengshan Road and Dong Ping Road, Zapata's is a wild, chaotic Shanghai nightspot that relies for its atmosphere on a cocktail of cheap alcohol, elastic opening hours and hot Asian weather. Joe arrived direct from the restaurant with Tom, Megan and Ricky, who led him across a crowded outdoor terrace where tanned, freshly showered expats sank Heinekens and talked shop in midnight temperatures of twenty degrees. Conscious of Zhao Jian's disclosure that Sammy, Miles's Pakistani contact, was a regular customer, Joe scanned the crowds for his face, but there were too many people to make an effective assessment.

A wooden staircase on the far side of the terrace led to a packed first-floor "cantina," where margaritas were on special offer and queues at the bar went three deep. Mike, who had come ahead in a separate cab with Jeff and Sandrine, had already bought a round of drinks which he was distributing from a small metal tray. Against a deafening background of Aerosmith and Run DMC, Joe thanked him and took a mouth-numbing slug of crushed ice and cheap tequila.

"What do you think?" Megan asked, looking up at him with wide, dark eyes. After a long campaign over dinner, she was still flirting, still apparently assessing his potential.

"Rammed," was all Joe managed to say before Ricky hooked a hand through her arm and dragged her away through the crowds.

"You're dancing," he told her.

Joe turned. There was a second, interior entrance towards which Ricky was leading the now laughing Megan. Joe followed them and found himself on a three-sided wooden balcony overlooking a thronging bar and dance floor. A Western girl wearing only a bikini top and a pair of skinny jeans had leaped up onto the top of the curved bar, where she was grinding and writhing her body to the chorus of "Walk this Way." Men and women alike clapped and whooped on the dance floor as a second girl joined in, removed her T-shirt and threw it into the crowd. Tom appeared at Joe's side and must have misinterpreted the look on his face because he said, "Now that's what I call a cultural revolution. Chairman Mao must be turning in his grave."

One of the barmen, a sinewy Chinese with the waxed, sculpted hair of a male model, reached out his hand and was pulled up onto the bar by the prettier of the two girls. Joe saw that he was carrying a bottle of tequila. The customers directly beneath him seemed to know what this signified because they turned around, tipped back their heads and allowed the barman to pour it neat into their opened mouths. More cheers, more whoops as the tequila was coughed and spat and swallowed. The inevitable "Billie Jean" replaced "Walk this Way" and Joe took out a cigarette.

"Interesting place," he said.

That was when he spotted him. On the left-hand side of the balcony, about twenty feet away, looking down at the chaos below. Sammy. The likeness was unmistakable, although Joe could now see that he was probably Persian or Arabic, not Pakistani, as Jian's photograph had initially suggested; a trick of the light had given the man's face a false structure and colouring. He was in his late twenties, good looking, well built and smooth, wearing a gold necklace, a smart, collared shirt, jeans and an expensive watch. He also appeared to be alone.

"Another drink?" Tom shouted.

"Sure. Can I have a beer?"

It was time to go to work. As Tom pushed his way back to the bar of the cantina, Joe kept his eye on Sammy, trying to make a rapid assessment of his circumstances and character. His body language—tight, withdrawn—continued to suggest that he was not with a friend nor part of any group. The bottle of Heineken he was holding was almost full, so it seemed unlikely that someone was fetching him a drink. He did not appear to be communicating with anybody down on the dance floor, but instead kept his gaze fixed on the activity at the bar, occasionally flicking his eyes back up to the balcony, as if scoping for girls. This seemed to be the most likely explanation for his presence in Zapata's: young Chinese women, mostly in their late teens and early twenties, were standing all around him. Joe knew that some of them would be looking for a rich Western boyfriend, while others would be prepared to go home with a foreigner in return for money. They were not full-time hookers, but students or workers looking to supplement meagre incomes. It was the same story in almost every Western nightspot in China.

Five minutes went by. Nothing appeared to change. Sammy didn't check his mobile phone or give any other obvious sign that he was waiting for company. Instead, he slowly sipped his beer, smoked a Marlboro Light and arranged his hair several times in a manner that Joe thought of as nervous and self-conscious. There were two Chinese girls to his left, close to the far wall, one of whom appeared to be building up the courage to speak to him. It was dark and crowded on the balcony, but Joe could see that the girls were not particularly attractive, and that Sammy seemed to have little interest in approaching them.

"You all on your own, mister?"

Megan had appeared beside him. She slipped her hand around Joe's back and he felt her fingers briefly move across his skin. The sudden contact surprised him, but he returned the gesture, placing his hand on the small of her back. It occurred to him that this was his first sustained physical contact with another person since he had embraced his mother on Christmas Day.

"Crazy in here, no?" she said.

"Crazy."

Sammy was about halfway through his beer and still scanning the room for girls. He seemed completely at ease in the Zapata's environment and Joe was fairly sure by now that he was a naturalized European or American. As Megan curled her hand further around his back, resting her fingers against the edge of his stomach, an idea came to him which combined a certain ruthlessness with the benefits of long experience in the secret world. He would use her for bait. She was by far the most attractive woman in the upper section of the club, and if he could manoeuvre her closer to Sammy, her looks and natural flirtatiousness might prompt him to make conversation. Joe could then introduce himself at a later point without arousing suspicion.

"Let's go over there," he said, nodding to his left, "where it's a bit less crowded."

Holding Megan by the hand, he waited until Sammy was looking down at the bar, then led her to within two or three feet of where he was standing. There was a Chinese girl positioned between them, but Joe knew that she had been waiting there, unapproached, for at least ten minutes.

"What happened to Tom?" he asked, releasing Megan's hand and formalizing his body language so that they would not look like a couple. Megan leaned against the balustrade and started moving her body to the music.

"No idea," she replied.

"He said he was getting me a drink. Wait here, will you? I'll see if he needs help."

Megan did not suspect a thing. As Joe walked off, making his way back towards the bar, she continued to look down at the dance floor, mouthing along to the lyrics of "The House that Jack Built." For the next five minutes Joe gave her the opportunity to work her magic, purporting to search Zapata's for Tom, but in reality killing time in the ground-floor bathroom. Walking back upstairs, he found Tom and Ricky at the bar of the cantina, took his bottle of beer and led them back to the interior door. As they emerged onto the balcony, Joe looked across and saw what he had wanted to see: Sammy, God bless him, smoothing back his hair and making awkward conversation with Megan.

"There she is," he said, pointing towards them. "That's where I left her."

After that it was easy.

"Oh there you are," she said, as if she had given up all hope of ever seeing Joe again. "I was wondering what had happened to you. This is Shahpour. Shahpour, these are my friends, Tom, Ricky and Joe."

"Good to meet you, guys."

The accent was American, born and bred, but the name was probably Iranian. Shahpour looked momentarily annoyed to have had Megan swamped by male admirers, but any irritation was soon replaced by a confident, conciliatory smile that Joe recognized as natural charm.

"Are you living here in Shanghai?" Tom asked.

"Yeah. Have been for about a year now."

"Shahpour used to work in construction," Megan said, making a joke with her eyes. "Now he's here in China selling software to small businesses."

By the tone of her voice, it was obvious to Joe that she had been bored by their conversation. Inadvertently, however, she had supplied him with two important pieces of information. "Construction" might mean Macklinson. "Selling software" could possibly imply that Shahpour was using the same cover as Miles.

"What about you guys?" he asked.

Tom and Ricky explained that they had been living in Shanghai for some time. Joe, deliberately standing behind them, added that he had arrived in the New Year. Shahpour did a good job of appearing to listen, but it was obvious that he was interested solely in their relationship to Megan. Was one of these guys her boyfriend? If not, could he take her off their hands?

"And what do you do, Tom?" he asked.

"I'm a yacht broker."

"You, Joe?"

"Pharmaceuticals." There was a danger of the conversation lasting no more than a few minutes. Ricky made a drunken joke about "making knickers for a living," but as far as Shahpour was concerned, he, Tom and Joe were just three British guys getting in the way of his plans for Megan. If Joe was going to find out what he needed to know, he would have to act fast. "I work for a small British company here," he said. "Quayler. We're trying to expand into China."

"Pharmaceuticals, huh?"

"That's right."

"Dancing Queen" sealed it. When Megan and Ricky heard the opening bars of the song, they both screamed in delight and announced that they were heading back to the dance floor.

"Great to meet you, Shahpour," she called out, disappearing into the distance.

"Yeah, great to meet you too."

There was a certain ruthlessness in the manner of her departure and Joe felt a pang of sympathy. He looked at Shahpour's face, where an uneasy mixture of loneliness and irritation crossed behind his eyes. Male pride had been wounded. Just as quickly, however, his frustration was replaced by a look of practised indifference.

"So what's her story?" he asked.

"Oh she's just crazy," Tom replied. "Forget about her."

An awkward silence lingered. To Joe's frustration, he could sense that both Tom and Shahpour wanted to end the conversation. They appeared to have little in common, and their reason for meeting had just disappeared downstairs. Joe was left with a dilemma. Try to keep them talking, a strategy which might arouse Shahpour's suspicion, or abandon the contact altogether. He could always tap Megan for answers later on.

"So you're from America?" he asked, opting for one last question.

"Nowadays I try to keep that a secret," Shahpour replied. His eyes were once again scanning the balcony and Joe could see that it was a lost cause. A man like that didn't want to be wasting his night talking to a guy who sold antibiotics for a living.

"Which part?" he asked.

"Pacific Northwest."

Another disinterested answer. Time to wrap things up.

"Well look, here's my card." As a tactic, this was not as cack-handed as it might sound; in China, exchanging business cards is common practice, regardless of social circumstances. "It was good to meet you."

Shahpour was well aware of the tradition and duly accepted Joe's card in a manner imitative of the Chinese, clasping it in both hands, studying the lettering carefully and even bowing his head for comic effect. He then returned the favour, as Joe had hoped he would, handing two cards of his own to Tom and Joe.

"Goodarzi?" Joe said, pronouncing Shahpour's surname. He had noted, with a leap of astonishment, that the card was embossed with the Microsoft logo.

"Goodarzi, yes. And yours? Lennox?"

Joe nodded. Had Shahpour put a slight stress on the surname, as if he had heard it before? Or was he simply checking its pronunciation? Joe could not be sure. "It's Scottish," he said.

Shahpour's eyes went to the roof of the club, as if he had been reminded of something, taken sideways into a separate life. Was Joe imagining this? It was like watching himself struggling with the memory of Ansary Tursun. Where had he heard the name before? Their eyes met but Joe was disappointed to see that Shahpour now looked just as bored and as indifferent as before. He was even angling past them as he shook their hands, heading back in the direction of the cantina.

"It was great to meet you guys," he said. "Dancing Queen" was coming to an end. "Maybe we'll run into each other sometime."

"I certainly hope so," Tom said, without feeling, and before Joe could add a farewell of his own, Shahpour Goodarzi had been swallowed up by a balcony of girls.

An hour later, out on the terrace, Joe saw Shahpour leave the club in the company of a young Chinese girl wearing torn denim jeans and a tight pink top. Turning to Megan, whose T-shirt was soaked through with sweat after a long session on the dance floor, he said: "Well, your Iranian friend got lucky."

"My Iranian friend?"

"Shahpour. The guy who worked in construction. You remember? The one you were talking to on the balcony."

"Oh *him*." She had forgotten their encounter entirely. "Were you jealous, Joe?"

He liked the way she went directly to the point. Her game was never over. "Inconsolably," he said, because he was now loose and drunk and strangely tempted by the idea of going to bed with her. "What was he like?"

"Didn't you and Tom stay and talk to him afterwards?" A line of German students squeezed past them, pushing Megan's body closer to Joe's. He caught the sweet toxicity of her breath as she held his arm for balance.

"Only for five minutes. He said he used to work in construction."

"That's right. Some big American company," Megan remembered.

Zapata's was emptying out. Joe could not afford to ask too many questions, at the risk of seeming unusually inquisitive. He offered Megan a cigarette and looked around the terrace.

"Where are the others?"

"Jeff and Sandrine went home about an hour ago. I guess Ricky and Tom are still dancing." Megan had not moved from her position, close to Joe. It was strange, he thought, how alcohol and the adrenalin rush of work could combine to push his longing for Isabella temporarily to one side. For weeks he had thought about little else but their first possible encounter, yet this alluring, flattering woman had worked her way under his skin. In Megan he detected something of the same rawness of spirit which had once captivated him about Isabella. Running his hand across her flat, cool stomach, he began to doubt the nature of his own feelings. How much of his need for Isabella was love, and how much a desire to get even? Did Joe want to possess Isabella again, only so that he could walk away? Seven years is a long time to harbour the grudge of heartbreak.

"So you think he was Iranian?" Megan asked, the palm of her hand gently brushing the hairs on Joe's arm. Here was another chance to discuss Shahpour, but all he could think about was the delicacy of her touch.

"Iranian Californian," he said. "A lot of them live over there. Families who escaped the Shah."

Megan nodded. They were communicating as much through silence as they were through words. The early hours of the humid Shanghai morning were a possibility into which they could pour their desire. Joe pulled Megan towards him so that his arms were completely encircling her waist. She leaned back against his chest. He lowered his face into her hair and closed his eyes to the smell of her. It was in this blissful instant that the name Ansary Tursun suddenly returned to him and he was alone again on the streets of Tsim Sha Tsui. The process by which Joe's brain arrived at the inspiration was as puzzling to him as the momentary loss of his desire for Isabella. He looked up at the night sky and smiled.

"So what are the rooms like at the Ritz-Carlton?" Megan whispered.

"What's that?"

Joe had heard her, but he needed time. His memory was racing back to the apartment, to Sadha and Lee, to stories of torture and betrayal.

"I said, what are the rooms like at the Ritz-Carlton?"

"A mess," Joe said, because he knew now that he ought to leave, to contact London, to speak to Waterfield before England went to bed.

"Don't they tidy up after you?"

"Not when I tell them not to."

Megan was waiting for an invitation. Of course she was. A woman needed more than code. He thought of the long night that lay ahead of them, the sudden end to his permanent solitude, the challenge and the excitement of taking a beautiful woman to bed, then the rapture of eventual sleep beside her. The twin, competing strands of Joe Lennox's personality, his immense tenderness and his ceaseless professional zeal, helixed in an instant that dizzied him. He wondered whether it was possible to do both: to love and to work; to lie and to please? He was drunk and he was out of answers. A weakness in him, or perhaps it was a strength, said, "Come home with me tonight."

Megan squeezed his arm so tightly that he almost laughed. He saw her twist away from him and turn and look up into his eyes in a way that was suddenly beyond lust and game-playing. Did this girl actually *understand* him? A few hours earlier Joe had been sitting beside her eating green curry, trying to sound clever about China. Yet his desire for her now was overwhelming. He wanted to kiss her, but also to save that kiss until they were alone and there was privacy and control. He did not want anybody to see them. He did not want those kinds of rumours.

"There are cabs outside," she said.

"Let's go."

Nine hours later, Megan was sitting up in Joe's wide double bed, a sheet wrapped around her body, picking at a room-service fruit salad. The curtains were drawn and she was watching BBC News 24 with the sound switched off.

"So is it true?" she called out.

Joe had stepped out of the shower and put on a dressing gown. He could still taste the sweetness of her body, the scent of the night on her skin. Drifting in and out of sleep beside this sensual, beguiling woman had been a waking dream of pleasure, by turns wild and then eerily calm. They were at ease with one another, and the morning had been blessedly free of any awkwardness or indifference.

"Is what true?" he called back.

"That you used to be a spy."

Joe searched for his reflection in the bathroom mirror, but found that his face was obscured by a film of steam on glass. *This is where it always begins. This is where I have to start lying.*

"What's that? Ricky's theory?"

"Everybody jokes about it." Megan had a cup of black coffee on the table beside her and she picked it up. When Joe came into the bedroom, rubbing a towel through wet hair, she clasped the cup against her chest and sneezed.

"Bless you. Who's everybody?"

"You know . . ." They were both tired and Joe simply smiled and nodded. He sat on the edge of the bed.

"To be honest with you, it always irritated me that they never asked. At Oxford, it was a sort of running joke that anybody studying Mandarin who could tie their own shoelaces would get talent-spotted by MI6. But the offer never came. Even when I was working for the Foreign Office, I never got the nod."

Megan sipped her coffee. "How come?"

"Search me. I can lie to people. I can drink Martinis. I've fired a gun."

She pushed her foot against his thigh and he felt toes wriggling through the fabric of his robe. "You'd have been good at it, I think."

"You do?"

"Definitely." She lowered the coffee and teased him with her eyes. "You're discreet. You're sensitive. You're reasonably good in bed."

"Oh thank you."

"Don't mention it."

He stood up and drew back the curtains. His room was on the forty-third floor of the Ritz-Carlton building, but the sound of the street below, the gridlocked traffic of that late Shanghai morning, was still audible through the doubled glass. Six blocks to the east, construction workers, obscured by a haze of sunshine, were steering a rust-coloured girder into the dark interior of a half-completed skyscraper. Joe followed the slow, gradual sweep of the crane as the girder inched home. Megan stirred behind him and he turned.

"I'm gonna take a shower," she said.

The bowl of fruit salad was resting on the bed beside a copy of *The Great Gatsby*, which Joe had been reading the previous afternoon. She lifted it up and he found himself captivated by the simple sight of her pale, slim arm. He knew every part of her now. They were each other's secret.

"What are you looking at?"

"Your arm," he said. "I love the shape of it."

"You should see my other one."

He took the book from her and she lifted the sheet around her body before walking to the bathroom. Joe picked a croissant from the breakfast trolley and ate it as he watched the news, finding that he enjoyed the noise of the shower running in the background. It was good to have company. It was good not to wake up alone. As he listened to Megan in the bathroom, gasping at the heat of the water, humming as it ran down her skin, he felt no disquiet over what had happened, no confusion or regret. Just a strange raw feeling in the base of his spine, as if he had done what he had done in order to protect himself from Isabella. Why was that? Was everything a calculation? With every step, with every Ansary or Shahpour, he was edging closer and closer to Miles. Now Megan was pulling him further and further away.

No more introspection. Time to dress. Time to work. Just after midday they made their way down to the lobby where Joe put Megan in a cab. She worked part-time at an investment bank in Pudong and was already three hours late. As he held the door for her, she put her arms around his neck and kissed him.

"I had a fantastic time," she said. "Can we do this again?"

"As soon as possible." He held her hand. "What are you doing for dinner?"

Megan laughed and ducked into the taxi. She turned in the back seat as the cab pulled away and Joe waved, aware that he was being watched by the doorman. It was only after the car had turned onto Nanjing Road that he realized he did not have her number.

The doorman smiled as Joe walked back into the lobby, a grin between men. It was good of him to risk it; Joe admired his cheek.

"My cousin from Malaysia," he said.

"Yes, sir. Of course, sir. Your cousin from Malaysia."

He called Waterfield that afternoon using an encrypted SIM smuggled into China in the spine of *The Queen of the South*. It was only the second time that the two men had spoken since Joe's departure from Heathrow. Waterfield sounded distant and groggy, as if he had been woken from a deep sleep.

"How are things?" he asked. It was nine o'clock in the morning in London.

"Things are fine," Joe replied, "but I need a couple of favours."

"Go on."

"On the river that day, you told me that you had a source in Garden Road back in '97. What are the chances of getting the American transcript of my interview with Wang?"

"The transcript from the safe house?"

"Yes."

An audible intake of breath. The original SIS document had been destroyed almost immediately by Kenneth Lenan. "Depends what steps Miles took to cover his tracks. If he was as thorough as Ken, I don't rate our chances. No harm in asking, though."

"It would help piece something together."

"Leave it with me."

Joe was sitting on a bench in Renmin Park, looking up at his favourite building in Shanghai, the J. W. Marriott Tower in To-morrow Square. It was a humid, sun-blinding afternoon and En-gland was truly half a world away. He tried to picture Waterfield in his tiny pied-à-terre in Drayton Gardens, working his way through a pot of Twining's English Breakfast while John Humphrys harangued somebody on the *Today* programme. The London of Joe's memory was Routemaster buses and Capital Radio, cafés on the Shepherd's Bush Road.

"You said a couple of favours."

Waterfield was waking up. A Chinese teenager with dyed hair and torn jeans curled past Joe on a skateboard. "Can you also run a check on a Shahpour Goodarzi, possible Cousin, possible former employee at Macklinson?" Joe spelt out the name as he wiped a sheen of sweat from his forehead. "He's American, probably second-generation Iranian immigrant, family resident in Califor-nia. Works for Microsoft, might be using the same cover as Miles." Joe was holding Shahpour's business card and read out the email address and cellphone details printed in the lower right-hand cor-ner. "I also need you to contact Amnesty International about a Uighur activist, imprisoned briefly in the mid-1990s. See if they have anything on an Ansary Tursun." He again spelt out the name. "Can you also try Human Rights Watch? Do they have a file on him? Anything unusual we should know?"

"Done."

Joe put Shahpour's card back in his pocket. "So how are things in the old country?"

"Same old, same old. You've heard about Rebiya Kadeer?"

Kadeer was a Uighur businesswoman who was arrested in 1999 while en route to meet a US Congressional delegation which had arrived in Xinjiang to investigate human rights abuses. Ka-deer had sent newspaper clippings to her husband, a Uighur exile resident in the United States, and was subsequently charged with "leaking state secrets" by the PRC. The Chinese also alleged that Kadeer had been in possession of a list of ten Uighur dissidents with "connections to national separatist activities."

"She's been freed, hasn't she?" Joe replied. The Kadeer story had been covered in the *International Herald Tribune*, copies of which were available to overseas guests in the business lounge of the Ritz-Carlton.

"Released last week as a sop to Condoleezza, officially on medical grounds. In reality, Beijing struck a deal to ensure that the Yanks dropped a resolution on Chinese human rights abuses at the UN."

"What a lovely story."

"Heartening, isn't it? And there's been a bus bomb in Jiangxi province."

"Yes. We heard about that one." On 17 March a double-decker bus had exploded in Shangrao, killing all thirty people on board.

"Who are the Chinese blaming?" Waterfield asked.

"Party line seems to be that it was a case of mishandled explosives. A worker travelling with some dynamite in his suitcase who didn't know what he was doing."

"Was a pig flying past at the time?"

Joe laughed. "Several," he said.

Humour was the simplest way of acknowledging the possibility that explosions of this sort could be linked to separatist activity. Waterfield sneezed, blew his nose and remembered something, saying, "One more thing."

"What's that?"

"Coolidge went to a funeral on a trip home six months ago. Young officer from the Directorate of Operations called Josh Pinnegar. Gave the address at the service, spoke about their 'close personal and professional' relationship, that sort of thing. Pinnegar was murdered by a Triad gang in San Francisco. Our source indicates that he also had links to TYPHOON. There may be a connection there."

"I'll look into it." Joe needed to put in an appearance at the Quayler office before the day was out and brought the conversation to an end.

"I'd better be off."

"Of course. Just a quick request before you go." Waterfield's voice briefly became a stern paternal rebuke. "Can you for God's sake move out of the Ritz bloody Carlton? Fifteen grand on board and lodging is in the general arena of taking the piss. Bean counters not amused. End of lecture."

The information Joe had requested arrived by diplomatic bag seventy-two hours later. It was sent to Beijing, where it was passed to me in Fish Nation, a tiny, British-style fish-and-chip shop, by the head of media and public affairs at the British embassy. To my knowledge, she thought she was handing over documents relating to Britain's recent decision to lift an embargo on the sale of arms to China. The package consisted of a padded A4 envelope in which Waterfield had placed two typewritten sheets of paper and a compact disc. I flew to Shanghai that night, placed the papers inside an edition of the *China Daily*, hid the disc inside a bootlegged copy of *Blood on the Tracks*, and presented both items to Joe at dinner. At about midnight, he left me in Park 97 with Tom and Ricky and returned to his hotel.

He soon discovered that London had been unable to trace a Shahpour Goodarzi either to Langley or to the Macklinson Corporation. All known aliases for Iranian-American Cousins under the age of thirty-five had been investigated. A database match of a photograph of "Sammy," provided by Zhao Jian, had also been attempted, without success. It was the same story with Ansary Tursun. Nothing from Amnesty, nothing from Human Rights Watch. London apologized for "any frustration this might cause."

The compact disc looked more promising. Booting up his laptop, Joe sat on the bed, inserted a pair of headphones, opened iTunes and was swiftly returned to the innocent spring of 1997.

> *Professor Wang, this is Mr. John Richards from Government House. The man I tell you about. He has come to see you.*

It was the live recording of the interrogation. Joe pressed the headphones against his ears and felt his skin prickle at the sound of Lee's voice. The take quality was poor; the room sounded faded and lifeless. Joe heard a creak of springs and remembered Wang rising slowly to his feet. He could picture the benign, intelligent face, the face that he had warmed to, the face that had later encouraged young Uighur men to kill.

> *Mr. Richards. I am very glad to make your acquaintance. Thank you for coming to see me so late at night. I hope I have not been any inconvenience to you or to your organization.*

Joe turned up the sound as Shanghai closed in around him. Now he was alone in the safe house, twenty-six years old again, and the pitch of his confident, entitled voice embarrassed him. This younger self was so innocent, so ambitious, so free of the pressures of age.

> *So I would say that you are a very lucky man, Mr. Wang . . . You survive a very dangerous swim. You are surprised on the beach not by Hong Kong immigration, who would almost certainly have turned you back to China, but by a British soldier. You claim to have information about a possible defection. The army believes your story, contacts Government House, we send a nice, air-conditioned car to pick you up and less than twenty-four hours after leaving China here you are sitting in a furnished apartment in Tsim Sha Tsui watching Lawrence of Arabia. I'd say that qualifies as luck.*

He was so sure of himself! Was that the man Isabella would remember? Had he changed so much that he would no longer be of interest to her? Joe lay back on the bed, his eyes closed, the side of his face resting on a fresh white pillow. Every trace of Megan had been erased by chambermaids and air conditioning.

> *At some point Ansary was taken into what he believes was the basement of the prison. His left arm and his left leg were handcuffed to a bar in a room of solitary confinement. He was left to hang like this for more than twenty-four hours. He had no food, no water. Remember that his crime was only to read a newspaper.*

On it went. As Joe listened to the recording, images flooded back from the discovered cave of his memory; he had arrived at

the name Abdul Bary before he even heard it. Wang said that
Bary had been imprisoned, that a toenail had been torn from his
foot by a laughing guard. It was like listening to an account of an
execution.

> *Other prisoners, we later learned, had been attacked by dogs,*
> *burned with electric batons. Another had horse's hair, that is the*
> *hard, brittle hair of an animal, inserted into his penis. And through*
> *all this, do you know what they were forced to wear on their heads,*
> *Mr. Richards? Metal helmets. Helmets that covered their eyes. And*
> *why? To create disorientation? To weigh them down? No. Ansary*
> *later learned from another prisoner that there had been an instance*
> *when an inmate had been so badly tortured, had been in so much*
> *pain, that he had actually beaten his own head against a radiator in*
> *an attempt to take his own life.*

The phone rang beside the bed. Joe was shaken from his semi-
hypnotic state and tore off the headphones, as if somebody had
burst into the room.

"Joe?"

It was Megan. He looked at his watch. "Are you OK?"

"Did I wake you?"

He stopped the playback. "No. It's almost two. What's happening? Are you all right?"

"I can't sleep," she said.

He was still under the spell of the recording, yet the prospect of
seeing her again was immediately enticing. He was thirsty and
stood up off the bed. "I'm wide awake," he said. "Do you want to
come over?"

"Would that be OK?"

They had spent two of the previous three nights together, always at the hotel, always sleeping late into the morning. Increasingly, Joe was living on London time. That was what Shanghai
did to you. "I have to check out tomorrow," he said. "I have to
move into my new apartment. But I'd love to see you."

I have often wondered if Joe had Megan vetted. He was
never prepared to say. When a spy meets a strange girl in a

strange restaurant, and that girl turns out to be as forthcoming as Megan, the spy has a right to feel suspicious. Why was she calling him at two o'clock in the morning? Why was it so important to Megan that they spend the night together? Joe was certain that she was legitimate, but as soon as he had hung up the phone, he removed the CD from the laptop and placed it in the small black safe located in the main wardrobe of his room. Afterwards, switching on the hot water in both the bath and shower, he created a room of steam to defeat the hotel fire alarm and burned the pages of Waterfield's report in the sink.

You could never be too careful. You never knew who you were dealing with.

Joe checked out the following morning.

His two-bedroomed apartment was part of a colonial art-deco complex set back from a dusty, tree-lined avenue in the heart of the French Concession. The contrast with the bustle and noise of Nanjing Road was stark: in Joe's new neighbourhood, traffic was more subdued and there was scarcely a high-rise in sight. The pace of life also slowed to a crawl: two blocks from his front door a carpenter sold lutes and handmade violins. All along the street middle-aged Chinese men played *majiang* and slumbered through long afternoons in the backs of wooden carts. From the window of his new kitchen Joe could hear birdsong and neighbourhood conversations. He was within walking distance of several small European-style cafés, as well as the Shanghai Library, the Ding Xiang Gardens and—more by accident than design—the main building of the Consulate General of the United States of America. The apartment was already fully furnished, with shelves of paperback books, broadband wireless internet, IKEA pictures on the walls and spices in the cupboards. Joe didn't need to buy sheets or pillows, lightbulbs or soap: everything was already in place. It must have felt like stepping into another person's life.

Two days after checking out of the hotel he went shopping for groceries in Xiangyang Market. It was raining heavily and Joe was carrying an umbrella as well as a briefcase full of documents from Quayler. The market, which has since been razed to the ground to make way for a shopping centre, was a crowded sea of stalls protected only by flimsy tarpaulin coverings which dripped water onto the ground. Butchers in white chef's hats took meat cleavers to joints of pork and chicken and failed to meet Joe's eye when he paid for them. At a vegetable stall he bought radishes and husks of white corn, beetroot for homemade borscht, as well as mangoes, bananas and apples to eat for breakfast. One of the pleasures of renting the flat was the opportunity he now had to prepare and cook his own food; from vast hessian sacks at the perimeter of the market Joe scooped dried mushrooms and black beans, nuts and rice, planning to host a flat-warming dinner party to which he would invite Tom and Megan and their friends. Weighed down with plastic bags, he eventually walked out onto Huaihai Road at about six o'clock, in the hopeless aspiration of hailing a cab. Every other shopper had the same idea. It was as if all of Shanghai was sheltering from the tropical rain beneath the eaves and awnings on the street. As the thick wet traffic fizzed past, Joe swore under his breath and knew that it would be hours before he saw a vacant taxi.

Sixty metres away, Miles Coolidge emerged from a branch of the Lawson's convenience store carrying a rucksack in which he had placed a box of Camel cigarettes, a bar of Hershey's chocolate, some aspirin and a packet of Style condoms. He had heard rumours of Joe Lennox's presence in Shanghai from two sources: a friend at the United States embassy in London who had attended his leaving party at Vauxhall Cross, and a young Chinese corporate lawyer who happened to mention that she had bumped into "a really interesting guy called Joe" at a bi-weekly meeting of the British Chamber of Commerce. The lawyer, who worked part-time for Microsoft—and full-time trying to fend off the advances of Miles Coolidge—was unable to recall anything about Joe's profession except that he "was a chemist or something." Miles had eventually discovered that Joe was staying at the Ritz-Carlton,

only to be informed twenty-four hours earlier that Mr. Lennox
had checked out, leaving no forwarding address. It was a measure
of how busy Miles was that he had given little further thought to
Joe's whereabouts until he glimpsed the tall, slim figure, weighed
down by plastic bags, sheltering under an umbrella on the opposite side of Huaihai Road.

Sixty seconds later, the bottom of his trousers soaked with rain
and grime, Joe was preparing to trudge home when he felt a presence behind him, a hand on his back, then a head popping up
under his umbrella like a jack-in-the-box.

"You just never know who you're gonna run into in this town."

Miles was just as Zhao Jian had described, just as he had looked
in the photos: thickset and shaven headed, only now with a heavy
black beard that aged in white streaks around the neck and ears.
This was it; the moment London had been waiting for. Joe had
rehearsed dialogue for their first chance encounter, but he was so
taken aback that it was three or four seconds before he was able to
remember his lines.

"Jesus Christ. Miles. I didn't recognize you with the beard.
What the fuck are you doing here?"

The umbrella had fallen to one side and the warm rain was
drenching his face. It ran through the tangle of Miles's beard; it
glistened the teeth of his grin.

"I was gonna ask you the same question."

"I live here."

"Well I do too."

They stepped off the street for shelter and found themselves in
a dumpling restaurant that smelled of rain and spilled vinegar. A
huddle of pedestrians were gathered in the entrance but Miles
barged through them like a commuter running late for a train. Joe
could see that he had no choice but to join him and followed the
American to a table at the back of the restaurant.

"You got time to talk, right?"

"Of course."

The table was constructed out of moulded orange plastic. A
waitress in a navy blue apron came over and Miles said, "Just tea,"
without looking at her. Joe put his bags on the floor and tried to

work out what was happening. Had Miles been following him? Was this just coincidence? It was impossible to tell.

"I'm trying to remember how I feel about you," he said, which was the first of the lines he had rehearsed. Miles, taking off his jacket, said, "Cute," and threw it on the chair beside him. Joe stared at his stomach, fat as an empathy belly, full of booze and lunches, and felt an immediate, visceral hatred of the man who had betrayed him. As he had long suspected, these first instincts were purely personal; they had nothing to do with the operation. He tried to arrange his face so that it would not reflect his anger and picked at a scratch on the table. He was forced to concede that Miles's beard gave his face a certain rugged grandeur, but the eyes had gone. Age had beaten the truth out of them: they were now just sockets of greed and lies.

"So you live here?"

Either man might have asked the question but Joe got there first. Miles nodded as he wiped a paper napkin over the dome of his head. He was staring at Joe, as if relieved that a long wait was over.

"That's right. I'm in software now," he said. "A free marketeer. You?"

"Pharmaceuticals."

"Oh come on." Miles laughed and shook his head, as if Joe had blundered the lie.

"Seriously. I got out six months ago."

"Pharmaceuticals? It's cover, Joe. Come on. You can tell me."

"There's nothing to tell. I'm serious." He looked around at the neighbouring tables, suggesting with his eyes that Miles was being childish. He wondered if Shahpour had shown him his card, or whether the rumours had filtered through from Grosvenor Square. Perhaps the whole thing really was just coincidence and every one of his carefully laid plans in Shanghai had proved pointless. "I got sick of working for an organization in thrall to a bunch of corrupt neocons, so I handed in my notice. If that makes you feel bad, I apologize. It's not personal."

Miles reared back in his seat. "Why would I give a shit?"

"I'm glad you don't."

There was a pause while Miles seemed to contemplate the philosophical implications of what Joe had told him. Finally, shaking his head, he said, "Seriously? You resigned out of moral disgust?" as if ethical behaviour should be anathema to men of their calling.

"People do braver things every day."

It looked as though Miles believed him, because a glint of guilt briefly flashed across his eyes. Joe had always been the principled one. The competitive rage of Hong Kong would soon return, because even marrying Isabella had not been enough.

"What about you?" Joe asked.

"What about me?"

"Why did you leave?"

The waitress set a pot of Lipton's tea on the table, looked quickly at Joe and walked away. Miles sniffed. "Why do you think?" he said.

"Money?"

"You got it."

Simultaneously they reached for cigarettes: Joe for a packet of Zhong Nan Hai, Miles for a soft pack of Camel Filters. Joe's pulse had settled now. He was able to relax and concentrate on the strategy he had put together with Waterfield.

"So what does 'software' mean?"

"I guess it means the same as 'pharmaceuticals.'"

What Joe had not anticipated was the abrasiveness of the conversation. Either Miles was working to a prepared script of his own, hoping to catch Joe off balance, or the years had rendered him even blunter and more aggressive than before.

"So you're not in computers? You're still working for the government?"

Miles ran a hand over his beard, acting as if Joe was being slow on the uptake. "Like I told you, man. I'm legitimate. I work ninety-hour weeks on software piracy. I travelled 100,000 miles last year trying to make sure Windows Vista doesn't develop a single-fold eyelid when we finally release in Asia."

Joe couldn't help but laugh. The lies. The casual racism. He poured the tea and rested his cigarette in a burn-scarred ashtray.

"Do you miss it?"

Miles lurched forward. "Like pussy, man," he whispered. "Like pussy."

Joe disguised another wave of consternation in a gentle, smiling shake of the head. A part of him had always admired Miles's sheer effrontery—brazenly lying about his work, about Linda, his mistress, about his marriage—yet the reply had been an implied insult to which he wanted to respond in kind.

"Speaking of which, how is Isabella?"

Miles sniffed again, pinned like an insect on his indiscretions. It had been a long time since anybody had challenged his natural authority.

"Oh she's great," he replied. "Why? You wanna meet up with her?"

Joe remembered the last time that he had seen the pair of them together, sitting on a sofa at a party in Causeway Bay. He had walked into the room and Isabella had immediately turned away, pretending to hold a conversation with the woman to her left. They had been separated for two months at that point and Joe had watched Isabella's hand link into Miles's arm, playing with the strap of his watch. Afterwards, out on a balcony, he had deliberately started an argument which had ended with both Miles and Isabella leaving the party. Those were the worst times and the humiliation of that period still ran through him like acid in the stomach.

"Sure. It would be great to see her."

"Dinner?" Miles suggested immediately.

Joe suspected that this was pre-ordained. Miles would want to maintain as much control over Joe as possible, to shunt him around town until he knew exactly what he was dealing with. Joe had planned to decline any initial invitation from Miles under the pretence of leaving Shanghai on Quayler business, but he was aware that he had several bags of fresh food resting at his feet and that such a tactic would now be impossible.

"Dinner sounds great."

"What about tomorrow? I know Izzy's free. I can get us a table at M on the Bund. She'd get a kick out of seeing you."

A kick? He had forgotten Miles's seemingly effortless slights and condescensions. He was acting as though Joe had been a mere footnote in the long narrative of Isabella's life. The rain was starting to ease off on Huaihai and he listened to the sound of the crawling traffic, to horns, the squeal of brakes.

"Fine," he said. "I'd like that." M on the Bund was a rooftop restaurant with views over the Huangpu and prices to match. Though he had imagined the circumstances of their reunion for seven long years, in that moment Joe had no conception of how he would react to seeing Isabella after such a span of time. What would he say? How would she behave? Why was he agreeing to meet both of them at the same time?

"You gotta cellphone?"

"Of course."

Miles was sipping his tea. He knew, as well as anyone, how much the separation had cost Joe in terms of his happiness and self-esteem and appeared to be enjoying his discomfort. Joe, realizing that he had been handed an opportunity, lifted his briefcase onto the table, flipped the catches and swivelled it towards Miles so that it was possible for him to view the contents. He looked quickly at his face and noted the eagerness with which the American scanned the leather interior.

"What you got in there?" Miles asked. "Vaccines? Viagra?"

"Just work," Joe said, "just work," closing the lid and passing Miles the card. "You got one of these?"

"Sure."

This was the second part of his plan. Miles took a card from his jacket and handed it to Joe, who carried off the act to perfection.

"Microsoft?"

Miles nodded. "Yup."

"I think I met a colleague of yours the other day. I've got his card in here somewhere."

Reopening the case, he scrabbled around for several seconds before emerging with what he needed. "Shahpour Goodarzi?" he said, as if struggling to pronounce the name. "Does that ring a bell?"

The deception had been simple and effortless and Miles fell for it like a hooked fish. "Shahpour?" he said, snatching the card out of Joe's hand. "Where the hell did you meet him?"

Joe strained, reaching for the memory. Eventually he said: "Zapata's? Maybe three nights ago. Matter of fact, I think he was trying to chat up my girlfriend."

"You've got a girlfriend already?"

The information had slipped out in the heat of the moment. It was his only mistake. There was no operational advantage in Miles knowing about Megan and Joe stubbed out his cigarette, annoyed with himself.

"Early stages," he said, "early stages," knowing that Isabella would now be told. How would she react when she heard the news? The only thing he feared was her indifference.

"Why don't you bring her along?" Miles suggested.

"Tomorrow?"

"Sure."

Joe agreed, although he had no intention of extending the invitation. The dinner would be complicated enough without throwing Megan into the mix. "Not a bad idea," he said. "I'll see if she's around."

"Maybe Shahpour can come too," Miles added. "The more the merrier, right?"

"Right," Joe said. "The more the merrier."

Forty seconds after Joe had left the restaurant, Miles took out his mobile phone, walked out onto Huaihai Road and called Shahpour on a secure number.

"Why the fuck didn't you tell me you'd run into Joe Lennox?"

"Who's Joe Lennox?"

"British. Ex-MI6. Works in pharmaceuticals. Ring any bells?"

"Miles, I don't have the slightest idea what you're talking about."

He did, of course. From the moment Shahpour had shaken Joe's hand in Zapata's, seen his card and registered the name, he had been weighing up the implications of their encounter. The look Joe had seen in his eyes was the look of a man who had found his salvation. Shahpour Goodarzi was Miles's right-hand man on the renewed TYPHOON, but he was also the greatest obstacle to its fruition.

"Hold on," he said. "Pharmaceuticals?"

"That's right." Water was dripping onto Miles's scalp. He looked up at the offending balcony, wiped the rain off with his hand and began walking east towards the metro station at Shaanxinanlu. "Six foot, dark hair . . ."

"Yeah. Oh yeah. Sure, I remember." Shahpour was smoking a joint in his apartment on Fuxing Middle Road and rested it on a table in the kitchen. "He gave me his card. I've got it here some-where. Who did you say he was?"

"Only the guy who first interviewed Wang Kaixuan. Only the guy who supposedly quit MI6 three months ago and now just hap-pens to be living in Shanghai. Only my wife's fucking ex-boyfriend. I told you about him, for Chrissakes. I told you two weeks ago there were rumours he'd been sent to Shanghai."

"Calm down," Shahpour said. "It's probably just coincidence."

"Coincidence?" Miles was barking into the phone as he walked. "What is this? A séance? Don't tell me to calm down, you prick. How did he get to you?"

Shahpour removed the phone from his ear, mouthed the words "Fuck you" soundlessly at the mouthpiece, and picked up the joint. "He didn't get to me," he said, dragging on the roach. "I was talk-ing to his girlfriend and his buddies came down on me like a SWAT team."

"Who's the girlfriend?"

"How should I know? Mary or Megan or something . . ."

"Well, she's coming to dinner tomorrow night. So is Joe. And so are you."

"Miles, it's the weekend. I have plans . . ."

"The only plans you have are to make it to M on the Bund by eight o'clock. Do your job, Shahpour. Fuck this up and you're on a cargo flight back to Sacramento."

Joe spent the next twenty-four hours trying his best to convince himself that he was ready to see Isabella.

He made dinner for Megan at his apartment, took her for a drink at the Cotton Club, lay awake beside her until almost four o'clock in the morning, then woke at nine to find her standing at the end of his bed bearing a tray of freshly cut mangoes and black coffee.

"I made us breakfast," she said.

For the first time their lovemaking felt pointless and forced, as if a memory of Isabella had slipped into bed beside them. After watching a bootleg DVD of *Troy*, Megan left the apartment at midday and Joe paced the rooms, the afternoon passing with a geological slowness. He fixed a leaking tap in the bathroom; he went running in Xujiahui Park; he read the same paragraph of the same article in the *Pharmaceutical Journal* eight times. How would Isabella react to seeing him? With indifference? With studied cool? He couldn't bear the prospect of a polite, bourgeois dinner where she asked meaningful questions about "Iraq and the war" while Miles joked about "the good old days in Hong Kong." He wanted Isabella to himself. He wanted to connect with her again.

Finally, as the sun went down behind the London plane trees of the French Concession, Joe took a shower and changed for dinner. It was six-thirty. Within two hours he would be sitting at a table making conversation with the woman who had colonized his thoughts for the best part of a decade. Pouring himself a drink, he settled in a deep armchair, took out his copy of *Gatsby* and finished it just before half-past seven.

So we beat on, boats against the current, borne back ceaselessly into the past.

The traffic running east along Yan'an Road was as slow as the midweek rush hour and Joe was twenty minutes late arriving at M on the Bund. A bald Italian steered him through the glittering dining room to a table on the crowded outdoor terrace which appeared to have been set for only four people. Shahpour was already in situ with his back to the Bund, looking crisp and laundered, but with a certain nervous intensity in his eyes. A cool breeze was blowing south along the river. Miles was seated opposite him and clambered to his feet as Joe came towards them.

"Joe. Buddy. Great to see you." He was wearing a black Polo shirt and his voice boomed around the terrace. "I believe you two have already met."

Shahpour also stood up to shake his hand. He looked more anxious and somehow far younger than Joe remembered from the club.

"Yeah, we met in Zapata's," he said. "Nice to see you again."

Joe scanned the two vacant places. Where was Isabella? Both napkins were still folded onto white ceramic plates with the chairs neatly pushed in. Making the obvious calculation, he realized that she was not going to be coming to the restaurant. The day had been a prolonged anti-climax. Sensing his confusion, Miles said simply, "Izzy couldn't make it," and Joe felt a terrible gnaw of disappointment. "What happened to your date?"

"Ditto. Last-minute crisis."

He wondered what had gone on behind the scenes. Joe had had no intention of inviting Megan and supposed that Miles had also lied about his plans. Did Isabella even know that he was living in Shanghai? That thought, in itself, was enough to drive him crazy with frustration. Yet the alternative was even worse: that Isabella knew of his presence in the city, but had told Miles she had no desire to see an ex-boyfriend who had lied to her throughout every moment of their relationship. Joe settled into his seat and ordered a vodka and tonic.

"So I guess it's just the three of us," he said.

At least it was a glorious evening on the Huangpu. Miles had secured one of the finest views in all Shanghai. From his chair, Joe could look directly across the river at the high-rise lightshow of Pudong while, ahead of him, the grand fluorescent curve of the Bund arced north towards Suzhou Creek. Long ago he had concluded that Asian cities were at their best at night: the chemistry of heat and neon was exhilarating. He lit a cigarette as two young Chinese waiters mournfully cleared away the empty space in which he had longed to find Isabella.

"So tell us about her."

"About who?"

"Megan," Miles said.

Joe looked at Shahpour, who had been drinking steadily since he arrived. Candlelight caught a look of disquiet on his face which suggested to Joe that he was either out of his depth or struggling to suppress feelings of anxiety. Hastily, Shahpour described his meeting with Megan and Joe in Zapata's, a story that Miles appeared to have heard before. There were predictable jokes about "sharking for chicks" and Joe was glad when his vodka arrived, sinking half of it almost immediately to quench his thirst. He had given some thought to the reasons behind Shahpour's presence at the dinner. It was possible that he was authentic Microsoft, and therefore a useful ally for Miles in trying to prove the legitimacy of his cover. More likely, however, Shahpour was also CIA and Miles had brought him along as a second pair of eyes. Yet he wondered why a trained intelligence officer would appear at a meeting of such importance looking so edgy. In Zapata's, Shahpour had seemed impressively self-assured, if somewhat vain and intense, and Joe had been struck by both his intelligence and charm. Either this current mood was an act, the purpose of which would eventually be revealed, or Miles had said something which had momentarily undermined his confidence. If that was the case, it certainly wouldn't have been the first time that Miles had belittled a junior colleague.

"So what do you make of Shanghai?" Miles asked. He might have been talking to a tourist just off a long-haul from Heathrow. A few feet behind him, the red flag of China was fluttering in an infrequent breeze and Joe reflected on the irony of the restaurant's predominantly Western clientele quaffing Martinis and New World Chardonnays beneath an icon of communist repression.

"It's like a frontier town, isn't it?" he said, lighting a cigarette. "I've been impressed with almost everybody I've met. People are ambitious here, sometimes reckless, but the intelligence and energy of the average person you come across is amazing."

"Han or *laowai*?"

"Both," Joe replied. "This is Shanghai's moment, isn't it? The feeling of tens of thousands of people—Chinese and foreigners—converging on a single city in search of fame and fortune."

"Try millions," Miles replied, as if he were only interested in correcting Joe's mistakes. Shahpour fixed his gaze at a point beyond Joe's head and broke his silence.

"I think it's a city of contradictions," he said, touching the gold necklace at his throat. "You got rich and poor, locals and *laowai*, the cultured and the hedonistic. All of it existing side by side. It's amazing like that."

Was he stoned? Joe looked at his eyes, dark and swimming, then down at the tense, sculpted jaw. There was evident awkwardness in Shahpour's relationship with Miles, yet the imbalance between them was so pronounced that Joe began to suspect an element of theatre. "So Miles is your boss?" he asked, trying to draw out more background.

"That's right. Got me my job, actually. I was working in construction out here and he hired me. Tell me about Quayler."

The immediate change of subject was telling: Shahpour was uncomfortable under questioning, as if he knew that Joe could quickly unravel his cover. Joe duly broke into his rote speech on

pharmaceuticals, a performance with which his dining compan-
ions seemed predictably bored.

"Gaining sixteen per cent every year, huh?" Joe had finished
talking about sector growth.

"That's right. Sixteen per cent."

Shahpour saved them. "So how do you guys know each
other?"

"We met long ago in Hong Kong." Here at last was a subject
about which Miles could talk for hours.

"We were good friends."

"Still are," he barked, resting a hand on Joe's back.

"Miles was always very enthusiastic about doing business with
China." The grip and sweat of his hand was like a dead weight on
Joe's shoulders. "I'm not surprised he's lasted as long as he has out
here."

Miles frowned at what was an accurate if harmless observation,
and promptly withdrew his arm. An Australian waitress brought
three menus to their table and began discussing the specials. Joe
ordered seared tuna as a starter followed by fillet steak and went to
the bathroom to wash his hands. He wondered if Miles had
watchers keeping an eye on him in the restaurant. Setting his cellphone to vibrate, he checked his reflection in the mirror, his
thoughts returning time and again to Isabella. He had believed that
they were only moments from seeing one another; her absence
from the dinner was like a broken promise. His work in Shanghai,
he realized, was dangerously entwined in the possibility of their
reunion; there were times when Joe felt that he could not rest, nor
make progress, without knowing, one way or the other, if they had
a future together. Was he mad even to think such things? How was
it that a person so calm and objective in every other area of his life
was held captive by this unrequited desire? He wanted answers. He
wanted hope, or to be free of her and to move on.

Back on the terrace, Joe found three glasses of Chablis on the
table and Miles waxing lyrical about the moral bankruptcy of Chinese businessmen. Shahpour seemed slightly more alert.

"You're just in time," Miles said with mock weariness.

"In time for what?"

"In time to hear me tell young Shahpour here that China will never succeed on the international stage until the guys doing business learn some manners."

"Manners?" Joe said, placing his napkin on his lap.

"That's right. The people here have no respect for us, no interest in our history, no understanding of our culture."

"Which culture would that be?"

"Mine." Miles swallowed an inch of wine and wiped his beard. "Let me tell you something about the Chinese, Shahpour. Joe, back me up here. For every man, woman and child in this country, it's about making money. Nothing else matters."

"You've changed your tune."

"What do you mean?"

"Ten years ago you were all for it. Let's make as much dough in China as we can, and to hell with the consequences."

"That's because ten years ago I hadn't experienced Chinese business practices at first hand." Miles didn't look too pleased to have been tripped up by forgotten memories of Hong Kong. He directed his next remark at Shahpour. "Fact is the Cultural Revolution stripped out individuality as you or I would understand it. So what are we left with? An organized, upwardly mobile, dedicated workforce that will stop at nothing to get what they want."

"The American dream," Shahpour muttered. Joe was beginning to like him.

"Don't be a smart ass." Miles gestured towards the glistening gold façade of the Aurora building. "Look at this place. Look at Pudong. What's it built on?"

"Marshland?" Joe suggested. The vodka was beginning to take effect and he had decided to try to enjoy himself.

"I'll tell you what it's built on. Corruption and lies." Shahpour caught Joe's eye and there was a shared beat of understanding between them. Both had sat through Miles Coolidge monologues many times before. "A Chinese real-estate developer comes along, he pays a bribe to a city official, then the police forcibly remove all the residents from the area on his behalf. Any people refuse, the developer sends in hired thugs who break their hands. This is happening right across China. Farmers ordered off their land with no compensation. Peasant workers who've been farming the same ten acres all their lives suddenly told to move fifty kilometres away where there's no agriculture, no community, no jobs. If they complain, they get fined or jailed. Then up goes a high-rise development built on soil they'd been working for generations. And who gets the profits? The developer."

Joe was stunned. In Hong Kong, Miles would have described such injustice as the natural consequences of rapid economic growth. Is that what TYPHOON had done to him? Had he developed a conscience?

"Is this your standard line at the moment?" he said.

"What do you mean?"

"In the old days, you always had a theory on every subject. You were like a politician on the stump, trotting out a favourite speech to anyone who would listen."

Miles did not seem offended. "You wanna talk politics? You wanna talk about capitalism with Chinese characteristics?" Most of Miles Coolidge's questions were rhetorical and he certainly wasn't expecting an answer to that one. He gestured towards the infinite skyscrapers of Pudong. "This is what it looks like. It looks like apartments that sell for a hundred dollars per square foot and fuck the men that died building them. Modern China is an entity of supercities built on the sweat of migrant workers who get paid less than ten bucks a day for doing it and told to sleep in a room the size of my bathtub. That's what they call progress here."

"What's your point?" Joe asked.

"My point, Joe, is that morality, the Judeo-Christian principle of love thy neighbor, is an alien concept to the Chinese."

"Well, I should be OK then," said Shahpour.

"How's that?"

"I'm Muslim."

That stopped the conversation dead. Joe sipped his wine and grinned at the Bund. Miles made an embarrassing remark about "how we're all trying to forget that" and struggled on. "Will somebody listen to what I'm saying, please?" He drained his Chablis. Their starters arrived and Joe began eating. His tuna had been rolled in sesame seeds which crunched between his teeth. "The

Chinese have no natural sympathy for their fellow man. Once you understand that, anything is possible."

"If you say so, Miles. If you say so."

In Joe's experience, there were two default conversations whenever groups of Western men gathered for dinner in China. The first, which usually took place in the earlier part of an evening, was a complex if largely theoretical discussion about the future of the country. Would China become the great economic superpower that the West had long feared, or would the economy overheat and go the way of the other Asian tigers? Had Beijing been wise to buy up $300 billion of US debt, and could America afford to pay it back? Would the country's increasingly well-educated, Westernized middle class eventually topple the communist government, having tired of the endemic corruption and repression of the one-party state, or were the great mass of Chinese too obedient, perhaps even too savvy, to undermine the political status quo? Miles ticked almost every one of these conversational boxes as the dinner continued, and Joe eventually realized that little had changed: the man who had taken Isabella from him was just as stubborn, just as confused and cynical about China as he had always been. One minute he was writing off an entire race on the basis that they didn't think like Americans; the next he was siding with disenfranchised Chinese workers because their plight handed him a convenient stick with which to rail at Beijing. Close his eyes and Joe could have been back at Rico's, defending Governor Patten against the latest Coolidge onslaught, or listening to one of his stock speeches about "the fucking futility of communism." Yet was there really that much difference between their two positions? Joe was equally jaded about the government in Beijing. He despaired for a country so contemptuous of its own citizens. But at least he *loved* China; at least he could see that to impose Western values on a country as complex and as historically damaged as the Middle Kingdom was a policy every bit as lunatic as the invasion of Iraq. Miles, on the other hand, had nothing but contempt for the place: his enthusiasm for TYPHOON, for example, had not been born of a desire to free the Uighurs of Xinjiang, or the migrant workers of Gansu, from the shackles of totalitarian repression; it had been born of a desire to undermine China, to bring bloodshed to the streets, and to profit from the ensuing chaos.

For his part, Shahpour remained on the periphery of the conversation, drinking heavily and offering only the occasional contribution to the intellectual slanging match taking place in front of him. At first, Joe put this down to a younger man's natural reticence in the presence of two age-old rivals. As the evening progressed, however, he began to sense that Shahpour shared few of his master's beliefs; indeed, he referred affectionately to his "many Chinese friends" and spoke with admiration of the way the country had "pulled itself up by its own bootstraps" in the previous fifteen years. It simply didn't make sense that Shahpour could be fighting alongside Miles on the same fool's errand as TYPHOON. Besides, surely Langley would have preferred to have one of their few Farsi-speaking officers operating in Iran? Maybe Shahpour was Microsoft after all.

The second default conversation, which usually takes place towards the end of dinner, concerns sex. Unsurprisingly, if unwittingly, it was Miles who instigated it when the mobile phone resting on the table beside him lit up and produced the opening bars of the "Battle Hymn of the Republic." Joe had just finished eating his main course. He could hear a woman's voice at the other end of the line when Miles picked up. He was certain that it was Isabella until Miles began replying in Mandarin and aimed a conspiratorial look at Shahpour.

"I gotta take this. Work," he said, and stood up from the table.

As he walked off the terrace, Shahpour leaned forward and said, "You know who that was, don't you?"

"Who?"

"His *ernai*."

Ernai is a Mandarin term for mistress or concubine. Shahpour's candour surprised Joe but he maintained an expression of vague disinterest. "Really? How do you know?"

"Her name is Linda. She has her own special ring. When she calls, you get the 'Battle Hymn of the Republic.' When it's work, you get the CTU phone from *24*. If his wife ever phones up, it's the training anthem from *Rocky*."

Joe found himself laughing, even as he noted that Zhao Jian had been correct about Linda's identity. "How long have they been seeing each other?"

"How do I know? Guy's some kind of sex addict. I never saw anything like it, not even by Asian standards. No disrespect to his wife, right, but Miles is running chicks all over town."

It was well past ten o'clock. The terrace was still packed with diners, most of whom had donned jackets or sweaters against the chill of the late evening. Cargo ships were moaning on the Huangpu. The lights of Pudong were as romantic and as breathtaking as any sight in China and Shahpour Goodarzi was casually shopping his boss to the Secret Intelligence Service.

"He doesn't try to keep any of this under wraps?"

Shahpour looked confused. "Why would he? He's not *British*, Joe. Every other guy in this restaurant probably has a chick shacked up in an apartment in Gubei. You know how things work over here." He ran a finger along the surface of the table. "Still, I gotta say that Miles is operating at a whole other level. He's tried to screw every Chinese girl from here to Beijing. One of my buddies calls him an MBA."

"What's that?"

"Married but available."

Joe laughed, because he knew that it was vital to appear unfazed by what Shahpour was telling him. The more relaxed he appeared, the more information he would be able to glean. "So Isabella knows?" he asked.

Shahpour shrugged. He was aware that Joe and Isabella had once been involved, but was clearly working on the assumption that Joe no longer harboured feelings for her. "I have no idea what she knows. I've never met her. I'm not even sure they still live together."

The revelation sent a fizz of satisfaction through Joe's body. That would explain why Jian had never photographed her. He offered Shahpour a cigarette, which the American lit from the candle at the edge of the table. His eyes caught Miles coming back from the restaurant's interior and Joe turned to find a rather forced look of regret on his face.

"Guys. I got a problem."

He was behind Joe's chair. The hot dead weight of his hand again.

"What's that?" Shahpour seemed to have anticipated what was coming.

"Goddam conference call from Redmond, starting in thirty minutes. I have to get to the office."

Joe balled his napkin onto the table and grinned in a way that was visible only to Shahpour. A waitress was clearing away their plates. "You have to leave?"

"'Fraid so. But listen, it shouldn't take long. Maybe I can catch you guys later? We got a lot of catching up to do. Shahpour, will you take care of this? Put it on Gates?"

"Yes, sir."

And with that he was gone, shaking Joe's hand and slipping off into the night. It seemed extraordinary that Miles should choose a few hours with Linda over the opportunity to probe more deeply into Joe's cover. His departure had either been prearranged, as part of a rather obvious American trap, or Miles was still as craven and as selfish as he had ever been. Zhao Jian had a fixed camera outside Linda's apartment complex which would at least provide Joe with evidence of whether he was telling the truth.

"Coffee?" he suggested, because he was tired after the sleepless night and needed a jolt to his wits.

"Sure. That'd be great."

He waved the waitress over, ordered two espressos and lit a cigarette. Shahpour had settled back in his chair, visibly relaxing in the absence of his boss. Two red kites appeared in the night sky above his head, the ropes attaching them to the ground invisible to the naked eye.

"So does he do that sort of thing a lot?"

"What? Take off like that? Sure. I've sat in on meetings where Miles excuses himself for an hour, gets a massage and comes back smelling of Chanel No. 5. He calls it 'sport fucking.'"

"What does Isabella call it?"

Shahpour acknowledged his point with a nod and said, "So what about you?"

"What about me?"

"What's your story with Megan? Is that serious? Is it something you hope might develop?"

Two hours earlier, Shahpour would not have dared ask such a question, but it was an indication both of how much alcohol he had consumed, and of his growing confidence in Joe's company, that he was now prepared to do so.

"It's early days," Joe replied. "I hope she was nice to you in Zapata's."

Shahpour exhaled smoke through a broad, self-confident smile. "That was funny that night. I'm sorry if I offended you."

"Not at all. To be perfectly honest, Megan and I weren't together at that point. In fact I'd only just met her."

"And yet she ends up talking to the one guy in the room who knows Miles Coolidge."

"I know. Amazing coincidence."

"Was it?"

The air went out of the conversation. Shahpour lowered his cigarette and fixed Joe with a look of such intensity that it forced his eyes to the table.

"Was it what?"

Everything was sober and still.

"Was it just coincidence?"

There are many ways that a spy is trained to deal with the unexpected, but mostly he must rely on his own judgment and common sense. Joe had been startled by what Shahpour had said, certainly, but he was not about to fold under pressure. He looked down at the fleets of ships on the Huangpu, boats so weighed down by cargo that they resembled submarines nosing south towards the East China Sea.

"You think I was trying to get to Miles?"

The American leaned forward. His gold necklace rocked against the base of his throat and Joe could see the sincerity, the seriousness which was at the very core of his character. What was striking was not so much the intensity of Shahpour's mood, but the sudden air of expectancy about him, as if he was trying to broker an understanding. He had about him the air of a man who wished to confess something.

"That's what Miles thinks," he said.

Joe dismissed the theory with a practised look of astonishment. "Miles still thinks I work for the British government?"

"Do you still work for the British government?"

"No."

Shahpour looked around him. The terrace was beginning to empty. He appeared to be weighing up the risks of his next re-mark. There were clearly consequences to what he was about to say and he did not wish to be overheard.

"What I'm about to tell you could get me fired."

"Then maybe you shouldn't tell me."

He leaned forward. "I'm like you used to be, Joe. Deep cover. I'm a NOC. I don't work for Microsoft." It was the drink talking. Alcohol and circumstance had handed a nervous, inexperienced spy the chance to confide in a colleague whose word he thought he could trust. "Same goes for our so-called buddy. Miles Coolidge knows as much about software as my Uncle Ahmed. We're both Company. We're both undercover. Miles has told me everything about your past."

"Shahpour, you shouldn't be telling me this. I am not who you think I am. I'm not with the Office any more . . ."

"Well, you see I just don't believe that." Joe's denial had been persuasively sincere, but Shahpour was sticking to his strategy. "I think you're here because of what happened to Ken. I think you're here because you know what we did to him."

"You're talking about Kenneth Lenan?"

Joe was mesmerized by the confession of CIA culpability in his murder, but there was barely a blink of surprise.

"Of course that's who I'm talking about. You wanna know why he was killed?"

Joe said nothing.

Shahpour wiped his mouth on a napkin. "Kenneth Lenan

worked for us, OK? He came over. Six months ago he gave up a Uighur CIA asset to the MSS because he had conflicted loyalties with his bank balance. Lenan identified the Agency officer who had recruited that asset out of Guantanamo and told the MSS where he was living in San Francisco. That officer got his body dismembered by a Triad gang in Chinatown."

"Shahpour, you're being unprofessional . . ."

Goodarzi shook his head. "The officer's name was Josh Pinnegar. You're telling me you never heard of him?"

"That's exactly what I'm telling you." Joe was trying to keep his mood light and detached, but the flood of information, confirming every detail of Waterfield's TYPHOON product, was breathtaking. "I work for a small pharmaceutical company because I got tired of this sort of—"

"Don't lie to me, man." There was a risk that Shahpour might shut down. Joe had to keep him talking. "My career is on the line here. My life. Now you came to me, Joe. I know why you've come to Shanghai. I know what it is that you need and I want to help you."

What perplexed Joe about Shahpour's entreaty was its extraordinary sincerity. He knew, with the vivid conviction of a blameless man proclaiming his innocence, that the American was telling him the truth. Somehow it couldn't be any other way. Yet Joe could not risk the obvious possibility that RUN was being flushed out as part of a clumsy, second-rate plot. He had to believe that Shahpour was putting on an elaborate performance.

"I can help you," he said. What was the best way of proceeding? He did not want to let go of the rope which now connected them. "I know British officials in China who will talk to you about this. I can put you in touch with—"

"I want it to be *you*."

"I'm out." For the first time, Joe raised his voice, as if he was offended by the repeated accusation. He had to play the role. He had to stay in character. "I've handed in my notice. I don't have the keys to the shop any more. I'm private sector. Why do you think I'd be any use to you?"

"Forget it then."

Their waitress had been waiting for a natural pause in the

conversation and she now approached the table as Shahpour turned and stared at the lights of Pudong. The espressos were placed on the table and Joe spooned sugar into his cup as he hit on a possible tactic. Somehow he had to draw Shahpour out without compromising his own position.

"Listen, what do you expect me to say? If I'd come out here under operational cover, I'd hardly be likely to blow that cover on the basis of what you've just told me. Why are you doing this? Why would you be so uneasy?"

A burst of sulphurous pollution drifted over the terrace, yet it did not disturb Shahpour from his mood. He continued to stare out over the river like a scolded teenager. It was as if he had played his final hand and there was nobody left to confide in. Then, a breakthrough.

"I'll tell you why." He was speaking into a southern breeze which took his quiet words out over the water. "I joined the Agency in the new year of 2002. I did it because I believed in America. I did it because I believed that I would be an asset to my country, that I could help prevent what had happened to us happening again." Now he turned, and Joe saw the disillusionment in his young eyes, the conflict of a decent man. "My father came to the United States in 1974. He had a place to study engineering at a college in Detroit, Michigan. You know how he came to choose Detroit?" Joe shook his head. "He was from Sari, a city on the southern shore of the Caspian Sea. He looked at a map of America, he saw a big blue lake with a city right beside it, and he thought it looked like home."

Shahpour turned, scraped his chair towards the table and sank his espresso in a sharp, controlled flick.

"When he arrived there, he saw that it was a good summer and that he'd made a good choice. Then the winter came. He'd never seen snow before, never seen ice on the roads. He had an uncle in Sacramento who invited him over to California. And what does my dad find? That it's seventy degrees outside in the middle of winter. So he finishes his degree, he moves to Sacramento, he gets a job cleaning dishes in my great-uncle's pizza parlor. But my dad was smarter than the other guys, you know? He worked hard and started up his own place, his own restaurant. Today he's a millionaire. He has six children, a grandson, five properties in three different states. He owns twenty-five pizza delivery outlets in the California area."

"American dream," Joe said. Shahpour silenced him with a raised hand.

"I'm not trying to sell you America," he said. "I'm not trying to sell you an ideal. I know that our country has its faults. But I could see past them, you know? I still can. I joined up because I wanted to make a difference, to show that a child of Iran could deal in something more than hate."

"I can understand that."

Shahpour looked relieved. "I think you can," he said. The cry of a bird went up over the Huangpu River. "Everybody heard about what you did, Joe. Everybody heard why you'd quit. I decided to talk to you because you have ideals, because you'll see the craziness of what's happening here. Because you're my best chance of getting out of this."

So that was it. Waterfield's plan had worked. The illusion of RUN's exit from Vauxhall Cross had convinced a compromised American spook that Joe Lennox was the answer to his prayers.

"Getting out of what?" To Joe's dismay, the waitress appeared again and punctured the conversation at a vital moment. Shahpour stared back at the entrance to the restaurant, as if to reassure himself that Miles was nowhere to be seen. "Getting out of what?" Joe said again. It had struck him, not for the first time, that at the tender age of thirty-four he was now regarded as a wise old hand by men who looked as young as he still felt.

"Getting out of what's happening."

"And what is that? What is happening?"

Shahpour twisted his narrow body to face Joe. He lowered his head. It was as if the open air could not bear the burden of such a heavy secret. Then he leaned towards Joe and looked up into his eyes. "Miles is planning something." He was whispering. "It has Pentagon approval, covert CIA backing. Funded through Saudi channels. An operation here, on mainland China. We have a Uighur cell asleep in Shanghai which may hit multiple targets this summer."

"Then you have to go to the police," Joe said immediately, because the role of a responsible citizen was the simplest role to play. "You have to go to your superiors. You have to try to stop that from happening."

"How can I? What can I do? I can't betray my country."

Isn't that what you're doing now, Joe thought. Abruptly, all of the neon, on both sides of the river, every brand and logo from Puxi to Pudong, blacked out. The terrace was cast into near darkness.

"Eleven o'clock," Shahpour said, without looking at his watch. "Happens every night."

"Answer my question," Joe said.

"What question?"

"Why don't you find a way of alerting the authorities?"

Shahpour actually smiled. "Don't you get it?" he said. "*You're* my way of alerting the authorities. I've thought of everything else, every possible way that won't come back and make me look like a traitor. I even tried with Wang, for Chrissakes. Last time I was in Beijing I spent five hours trying to persuade him to go to the MSS and tell them what was happening."

"Wang Kaixuan?"

Shahpour stopped. "Of course," he said, as if he had forgotten a vital piece in the puzzle. "You were the first person to meet him, weren't you? That's quite a serious mark on your résumé, Joe."

"Professor Wang Kaixuan?" Joe said again, because he needed time to think. "What does he have to do with this?"

Calling for the bill, Shahpour spent ten minutes outlining Wang's role in TYPHOON, an account of the operation so close in character to Waterfield's own descriptions that Joe began to suspect that Shahpour was London's source at Langley.

"And now he's in Beijing?" he said, the only question he allowed himself to ask about Wang's predicament. "You've seen him up there?"

"Sure." Shahpour seemed bored by the detail. "Teaches Chinese to corporate suits at one of those language schools in Haidian. He doesn't want anything to do with me. He doesn't want anything to do with Miles. For professional purposes he's changed his name to Liu Gongyi. Says he's lost faith in the concept of armed struggle. But the only people he hates more than Americans are the Chinese, so he won't tell them about the cell."

Language school? Joe remembered that Macklinson had set up free language schools on construction sites as a means of recruiting disenchanted labourers. Were the two connected, or was this yet more obvious bait? "And who's in the cell?" he asked, his desire for information briefly causing him to forget that he was supposed to be playing the role of a disinterested observer.

"What do you care?" Shahpour had poured himself the last of the wine, which he finished in three long gulps. "Uighurs. Kazakhs. Guys with nothing to lose." The wine caught in his throat and he coughed. "All I know is that in Christmas 2002 I was getting ready to move to Tehran when I was told to pack my bags for China. Have SIS check me out if you're in any doubt. My real name is Shahpour Moazed. My father's name is Hamid Moazed. I also have an American name—Mark—because that's what all good Iranian-American boys do so that they can get along in California. Ask your people in London to check the employee register at Macklinson Corporation. They'll tell you that a Mark Moazed was working in Xi'an between 2002 and 2004. What they won't be able to tell you is that the CIA spent three years routing weapons and explosives through Macklinson to Uighur separatists who blew up innocent women and children all over China. What they won't be able to tell you is that I spent two years trying to clean up the mess. Tell them to give Microsoft a call while they're doing that. They'll tell you that Mark Moazed joined them late last year. They might even be surprised to learn that two of their employees are in league with clandestine elements within the Pentagon and have recruited a cell of Islamist radicals prepared to kill hundreds of innocent people in Shanghai. And why? Why have we decided to do this? Why am I dedicating my life to an operation with no value or purpose or principle? I really have no idea at all."

39 | PERSUASION

As soon as he left the restaurant, Joe took a cab back to his apartment, telephoned Waterfield on a secure line and gave him chapter and verse on Shahpour's extraordinary gamble.

"It's a trap," Waterfield said when he had finished, and Joe knew that he would now be alone. Whatever he told them, London would never believe that Shahpour Moazed had just dropped out of the sky to make a hero of Joe Lennox. "Think about it," Waterfield said. "I know you want product, Joe. I know you're looking for answers. But this is too simple. He's a poisoned pawn."

Joe was not a chess player and ignored the metaphor. "So you don't think Miles had Lenan killed?"

"I didn't say that."

"You don't think there's a cell planning a hit in Shanghai?"

"I didn't say that either."

"Then what are you saying? It seems perfectly obvious to me that Miles couldn't give a flying fuck what I'm up to out here. He has bigger things on his mind. I sent a text to Zhao Jian on my way home. Guess what? Miles really did leave in the middle of dinner so he could get his cock sucked in Gubei. That's how much my presence in Shanghai means to him. He doesn't care that we might find out what happened to Ken. What are we going to do? Arrest him? Run crying to Washington? The Office is irrelevant in all this. A bit-part player. Even if half of what Shahpour just told me is correct, this thing has taken on its own momentum and is going to happen, with or without British interference."

There was a long silence. Joe sensed that he had found a route through Waterfield's objections, but he was mistaken.

"Let's suppose that it is true. How do you know the cell isn't penetrated? Every other Miles Coolidge operation in China has gone tits up. What's so different about this one? The man has an inverse Midas touch. Besides, Cousins don't suddenly walk off the plantation and start baring their souls. Your American friends were trying to provoke exactly this sort of reaction. They'll be watching you from now on. They'll want to find out whether you respond to what you've been told. This is basic stuff. Page one."

"Then at the very least let's try to find Wang."

"No. Aren't you listening to me? They'll have eyes all over him. You try to flush Wang, you'll draw MSS, CIA, and God knows how many other services into a shitstorm of unimaginable proportions. Leave well alone. Your assignment is to get close to Coolidge. Your operation is to discover how much local liaison knew about Lenan's activities and whether they can be traced back to London. Now I have to go into a meeting."

"David, with the greatest respect, those are side issues now . . ."

"I said I have to go into a meeting. You're obviously very tired, Joe. It's late out there. Get some sleep."

Joe heard the hollow click of Waterfield hanging up and shook his head with frustration. He was sitting at his desk in the second bedroom of his apartment, which he had turned into a makeshift office. The walls were uncovered save for a large National Geographic map of China and a pin board onto which Joe had tacked documents relating to Quayler. The conversation with Waterfield had served only to remind him of the pettiness and obstructive bureaucracy which had characterized the Office in recent years. Where was Waterfield's willingness to take a risk? What was the purpose of Joe's being in Shanghai if not to discover what America was up to? Taking a drawing pin out of the board, he pushed it repeatedly into the soft wooden surface of his desk and felt the utter frustration of his solitary trade. He would never make progress. He would never see Isabella. Joe was convinced that Shahpour was telling the truth, that he was trying to find a way of destabilizing the cell which would bring dishonour neither upon himself nor upon the American government. But how to convince Waterfield of that when he was thousands of miles away?

Just before 2:30 in the morning, with a glass of whisky at his side, Joe sent me a text message in Beijing. He had made the decision to ignore Waterfield and to follow his instincts. If he was wrong, so be it; he was deniable to London. If he was right, Waterfield could take credit for his foresight in sending RUN to Shanghai.

I was sitting in the lounge bar of the Kerry Centre Hotel with a government official who was helping me with a story I was writing about the Olympics. A group of Japanese businessmen were sitting on the sofa next to mine drinking Californian Merlots and watching coverage of a golf tournament on ESPN. Jumbo Osaki sank a monster putt at the seventeenth and a roar went up as my phone beeped.

"Ring your sister," the message said, and I experienced one of those strange, out-of-body surges which are the perks of life as a support agent. Making my excuses, I took a cab back to my apartment, found a clean SIM and called Joe in Shanghai.

His instructions were simple: to find Professor Wang Kaixuan. He was teaching English as a foreign language at one of the schools in Haidian district. What was the name of the school? Where was it located?

As tasks go, it was not particularly taxing, certainly for a reporter of long and weary experience in investigative journalism. A quick search of the internet provided me with an exhaustive list of language schools in the Beijing metropolitan area and I simply cold-called each and every one of them in Haidian throughout the course of the next morning. Joe had given me a simple cover story: to pretend that I was a former student in Mr. Liu Gongyi's class who wanted to send him a book through the post. Predictably enough, the first eighteen receptionists insisted that they had nobody of that name teaching at their school and that I had dialled an incorrect number. The nineteenth school, however, was only too happy to provide me with a full postal address and were certain that "Mr. Liu" would be delighted to receive his gift.

I called Joe with the good news.

"Not bad for an ageing hack with a drink problem," he said. "I'm coming to Beijing."

40 | BEIJING

Fourteen hours later, the old Shanghai sleeper rumbled into Beijing station like a faithful dog. I was waiting at the end of the platform with a cup of coffee and saw Joe emerge from the train in conversation with a stewardess who had her hair in a bun. She laughed at something he said as weary passengers disembarked all around them. Then Joe caught my eye and shook her by the hand, rolling his suitcase towards me like the anonymous, nondescript pharmaceuticals salesman he was supposed to be.

"Nice day for the time of year."

"Welcome to Peking, Mr. Lennox."

We escaped the pressing crowds in the great vault of the old station and went into a virtually deserted shopping mall nearby, where I told Joe what I knew: that I had been to the language school the previous evening and discovered that Wang gave classes every afternoon, Monday to Friday, beginning at two o'clock and ending at five. Joe was noticeably more intense than he had been on my recent visit to Shanghai, and seemed to be calculating moves and implications all the time. At this early stage, he said very little about his dinner with Miles and Shahpour and nothing at all about the cell. As far as he was concerned, I was just a support agent of the Secret Intelligence Service doing the job that I was paid to do. It was neither my concern, nor my particular business, to know anything more than I needed to. At such times, Joe had a way of keeping our friendship at arm's length and I knew not to press him on operational details. There was a lot at stake, after all. For a start, RUN would almost certainly be blown if Joe was observed talking to Wang; if Waterfield found out about it, he would be called home. Looking back on the two eventful days that followed, it occurs to me that Joe still didn't know to what extent Wang was involved in separatist activities. In spite of what Shahpour had told him, there was still a more than plausible chance that he was an American agent. If that was the case, Joe was ruined.

"There are known knowns," he said, lightening the mood with a joke as we walked to his hotel on Jianguomen Road. It was a typically hot, dry spring day in the capital, traffic and cyclists warring on the wide, featureless streets. "There are things we know that we know. There are things that we know we don't know. But there are also unknown unknowns."

Two days had passed since the dinner at M on the Bund, a period in which Joe had laid the foundations for his trip to Beijing. On his way to the railway station in Shanghai, for example, he had carried out a two-hour counter-surveillance exercise designed to flush out any American watchers before he departed for the capital. On the train itself, he had called Guy Coates from the dining car to arrange a meeting at the nascent Quayler representative office in Beijing, just in case Miles had put eyes on it. He then stayed up most of the night on the top bunk of his four-berth compartment listening once again to the recording of the safe house interrogation with Wang. All of this was a way of preparing himself for their inevitable second encounter. There might be clues in the conversation; there might be leads.

I am regarded as a political undesirable, a threat to the Motherland. My actions as an academic drew me to the attention of the authorities in Xinjiang, who jailed me along with many of my students.

The plan to get to Wang was straightforward: to keep a watch on the entrance of the Agosto Language School on Yuanda Road and to follow him to a point where Joe could make secure contact. Given that SIS Station in Beijing had been told, along with everybody else in the intelligence fraternity, that Joe Lennox had quit the Service, we could not call on the British embassy for additional operational support. Nor was Zhao Jian available: Joe had left him and his brothers in Shanghai with instructions to gather more information about Shahpour Moazed and Ansary Tursun. Besides, Joe couldn't risk a rumour filtering back to Vauxhall Cross that three of their finest Shanghai pavement artists had suddenly been called to Beijing. So it was to be just the two of us, a pair of white faces in a crowded sea of Chinese, trying to follow a renegade academic with years of counter-surveillance experience in one of the busiest and most populous cities on earth. I had long ago received basic training in foot surveillance at a course in Bristol, but Joe knew that I was out of practice; indeed, if the truth be told, I don't think he fancied our chances that much. On the Tuesday evening, after he had sat through what he characterized as a "skull-numbing" meeting at Quayler, we met for dinner at Li Qun, a Peking duck restaurant off Qianmen East Road, and Joe could speak about little else but the task which lay ahead of us.

"We have to be prepared for every eventuality," he said. "Does Wang ride a bike? Has he got a car? Does he live within walking distance of the school or, more likely, is he going to want to get on a bus and ride across the city? This is how it's going to work. He knows what I look like so I can't get close to him. You, on the other hand, can be standing outside the school entrance with a bike speaking to me on the phone when he comes out. I'll identify him for you and we can work it from there. We've got to hope he has some kind of hat on, or a distinguishing characteristic in his dress, because he's going to get lost in the rush-hour crowds within seconds of being on the street. If he's on a bike or in a car, you'll have to try to stay on his tail. Don't worry about getting too close—it's normal to ride in packs and you'll get lost in the vehicles surrounding him. If he runs a red light, follow. If you sense that he's about to stop, try to get directly behind him so that he's not aware of a Caucasian hanging on his shoulder."

"What if he walks?"

"Take the bike but follow on foot. Again, try to anticipate when he's going to stop. Get on the opposite side of the road as much as you can. If he doubles back more than once, chances are he's conscious of you and will try to shake you at a choke point. But if he walks, it's probably because he's heading for a bus stop. If that's the case, hang well back and, once he gets on board, just tail the bus for as long as you can. I'll have a cab waiting on the corner outside the school. Once you have a good idea of the mode of transport he's using and the direction he's heading in, I'll follow in the vehicle. More than likely I'll try to get close to where you are and we can work him in parallel."

"How do you know the cab will stick around?" I asked, beginning to feel anxious about the demands Joe was placing on me. "Wang might not come out of the school for an hour. The driver could get itchy feet."

"Because I'll pay him to stick around," Joe said, as if my basic understanding of the pathology of taxi drivers needed fine-tuning. A ragged Chinese boy, no older than five or six, came into the restaurant and handed one of the waiters a few coins in exchange for a bagged-up duck carcass. His family would use it for soup. "Another thing," Joe said. "Charge your phones up overnight so they don't run out of juice."

"Phones?" I replied. "Plural?"

"We could be talking for up to three hours. If one of them drops, I need to know that I can reach you quickly. To blend in, wear a plain white T-shirt and a pair of sunglasses. If Wang turns round, you don't want him looking into your eyes."

This went on for another half-hour. Every angle was covered, every nuance of Wang's possible behaviour anticipated and thought through. Then Joe settled the bill and headed back to his hotel for an early night. The next morning he was at my apartment by eight and we travelled north to scout the immediate area around the language school. Feeling somewhat ridiculous, I practised cycling around while talking to Joe on the phone, using an earpiece and a microphone clipped to my shirt. By midday, I knew every bus stop, restaurant and traffic light within a two-block radius. That said, Haidian is the university district in Beijing and I did not feel that I knew the rest of the area particularly well. Having lived in the city for just a few months, I was still frequently spun round by the grid system of seemingly identical streets; there are very few landmarks in Beijing, no hills, nothing to give you a bearing. My worry was that Wang would vanish in a section of the city that I simply did not know or recognize. There were times when every corner in the capital looked the same. How would I then be able to give Wang's location to Joe, who might be five or six blocks away in a cab?

As things turned out, we got lucky. At 4:45 p.m. on the Wednesday, I leaned my bicycle against the exterior wall of the Agosto and dialled Joe's mobile. We were both using clean phones purchased the previous day. He was fifty metres away, on the opposite side of the street, sitting on a metal railing with a street map of Beijing open on his lap.

"You look like a tourist," I told him.

"And you look like a sad middle-aged man who can't afford to buy a decent bicycle."

It was a grey, smoggy day and there was plenty of traffic between us. When Wang came out, he would be unlikely to spot Joe through what amounted to a permanent, moving screen of dust and cars. The cab driver was waiting on the next corner, reckoning it was his lucky day, because Joe had picked him from five different drivers that he'd spoken to at the rank outside his hotel and handed him the equivalent of a hundred and fifty dollars to be his chauffeur-on-call all day. At about five to five, a gorgeous Chinese girl wearing a knee-length *qipao* walked past me and Joe made a joke about giving me the rest of the day off to follow her. I was grateful for his easy humour because it cut through the tension of the long wait. I was ashamed by how edgy I was feeling; at this early stage, to avoid drawing attention to myself, I had my phone in my hand and the hard plastic casing was sticky and damp against my ear.

"Not long now," Joe said. "Try to look as though you're waiting for your girlfriend. A lot of washed-up European perverts get lucky at foreign-language schools."

I looked across the street and Joe was smiling at me, looking extraordinarily relaxed; he'd done this sort of thing dozens of times before. Just then, the first of the students started trickling out of the entrance and he said "Here we go" in a way that made my pulse kick. About five of them hung around on the pavement in front of me, all Caucasians in their late twenties, and they were soon joined by a flood of others. This went on for about ten minutes until I was lost in a thick swarm of foreigners.

"I can't see you," Joe said. "That's good. Blend in. Try to keep the camouflage. And don't look at the door. When he comes out, I'll tell you."

I must confess that Professor Wang Kaixuan had become so mythologized in my imagination that I was half-expecting him to look like Pat Morita, the wizened martial arts guru who offers instruction to Ralph Macchio in *The Karate Kid*. I had said as much to Joe over dinner and he had attempted to describe Wang's basic physical characteristics.

"He's stocky and fit. At least he used to be. A broad face with smooth, dark skin. No distinguishing characteristics except intelligent, contemplative eyes, the sort that encourage young people to do things that they shouldn't be doing. I probably wasn't the last person to fall for them."

"And you say he's about sixty now?"

"About that. Might look younger."

Wang finally came out at five-fifteen. Joe recognized him instantly and I heard his voice quicken with excitement.

"OK, he's here. White, short-sleeved shirt. Black flannel trousers. Coming down the steps carrying a blue canvas bag over his shoulder. Stay where you are, Will. A student is going towards him. Tall black girl in the red T-shirt. A smile, he knows her. Looks like she's thanking him for his class. Our man seems very popular with the students. Apples all round for Professor Wang. He's facing in your direction now. His head is completely shaved . . ."

"I see him," I said.

Joe's commentary ran on as Wang loitered on the pavement in

front of me. He was no more than ten feet away. I kept him in my peripheral vision with my eyes on the entrance to the school, as if waiting for somebody to come out. Joe became increasingly certain that Wang was waiting for a lift.

"It probably won't be a taxi," he said. "Not on a teacher's salary."

Sure enough, after three or four minutes a dark blue Hafei Saima with Beijing plates, driven by a blonde woman who can't have been more than twenty-two or twenty-three, pulled up on the street in front of him.

"That girl came out ten minutes ago," Joe said quickly, and I was astonished by his powers of recall. "Probably one of his students. Let's bank on that. She's probably giving him a lift somewhere."

Wang was talking to a tall, extraordinarily ugly German with tattoos on his arms as the car came to a halt. He shook the German by the hand, said "Now go home and study" in Mandarin, and then ducked into the front seat. I looked across the street. Joe was already walking east towards his waiting cab. Both of us were muttering the Lord's Prayer into our phones as a way of looking like we were talking.

Our father, who art in heaven, hallowed be thy name.

Taking my bike off the wall, I plugged the earpiece into my cellphone, clipped the microphone to my T-shirt and fell in behind the car.

"Are they moving?" Joe asked. It sounded as though he was already inside the cab.

"Just taking off now."

I managed to stay with the Hafei for the next fifteen minutes. The driver headed south in dense traffic on Landianchang Road, which runs along the western side of the Jingmi Canal. Joe was in my earpiece the whole time, talking openly about Wang's position because he had made sure that his driver didn't speak a word of English. It was extraordinarily hot and the pollution in my mouth was like a chemical liquefying on the lungs. God knows what I must have looked like to passers-by: a sweating, panting *laowai*, riding a second-rate bicycle surrounded by mellow, drifting flocks of Beijing cyclists. I became concerned that the Hafei would make a turn on Fushi Lu towards either the second or third ring roads which surround downtown Beijing. As soon as that happened, Wang would be on a three-line highway and I would no longer be able to follow him on the bicycle. Yet the car continued as far south as Fuxing Road.

"You've done well," Joe said, passing me for the fourth time and accelerating ahead to stay within touching distance of Wang. We were on a wide avenue, surrounded by billboards advertising Western brands of clothing and cigarettes. At times it was difficult to hear precisely what he was saying because of the noise of the traffic. "It looks like he's following signs to Tiananmen Square. Don't worry if you lose us. There's nothing more you can do. I'll call you when I get a fix on his position."

Two minutes later the Hafei was travelling east on Fuxing Road, doing an average of about twenty miles per hour. The line went dead in my ear and Joe's cab was nowhere to be seen. I looked ahead at a blur of traffic near the subway station at Wan-shou Road and tried to reach him on a different number. There was no answer and therefore nothing more that I could do. If Joe had him, he had him. If Wang had disappeared, he would doubt-less call me back and we would have to go through the whole, exhausting process all over again at the same time tomorrow.

41 | HUTONG

Wang stepped out of the Hafei at the southern end of Jingshan Park, having taken a somewhat circuitous route to get there. Jingshan is just to the north of the Forbidden City, in the very heart of old Beijing, and the young female driver, perhaps ignorant of the city's basic geography, could have cut east far earlier in their journey. Carrying the blue canvas bag over his shoulder, Wang headed directly towards an outdoor exercise area, where he proceeded to change into a pair of shorts and a T-shirt. Joe kept a distance of between seventy and eighty metres between them, settling on a bench with a novel in his hands while Wang stretched and worked out. He was still in excellent physical condition, bench-pressing weights which would have troubled a man half his age.

He remained there for about twenty minutes. During this time Joe removed a green long-sleeved shirt he had been wearing to reveal a grey T-shirt underneath. He also took a red baseball cap from a moneybelt around his waist and placed it on his head to effect a basic change in his appearance. While Wang was doing pull-ups, Joe moved to a grass clearing two hundred metres away and made conversation with a small group of tourists so as not to draw attention to the fact that he was on his own.

Just after six o'clock, Wang crossed to the north corner of the gym area and drank water from a public fountain. He had changed back into his work clothes and draped a towel around his neck and now began to walk slowly towards the north-eastern corner of the park. Joe tailed him through an oasis of dappled light and evening birdsong, blending easily with the large numbers of tourists who were passing through the park on their way back from the Forbidden City. Throughout this time I was waiting for Joe to call me in, but he had decided not to risk the small chance that Wang might see me and recognize my face from the school. He was also certain that Wang lived nearby; with any luck, he would not have to tail him for more than a few blocks.

The professor left the park via a gate on Jingshan East Road, walked for three minutes along a crowded side road, purchased a copy of the *Beijing Evening News* and then turned into a *hutong* a few hundred metres from the Times Holiday Hotel. *Hutongs* are quiet, crumbling Chinese neighbourhoods, characteristic of old Beijing, most of which have been gradually and systematically torn down by the communist government in recent years to make way for yet more concrete-and-glass skyscrapers with no discernible purpose; in Shanghai, they are more commonly known as *shikumen*. As Wang disappeared, Joe broke into a sprint to catch up with him. Turning into the *hutong* he saw the professor up ahead at the end of a narrow alley criss-crossed by washing lines. There was nobody else nearby and he decided to take a chance.

"Excuse me!"

Wang stopped and turned round. It was as if his eyesight was failing him because he squinted and took several paces forward. Joe had spoken in Mandarin and the professor seemed unsure whether or not he was the person being addressed. Caged birds were singing on the balcony of an apartment building high above their heads. The two men moved closer together.

"Are you speaking to me?"

Joe was within fifteen metres now and yet still Wang seemed not to have recognized him.

"Professor?"

"Yes?"

"We met in Hong Kong several years ago. I wonder if we could go somewhere private to have a talk."

Wang was holding both ends of the towel around his neck. He tilted his head to one side and stared at Joe as if he were a strange and rare bird.

"Were you followed here?" he asked.

"I really don't know." Joe was surprised that he had been so frank. "Which makes it all the more necessary that we go inside as soon as possible."

Wang looked quickly to his left and, for an instant, Joe was concerned that he was going to try to run for it, to lose himself in the labyrinth of the *hutong*. Instead, he took a further step forward, frowning as he struggled to throw his memory back into a forgotten past.

"Let me put you out of your misery," Joe said. An insect flew into his face and he waved it away. "You knew me as John Richards, a representative from Governor Patten's office in Hong Kong. I interviewed you at a safe—"

"How extraordinary." There was no artifice in Wang's interruption, nor in the portrait of surprise painted on his face. He removed the towel from his neck and studied Joe's eyes. "Why are you here?" he said, as if talking to an apparition. "I thought it was over."

"Well, you see, that's exactly what we need to talk about."

Wang shook his head and turned. There was a certain fatalism in his movements. A woman carrying fresh cherries and lychees in baskets braced across her shoulders passed them and greeted Wang with a singing hello. This was clearly his neighbourhood, a place where he was known to the locals. Joe followed the professor to the end of a second narrow alley, perpendicular to the first, where he stopped and pulled out a key. His house appeared to be little more than a single-storey shack. The front door was made of rotting wood which clung to a rusty hinge. A blue shirt, frayed at the collar, hung on a coat hanger from a stretch of electric cable outside. Joe accidentally kicked an old tin of paint as he ducked to pass into the living room. It was dark inside until Wang switched on a bare lightbulb and closed the door behind them. The ceiling was less than six feet high and Joe lowered himself onto a hard wooden sofa to avoid banging his head.

"This is your home?" he said. He wasn't feeling sentimental about their reunion and was not concerned if he caused any offence with the question. The room was barely larger than his bathroom in Shanghai.

"I am shortly to be relocated," Wang replied, and said something about the entire *hutong* being razed at the end of the summer. Ahead of them was a tiny bedroom with a bare mattress, boxer shorts and books on the floor. There was a faint, possibly ineradicable odour of vermin. Wang went into a small kitchen where he lit a gas stove and filled a pan with water. "Tea?" he said and Joe accepted the offer, setting each of his phones to vibrate. While the water boiled, Wang went into the bedroom and put on a thin brown cardigan and a pair of trousers. His feet, Joe noticed, were unwashed and black and he wondered what had brought Wang to such lowly circumstances.

"So what do you want?" the professor asked. There were no pleasantries, no gentle probings to establish the other man's character and credentials. Wang Kaixuan had spent eight years dealing with spies: they were all the same to him now. "I have told your people I have nothing left to say. I have abandoned the struggle. I wish to live my life in peace."

Joe had calculated that it was safe to talk in Wang's home, on the simple basis that he had survived undetected by the MSS for more than a decade. "And who are my people?" he asked, mesmerized that the charming, confident crusader of his memory had become little more than a paranoid loner hiding himself away in the depths of old Beijing.

"MI6. CIA. Does it make any difference? Why have they sent you this time? Why did I never see you again after our conversation in 1997?"

"I've been asking myself the same question," Joe replied. Wang caught his eye and there was a flicker of confusion. The water was boiling on the stove and he went back into the kitchen, returning with tea.

"I cannot help you," he said, sitting on a rickety wooden chair.

Wang looked like an old man waiting in line to see a doctor. "You have risked my life coming here. I am not interested in any more of your propositions. You have lied to me before and you will lie to me again."

"When have I lied to you?"

Wang looked as if he was about to spit on the floor. "You were actually the first of them, Mr. Richards," he laughed. "You have that unique distinction. You presented yourself to me as a representative from Government House, did you not? And you would have carried on lying if only the others had given you the chance."

"We both lied that night," Joe said.

"Did I? Did I mislead you?" Wang's contemplative eyes appeared to concede that he had been playing a complicated game, but there was no sense of regret or apology in them. He tried to sip his tea but found that it was too hot. "What is your real name?"

"My real name is of no concern to you." A motorbike gunned in a lane behind the house. "You told me that you were not permitted to leave China. You told me that you had lost your job at the university, that you were a political undesirable regarded as a threat to the Motherland. You made a song and dance about human rights abuses in Xinjiang when all you were concerned about was encouraging young Uighurs to commit acts of terror."

He had gone too far, but he had done so deliberately. Joe was convinced that beneath the complex layers of Wang's personality, hidden behind the vanity and the lies and the self-delusion, lurked a decent man. He wanted that man to emerge again, to engage with him, to see that Joe Lennox was somebody whom he could trust.

"You may say anything you like about me," Wang replied quietly. "You may say that I was responsible for the deaths of innocent people. That is probably true. You may say that I used what talents I was given to trick and to confuse my own people. But do not ever say that I did not care about what I was doing. Never say that. It is others who did not care and others who betrayed me. Did you leave that night and resolve to do something about what was happening in Xinjiang? Did you use your powers to investigate the abuses which were being carried out every day in cities across Eastern Turkestan? Did you, Mr. John Richards? Or were you just like everybody else in the West? You heard that a terrible thing was going on in a land far away and you did nothing."

The speech had been heartfelt and powerfully delivered, and Joe had to remind himself that he was dealing with an actor of considerable gifts. He felt the dull pulse of his conscience, of his own moral shortcomings, but the feeling was not new. He looked at the wall nearest the kitchen where Wang had taped a photograph of a young Chinese man.

"Who is that?" he asked.

Wang turned slowly and looked at the picture. His eyes narrowed to a confused frown and he shook his head. "Excuse me?"

"Who is that man in the photograph?"

Wang produced a hollow laugh. "What is happening?" he said, speaking now in Mandarin. "Why are you here? I thought you were one of them. Have they not explained to you?" He was talking as if Joe were a child who had been protected from the truth.

"Explained what? One of whom?"

"One of the Americans. Did they not tell you about my son? Do you not know about him?"

"Nobody has sent me," Joe replied. "I am not with the Americans. I have come here of my own volition. Nobody has told me anything."

Wang had not expected this. The professor buttoned his cardigan to the neck and crossed to the front door. He opened it, peered outside, and came in again like a neighbour with a piece of gossip. Sitting down in his chair, he continued to stare at Joe, almost as if he had misjudged him.

"This young man was the reason for everything. Did you not work it out? This boy was my son."

"I don't understand." Up to this moment Joe had felt that everything had been within his control. Now there was a new factor in play. He looked down at the cold concrete floor, craving a cigarette.

"My son, Wang Bin, was shot dead during a riot in Xinjiang. He was starting to become active in the independence movement. I was a grieving father when you met me. I was crazed with anger and the desire for revenge. I wanted to bring about change in my country. I wanted to bring back Wang Bin. I thought in my madness that my salvation lay in England."

This is an act, Joe kept telling himself. These are lies. Wang's dignity and his rage are identical faces that he can put on to achieve any end. "Your son?" he said.

"Yes, my son." Wang touched the broad, happy face in the photograph. The young man could not have been older than nineteen or twenty. "You were too young to understand, Mr. Richards. Perhaps that is why I did not tell you. A man without children cannot understand the impact of a child's loss." Joe was staring at Wang's blackened feet. "Your colleagues, on the other hand, were cleverer than you were. Or perhaps I should say they were more cynical. They realized that my grief would compel me to act. And so that is what I did."

Joe assumed that Wang was speaking about Lenan and Coolidge and felt, in his confusion, a small sense of relief that Wang's story chimed with the versions he had heard both in London and from Shahpour. "Those men were not my colleagues," he said. "The man you knew as Lodge was a British intelligence officer who was working for the Americans without our knowledge. TYPHOON was an American operation."

Wang held up his hands. "I do not want to know," he said, although Joe could sense his fascination. Wang had spent a lifetime absorbing secrets; he thrived on information. "As I have told you, my work with your organization is over."

"I don't think it's that simple," Joe said.

"And how is that?"

"Because I think you still know things that could be important for us."

"Us?"

The repetition was a taunt. In this game, nobody helped anybody. Nobody loved thy neighbour.

"Yes. For me and for you. For the British in bringing an end to the violence, and for you, in saving hundreds, possibly thousands of innocent lives."

Wang looked confused, as if Joe were trying to trick him with words. They were speaking in English again, switching between the two languages like a struggle for power. The professor finished his tea and went into the kitchen, reigniting the gas on the stove. As he did so, Joe opened his moneybelt and withdrew the surveillance photograph of Shahpour Moazed and Miles Coolidge arguing at Zapata's. It had been folded and a faint white line was visible between the two faces. "I'm going to show you a picture," he said. "I want you to tell me what you think of these men."

Wang turned away and sniffed, a man of long and weary experience who was above playing such childish games. But Joe had judged him correctly. As he held out the photograph, the professor snatched at it and studied the image closely.

"These men? What do I think of them?" He laughed again, but without feeling. "I think you know how I feel about Miles Coolidge. And I believe that his friend has a big problem."

"And why do you say that?"

"Because he has discovered that the world is not as straightforward as he would like it to be. Is he a friend of yours, Mr. Richards? Because he is very much like you. He allows unscrupulous men to control him."

"I'm not like that any more," Joe said, and regretted it, because the response sounded feeble. The photograph was a test, of course. Joe's decision to come to Beijing and to seek out Wang was based on a simple premise: that Shahpour had been telling him the truth. Everything flowed from that. If Wang now confirmed his story, Joe would know that his instincts had been correct. "What kind of problem does he have?" he asked.

"His problem is that his employers are still determined to continue with their policy of chaos in China. Even after everything they have learned. Even after everything they have seen with their own eyes, they maintain fantasies of influence. They believe that by mimicking the activities of the same Islamist fanatics who have so troubled their own country in recent years, they will bring about rebellion in China. I would assume that this is the reason the British have sent you to talk to me." Joe felt a surge of excitement, the certainty now that TYPHOON was reborn. He wanted to ask Wang to elaborate, but his host needed no prompting. "The politicians and spies in Washington to whom you have allied yourself, the men to whom your Iranian friend is answerable, have tasked him with recruiting agents at the Olympics site here in Beijing. Did you know that? Construction workers, security guards, officials at the Olympic village. These are the new targets."

"Shahpour is recruiting them?" Joe asked. He experienced a moment of fear because the American had said nothing about this at M on the Bund.

"Shahpour?" Wang replied. "I know him only as Mark. All of you have so many personalities." Joe shifted on the hard, unforgiving sofa. "He has certainly been instructed to recruit them. Whether his divided conscience will allow him to do so is a different matter. When I worked for Miles, he convinced me that we could bring about change in Xinjiang. I realize now, of course, that he was lying. He was interested in change because he was interested in oil and gas."

Wang suddenly stood up and went into the bedroom. He was gone for some considerable time and Joe was concerned that the flow of information might now stop. He recalled how difficult it had been to draw out Wang's secrets on that long-ago night in Hong Kong. He heard a rustle of papers, the scraping of a box, then the flap of what sounded like newspaper. Wang eventually emerged holding a cut-out article from the *China Daily* which he thrust into Joe's hand.

"Read this," he said.

MACKLINSON, PETROSINA SIGN JOINT-VENTURE

CHINA: An international consortium in which the local Petrosina and Macklinson Corporation of the United States hold a 74% and 26% stake respectively is gearing up to develop the Yakera-Dalaoba gas field in Xinjiang province. The front-end engineering and design contract was awarded for a planned US$600,000,000 upstream facility in the Tarim basin and is scheduled for completion by some time during the first quarter of 2008.

"This is a recent article?" Joe asked. Wang was stretching a muscle which had tightened in his arm.

"Very recent," he said. "Did you read what was written? A six hundred million-dollar joint venture, brokered by your good friend Mr. Lambert. His company now has all that they required from the Uighur people. They have their land, they have their oil and they have their gas. The Central Intelligence Agency may have failed in its efforts to destabilize Xinjiang, but it has surely succeeded in filling the bank accounts of America's richest men."

"But what about Beijing? Why would they start all over again? If you believe that about the CIA, this new operation makes no sense."

"Oh it makes sense, Mr. Richards." Joe was desperate to reveal his true identity, if only to stop Wang's incessant, taunting repetition of the cover name. "Their goal for China is a loss of face. This is what Miles has stooped to. America understands that the Games of 2008 represent an opportunity for the People's Republic to present a civilized face to the world. Think of it as a coming-out party, if that phrase is still used in England. In three years' time, China wishes to announce itself as a superpower competing on an equal footing with the United States of America. This is the dream of the apparatchiks in Tiananmen Square and they are determined to realize it. They have already relocated tens of thousands of people from their homes, and they will relocate tens of thousands more, myself and my neighbours included, to make way for their roads and stadiums. They will drive tramps and beggars out into the countryside. They will seed clouds to control the rain, fill the streets with smiling volunteers. And the world's press will come here and they will photograph the gleaming buildings and the successful athletes of the Chinese economic miracle and these journalists will tell the world that this is what the future looks like."

"And the Americans want to stop that?"

"Of course they want to stop that. There can be only one superpower. There is no place for China at the top table. These few men who wish to do this are as unrepresentative of the American people as you, an Englishman, or I, a Chinese. And yet they hold the absolute power. They will do whatever it takes to humiliate Beijing."

"And will you stop them?"

Wang flinched at the question, tired of Western temptations. He stood up and went back into the kitchen, preparing himself a second cup of tea.

"I no longer believe that terror is the answer," he said, pausing in the tiny kitchen, as if delivering one of his lectures. "I looked back and added up the cost of every Uighur bomb on every bus and in every restaurant in China. What was the result? The people of Xinjiang are now worse off than they were when you and I first met, Mr. Richards. I have looked at New York and Bali and Madrid, and I have seen that nobody has gained from terror, not the victims nor the perpetrators. So my attitude to what is being planned for Beijing is pessimistic. If attacks are successful, the Chinese government will lose face, certainly. The Olympics will be remembered as a tragedy, a fiasco, and the world's press will move on. But China will soon recover. Nations are larger than bombs. Meanwhile, any atrocity will be blamed on external forces, almost certainly Uighur separatists with tenuous links to al-Qaeda. As a result, innocent Muslims throughout Xinjiang will continue to suffer."

"If you believe all that, then why didn't you agree to help?" Joe asked.

"Help who? Mark? Let him help himself. I am finished with politics. My wife abandoned me because of politics. She believed we would be arrested and sent to a gulag. My son is dead because of politics. My only concern now is to wake up tomorrow morning and to go to work."

"I'm afraid I cannot allow you the luxury of that decision," Joe said, arriving at the most distasteful part of his chosen trade. "If you don't give me the information I need, the British government will find a way of letting their Chinese counterparts know the full extent of your activities over the past eight years."

Wang was in the process of sitting down as Joe spoke and he was silent as he absorbed the threat. He drew the palm of his hand across the smooth shaved expanse of his scalp and breathed slowly.

"I have two reactions to that," he said finally. Birds were singing in the *hutong*. "The first is that I do not have the information that you require. The second is that I do not believe you are the sort of man who would carry out a threat of that nature. Black-mail does not become you, Mr. Richards."

"Try me," Joe said.

Wang smiled. He was like a disappointed father with a reckless son. He had faith enough in Joe's decency, but the effort was costing him something in terms of his own patience. "Not far from here, at the eastern side of Tiananmen Square, a clock is ticking down to the start of the Games," he said. "No doubt you have seen it on your visit to Beijing. I credit the Chinese MSS with enough common sense and intelligence to put a stop to whatever operations the Americans are planning between now and then. They have already had great success in dismantling TYPHOON. I see no reason why they should not succeed again."

"And what about Shanghai?" Joe asked.

"What about it?" Wang actually looked bored.

"There is a Uighur sleeper cell in Shanghai."

"You are only telling me what I already know. You are only repeating what Mark has already said."

"Did he tell you that Ansary Tursun may be a part of it?"

Wang had been in the process of taking an apple out of a bowl. His hand froze and he replaced the fruit, turning to face Joe. "Ansary is alive?" It was as if Joe had spoken of Wang's son. Any lingering doubts he may have held about the wisdom of his decision to come to Beijing were dispelled in this moment.

"Alive and well and working in a Muslim restaurant in Shanghai. Given that he has suffered as much as anyone else at the hands of the Chinese, it seems logical to me that he might be involved in a plot to harm them."

"What do you mean by that?" Wang's question carried a false note. It was possible that he was testing the extent of Joe's knowledge.

"Eight years ago, you told me that Ansary had been tortured in a Chinese prison. I suspect that he was one of the first people you turned to when the Americans engaged your services. You also mentioned a second man, a student of yours, Abdul Bary. I suspect that he, too, became instrumental in the struggle for an independent Eastern Turkestan. Am I correct?"

Wang nodded admiringly. "You are not incorrect," he replied. There was a sound outside the door. It would not have surprised Joe if uniformed officers of the PLA had suddenly burst into the room. He had exercised the minimum precaution in reaching Wang's home and had acted with wild impulsiveness in seeking him out. But it was just an animal scratching around in the dusty passage outside. "I did not know that Ansary was still alive," Wang said quietly. "We were once very close. It is true. But we have not spoken for a number of years. We had what you might describe as a falling out."

"What sort of falling out?"

"It was the same with Abdul," Wang continued. He was nervously scratching his arm. "They became radicalized after 9/11 and fell under the influence of a Uighur fighter named Ablimit Celil. They are not the men they once were. It is one of the unfortunate consequences of your war on terror that it obliges good men into alliances they would once have considered foolish. It becomes more important to fight the war than to fight the war for a meaningful purpose. Does that make sense to you?" Joe nodded. Wang brushed an insect from his sleeve. "I never trusted Celil," he said. "I never liked him. He was the kind who was emboldened by the actions of al-Qaeda and who allowed the independence movement to be infiltrated by external elements. We had a fight, a series of arguments. I believed that they had lost sight of the cause for which we were all once fighting. You say that this cell has American backing?"

Joe was confused by the inference behind the question. "Possibly," he said.

"I doubt this."

An expression of profound concern had formed on Wang's face. He looked like an organized, resourceful man who had allowed a moment of stupidity to cloud his thinking.

"What do you mean?"

"Ansary and Abdul would have no business with Americans," Wang said. "On the day of September 11th I was sitting with them in a hotel room in Kashgar. Tears were streaming down Ansary's face as the second plane hit the tower. I looked at him and I saw in his eyes that they were tears of happiness." Joe wiped a droplet of sweat from his forehead. "Ablimit spent a year at a training camp in the Pamir mountains. He became an agent of the Pakistani ISI. Surely the Americans know this?"

Joe was perplexed. "Not unless you've told them," he said. "Did you say something to Mark?"

"I never thought to tell him," Wang replied. "It was not my business. He spoke of a cell in Shanghai but he did not speak of names."

"Celil?" Joe said, trying to remain thorough and logical. "How would you write that?"

Wang spelled out the letters. "The last I knew of him, he worked in Urumqi as a hotel doorman." Wang wrote an address on a small piece of paper using a pencil which he had retrieved from the floor. "If you find him, let me know. Because if you find Ablimit Celil, you will find Ansary Tursun. And I would very much like to see him."

Miles Coolidge was going to the movies.

In a city built on commerce, Xujiahui—pronounced *Shoo-ja-hwe*—is a modern Mecca of Shanghai shopping. Seven separate malls and department stores are located at the junctions of Hengshan, Hongqiao and Zhaojiabang roads, about a mile south-west of Joe's apartment in the French Concession. At all hours of the day, but particularly in the early to late evening, Xujiahui teems with tens of thousands of Chinese, buying and selling everything from computers and electrical equipment to children's toys and the latest clothes from East and West. You would not describe it as an area of outstanding natural beauty. Traffic clogs the packed streets. Subway exits lead to a warren of interconnected underground tunnels which are so hot in summer that to pass through them is to be suffocated by stagnant, putrid air. Horns and jackhammers puncture the atmosphere. A pretty steepled church and an old library, set back from nearby Caoxi Road, are all that remain of the colonial era. Progress has claimed the rest.

Miles pulled up in a cab outside the Paradise City mall, the huge, seven-storey edifice where, just a few weeks later, TYPHOON would reach its horrific zenith. He passed a twenty-yuan note through the driver's perspex separator and waited as his receipt chugged out of the meter. A vast, fifty-foot-high photograph of David Beckham gazed down at him from an advertising hoarding slung from the façade of the Metro City mall on the opposite side of the intersection. Miles stepped out of the taxi and held the door for two Chinese girls dressed head to toe in Western brands. A moped swept past him, buzzing its horn. He tried giving one of the girls the eye, but she ignored him and slammed the door.

The Paradise City was a sanctuary of air conditioning which released Miles from the cloud-trapped pollution outside. Surveillance footage shows him stepping around a salesman handing out leaflets for skincare products and taking an escalator to the first floor. He bought a latte and a chocolate muffin from a branch of Costa Coffee. Tables were arranged at the perimeter of a balcony which afforded panoramic views of the gleaming white atrium. Ahead of him, Miles could see all seven floors of the mall, the branches of French Connection and Nike Golf, the bubble lifts and sliding banks of escalators, the giggling girls gassing on mobile phones.

The meeting was set for seven-thirty. At half-past six, he walked round to the opposite side of the atrium, where he caught a lift to the seventh floor. Heading to the north-western corner of the mall, Miles entered the Silver Reel cinema multiplex and purchased a ticket for the 6:50 movie showing in Screen Four. There were extensive queues at the popcorn concession but he waited in line under the watchful eye of Elmo and Bugs Bunny, purchasing a tub of salted popcorn and half a litre of Diet Coke. This was his usual routine. There was no security as he handed over his ticket, just a Chinese girl standing at the gate who said, "Hello, sir," in English, indicating the entrance to Screen Four behind her. Miles made his way along the darkened corridor, entered the cinema and sat in his usual seat at the end of row Q. The advertisements had already started and he leaned back in his chair, waiting for Ablimit Celil.

London had gone silent. Upon returning to Shanghai, Joe had put in a request for information on Ablimit Celil. Five days had passed and he had heard nothing back.

It was partly his fault. Under normal circumstances, Joe would have filed a CX report about his meeting with Wang Kaixuan, detailing the significant allegation that Celil maintained links to the Pakistani ISI. But Waterfield had effectively forbidden him from pursuing Wang as a line of enquiry; until Joe had firm intelligence that the professor was telling the truth, he could hardly admit to having ignored London's basic instructions. That was the trouble with the secret world; only on very rare occasions did all the rumours and the leads and the theories converge to paint a perfect picture. There was no such thing as the truth. There was only product.

Joe had also been in touch with Zhao Jian, who had never heard of Ablimit Celil, far less seen him in the company of Miles Coolidge. As for Shahpour Moazed, Zhao Jian's brothers joked that they had developed bunions waiting for him to emerge from his apartment building on Fuxing Road. Miles's right-hand man had gone to ground. Nobody had seen hide nor hair of Moazed for almost a week. When Jian had telephoned the Microsoft office in Pudong, a secretary had informed him that Shahpour was sick. They were expecting him back at work on Monday.

Shahpour was indeed sick, but not with stomach cramps brought on by dodgy tofu, or with a nasty dose of the flu. He was suffering from a sustained bout of regret and paranoia. For five long days he had bunkered down in his apartment, surviving on a diet of counterfeit DVDs, Thai marijuana, Chinese hookers and takeaway food. To his longstanding doubts about the moral rectitude of TYPHOON was now added a second, shaming regret that he had spilled his guts to Joe Lennox. Prior to leaving for M on the Bund, Shahpour had smoked a pre-dinner joint, then sunk two bottles of white wine, a cognac and a vodka Martini at dinner before calmly informing a former officer of the British Secret Intelligence Service that the CIA was bankrolling terrorism in China. He had somehow persuaded himself that Joe Lennox was his saviour. The reality, of course, was that Joe was now a private citizen who would surely have gone straight to SIS Station in Shanghai and informed them about the plot. Shahpour was amazed that he had not yet been called home. He was stunned that he had not, at the very least, received a visit from an irate Miles Coolidge. He had already drafted his letter of resignation and was preparing to pack.

"So nobody's seen him for a week?" Joe asked Zhao Jian.

"That is correct, sir. Nobody has seen him since your dinner on the Bund."

"And you're convinced that he's still in his apartment? You're sure he hasn't flown the nest?"

"Convinced, sir. Convinced."

There was only one thing for it. On a damp Friday evening, Joe walked the short distance from his apartment in the French Concession to Central Fuxing Road. He paused outside a barber's shop where an exhausted-looking businessman was receiving a head massage and called Shahpour's mobile.

"Hello?" The voice was gravelly, only half-alert.

"Shahpour? This is Joe. Joe Lennox. How are you doing?"

Shahpour thought about hanging up, but was intrigued. He had heard nothing from Joe since their conversation at dinner, only a rumour that he had left town for a few days on Quayler business. He looked at the clock on his kitchen wall. A dried chunk of spaghetti sauce obscured one of the digits but he could see that it was after eight o'clock.

"Hi, Joe. I guess I'm doing fine. It's good to hear from you. What's up?"

"Well, I was just passing your door and I wondered if you fancied a drink? It's Friday, Megan's away and I hoped you might be at a loose end."

"How did you know where I live?"

It was the first indicator of his paranoid state. "You told me. At dinner. Fuxing Road, right?"

Ten minutes later Joe was in a lift riding to the fourth floor of an apartment block built in the hideous neo-Grecian style which is considered luxurious by certain Chinese architects. Shahpour lived alone at the end of a long corridor crowded with old boxes and plastic bags. Joe rang the doorbell and waited up to a minute for the American to answer.

A stewardess once described to me the smell which emerges from an aeroplane when the doors are opened for the first time after a long-haul flight. Joe experienced a comparable odor as he stepped into Shahpour's apartment to be greeted by a noxious cocktail of stale air, farts and socks which almost made him gag with its intensity. Shahpour had grown a substantial beard and was dressed only in a pair of torn jeans and a Puma T-shirt. He had taken on the countenance of a brilliant, insomniac postgraduate student who has been toiling in a laboratory for days. The air conditioning in the apartment had been switched off, and there was no natural light to speak of. Plastic DVD cases and pizza cartons were scattered on a *kilim*, dirty clothes strewn on an L-shaped white leather sofa. On the table nearest the door Shahpour had placed a laptop computer and a Tupperware box containing enough marijuana to earn him a seven-year prison sentence. An iPod glowed in the corner.

"Have I come at a bad time?"

"The place needs to be cleaned up," Shahpour muttered, walking into the kitchen. Joe saw that he had already begun to make a start on five days of washing up. A bin bag in the corner had been hastily tied together and the floor was sticky under his feet. "I haven't been out much."

"Let's go out now," Joe suggested, as much to relieve his own discomfort as to offer Shahpour a release from his torpor. "Why don't you have a shower and I'll take you out for dinner?"

"OK." Shahpour sounded like a drunk preparing to sober up. "Might be a good idea. Give me five minutes."

It took fifteen. Joe waited in the deep-litter sitting room, sipping from a can of lukewarm Tsingtao and flicking through a copy of *City Weekend*. He wanted to draw the curtains, to open a window, to tidy some of the detritus from the floor, but it was not his place to do so. Eventually Shahpour appeared, with the beard slightly trimmed, wearing a clean T-shirt, worn jeans and a pair of trainers. The transformation was remarkable.

"I needed that," he said.

"Let's go."

At first they walked in near-silence, heading west in the general direction of Joe's apartment. He felt like a visitor to a sanatorium, strolling in the grounds with a patient on day release. Cyclists and passers-by cast strange looks at the tall, bearded Persian in Joe's company, and he was concerned that they would soon attract the wrong sort of attention from the wrong sort of Chinese. Joe suggested going to Face, a bar in the Rui Jin Guest House a few blocks away, where expats could blend into a gin and tonic in relative obscurity, but Shahpour was apparently enjoying the fresh air.

"Do you mind if we just walk a while?" he said. "I haven't been outside in a long time."

"What's the matter?" Joe asked. "What happened?"

The answer was a long time coming, and its content did not surprise him.

"I guess I feel like I owe you an apology," Shahpour said finally. "I was out of line the other night."

"How so? I had a great time."

Shahpour's humid eyes stared into Joe's, who saw that there was no energy left in them for British *politesse*.

"I've been under a lot of pressure lately. I'd heard things about you that I had misinterpreted."

"What kind of things?"

"That you were the only man left on either side of the Atlantic with any principles. That all the secretaries at Vauxhall Cross were crying in the restrooms at your farewell party. That Joe Lennox was a guy I could talk to, whether or not he was working for Quayler Pharmaceuticals."

"What if I'm not working for Quayler Pharmaceuticals?"

They were standing beside a fruit stall on the corner of Shanxi Road. A gap-toothed Mongolian was preparing slices of water-melon on a chopping board erected in the street. Shahpour came to a halt beside her and turned to look at Joe.

"Keep walking," Joe said quietly. "Keep walking."

They went north.

"What did you mean by that?" Shahpour was running a hand through his hair, looking behind him, as if concerned that they were being followed. They had not passed another foreigner since leaving the apartment.

"Tell me about Beijing," Joe said.

"What about it?"

"Tell me about the Olympics."

Shahpour stared at him. "You've seen Wang, haven't you?"

Right on cue, a phalanx of uniformed PLA guards turned the corner ahead of them and marched two abreast along the opposite side of the street. Shahpour swore under his breath.

"I'm going to take a chance," Joe told him. He had prepared precisely what he was going to say. A passer-by, observing their conversation, would have suspected that Joe was talking about nothing more pressing than the weather. "If my instincts are correct, you and I can possibly save a lot of innocent lives. If they're wrong, I'm going to look like the biggest idiot this side of the Yang-tze River." A man stepped in front of them and opened up a brief-case of counterfeit watches, following for several paces until Joe waved him away. "You were right about Zapata's. Our meeting was not an accident. I used Megan to draw you on."

"I knew it!" Shahpour was like an excited child. Joe would have told him to calm down if he had not quickly done so himself. This wasn't a game. He needed Shahpour to concentrate.

"But you neglected to mention Beijing. I want to know what's being planned for the Olympics."

There is a certain, undeniable thrill in running a successful agent, a feeling of absolute control over the destiny of another human being. Joe experienced something of the same pleasure as he observed the gradual shift in Shahpour's body language, the softening of his demeanour. It was obvious that he trusted Joe implicitly. He had found the one man who offered him release from his wretched predicament.

"The only reason I didn't tell you is that there didn't seem any point. I bought your story, man. I really thought you were out. I can't believe this."

They had come to an intersection. Shahpour was a decent man, erratic of temperament and occasionally immature, but Joe liked him. He had concluded that he had been selected in haste by the CIA in the aftermath of 9/11 and rushed through training at the Farm, probably for reasons of racial profiling. He would have been more suited to a career in sales or, indeed, computing. As if to confirm this basic impression, Shahpour now lit a cigarette and walked straight into what appeared to be a clear road, having apparently forgotten that in China it is best to look left and right, up and down, front and back, before stepping out into traffic. He was quickly assaulted by the horn of an oncoming cab, angling towards him on the wrong side of the road. Joe grabbed his shirt and pulled him back.

"Jesus!"

"Let's try to keep you alive."

Safely on the opposite side of the street, Shahpour began to extrapolate on Wang's description of the CIA's plans for Beijing. Miles apparently wanted several incidents, at least one "on the scale of Atlanta," which would concentrate media attention on casualties and civil unrest, rather than on the gleaming economic miracle of modern China. Using his cover at Microsoft, Shahpour had been tasked with recruiting underpaid, overworked Chinese employees inside the stadium complex, as well as television and advertising personnel in the city. He was due to move to the capital in the late summer. Meanwhile, Miles was working on a plan to bring a Uighur cell into Beijing to bomb the Olympic village.

"The same cell that's in Shanghai?"

"I have no idea. Miles only tells me what I need to know. But it's compartmentalized. There could be hundreds of officers working on this, could be just me and him."

Joe shook his head and lit a cigarette. That the operation appeared so chaotic was, he concluded, an indication of its absolute secrecy, rather than an illustration of CIA or Pentagon incompetence. Shahpour continued.

"Miles thinks it's gonna be easy falsifying documentation to get into the village. I told him the Chinese won't let anybody move in there unless they can prove they're legitimate. How the fuck are we supposed to get a bunch of out-of-shape Turkic Muslims into an elite training area for the world's finest athletes? I'm telling you, the whole plan is a mess."

"It can't be the same cell that's here in Shanghai," Joe concluded. "If they carry out an attack this summer, they'll be arrested. Miles can't expect the cell to survive undetected for three more years."

Shahpour tossed his cigarette into the street. "I guess you're right," he said.

"How much do you know about the cell?" They were forced to walk around a pool of water flooding out of a canteen halfway down Xinle Road. Crowds of Chinese were hunched over tables, shovelling rice and cuts of pork into their mouths, oblivious to the chaos around them. "When did Miles recruit them?"

"I think they're the dregs," Shahpour replied. "I only look out for one of them. Memet Almas. He's Kazakh, kind of devout, so he likes it that I'm a fellow Muslim, you know? Has a wife back in Kashgar. Miles doesn't give me any other names. The less people that know, the better, right?" Joe asked for a spelling of Memet

Almas. "But I get the impression he's using fanatics. In the old days, TYPHOON was what you might call a secular operation. They were lapsed Sufis, fighting for a political cause. Far as I can work out, a guy like Memet just wants to blow things up. The whole thing has become radicalized."

"What about Ansary Tursun? Abdul Bary? Do those names mean anything to you?"

Shahpour shook his head. It was dark and two mopeds without headlights were coming towards them on the opposite side of the street.

"Ablimit Celil?"

Another shake of the head. Joe was bewildered that Shahpour seemed to know so little about the operation. "What makes you think they're all radicalized?" he asked.

"Just listening to Miles talk. Maybe he's bought into the whole Chinese state propaganda thing that all Uighurs are terrorists. How do I know? The whole thing's gotten fucked up."

"Wang thinks Celil is the head of the cell. He also thinks he might be ISI."

"He thinks *what*?"

Shahpour had stopped in his tracks. Joe again asked him to keep walking and put a hand around his back. His body was powerfully built and sweat had collected at the bottom of his shirt. "He told me Celil spent time at an al-Qaeda training camp a few years ago. He thinks the cell may be being controlled from Islamabad."

"Then Wang is full of shit." An elderly man in a rocking chair was staring at them from the darkened entrance of a *shikumen*.

"Why do you say that?"

"Because he's been full of shit about things in the past so he'll be full of shit about things in the future." Joe's memory was thrown back to the basement of the nightclub in Wan Chai. What was it that Miles had said to him? *Wang Kaixuan is a myth, a spook story. Nothing that old fuck told you has any meaning.*

"Is that you talking, or Miles?"

Shahpour appeared offended by the criticism implicit in the question. He stepped out in front of a cyclist and separated himself from Joe by crossing the street. They were on a narrow, dimly lit road in the heart of the French Concession, the dark plane trees bending low over their heads and stretching like a tunnel into the distance. Without hurrying, Joe caught up with him and simply picked up where they had left off.

"How do you meet Almas?" he asked.

Shahpour did not hesitate before responding. He was eager to dispense of operational secrets which had been weighing down on him for too long. "We go to a bar on Nanyang Lu. Place called Larry's."

Joe knew it. Larry's was a block behind the Ritz-Carlton, a split-level American-style pub with big-screen sports and pool tables. He had eaten there, watching coverage of a one-day cricket international between England and South Africa. It was popular with twentysomething *laowais* who liked burgers and French fries. "You meet him in the open? In a restaurant?" He did not want to risk incurring Shahpour's wrath by asking further questions about the sloppiness of his tradecraft.

"Sure. He blends right in. We sit in the corner, get a cheese-burger, we watch a ball game and act like a couple of Americans a long way from home. Chinese can't tell the difference. We all look the same to them."

"How often does this happen?"

"Twice, maybe three times since he came to Shanghai." From the slightly obstinate tone emerging in Shahpour's voice, Joe sensed that he was feeling defensive. Best not to push too hard.

"How do you contact him?"

Shahpour scratched an itch on the lobe of his left ear. "Text message." He waited until he was clear of an elderly lady washing plates in a plastic tub at the edge of the street. "I gave him a cell-phone. There's language I use that indicates a desire to meet. Memet speaks English and we just code the time and date."

Joe nodded and asked how it worked from Memet's end.

"Same thing, more or less. He sends a text from a cellphone sourced in the US telling me to contact my grandparents in Sacra-mento."

"Because your grandparents in Sacramento are no longer with us?" Joe was always fascinated to glean titbits of Cousin tradecraft.

"No, they're still with us. But they live in Tehran."

Joe smiled. "What about Miles?"

"What about him?"

"How does he do it? How does he meet the cell?"

"I have no idea." Shahpour was shaking his head. Briefly, it looked as though he had no more to say on the subject. Then: "All I know is that he sometimes uses his wife."

Joe felt a lurch of surprise which quickly turned to indignation. "Isabella?"

"Sure. For cover. You guys know about that, right? Take a chick with you, pretend like you're going shopping or something, then meet your contact along the way. Isabella makes Miles look normal. But ask me where the hell he takes her and I'll tell you I have no idea."

"**Where is your** wife?"

The whispered voice of Ablimit Celil was audible above the screams and gunfire of an American disaster movie. He had taken the vacant seat beside Miles Coolidge at the far end of row Q, entering the cinema shortly after the film had begun.

"She couldn't make it," Miles replied. "Women's troubles."

He enjoyed taunting Ablimit's religious beliefs, sexualizing women in his company, occasionally referring to his own agnosticism. He wasn't going to be dictated to by a fanatic. Miles needed Celil, certainly, but Celil also needed Mike. Without American money and American explosives, he was just another two-bit saboteur.

"You wanted to talk."

Miles had not yet looked at his agent. Three rows ahead of them, a man wearing a baseball cap was making his way through a tub of ice cream and laughing at a snatch of dialogue on screen. Had he turned around, he would have been met by the incongruous sight of two overweight middle-aged men, one with a thick beard, the other clean shaven, leaning towards one another like lovers in the back row. A vivid montage of flickering light reflected in the blackened eyes of Miles Coolidge and Ablimit Celil as they spoke reverently and quietly, like mourners at a funeral.

"How are you doing?"

"We are fine," Celil replied. "But we must have more money."

"So what else is new? Patience, for Christ's sake."

"Ansary has been ill. He does not work. He questions the direction we are taking."

"I saw him last week. Ate a good dinner at Kala Kuer. He looked fine to me."

Miles popped a single kernel of popcorn into his mouth, allowing it to melt on his tongue.

"I mean he is anxious for action. We all are. We wonder why we are waiting."

Celil was speaking quickly, in Mandarin, and the whisper of his voice was almost lost amid the wail and crash of an action sequence. The film appalled him, the violence and the blasphemies. He tried not to look at the screen.

"I've been working up some possible targets," Miles said, passing a package across the armrest. Celil placed it on his lap, straining to listen. "Factories. State-owned banks. A Sichuan restaurant in Pudong. I don't want Americans hit, I don't want Europeans. We've suffered enough." Not much came back from Celil by way of a reaction, just a blank stare into the middle distance. "I want you to think about switching jobs. Leave Abdul at his factory, but Ansary can take a job washing dishes at the restaurant. I can get you security passes for the banks, access all areas. We have a lot of time."

Celil sniffed violently. The American's ignorance of Chinese affairs was still breathtaking to him. "This is not easy for Uighurs," he said. "We cannot just walk into jobs in such places."

"It's all in the file," Miles replied.

His apparent ignorance was, in fact, a front. After a recent meeting with his contact at the Pentagon, Miles had been persuaded that any successful attack in Shanghai would only strengthen Chinese resolve to protect the Games of 2008. There was also the added, obvious risk of losing the cell entirely. Every Uighur within a hundred miles of Puxi would be arrested and interrogated in the wake of a co-ordinated terrorist strike. Washington therefore had no intention of green-lighting an operation for the forthcoming summer. The information Miles had passed to Celil in the envelope was sketchy, at best; if the members of the cell succeeded in securing the positions he had described, Miles would simply pull them at the last minute, citing intelligence indicating that the operation was blown. He had also slipped fifteen thousand American dollars into the package, which would be more than enough to buy off Celil's frustrations for several more months. Beijing was now the sole target. Both parties would eventually get what they wanted: the Uighur cause on a global stage; carnage to overshadow China's precious Olympic Games.

"How are the others?" Miles asked. "How are Abdul and Memet?"

The audience suddenly burst into laughter. Miles looked up at the screen. A character appeared to have fallen over accidentally and was attempting to stand up. The Chinese love a pratfall.

"Memet I never see. Abdul also. It is the way we want it, the way we have always operated. I only know about Ansary because I visit his restaurant and they tell me he is sick. It is too dangerous to be seen with them. We want action. We want to hit the Chinese. We are tired of waiting."

"And action's what you'll get." Miles was irritated by these repeated calls for progress. The cell's bloodlust was entirely of Celil's making; he had brought a new fanaticism to their work. At the high tide of TYPHOON, there had been no undercurrent of religious fervour. The men had regarded themselves as soldiers, fighting for a just cause. Now stalwarts such as Tursun and Bary were no better than the maniacs of Baghdad and Atocha. "You just have to trust me," he said. "You have to listen."

"I will listen," Celil replied.

A hiss went up from somewhere in the cinema. Their conversation had gone on too long. "You'd better get going," Miles whispered. "Read the file."

Celil placed the package in a plastic bag and walked out of the cinema. The lobby was empty and he was soon in the main atrium of the mall, descending by lift to the ground floor.

Each of his visits to Paradise City was now of vital importance to the cell. Why? Because they were indeed under new instructions, just as Wang had disclosed. Celil's apparent obeisance in the presence of Miles Coolidge had been an act; the Americans were yesterday's men. By allying the Uighur cause to the ISI, Celil had guaranteed frequent and effective action on the ground.

I don't want Americans hit, I don't want Europeans. We've suffered enough. Wasn't that just like the hypocrisy of the West? They wreak havoc in foreign lands and then make efforts only to protect themselves. For too long, Ablimit had allowed himself to be blinded by American promises that had never borne fruit. The CIA had aided the cause of Uighur separatism not because they believed in the right of his Muslim brothers to live in their own land, free of Han oppression, but because they coveted yet more oil, yet more gas, to fuel their bankrupt economy.

He looked around him. He looked at the mall. Ablimit Celil saw the evidence of another defunct culture, a China imitative of all that was worst in the West. He thought ahead to the glorious release of 6/11, and was never more certain that he had taken the correct decision.

Let's face it: Joe didn't need to go and see Isabella. He could have asked Zhao Jian to track her. He could have waited patiently for London to contact him with the information he had requested about Ablimit Celil. Shahpour's disclosure that Miles used her as cover for his meetings with the cell was valuable product, certainly, but it didn't necessitate a visit to her home in Jinqiao. What was Joe expecting? A confession? A full report on Miles's clandestine movements in China? Isabella was hardly going to betray the man she had married, particularly to a former boyfriend who had once betrayed her himself. Yet the temptation proved too hard for Joe to resist. It was the perfect opportunity to see her. After all, Waterfield had tasked him with getting close to Miles Coolidge. Well, getting close to Miles Coolidge meant getting close to Isabella. And who knows a man better than his own wife? From a certain point of view, Joe was just doing his job.

Jian gave him the details. Every weekday morning, regular as clockwork, Isabella bicycled to Century Park where she joined a public tai-chi session between eight-fifteen and nine o'clock. By then, Miles had left for the office. She was always alone. It would simply be a case of finding her and taking things from there.

Travelling east on the Line 2 Metro into Pudong, Joe realized that he was blurring a dangerous professional and personal boundary which could only end in disappointment. He had hardly slept. He had deliberately avoided Megan for days. He had not prepared what he was going to say, nor thought through the consequences of his actions.

The train was packed. He stood in the pristine, swaying compartment, a *laowai* spy of thirty-four, thousands of miles from home, racing towards his destiny. It was 7:45 in the morning. What if Isabella simply turned on her heels, ignoring his entreaties? What if she phoned Miles and told him that Joe had been to see her? How would he explain that one? He was supposed to be an employee of a niche pharmaceutical company, not a British spook asking sensitive questions about the activities of the CIA. If she asked him what he was doing in Shanghai, Joe was going to tell her. He had already decided that. He could not lie. It was lies, after all, which had brought about their undoing eight years earlier. But to tell her was to jeopardize everything: the operation, his cover, the successful pursuit of the cell. If Joe had possessed even an ounce of common sense on that humid mid-May morning, he would surely have turned round at Dongfanglu and headed straight back to Puxi.

He found the location easily. He had no need of the map which he had brought with him. The tai-chi session was taking place at the southern edge of an artificial lake, a short walk from Century Park station. In the distance Joe could see a large group of exercising Chinese, mostly men and women of retirement age, stretching and revolving in slow motion, communing with invisible gods. He moved towards them. He saw a bearded Western man in his late fifties, and another *laowai* woman of a similar age wearing tracksuit trousers and a T-shirt which appeared to have been dyed pink in the wash. They looked out of place in a group of perhaps thirty or forty Han, with no sign of Isabella among them. Joe sat on a bench in the shade of a tallow tree. He wondered if he was observing the correct group. Had Zhao Jian sent him to the wrong section of the park? It would take at least forty minutes to scout the entire area, a period in which Isabella might easily return home.

An aeroplane flew in low overhead, descending east towards the airport. The decelerating noise of its engines smothered the wail of Chinese folk music issuing from a portable CD player at the edge of the lake. Joe stood up. To the north he could discern the faint outline of the Jin Mao Tower, obscured by smog. He lowered his gaze and stared again at the group, moving two paces to his left so that his line of sight was no longer blocked by four men wielding wooden swords.

And then he saw her, the haunting, seductive revelation of Isabella Aubert, her face and body as familiar to him as the morning breeze. She was wearing black cotton yoga trousers with a band in her hair, bare slender arms stretched out in front of her, shoeless feet rotating on the dew-kissed grass. Joe's first reaction was to smile, because there was a look of intense, almost childlike concentration on Isabella's face as she geared through the complex movements of the tai-chi. In this first instant he realized that all of his pain, all of his heartache and longing, had not been wasted. She was still as vivid and as beautiful to him as she had ever been, and it had been right to come back to her. He returned to the bench. Joe's heart was racing and he lost himself in a flood of memories, recalling the first time that they had seen one another at the wedding, their first hypnotic nights in Kentish Town, the arguments which had raged between them in the desperate week of *wui gwai*. He continued to watch her, thinking of Miles and Linda and the lies in their lives, and it was almost impossible to imagine how close Isabella was living to a terrible secret. How was he going to break it to her? What the hell was he going to say?

The music stopped. There was laughter and a coming together of friends. Isabella appeared to know one of the elderly Chinese ladies on her left because they immediately fell into conversation when the exercise ended. A gull flew in front of them and settled at the edge of the lake. Joe stood up and began walking through the crowds. He was forty metres away. Thirty. Isabella put on a pair of soft shoes and shook out the long dark curls of her hair, movements that were almost melancholy in their practised simplicity. It was at this point that she seemed to sense his approach and it surprised Joe that Isabella smiled as he came towards her, as if they had made an arrangement to meet, almost as if she had been expecting him.

"Oh my God." The smell of her as they hugged was an opiate of memories. She was on tiptoes, squeezing his back, saying things into his body that he could barely hear. "What are you doing in Shanghai? I don't believe this."

They parted and looked at one another. Isabella's face was flushed with exercise, but it was also alive to the pleasure and surprise of seeing him. The final, dreadful months in Hong Kong appeared to have been forgotten. Time had erased all ill feeling between them.

"What are you doing in Shanghai?" she said again. "This is so unbelievable."

"It's a long story."

It was only after several seconds that Joe realized what she had revealed: that Miles had told her nothing. Had he deliberately withheld the fact that Joe was living in the city? Or was what Shahpour and Zhao Jian had told him correct? That Mr. and Mrs. Miles Coolidge no longer lived together, no longer shared the same bed?

"I didn't mean to surprise you," he said. "Didn't Miles say anything? Didn't he tell you I was living here?"

Isabella shook her head, the rueful smile on her lips providing him with the answer to his question. *Miles doesn't tell me anything. My husband is a basement of secrets.*

Joe lowered his gaze. He saw the battered gold wedding band on her finger. "Well, that's not what I expected," he said. Isabella spluttered out a laugh. "I had dinner with him in April. We bumped into each other on Huaihai. He never said anything?"

"Nothing," Isabella replied.

It was possible, of course, that she was lying; after all, it would be easier to blame Miles than to admit that she had been deliberately avoiding the very confrontation that Joe had now engendered. Yet that wasn't Isabella's style. It never had been. She wasn't a coward. She wasn't a fake. She spoke her mind and called things as she saw them. Besides, why deny something so straightforward? She picked up a broad-brimmed sun hat from the grass and began walking towards the lake. There was a note of fatalism in her voice as she said, "Miles has been very busy. He's away a lot."

It sounded like a wife's hollow excuse. Falling in step beside her, Joe could sense that Isabella barely possessed the energy to defend him. She knew instinctively that Miles had been trying to keep them apart. They both did. That was the obvious, embarrassing conclusion to be drawn. To save her further discomfort, Joe paid Isabella a compliment, saying that she looked exactly the same as she had done when he had last seen her eight years earlier.

"God. Is that how long it's been?" The lovely cascade of her hair, the life in her voice, were returning to Joe like forgotten photographs. "Christ we're getting old," she said. "So is this an accident? Are you in Pudong on business?"

Joe had set himself only one rule for their reunion: that he would never again lie to Isabella Aubert. Already that rule was under scrutiny. It was too early in the conversation to reveal the true nature of his quest.

"Like I said, it's a long story. Do you have time for a coffee?"

Isabella's face suddenly contracted with worry, and she placed a hand on Joe's arm. The contact was like a physical guarantee of her affection for him. Sensing her distress, Joe said, "Don't worry, it's nothing serious," and if he had been more certain of Isabella's feelings towards him, if there had not been so much history between them, so many doors to be reopened, he would have lifted her hand from his arm and held it, to reassure her. There still existed an extraordinary physical and emotional connection between them which he could sense as vividly as he could feel the morning sun burning in the sky. He was certain that Isabella could sense it too. There is a magic in first love; it never leaves you.

"There's a café over there," he said, pointing north towards the black glass structure of the Science and Technology Museum. He had been there once before, on a bored early weekend in Shanghai. "We could get breakfast and talk."

"Let's do that," she said. "And I'm paying."

They found an outdoor table set in a pseudo-futuristic courtyard overlooked by the dark polished curves of the museum. The humidity of mid-morning was kept at bay by a gentle breeze which ran free across the undeveloped marshlands of southern Pudong. Children were decanting from fat, gleaming buses. They played in the spray of a fountain, giggled as they waited in line.

"So are you married?" Isabella asked. "Have you got children? Are you still working for your secret bloody brotherhood?"

Eight years as the wife of an American spy appeared to have normalized her attitude to Joe's chosen trade. She had grinned as she asked the list of questions and he had no hesitation in replying.

"I'm not married," he said, adding quickly, "Not divorced, either," because he saw what he interpreted as a look of confusion on Isabella's face. "I don't have any children. At least I didn't last time I checked."

"And the Foreign Office?"

Joe noted that there had been a little blink and swallow as she had absorbed the news that he was single. "Are we back here again?" he said. He could afford to risk the joke because there was no more pain between them. He stared at Isabella's face, at the eyes he had kissed, the neck he had touched, and marvelled that their conversation was so effortless. "Actually I made a private vow to myself eight years ago that if we ever met again I wouldn't lie to you about what I do for a living."

"And yet here you are about to do exactly that." She waved away her indiscretion. "I'm sorry," she said. "I shouldn't have asked." Their eyes met in a moment of quiet understanding. Joe could see that Isabella was now all too aware of the unique, private frustrations of the secret life.

"Can I say something about that?" she said suddenly.

"About what?"

"About the way I behaved in Hong Kong." It was not yet ten o'clock, but she had plainly made the decision to clear her conscience as quickly as possible. "I was very hard on you." She swept a strand of hair out of her eyes. "You didn't deserve it. It took me a long time to realize that, and by then I was in Chengdu with Miles. I'm so sorry." Joe tried to stall the confession, because he was shocked both by its candour and by the impact that Isabella's words had on his heart. They had come too late, and yet they were all that he had longed to hear. "The truth is that I wasn't really ready for what we had. I was too young. I used what I discovered about you as an excuse to end what we had between us."

"Izzy . . ."

"No, please. Let me finish. For all I know it'll be another eight years before I see you again and I've been wanting to say this for ages." She lowered the cup of coffee she had been holding and placed it on the table in front of her. Joe suddenly glimpsed an extraordinary solitude in her eyes, as if there was no one in Shanghai to whom Isabella could speak as frankly and as passionately as she was now doing. "I wasn't as kind as you thought I was," she said. "You deserved better. I had a habit of pushing men away who were good to me. I did it with Anthony and I did it with you. It was heartless."

"I lied to you," Joe said, trying to protect her. "I should have been more honest from the start."

"No. How could you have been?" She had thought it all through. She was trying to demonstrate her desire to mend their shared wound, as if they could not speak of anything else until the past had been laid to rest. "It was the nature of your job," she said. "You couldn't have done it if you were going around telling everybody the truth."

"Perhaps," Joe said. It occurred to him that there were other things, more damaging things, yet just as truthful, that Isabella might now have added. That Joe had been just a little bit too sensible, a little bit too buttoned up, a little bit too withdrawn and conservative for a girl of her background and character. A part of him had always known that Isabella had discovered his dark secret just at the point when she was beginning to tire of him. The timing was immaculate. Had he asked her to marry him, she might well have said no. These were less consoling truths and Isabella was being kind not to speak of them.

"And what about now?" he asked. He was trying to smile, trying to get her to relax and enjoy the morning. "Are you happy? Did it all work out the way you wanted it to?"

She stared across the blinding courtyard, the sun burning the concrete and glinting off the surface of the water. How much does a woman tell a man about the secrets in her heart? How much can a wife disclose about the failures of her marriage?

"Isn't that why you've come?" she said.

Joe lit a cigarette. "I don't understand."

"To talk about Miles."

He took the first smoke deep into his lungs and exhaled at the cloud-smothered sky. "It's partly why I've come," he conceded, though he could not imagine what Isabella knew.

"To talk about Linda?"

This stunned him. "You know about that?" he said, before he had a chance to consider the wisdom of betraying Miles.

There was silence.

"Izzy?" Joe experienced the extraordinary sensation that she had been waiting eight years to break her silence. He suddenly felt as though she regarded him as her closest friend in the world, and that he had ignored that friendship out of sheer spite.

"It doesn't matter," she said. She took one of his cigarettes. She wasn't going to break down or cry. That wasn't her style. "It's the lot of the expat wife, the *tai tai*. We make our beds, we lie in them."

"I don't understand."

She lit the cigarette because he had forgotten to do it for her. "I mean that we come out here on six-figure packages, we get our club-class air tickets, our tennis lessons and our houses in Jinqiao. And what's the trade-off? Husbands who are away two hundred days a year with a girlfriend in every port and a permanent hang-over on weekends." She met his eyes. "Don't tell me you don't know what I'm talking about, Joe. How long have you lived in Asia?"

"For ever."

"Exactly. And it was the same story in Hong Kong, the same in KL, the same in Singapore, right?" He didn't wholly agree with her, but knew better than to interrupt. "The Empire lives on. In the 1930s, corporate wives went to the Del Monte and the Cathay. Nowadays we go to Bar Rouge and M on the Bund. There's no difference. We're still bored and frustrated. We still have more money than the locals. We still have servants. We still dress up and play the Empire game. Meanwhile, our beloved husbands fuck as many Chinese girls as they can get their hands on and convince themselves they're part of a master race."

In truth, this was not the first time that Joe and Isabella had had a conversation of this kind. Her father, Eduard, the French insurance broker, had been a serial womanizer whose philandering was a frequent source of anguish for Isabella, even ten years after his death. When she had left Joe for Miles, a part of him rationalized the switch on the cod-Freudian basis that all women eventually married their fathers. Nevertheless, as he listened to Isabella on that summer morning, Joe experienced something of the same uncertainty that he had felt in the early stages of his conversations with Shahpour and Wang. *Is everybody lying to me, or is everybody telling the truth?*

"Where's this coming from?" he asked. "I don't know how I can help you. I don't know what it is that you want me to do."

She laughed. "Oh, Joe. You're so sweet. You were always so old-fashioned. I don't want you to *do* anything. It's just lovely to see you again. It's just lovely to talk. I had no idea how much I missed you. This place is so . . ."—she gestured north—"exhausting."

Joe would have reached out to touch her hand, but he lacked the confidence. Isabella had stripped that away from him. In the eight years without her he had put on skins, layers, a carapace of emotional toughness to prevent him from falling prey to another woman. It had worked, by and large. Megan had broken through for a little while, but as he sipped his coffee and reflected that his heart was still anchored to Isabella, he resolved to end that relationship as soon as possible. It didn't feel right. It wasn't going anywhere.

"Why do you stay with him?" he asked.

It was a brave question. Isabella ground out her cigarette.

"Because I made a vow. In church. In front of God."

Joe wasn't sure whether this was a statement or a question. His own faith had become a nebulous thing; he admired any expression of devotion. "Nothing else? Are things that bad between you?"

"They're like any marriage." She placed the sun hat on her head. "When they're good, they're good. When they're bad, they're bad.

The trouble is that the good times come along less and less often. So you're left with consolations. You're left with Jesse."

"Who's Jesse?" Even as Joe uttered the question he discovered its ghastly, inevitable answer. Jesse was their child. Miles and Isabella had a son.

"Miles really hasn't been too forthcoming with the information, has he?" she joked. Joe felt a void opening up inside him like a sickness. "Jesse's our son. My little boy."

"Where is he?" Joe had buried his shock in the only question he could think of. He felt betrayed and humiliated. Why had Miles not seized on the opportunity to wound him with the news when he had met him on Huaihai, or at M on the Bund?

"He's back at the house with Mary." Joe assumed that Mary was an *ayi*, a Chinese live-in nanny. "Do you want more coffee? Do you mind if I get something to eat?"

He knew that she had said it to relieve his sadness. He shook his head and smiled, saying, "No, but you go ahead," and Isabella stood up, making her way into the café. Why was he so distraught at the gift of a child? People got married. People had children. Miles was ten years older than Isabella; a pregnancy had been inevitable. The child was probably the one constant happiness in his mother's life. Why resent it?

Joe's mobile pulsed in his pocket. He took it out and saw that Waterfield was calling from London. The phone was not secure, so any conversation would have to be short and non-specific.

"Joe?"

He was grateful for the immediate distraction of work. "David. How are you?"

"Sorry to have been out of touch."

"It's all right."

A little boy walked past him eating a toffee apple. Waterfield moved straight to business. "No news on your doorman, I'm afraid. Sally's never heard of him. Ditto the chef."

The doorman was Ablimit Celil. The chef was a nickname for Memet Almas. "Sally" was agreed language for the database at Vauxhall Cross. Joe leaned his elbows on the table and took a chance.

"Have you tried asking in Pakistan?" He wanted to verify Wang's theory about the ISI. "I heard a rumour they'd worked in Islamabad. Might be worth checking."

"You're sure about that?"

"Not entirely."

Waterfield coughed. "I thought it was American owned?"

It amused Joe to hear him improvising with the coded language. Waterfield was part of the telegram generation. Speaking about an operation on an open line was contrary to every instinct he possessed for secrecy.

"I thought so too," he replied. "That still might be the case. It would just be interesting to know if the doorman ever had a job there."

Isabella was coming out of the museum. When she saw that Joe was on the phone, she stopped, offering to grant him some privacy. Seeing this, he shook his head and waved her over, telling Waterfield that he had to go.

"I'm having a coffee with Isabella," he said, because it would raise his stock in London.

"You are? Well, good for you. Be sure not to send her my love."

"Work?" Isabella asked when he had hung up. She had bought two bottles of water and a brace of dehydrated croissants.

"Work," Joe replied.

46 | THE LAST SUPPER

On the fifth floor of a Minxing Road apartment block, seven kilometres from downtown Puxi at the edge of a featureless, traffic-clogged freeway, Ablimit Celil set out the plan for the co-ordinated attacks of Saturday 11 June, codenamed ZIKAWEI.

It was 9 p.m. on the evening of Sunday the 5th. The one-bedroomed apartment was rented in the name Chan Chi-yung, a known associate of Mohammed Hasib Qadir, an officer of the Pakistani ISI. Celil was seated at the head of a low rectangular table in the living room. To his left was Memet Almas, unshaven and sipping from a bottle of water. To his right, Ansary Tursun was smoking a cigarette, dressed in a short-sleeved cotton shirt and denim jeans. Abdul Bary was directly opposite Celil, his pale face partly obscured by a baseball cap pulled low over the eyes. An hour earlier, the four members of the cell had been eating *kurdak*, a sweet and sour Uighur stew prepared with lamb, carrots and potatoes. The plates and cutlery had now been cleared away from the table and replaced by three improvised explosive devices, each consisting of 22 pounds of Goma-2 ECO gelignite, three detonators and three mobile telephones. Celil had spent forty minutes explaining how to arm the IED and to trigger it using the alarm clock on the phone.

He reminded the men that an unexploded bomb from El Pozo station in Madrid had failed to detonate on 11 March 2004 because the alarm had accidentally been set twelve hours late.

Standing up from the table, he started to detail the specifics of the plan.

"Remember this," he began. "Our brother Ansary was arrested by the Chinese authorities for owning a newspaper." He looked at Tursun and briefly clasped his hand. "He was tortured and brutalized for this harmless offence." Celil looked across the room and found Bary's eyes beneath the shadow of his cap. "Our brother Abdul was imprisoned for insulting a Han." Celil appeared to wince, as if somehow sharing the memory. "He was tortured and beaten for exercising his right to speak." Moving behind Almas, Celil now squeezed the muscles of the Kazakh's shoulders and stared directly ahead at Tursun. "Our brother Memet has come to us to free his Turkic brothers from the yoke of Chinese oppression." Almas bowed his head. "And we remember those who have died for our cause, who now regard us from paradise. We remember, in particular, our brother Enver Semed, a proud Uighur fighter held in the gulag of Guantanamo and later betrayed by the American infidel. We remember our Muslim brothers and sisters who are tortured daily at Abu Ghraib. We fight on behalf of all Muslims who find their lands occupied by imperial powers."

Celil picked up the pad. Five floors down, in a dusty Chinese courtyard, children were laughing.

"Here is what we plan. The Americans have paid us in dollars and blood. They believe that they control us. But their government has sided with the pigs of Beijing who occupy our land. We are stronger than the infidels. We will defeat them."

Abdul Bary was the most intelligent and thoughtful of the four men gathered in Shanghai that evening. He removed his baseball cap and placed it on the table. The edge of the cap touched a detonator and he separated the two objects like a superstition. Bary felt that the language of *jihad*, its grammar and vocabulary, sat uneasily on the tongue of Ablimit Celil, who was no more a man of God than the cats and dogs who roamed the filthy, dilapidated corridors of the anonymous apartment block in which they had found themselves. Every molecule of Celil's shabby, corrupted face spoke of violence and a zeal for blood. Did he truly believe in the possibility of an Eastern Turkestan, or had he moved beyond politics into the facile, deadly playground of violence for its own sake? Yet what choice did Bary now possess but to follow such men? How else could he bring about change in his country, if not through bombs and terror? It had never mattered to him who bankrolled the safe houses, who smuggled the explosives, who prepared the bombs or drew up the plans. All he wanted was results. He wanted the Chinese to stop shooting unarmed Muslim boys and girls. He wanted to stop innocent Uighurs being suspended from the ceilings of Chinese prisons and beaten repeatedly by their guards. He wanted an end to electric shocks, to torture, to imprisonment without trial. He wanted Uighurs to be free to express themselves without fear of execution for "political crimes." He wanted justice. This is what the Americans had promised them; this is what their new masters in Islamabad now seemed prepared to guarantee. If the short-term price of independence was an Islamist state, an Eastern Turkestan ruled by shariah law, so be it. The Uighur homeland would, at least, be independent. Chinese Xinjiang would have ceased to exist.

"Abdul?"

"Yes?"

He had not been listening. Celil fixed him with an impatient gaze. "You must concentrate. You must listen. It is the inspiration of our benefactor that we should kill the infidels who have betrayed our cause."

Abdul placed the cap back on his head. He did not immediately understand the significance of what Celil was saying.

"The attacks will take place six days from now, on the night of Saturday June the 11th. After that, we will not see each other again for many months. They will be simultaneous attacks, inspired by the bravery and the courage of our brothers in New York, our brothers in Egypt and Madrid. It is our destiny not only to bring destruction to the infidel Chinese, but also to the Americans who have made their homes among them. Our attacks will also claim the lives of Miles Coolidge and Shahpour Goodarzi, spies who will pay for their treachery and cunning."

348 / Charles Cumming

"How do you propose this?" Abdul asked. His experience, his gut, immediately reacted against any unnecessary complications.

Celil paused. Did he sense Abdul's reservations? To remove Miles and Shahpour had been the initiative of Hasib Qadir. It was the sole condition of the ISI's co-operation, and one that Celil readily agreed to. The plan was otherwise as straightforward as it was barbarous. It would bring ruin to Hollywood and terror to the streets of Shanghai. On the evening of 11 June, Ansary Tursun was to make his way to Paradise City and purchase a ticket, using cash, for the advertised 8:15 performance in Screen Eight of the Silver Reel Cinema. It would be a Saturday night; the multiplex would be packed. Once the film was under way, nobody would notice when Ansary exited the auditorium after thirty minutes, leaving a rucksack under his seat.

At the same time, Ablimit would arrange a crash meeting with Miles Coolidge for 8:45 p.m. He would arrive at Screen Four for the 8:25 performance, conceal his IED beneath his seat in the back row, and leave by the western fire exit before the film had begun.

On the morning of Friday 10 June, Memet Almas was to send a text message to Shahpour Goodarzi, asking him to telephone his grandparents in Sacramento. Memet would then arrange an emergency meeting with Shahpour at Larry's bar on Nanyang Road. The American would be asked to arrive at eight o'clock. Memet would go to the bar an hour earlier, leave his rucksack in the cloakroom, purchase a drink and a small plate of food, then leave before half-past seven.

The final member of the cell, Abdul Bary, was to take his wife and daughter to the sixth floor of the Paradise City mall and order a meal at the Teppenyaki Shinju, which was one of four restaurants located immediately beneath the seventh-floor foyer of the Silver Reel multiplex. On a Saturday night, each of the restaurants would be packed with diners, but it would be unusual for an impoverished Uighur family to be among them. Therefore, to avoid drawing the attention of passing security officials, Abdul was to dress as smartly as possible in the hope of passing himself off as a businessman visiting from overseas. At 8:15 he would begin to complain of a stomach cramp and go to the washrooms. He would take his rucksack with him, telling his wife that it contained necessary medicines. He would then withdraw the IED, place the device in the metal bin of the disabled washroom and return to his family. At 8:30, still complaining of sickness, Abdul would ask for the bill and leave the restaurant.

Celil now looked at each of the four men in turn. He had arrived at the most vital part of the meeting.

"You will go to the locations in order to prepare yourselves this week," he told them. "Each of the four devices will be timed to detonate at exactly nine o'clock. You are responsible for this. God has provided us with the tools to carry out his sacred work and now you must perform his task. I leave your bombs with you now." He indicated the three devices on the table. "Remember," he said, "this is only the first stage of our battle, a first phase in our work. There is more to come. Now let God be in your hearts. May he bring us together soon in Beijing."

47 | PRODUCT

The conversation with Waterfield had prompted Joe to act. If he was going to engage Isabella's co-operation in finding Ablimit Celil, this was the moment to do so. He did not feel that he was manipulating her by taking advantage of her mood of candour. On the contrary: she possessed vital information that it was his duty to extract.

"Can I ask you a question?"

"Of course."

"How much do you know about what Miles has been doing in China since 1997?"

Isabella had removed her hat because the sun had been obscured by a bank of yellowed clouds. She did not look at Joe as she said, "Very little."

"Are you interested in knowing?"

She touched her face. "Not really."

"Why?"

"Because we're not in business together, are we? We're husband and wife. I think it's better that I don't know things like that."

"He doesn't talk to you about his work? He doesn't complain or celebrate or use you as a shoulder to cry on?"

"Never." Isabella touched the fabric of her shirt. "Since when did Miles Coolidge ever need a shoulder to cry on?"

Joe met the remark with a nod of assent and tried a different, more combative tactic. "What if I told you that he was being investigated? What if I told you that MI6 has sent me to Shanghai to find out what he's up to?"

It was an extraordinary gamble, not least because it assumed that Isabella's loyalties lay with Queen and Country, rather than with her husband, the father of her child. Joe witnessed its impact in a moment of brittle shock which seemed to tighten Isabella's entire body. She looked at him in a way that she had not looked at him since the eve of *wui gwai*. With disbelief. With disgust.

"Are you still not who you appear to be, Joe?" she said quietly, and Joe knew that he would have to be extremely careful with his answer. One false move, one glib remark, one overly defensive plea for understanding, and she would leave the café. His only hope lay in complete honesty. His only way of convincing Isabella to help him now was to tell her the truth.

"I'll tell you who I am," he said. His voice was very steady, very controlled. "I have nothing to hide from you any more." He leaned forward, so that she could see directly into his eyes. "At the end of last year, I was on the point of leaving the Service. I'd been offered a job in Beijing and I was going to take it. I was sick of what was happening in Iraq, sick of the mood of defeat in London. Then David Waterfield came to me and told me that Miles had been at the forefront of a four-year American effort to destabilize Xinjiang."

"That doesn't surprise me," Isabella said quickly, though the remark was designed not to placate Joe, but somehow to restore her rapidly evaporating self-confidence.

"The operation was called TYPHOON. It was disbanded after 9/11 when Washington, in its infinite wisdom, more or less decreed that all Uighurs were terrorists. But in the last two years a clandestine unit within the CIA, mounted with Pentagon approval, has been trying to revive TYPHOON in mainland China. Miles has been at the forefront of that effort because he maintains links with Uighur separatists who were involved in acts of sabotage prior to September 11th." Joe saw that tears had welled in Isabella's eyes but that she was willing them away. "Elements within the American government, as far as we know without presidential approval, are planning a terrorist atrocity at the Beijing Olympics. Miles is at this moment attempting to recruit the men who will carry out that attack. There is also an al-Qaeda cell somewhere in Shanghai planning a hit this summer. That cell has American backing. It's what I'm here to try to stop. You ask me who I am. I've told you."

Isabella tipped her head back and looked at a point in the sky, breathing very slowly. She reached down for the hat and again placed it on her head, as if to shield herself from what Joe was telling her. He wanted to say "I'm sorry," he wanted to help her, but there was nothing he could do. Her husband was aiding and abetting terror.

"Why?" she said, shaking her head. She was staring at him, as if the whole thing was Joe's fault, another ghastly, unforeseen consequence of his secret identity.

"I really don't know," he said, and began talking again, because he felt that by doing so he would at least keep Isabella at the café. "The Americans want a massive loss of face at the Olympics. That's the simple answer. They want to show the world that China isn't as modern and sophisticated and peaceful as she says she is."

"How does killing people do that?"

Joe was briefly silenced, both by the question, with its unarguable logic, and by a passing security guard, who stared at him intently as if he were one of the exhibits at the museum. "The bombs would have a Uighur signature," he said finally. "They would bring the world's attention to the plight of the people of Xinjiang, to human rights abuses which have escalated tenfold since 9/11. The Americans would again start pressing for independence in Eastern Turkestan. If that happened, they would ultimately control the flow of oil into China, Japan and Korea."

"Are you mad? Do you believe this stuff? Have you listened to what you're saying?"

"Izzy, I'm not the guy who thought this up." He had briefly lost his temper, but the effect of his words was startling. Isabella made a gesture of apology, muttering, "All right, sorry, OK," as she sat back. Joe realized that he might quickly become her sanctuary. Who else, after all, did she have to turn to? "It's a new version of the Great Game," he said. "Who knows what Washington ultimately wants? To break up China? To make China more authoritarian? To bring sympathy to the Uighur people or to tar them with the same brush as al-Qaeda?" He unscrewed a bottle of water and poured its contents into a plastic cup. Isabella picked it up and drank from it without saying a word. "It's like Iraq. They've ended up with the exact opposite of everything they said they hoped to achieve, so maybe chaos and instability is what they wanted in the first place."

An announcement came over the public address system, praising "The Motherland, the Party, the Great Advance of Chinese Technology." Joe saw that Isabella understood what was being said and realized, with a feeling of almost sibling pride, that she had learned to speak Mandarin. He waited until the announcement had ended before continuing.

"Have you heard of a man called Shahpour Moazed?"

"Of course I have. I know Shahpour."

"Do you know what he does for a living?" Joe hoped that Isabella already knew about the CIA's arrangement with Microsoft, or things were going to get even more complicated.

"I know what he does for a living," she replied quietly.

"And what do you make of him?"

"What do I make of him?" She plainly regarded the question as an almost complete irrelevance. Nevertheless her response helped, in small measure, to lift the air of gloom which had descended on the conversation. "I think he's the sort of person Miles would like to be."

"What do you mean by that?"

"Not Shahpour, specifically. I mean the lifestyle of the Iranian male. Iranian wives do all the cooking, keep the house spotless, raise the children. They're completely subservient to their husbands. It's Miles's idea of paradise." A dog began barking in the distance. "So is that who you're following? Is Shahpour the traitor? Please don't tell me that or I think I might be sick."

Joe extracted a cigarette. He offered one to Isabella, who declined with a rapid shake of the head. She was grinding her teeth, the bones at the back of her jaw bulging like pearls. Had he been wrong to tell her? Had an impulse of cruel power, the wrath of his damaged subconscious, forced him to shatter what little happiness Isabella still possessed? Joe felt the sudden heat of guilt, as if he had deliberately exacted his revenge on a woman simply because she had failed to love him.

"Shahpour is one of the good guys," he said, a statement which appeared to make no impact upon her at all. Isabella was trying to be brave, trying to maintain her dignity in the face of his revelations, but she was pale and drawn with worry. He longed to hold her. "There are two reasons why I came here today," he said. "I wanted to see you because I needed to know that you were all right. I knew about Miles and I knew about Linda. I had some strange idea in my head that I could help you." Isabella was absolutely still and made no reaction. Joe could not tell if she wanted him to stay and to keep talking, or to leave and never to see her again. It occurred to him that she had no idea of the depth of his love for her, no idea of the extent to which she had haunted his dreams for eight long years. "The second reason is that I think you can help to stop what's going on. Shahpour has told me that Miles sometimes takes you when he meets the leader of the cell."

Her lovely eyes flicked up at him like a frightened animal. Joe saw the pain that he had caused her and which he longed to take back. "What do you mean by that?" she said.

"I mean that Miles uses you as cover when he contacts a man named Ablimit Celil. You may not be aware that he's doing it. Sometimes wives are informed, sometimes they're–"

"I'm aware of it."

Joe was startled. He had assumed that Isabella had remained completely unblemished by the tricks and prisms of tradecraft. "So you know Celil?"

She shook her head.

"But you're aware when Miles meets him?"

"I can guess when it happens."

A line of schoolchildren funnelled out of the café and colonized a nearby table. They were dressed in identical uniforms, navy blue satchels slung over their backs. One of them, a tall nine- or ten-year-old boy, slapped a classmate over the head and was reprimanded by his teacher. Isabella looked at the child and closed her eyes. She had sat up in a crouch on the chair, resting her chin on her knees.

"Would you be prepared to tell me about that?"

There was a flicker of a smile, an irony. So this is what Joe had come for. He wasn't a friend. He wasn't an ally. He was just a spy tapping her for information. Joe saw this and tried to defend himself.

"You must know that I wouldn't ask if it wasn't completely necessary and important." He looked down at his cigarette and felt as though he was smoking in church. "Nobody is using you, Izzy." He let it fall to the concrete. "The last person in the world I want to hurt is—"

"We go to the cinema," she said. Her voice was a flat, low confession, a whisper of secrets. It was like Wang breaking his silence in the safe house. Joe felt the familiar twin motors of elation and self-disgust.

"What do you mean?"

"Miles must meet this man in the cinema."

"What makes you think that?"

She looked at the ground. "Because we always go to the same place, to the same screen, the same mall. The Silver Reel at Paradise City." She released her legs and let them drop to the floor. There was an odd sort of defiance in her mood now, a preparedness to play things out. "Halfway through the movie, Miles gets up and goes to the back. I never ask him what he's doing, he never tells. Afterwards, when the film's finished, we meet for dinner downstairs. There's a Vietnamese restaurant there. A good one. On the sixth floor."

"You're sure?" Joe said.

"I'm sure."

Everything happens quickly now. The cell is in play.

On the late afternoon of Saturday 11 June, Ansary Tursun strolled along the broad walkway of the Bund, smoking a cigarette, his mind turning over the final details of the plan. Secured on his back, pulling down on his shoulders like the dead hard weight of a stone, was a small polyester rucksack in which he had placed a detonator, a telephone and a bomb.

Less than a mile to the south, amid the crowds and stalls of the ancient market at Yunyuan, Abdul Bary was buying a coconut. He removed his own rucksack from his back and extracted a small leather purse from the side pocket. He passed a crumpled twenty-yuan note to the stallholder and received a handful of coins in change. The husk of the coconut had been punctured with a pink straw and he handed it to his smiling daughter, who sucked hungrily at the cooling milk. His wife, who was on the eve of celebrating her twenty-seventh birthday, smiled at the child and reached for her outstretched hand.

The third member of the cell, the Kazakh Memet Almas, was in Nanshi district, waiting in the bored, miserable straggle of a bus queue. Twenty-four hours earlier he had sent a text message to Shahpour Goodarzi requesting that he contact his grandparents in Sacramento at the first available opportunity. Almas saw the bus coming towards him. It turned in the road, moving slowly towards the bus stop through a thin, shiftless mist of pollution. He spotted a seat towards the back of the packed interior, claimed it and sat down.

All three men had been captured on closed-circuit television, though it would be many weeks before the team investigating the events of 11 June were able to put together an exact picture of the cell's movements at this early stage of the evening. Ablimit Celil, for example, was seen for the first time stepping out of a taxi near the Xiaotaoyuan mosque, not far from Shahpour Moazed's apartment on Fuxing Road. The driver of the taxi, who happened to be a Hui Muslim, was interrogated for four subsequent days under suspicion of consorting with the plotters. He told a female officer of the People's Armed Police that Celil had recognized him as a fellow Muslim and that they had discussed a passage in the Koran during their short and otherwise uneventful journey. A surveillance camera, positioned in the roof of the Xiaotaoyuan, had photographed Celil at prayer, but the plain-clothes officer of the MSS, prostrated no more than ten feet away from him, had assumed from Celil's dress that he was a Turkic businessman or tourist visiting Shanghai from overseas. As a result, he had taken no further steps to follow him.

Celil had been fortunate in the timing of his contact with Miles Coolidge. He had sent a text message earlier in the day requesting a crash meeting at the Silver Reel cinema. Miles had been standing in the master bedroom of his villa in Jinqiao, preparing to leave on a five-day business trip to Beijing. Had Celil sent the message just three hours later, Miles would have been taxiing on the runway at Hongqiao and his planned demise amid the carnage of the Paradise City mall would have been rendered impossible.

Jesse was in his father's arms as the phone beeped in his pocket. Isabella was washing her hands in the bathroom. Two of Miles's battered leather suitcases were packed and waiting in the hall. To his startled, frustrated eyes, the contents of the message were straightforward enough; to anyone who happened to be looking in—a Chinese spook, say, or a paranoid, nosey wife—they were at best a number plate, at worst a line of garbled cyber nonsense.

SR4J 825M

"SR4" was Screen Four of the Silver Reel multiplex, their habitual meeting place. "J" was the first letter of *Jīnwǎn*, the Mandarin word for "tonight." "825" was the time of the screening, to which Miles routinely added twenty minutes in order to allow Celil time to find his seat. "M" was an arranged code to imply that the meeting was urgent.

"Fuck," Miles said, lowering the boy to the ground.

Turning her face from the sink, Isabella shot her husband a look of frustrated annoyance and eyeballed their sleepy son. Jesse was three years old. Use that kind of language in his presence and he'd be repeating it until Christmas.

Miles pressed "Reply" and began texting his response. Jesse said, "Carry me, Daddy," as his father typed the simple word "OK."

"Looks like I'm not going to Beijing after all." Miles looked up. "You feel like going to the movies tonight, honey?"

For Shahpour Moazed and Joe Lennox, the evening of Saturday 11 June had also assumed a vital importance.

As soon as Shahpour had received the text message mentioning his grandparents, he had contacted Joe and arranged to meet him for a late Friday drink at Bar Rouge. A stylish lounge where beautiful Chinese girls sip cocktails and size up the wallets of Western businessmen, Bar Rouge has a large outdoor terrace overlooking the Huangpu River, with clientele as fashionable—and frequently as vacuous—as any you will encounter in Shanghai.

"Memet wants to meet," Shahpour said. "At Larry's. His suggestion."

Joe, looking out at the warm neon river, took a sip of his vodka and tonic and said, "When?"

"Tomorrow night. Eight o'clock. I got a call at my office this afternoon."

The plan that Joe had devised was straightforward. Shahpour would go to the bar at eight. He would meet Almas and listen to what he had to say. He would buy him some drinks, order some food, tutor him in the ways of American football. Meanwhile, Joe would occupy a nearby table and follow Almas when he left the bar. At a suitable opportunity he would confront him, attempt to lead him to one of the quieter establishments near Nanyang Road and declare himself as an officer of the British SIS. This seemingly wild strategy possessed an absolute logic and coherence. While Almas struggled to work out what was happening to him, Joe would reveal that MI6 knew of the cell's plans to carry out an attack in Shanghai. He would name Ablimit Celil and Ansary Tursun as two of his co-conspirators. He would then present Almas with a choice: to become an agent of British intelligence, informing on the activities of the cell, or to face immediate incarceration, and probable execution, at the hands of the Chinese authorities. Joe was in a position to offer Almas's wife, whom he knew was currently living in Kashgar, residence in the United Kingdom. In due course, if he so wished, Almas would be able to join her. All that Joe required in return for a comfortable life in the West was three years of co-operation: product on the Shanghai operation and full details of any subsequent activities in the run-up to the Olympics of 2008.

It was the sort of snap recruitment in which Joe Lennox specialized and, in different circumstances, it might well have worked. It was just that it was happening far too late. This time, Joe Lennox was behind the game.

As he had been preparing to leave the Agosto Language School on Yuanda Road four days earlier, Professor Wang Kaixuan had been called into the secretary's office to receive a telephone call. He had assumed that it was a student contacting him to discuss a recent assignment or to arrange private tuition. He had assumed wrong.

"Teacher."

The low, hollow voice of Abdul Bary cut short his breath.

"Abdul?"

"Say nothing more." Bary was whispering. "I have a warning."

Wang, his back turned to a group of American students paying fees in the office, had covered the mouthpiece and stepped closer to the wall.

"An operation is in motion. An operation for Saturday. It is the plan to start a new era and to destroy our former friends. I am calling only to warn you. If you are travelling to Zikawei, turn back. Do not come to Shanghai this weekend. If anybody from our past has invited you, they are traitors. Do not trust them. I am telling you this only to protect you. I am telling you this in thanks for all that you have done."

"Zikawei?" Wang had replied. "Zikawei?" Nobody had invited him to Shanghai. He had not even spoken of TYPHOON since John Richards's visit in May. "Are you there?"

The line had gone dead. Behind him, an American was shouting, "Dude! No way! Dude!"

Bary was gone.

Ablimit Celil left the Xiaotaoyuan mosque at half-past six. He had decided to walk the relatively short distance south to the confluence of shopping malls at Xujiahui. It was a close, humid evening, gluey sweat forming beneath the straps of his cheap polyester rucksack, yet the weight of the bomb, the pressure of the operation, had been lifted by his hour of prayer. It had been Celil's first visit to a mosque in more than two years; breaking his self-imposed exile had remade him.

In Jinqiao, in the kitchen of their villa, Miles and Isabella were edging round an argument.

"So what movie are we going to see?" she asked.

Miles was replacing a broken plug on a microwave oven and flashed his wife a look of impatience. Isabella knew as well as he did that his trip to Beijing had been cancelled because there was an emergency in Shanghai. He needed to get to the Silver Reel by half-past eight. It would look better if she went with him.

"It's Chinese," he said. "You'll like it."

"What's it about?"

Isabella must have been in one of her moods; she didn't normally ask so many questions. Lately she'd been behaving strangely. He wondered if she knew about Linda. He had checked the Silver Reel listings online and now proceeded to describe the basic outline of the film.

"What else is on?" she asked when he had finished.

He dropped the screwdriver. "Honey, if we were going on a date, we'd be going to Xintiandi, right?" Miles was referring to the cinema complex at the Xintiandi development, which was closer to Pudong and more popular with expats. "Now, do you wanna come, or don't you? I gotta leave in twenty minutes."

"Do you *need* me to come?" she asked. She was wondering how she was going to alert Joe.

"Sure I need you to come. So will you make up your mind? There's gonna be traffic."

Professor Wang Kaixuan was haunted by the conversation with Abdul Bary. He tried, as best he could, to recall every word of their brief and disturbing exchange.

It is the plan to start a new era and to destroy our former friends.

What exactly had Bary meant by this? What was the nature of the new era? By "friends," had Bary meant the Americans, or did the word now carry a different meaning? In the middle of a language class, or during a work-out in Jingshan Park, the professor would find himself thinking about the conversation. Was it a trap? Had Bary betrayed him? He could not work out what it was that he was expected to do.

The answer came to him while he was walking in the streets near his home. He had a duty to warn the authorities of what was about to happen in Shanghai. Wang could no more pretend to be a political agnostic than he could return to the Xinjiang of his youth and alter the path that he had taken as an academic and radical. But how to inform the Chinese of what was happening without risking his own wellbeing? An anonymous phone call would likely be ignored. Besides, why give the government the satisfaction of preventing an atrocity that would further undermine the Uighur cause?

Wang was also concerned for his former students. Bary and Tursun might have attached themselves to a religious code which he believed to be both counter-productive and ideologically bankrupt, but they had only embraced radical Islam because there were no further options left open to them. The Chinese, the Americans and, now, the government in Islamabad had effectively turned two idealistic young men into terrorists. All his students had ever wanted was their land back; now they stood to set back the cause of liberation by a generation.

He decided to send the warning in the form of an email. He was taking an extraordinary personal risk in doing so. Trace the message and the Chinese would lock Wang away for life. Send it out into cyberspace and he would have no clue as to its ultimate destination.

He chose a small internet café far from his home. For half an hour he watched the entrance from a restaurant across the street, concluding that enough customers passed through the door for his own brief appearance to be ignored or even forgotten. Wang ascertained that there were no surveillance cameras operating near the premises, though he was certain that there would be at least one camera recording activity in the café. Leaving the restaurant, he put on a pair of bifocal spectacles but otherwise effected no further changes to his appearance. The trick was not to draw attention to oneself, but to appear as bland and as unremarkable as the millions of other Chinese men who lived and worked in Beijing.

There was one small obstacle. In order to use a public computer in China, it is necessary to present an identity card—a *shen fen zheng*—to the operator of the internet café. Wang had kept only one false ID from the era of TYPHOON, a laminated card, prepared by the CIA's Graphics and Authentication Division, which stated his name as Zhang Guobao. Upon entering the café, Wang presented the card to the young man behind the desk and was relieved when he began recording its details, as required by Chinese law, in the café's log book, without bothering to compare Wang's bespectacled face with the outdated black-and-white photograph in the *shen fen zheng*. Wang then purchased a twenty-renminbi card which gave him thirty minutes of screen time. He sat at a terminal with his back facing the small security camera bolted on the rear wall. Settling into his seat, he then accessed a dormant email account which he had used several years earlier to communicate with Kenneth Lenan.

Wang Kaixuan was on the point of composing his message when he looked up and saw that a uniformed officer with the Beijing police had walked into the café. The policeman was moving slowly, glancing idly around the room. Suddenly it occurred to Wang that he was at least twenty years older than almost every other customer in the café; bored, glassy-eyed teenagers were slumped in front of the other monitors, others huddled in groups of three or four taking turns to play online games. Wang looked out of place among them; he wasn't a part of the cyber generation.

A less experienced man might have panicked at this point, but the professor ignored the chill he felt on the surface of his skin and simply signed out of the email account and typed in the web address of a local daily newspaper. The policeman was now making idle conversation with the assistant behind the counter. They lit cigarettes and eyed up a girl. The cop began flicking distractedly through the pages of a magazine and did not seem particularly interested in using one of the terminals himself.

Wang looked to his left. There was an exit three metres from his chair. He could make a run for it, but if the police had come for him, chances are they would have already sealed off the rear of the building. Yet there was surely no possibility that they could know what he was doing: Zhang Guobao's personal details—his place of birth, ID number, the city in which he was registered to live—had been recorded only moments earlier. It was far too soon for the authorities to have noticed. Perhaps the password on his email account had alerted them. Wang knew that Lenan had been murdered in suspicious circumstances, and that most of the networks with which he had been involved had been rolled up by the MSS. It had been foolish to use the account, foolish to use the Zhang Guobao identity. But what other choice did he have?

A further five minutes passed. The professor remained in his seat, watching the cop, watching the doors. He wanted to take his glasses off, because they had begun to hurt his eyes, but it was important not to change his appearance or to draw attention to himself with even the slightest movement. Then, to his horror, he saw the policeman reach for the log book and begin to study the list of recent entries. Wang kept his head down but could sense the policeman looking up and checking activity at the terminals. Was he looking for Zhang Guobao? In time, a woman in her mid-thirties, seated at an opposite terminal, stood up and walked out of the café. When the police officer did not bother to turn round and look at her, Wang felt that he was safe; this cop was clearly just passing the time. According to the clock in the lower left-hand corner of his computer, he had sixteen minutes remaining. As long as the official left within that period, everything would be all right.

Wang waited. He clicked through random pages—news stories, classified ads, letters—and rehearsed the details of Zhang Guobao's cover in the event of a brief interrogation. He was an engineer, born in Chongqing, registered to live in Beijing. Surely none of these personal details would be necessary? The police officer was not about to interview every one of the twenty or twenty-five customers in the café. He was just a friend of the proprietor, stopping by for an idle chat. At the very worst he might walk around on a power trip, looking over shoulders, the personal embodiment of state power.

A further ten minutes passed. Wang could not risk returning to the desk and purchasing another half-hour of time if the cop was still there. Why had he spent so little money? Why had he not bought two or three hours and spared himself these agonies? He began to develop a migraine and longed to return home. He considered briefly the possibility of returning at a later point in the day, but knew that time was a factor if he was to influence events in Shanghai. Eventually, with only five minutes of credit remaining, the police officer walked outside.

It was as if the entire room breathed a sigh of relief. Wang returned immediately to the dormant Lenan account. The email address had been given to him by Mr. John Richards, a man whom Wang trusted and admired. He had looked into the eyes of Joe Lennox and realized that he alone possessed the power to stop the bombs. An old man who had seen too much blood still believed that his salvation lay in England.

He began to type:

An attack is set for Saturday, Mr. Richards. The code they have used is "ZIKAWEI."

49 | CHATTER

On Nanjing Road, not far from the triple towers of the Ritz-Carlton hotel, Memet Almas stepped down from the crowded, shuddering bus, shouldered his rucksack and began walking north along Tongren Lu. Celil had suggested that he arrive at Larry's at seven o'clock, but he was fifteen minutes early.

Almas's movements between 6:45 and 7:00 p.m. remain a mystery: traffic cameras lost him in a black hole on the corner of Tongren and Nanyang Lu. Unimaginative, yet thorough by nature, it seems likely that he waited on a deserted stairwell close to the bar, making a last-minute adjustment to his IED. Satisfied that he could do little more than pray for the successful outcome of the operation, the Kazakh entered Larry's just after seven o'clock. Staff at the bar remembered a man, whom they took to be a tourist from Central Asia, ordering a bottle of Michelob, eating a plate of nachos and leaving before half-past seven. The coat-check girl, to whom Almas had handed his rucksack, recalled only that the customer had seemed quiet and polite. Confronted with his photograph forty-eight hours later, she recalled that she had joked that the rucksack seemed unusually heavy. No, she had not witnessed him leave. It was happy hour, the bar was busy. She wished that she had been paying closer attention.

Shahpour Moazed was hailing a taxi on Fuxing Road just as Almas was walking out of the bar. He had cleaned his apartment. He had shaved off his beard. The prospect of the meeting filled him with an excitement that was as new as it was unexpected. This was the impact that Joe Lennox had had on his life; there was now vigour and meaning to his work. If Joe succeeded in his recruitment of Almas, Shahpour's years in China would not have been wasted. Together they would put a stop to the bombs. Together they would bring Miles Coolidge to his knees. Shahpour had adjusted to the probing, thorough approach of the British. He trusted Joe implicitly and believed that the evening would be an unqualified success.

For his part, Joe had spent most of the day fielding Quayler-related calls at his apartment in the French Concession. In mid-afternoon, seemingly oblivious to the fact that it was a Saturday, a representative from a German pharmaceutical company had telephoned requesting detailed information about Chinese patent law. At 4:50 Joe had taken a call from his father. At about 5:15 he had switched off his phone and taken a nap, waking an hour later to discover a text message from Megan—"Dinner?"—and a follow-up from Tom which convinced him that they were working in tandem. He had broken things off with Megan ten days earlier. She had taken the news calmly, but appeared to be trying to hold on to the possibility of a reconciliation. As things turned out, it would be several months before they would see one another again.

Isabella rang just after seven. Her number was programmed into Joe's mobile and his excitement at seeing the read-out was tempered only by the thought that she might be calling with bad news.

"Joe? It's me. Izzy."

Her voice had a quality of defiance perhaps even of mischief. She was standing in Jesse's bedroom at the villa in Jinqiao, watching Miles drinking a glass of white wine in the garden below. For days now she had been looking at her husband as if he were an apparition. Even given all that she knew about Miles Coolidge, it was impossible to imagine that the man she had once loved had organized an operation on the scale of TYPHOON, given his blessing to a terrorist cell which planned to kill thousands of innocent Chinese.

"It might be happening tonight," she said. She was betraying the father of her child and yet her words felt like an act of liberation. "He's taking me to the cinema."

In view of Joe's plans for Larry's, the timing was disastrous. Yet to hear Isabella's voice was thrilling. She had kept her word.

"Where?" Joe said.

"Silver Reel. Eight twenty-five in Screen Four. It's the usual place."

"That's in less than two hours. When did this get decided?"

"This afternoon. Miles got a text message. He was on his way to the airport. Cancelled everything."

Isabella looked outside. To her horror she saw that Miles was no longer in the garden. She looked directly below the window but saw no sign of him on the patio. How long had he been gone? Was he already in the house, listening to everything she had said? For a moment she froze, unable to know what to say or do.

"Isabella?"

"I have to go," she whispered.

"What?"

"I said I have to go. He's coming."

Joe ignored her concerns. He was frustrated that it had taken her so long to ring him. Why had she waited? What was the reason for the delay? "Screen Four?" he said.

Isabella was listening at the door of the bedroom, torn between her loyalty to Joe and the pure fear of losing everything. She crossed the room and again looked out of the window. Miles's empty wine glass was toppled over on the grass. Against her better judgment she whispered, "Yes. Screen Four."

Footsteps on the staircase. At the top or the bottom? It sounded as though Miles was already upstairs. Jesse, God bless him, was splashing and shouting in the bath. Miles would surely have assumed that Isabella was with him. And there was indeed a look of surprise on his face when she emerged from their son's bedroom, holding the phone.

"Who you been talking to, honey?"

She longed to say the single word "Joe," just to see the look on Miles's face, just to let him know that the game was up. Instead she lied and told her husband that a friend had called from England.

"So you ready to go?" he asked. Mary, the *ayi*, emerged from the bathroom with Jesse wrapped in a towel. "The driver's waiting downstairs."

"I'm ready to go," she replied. "I've been ready for ages."

By the time Isabella and Miles were on the Yan'an Road, making their way through Saturday night traffic towards Xujiahui, Abdul Bary had told his wife that, as a surprise on her twenty-seventh birthday, he was taking her to the Teppenyaki Shinju restaurant on the sixth floor of the Paradise City mall. He explained that he had been saving up for weeks, although the money to pay for the dinner had actually come from Ablimit Celil. He said that he knew how much she loved Japanese restaurants; this one had a fish tank which their daughter would adore.

Ansary Tursun had bought his ticket, using cash, for Screen Eight of the Silver Reel multiplex. He saw to his satisfaction that the cinema was going to be packed. Unusually for China, two American summer blockbusters had been released in the space of two weeks: the first was showing in Screen Three, the auditorium immediately adjacent to Screen Four, the second in Screen Eight. Under the disinterested eyes of an elderly guard, Tursun wandered out of the lobby, past the life-size cut-outs of Elmo and Bugs Bunny, and headed down to the fifth floor. He looked idly at some shirts in French Connection and spent half an hour browsing in a branch of the Xinhua bookshop. Closed-circuit television recordings suggest that he read the first few pages of a historical study of ancient Egypt before replacing the book on a shelf.

As he returned to the seventh floor, walking back into the cinema, it is possible that Ansary Tursun would have passed Ablimit

Celil. Did they look at one another? Did they find some way of acknowledging the enormity of what they were about to set in motion? The lobby was packed with teenagers on dates, students queuing for popcorn, *laowais* trying to work out which films were dubbed and which ones had English subtitles. Beneath a bank of television screens playing trailers for forthcoming features, Celil paid for his ticket using a credit card. The card had been registered in a false name, to a Dubai postal address, by Mohammed Hasib Qadir. Ablimit had used it many times and it had never given him any problems.

It was 8:15 p.m.

Joe Lennox had a decision to make. He had gone directly to the Silver Reel on the afternoon of his meeting with Isabella. He knew that there were three separate exits from Screen Four, all of which it would be impossible to cover alone. Without the assistance of Zhao Jian, he was stymied. With a man covering the western fire exit, another in the lobby and a third on the staircase which linked the multiplex to the restaurants on the sixth floor, it might be possible to track Celil. But he had been counting on Shahpour's assistance when the day came. It seemed an act of the cruellest fate that both Almas and Celil had requested crash meetings at the same time. Perhaps there was a problem with the cell, an ideological conflict, a clash of personalities. He would be fascinated to learn what Almas told Shahpour during their meeting at the bar.

He rang Zhao Jian's number. There was no reply. He waited two minutes and tried again. An answering machine kicked in and Joe left a message, requesting that Jian contact the offices of Quayler pharmaceuticals as soon as possible.

Joe had a second number for Jian's brother, Yun, which he had never had cause to use. He dialled it. This time, someone answered.

The voice at the end of the line was impatient and tired. "Yes?"

"This is Joe Lennox."

"Who?"

An inauspicious start. "I'm a friend of your brother."

A dawning recognition. "Oh, Mr. Joe."

They were speaking in Mandarin. If Yun was alarmed by the fact that he was speaking to an undercover British intelligence officer on an open line, he betrayed no sign of anxiety. He asked after Joe's health and informed him that Jian was at a funeral in Yancheng.

"And what about you? What are you up to this evening?"

"I have a stomach cramp, Mr. Joe," Yun replied.

"You'll feel better after a cab ride. How soon can you get to Xujiahui?"

A long pause. Joe felt that he could hear Yun sitting up, stretching, checking his watch. "After eight o'clock?"

"That's good of you. I have urgent business. Is your other brother there?"

"My other brother also at the funeral."

Joe had been walking around his apartment as he spoke, filling a shoulder bag with a back-up mobile phone, his wallet and a street plan of Shanghai. "Meet me at the entrance to the Paradise City mall," he said. He was looking for his keys. "Get there as soon as possible."

Shahpour was on his way to Larry's when Joe called with the bad news. He explained that Celil had also called a meeting with Miles at the Silver Reel multiplex. The opportunity was too good to resist: he was going to meet Yun at Paradise City and attempt to follow Celil to his home. Once he had established where he was living, Joe would alert the MSS, anonymously, that Celil was a Uighur separatist planning a terrorist atrocity in Shanghai. After that, he was China's problem.

"Where does that leave me?" Shahpour asked. He felt a cramp of frustration. This wasn't what he wanted. This wasn't what they had planned. "Where does that leave my meet with Almas?"

"It leaves it exactly where it was. Chances are I won't even get close to Ablimit tonight. He's too cautious. Neither Yun nor I even know what he looks like. I'm taking a gamble that he's either going to leave by the western fire exit or take the stairs to the restaurants. You'll have to try and keep Memet at the bar for as long as you can. Make regular trips to the bathroom. Go out and buy chewing gum if you have to. Get him drunk. Get him a girl. If I haven't had any luck with Ablimit by quarter-past nine, I'll jump in a cab and come to you. Is that all right?"

Shahpour looked at the digital clock in his taxi. At most, he would have to kill ninety minutes in Memet's company. It wasn't too bad. He had done it before. "That's all right," he conceded. "I can take care of it."

Shahpour soon became snarled in traffic at the edge of the French Concession. The driver was listening to coverage of a ping-pong tournament on the radio. With only five minutes to go until the meeting, Shahpour paid his fare and jogged the last quarter-mile to the bar, arriving in a breathless sweat. Almas usually waited on the second floor, in one of the quieter corners of the bar, away from televisions and the clack of pool, so Shahpour walked upstairs and scanned the customers. There were between thirty and forty of them, almost all exclusively expat males from Europe and North America. Rock music was playing on the sound system. Draught beers and burgers were flowing. He made a complete circuit of the room but saw no sign of Almas. Downstairs it was even busier: Chinese girls in short skirts flirting with customers; Australians watching highlights of a rugby match; Brits and Americans telling stories and quaffing margaritas. Still no sign of Almas. Shahpour checked the bathrooms, checked the street. He told himself to re-lax and buy a drink. The Kazakh was probably caught in the same traffic which had delayed him on his way from Fuxing Road. Shanghai on a Saturday night was always chaotic. Shanghai on a Saturday night was murder.

Joe took one look at the cars and mopeds clogging up the French Concession and decided to walk to Xujiahui. It was a stifling night, horns and engines adding to the bass notes of heat and pollution which thrummed through the Chinese summer. He headed south along Hengshan Road, passing Zapata's, passing a strip of bars where girls whistled at him as he walked by, trying to lure him inside for a drink. He made it to the entrance of the Paradise City at 8:15, by which point Abdul Bary, eating sushi with his wife and daughter in the Teppenyaki Shinju, had begun to complain of a stomach ache. His wife, wearing a necklace which her husband had given to her as a birthday present at the start of the meal, placed her chopsticks in their holder and put a protective hand on his back.

"Are you all right?"

The restaurant was almost completely full. Abdul Bary looked up and winced. His daughter was on the far side of the room, gazing into a fish tank.

"I'll be fine," he said. "It's your birthday." He managed a brave smile. "There is medication in my rucksack. I will be fine."

Moments later, Bary had locked the door of the disabled bathroom. All around him he could hear the steady murmur of laughter and conversation, the lives of the men, women and children his comrades planned to kill.

He lifted the lid of the bin and removed several handfuls of damp paper towels, a crumpled sheet of newspaper and an empty packet of cigarettes. He unzipped the rucksack, removed the IED, and placed it at the base of the bin. The phone, he saw, was active. The read-out said 8:23 p.m. He covered the bomb with the newspaper, camouflaged the device with the towels and closed the lid. Someone was knocking on the door. Bary flushed the toilet and washed his hands. He placed six rolls of toilet paper in the rucksack to give it weight and bulge, and smiled as he opened the door.

On the seventh floor, barely thirty or forty metres away, Ansary Tursun stood up in Screen Eight of the Silver Reel multiplex. The rows surrounding him were almost completely full. He had been among the first people to arrive in the auditorium, placing the rucksack under his seat as soon as he had sat down. As the advertisements began, he could feel the bomb resting against the heels of his shoes. It was wedged against the wall. Nobody would know it was there. Nobody would suspect a thing.

Ablimit Celil saw Miles Coolidge enter the cinema at half-past eight. His wife was with him. The cinema, to his frustration, was half empty, a flaw in the plan which he blamed on the Han appetite for bankrupt American culture. Miles and Isabella sat down. Ablimit was in his usual seat, alone, at the far end of row Q. Just as Ansary had done, he had wedged his rucksack against the rear wall of the cinema. When Miles approached in twenty minutes' time, he would have no idea that it was there.

A message shown on the screen requested that patrons refrain from using phones during the film. Ablimit smiled and thought that he saw Isabella dutifully switching off her mobile.

The lights in the cinema dimmed like an eye test.

Professor Wang Kaixuan's email had been sitting on an SIS server for three long days. By a stroke of good fortune, an alert analyst in the Far East Controllerate, one of the few with knowledge of RUN's operation in Shanghai, had noticed that Joe had failed to download it. Late on the morning of Saturday 11 June he had telephoned David Waterfield and given him the news.

Within two minutes Waterfield was dialling Joe on a scrambled line to Shanghai. There wasn't time for contemplation or delay. He was enraged.

"Joe?"

Joe had just spotted Zhao Jian's brother at the entrance to the Paradise City. He was walking up the steps towards him, his clothes and body soaked with sweat.

"David?" He wondered why London was calling on the Quayler mobile and assumed that the conversation was encrypted. "It's not a great time."

"I'll be brief then. Have you checked your emails lately?"

"David, at the last count, I had seventeen separate email addresses. The answer is no. Probably not. I haven't."

"Didn't think so." Waterfield was staring at the printout in front of him.

An attack is set for Saturday, Mr. Richards. The code they have used is "ZIKAWEI."

"Something rather odd has crossed my desk," he said. "Something rather disturbing."

Joe was struggling to hear above the noise of the intersection. The giant, fifty-foot-high photograph of David Beckham gazed down at him from the façade of the Metro City mall like an image from a parallel world. He raised a hand at Yun and waved him inside. The blessed chill of air conditioning greeted them both like a soothing balm.

"Go on."

"Do you want to tell me what you're up to?"

Joe didn't need this. Not now. Not with everything that was going on. London had effectively abandoned him, so he had abandoned London. It was that simple. This wasn't the moment for a lecture about the team ethic, for warnings about "going off piste." He would rather Waterfield just left him in peace and allowed him to get on with his job.

"David, I might have to call you back."

"And I might have to start worrying about your position."

"What's that supposed to mean?"

"Guy Coates said you had a meeting in Beijing the other day." Waterfield had put two and two together. "That wasn't on the books. Do you want to explain why?"

Joe removed the phone from his ear and swore under his breath. Why was Waterfield bringing this up now? Yun was staring at him, waiting for further instructions. "Can this not wait?" he said.

"You weren't pursuing your little infatuation with the professor, by any chance? Tell me that isn't the case because I warned you about that."

Joe thought about hanging up, but it wasn't his style. He didn't like admitting defeat. Besides, to do so would be to indicate culpability. "What makes you say that?"

Waterfield tried a different approach. "When I called the other day, where were you?"

"With Isabella. I told you. Why?"

"Don't lie to me, Joe. For God's sake don't lie."

"David, what the hell is going on?"

"I have said before and I will say it again. You are in Shanghai to get close to Miles Coolidge. You are in Shanghai to find out what the hell happened to Kenneth Lenan. Now I want to know what progress you have made."

It was like being scolded by a schoolmaster, a humiliating, infuriating interjection by someone who had lost all trust in his abilities. A salesgirl approached him and attempted to spray aftershave onto his wrist. Joe waved her away.

"David, it sounds to me as though we should have this conversation at a time that's convenient for both of us. I will explain myself to you at that point. Now I really have to—"

"Does the word 'Zikawei' mean anything to you?"

Joe again removed the phone from his ear, gesturing at Yun to apologize for the delay in issuing him with instructions. "How are you spelling that?" he said.

"Z–I–K–A–W–E–I."

Joe couldn't think straight. He was still incensed. It would take him about a minute to work out the implications. Meanwhile he was heading towards a bank of escalators and wondering why Waterfield was wasting his time.

"I'm going to read to you the contents of an email that was sent to one of your addresses on the Office server."

"Go ahead," Joe said. He didn't care if he sounded insubordinate. Yun was walking alongside him now. They had twenty minutes, at best, to be in position.

Waterfield continued, "The message reads: 'An attack is set for Saturday, Mr. Richards. The code they have used is "ZIKAWEI."'"

Joe stopped at the bottom of the escalators and felt a jab at the base of his gut. Mr. Richards. The professor was trying to contact him. Why the hell hadn't he checked his emails? "Can you repeat that?" he said.

"Of course." There was a controlled superciliousness in Waterfield's voice as he read the message a second time. "Wasn't Richards the name by which you were known to our friend?" he asked.

"Yes it was," Joe admitted.

"So you have been to see him?"

Joe was wondering how to play it, working out if he had the

time to lie. "Attack?" he replied, ignoring the question. "He says an attack is set for Saturday?"

"That is correct. And the code associated is this word 'ZIKA-WEI.'"

The full meaning of the email was beginning to dawn on him. "Can you Google it?"

Waterfield had to admire RUN's nerve. Sitting down in front of a Vauxhall Cross computer, he opened Internet Explorer, hit a Favorite for Google and typed "Zikawei" into the search bar. "Sorry," he found himself muttering. "Should have done this before."

"What does it say?" Joe asked.

Waterfield read out the contents of the top line:

> The Xujiahui Library of Shanghai. Pronounced "Zika-wei" in the local dialect.

"Must be Shanghainese," Waterfield said. "Do you want me to go on?"

Joe Lennox froze in the blinding white atrium of the Paradise City mall.

Zikawei. Xujiahui.

9/11. 3/11. 6/11.

The attack was happening now.

He should have gone to the fire alarms first, should have immediately alerted a guard. Instead, his first overwhelming instinct was to protect Isabella. Joe hung up on Waterfield and dialled her number.

Her phone was switched off.

Zhao Jian's brother was staring at him as if he had lost his mind. Joe dialled the number again. He swore aloud when he heard the message a second time and offered a silent prayer that Isabella had decided to remain at home.

"Izzy, it's Joe. If you get this, call me. Straight away. It's not safe. For God's sake, stay away from Xujiahui. Tell Miles to get out of there. There are bombs. It's a trap. For Christ's sake, stay away."

He turned to Yun.

"There's going to be an attack." He was holding Zhao Jian's brother by the arms, hands gripping his shoulders. "Find a fire alarm," he said. "Alert the guards. Tell them to evacuate all the malls in Xujiahui as soon as possible. Do this as fast as you can."

Joe did not wait for a reply. He was already pounding up the escalators, desperate to reach the cinema. Between the fourth and fifth floors, hordes of Chinese shoppers staring at him as he pushed past, he realized that Shahpour was also in danger. Almas, after all, had called the meeting. How could he have been so stupid, so short-sighted, as to ignore that coincidence?

Shahpour was on the ground floor of Larry's when his mobile lit up on the bar. Alice Cooper was screaming out of the sound system. He moved his gin and tonic to one side and looked at the read-out.

"Joe. Hey buddy. What's going on?"

Joe had to shout against the pounding rock music. "Shahpour?"

"I'm here."

"Memet hasn't shown up, has he?"

Shahpour frowned. He could barely hear what was being said. He picked up his drink and moved towards the entrance. It would be easier to talk out on the street. "How did you know that?" he shouted.

Joe prayed that Shahpour would have the courage to do what he was now going to ask him to do. "I think he's already been and gone . . ."

"What do you mean?"

"Listen to me. Don't interrupt and don't question what I'm going to tell you. There's going to be an attack on Larry's. At any moment. You've been lured into a trap. Xujiahui is going too. It's a multiple strike. Get everybody out of there as soon as possible. And I mean everybody. Do it now and do it fast."

"Joe, man." Shahpour had started to laugh, but he felt a fear inside him as cold as the condensation on the rim of his glass. "Are you sure about this? Are you sure?"

"Do it, Shahpour. Hit the fire alarm. Do it now."

At that moment, fifty metres short of the Silver Reel lobby, exhausted by his race to the seventh floor, Joe heard the Paradise City alarm. Yun had done his job. The vast white atrium screamed.

A Chinese guard in a pale blue shirt was standing in front of him. When he heard the piercing siren, his eyebrows wormed with frustration. Another false alarm. Another problem.

"Listen to me," Joe said. To his despair, he saw only a typical Chinese ambivalence in the guard's exhausted eyes. He held him at the elbows, as if trying to shake him from a deep sleep. "You have to evacuate the area." He was speaking in Mandarin. "You have to help me. Will they hear the alarm in the cinemas?"

It was useless. It was like talking to a child. Joe released him and sprinted into the cinema.

In the lobby, lined with posters of Harrison Ford, of Humphrey Bogart and Bruce Willis, staff were staring up at the ceiling, convinced that the alarm was a momentary problem that would soon go away. Customers, covering their ears, continued to queue up at the popcorn concession. Teenagers continued to kiss.

"Get out of here!" Joe shouted, a madman, a *laowai*. At first nobody seemed to know what to do. One woman actually laughed. Joe screamed at a member of staff to help him as the guard came up behind, raising his voice now, trying to grab Joe and to pin him down.

He shook himself free. The alarm was unrelenting. Up ahead, to Joe's relief, he saw a bewildered shoal of people apparently filing out of the cinemas, moving in bored slow motion along the darkened corridor. The ticket girl looked confused. Everybody looked confused. Joe went past them, shouting at them to hurry, urging them to get down the stairs and out onto the street. He ran down the multiplex corridor, past the numbers of the screens glowing like lights on a runway. He burst into Four, eyes blacked out by the darkness, his senses adjusting to the deafening noise of the cinema.

"Get out of here!" he screamed in Mandarin. "Everybody, everybody get out!"

He realized that the volume of the film had rendered the alarm inaudible. The audience tutted at him to sit down.

"Isabella!" Joe now tried shouting in English. "Isabella! There's a bomb in the cinema. It's a trap. Get out of here! Move! Run!"

Two of the four bombs exploded.

Shahpour Moazed's first reaction to Joe's warning had been to close his phone and to stand stock still in the entrance of the bar, in what he would later describe as a state of suspended animation. He was just a few feet away from the cloakroom. Shahpour caught the eye of a young British man making his way up the steps from Nanyang Road. He wanted to reach out and grab him, to warn him to stay away, but his courage was lacking. It was 8:47 p.m.

"Christ," he whispered and, with the resigned deliberation of a man with no choice other than to make a fool of himself, he placed his gin and tonic on a nearby step and walked back into the bar. Alice Cooper was still wailing from the stereo. Standing between two waitresses, Shahpour spoke to the oldest of the four bartenders, a New Zealander wearing an All Blacks T-shirt.

"Turn the music off," he shouted. He was still trying to find his courage. His voice lacked impact.

"What's that, mate?"

"You've got to turn the music off. Get everybody out of here. There's a bomb in the bar."

The Kiwi was shaking his head. Either he couldn't hear what

382 / Charles Cumming

Shahpour was saying or had written him off as a drunk. Neither of the waitresses, both of whom were Chinese, reacted to what Shahpour was saying. He could see the hi-fi system on a shelf behind the bar, obscured by a pile of napkins.

"I'm serious, man. Turn the fucking music off. We have to get everybody out of here."

An American woman, paying for a round of drinks, turned towards him and said, "Did you say there was a bomb in here?"

"Yes I did." At last Shahpour felt as though he was being listened to. He was now committed to what he had to do. Lifting himself onto the bar, he swung his legs over into the service area and killed the power on the sound system. One of the staff grabbed him and shouted: "Hey!" but Shahpour pushed him back and shouted as loudly as he could.

"Listen to me. Everybody. We have a very serious situation. I am not kidding around. Everybody needs to clear this area as quickly as possible." The Kiwi attempted to restore the sound on the hi-fi and Shahpour swore at him. The American woman later told me that this was the moment when she realized that something was seriously wrong. Shahpour then ran out into the main area of the bar and began physically manhandling customers in what must have looked like an act of lunacy. But the music remained switched off. People began to react. Shahpour heard stools and chairs scraping back, confused, murmured conversations. Several customers on the upper level were staring down at him from the balcony, trying to work out what was going on. Shahpour went from face to face, group to group, saying the same thing to each of them, over and over again.

"I work for the American government. Get out of here. There may be a bomb in the bar. Larry's has been targeted as a place where Westerners drink. Leave quickly. Leave now."

Several customers—those of a more credulous and biddable nature—began moving slowly towards the exit. Others—those, for example, who had just bought an expensive round of drinks, or waited patiently for their turn at a game of pool—swore at Shahpour and told him to leave them in peace. One of them said,

"Sit down you fucking idiot, this isn't funny," but was met with a stare of such intensity that he immediately began encouraging his friends to leave. At the same time, somebody had the presence of mind to hit the fire alarm. As Shahpour ran upstairs, he could hear the Kiwi barman saying: "OK, let's do this. Everybody leave," in a steady, level voice. It was now a matter of Shahpour's personal pride, as much as it was of saving lives, that he should succeed in evacuating the building.

"Didn't you fucking hear me?" he shouted at a group of bewildered customers huddled at the top of the stairs. They were holding bottles of beer, pool cues, staring at him as if determined to make a point. "Get out of here. There's a fucking bomb."

Others were still eating. They had belongings. In all, it took about three minutes to clear the upper level and a further four to search every nook and cranny of the building—including the kitchen, the bathrooms, the office at the back—and to be certain that Larry's was empty. This was an act of extraordinary bravery on Shahpour's part because, for all he knew, the bomb could have gone off at any moment. Finally, when he was done, he walked out onto Nanyang Road and saw to his disbelief that most of the customers were standing within ten feet of the entrance. Still fired with adrenalin, he shouted at them to move "at least one hundred meters back down the street." Staff from a neighbouring Chinese bar received the same instruction in Mandarin when he saw them staring blankly outside through an open door.

"Get inside!" he shouted, a raised voice in China as rare as it was potentially humiliating. "Get to the back of your building! It's not a fire!" and while three of them joined the crush of bemused local residents and Westerners on the road, two remained rooted to the spot, not prepared to lose face at the hands of a wild-eyed, screaming Arab.

They were two of the eighteen people who suffered minor injuries as a result of the subsequent explosion. Shahpour remembers feeling the eyes of perhaps 200 people boring into him as he began to suffer the awful, humiliating possibility of being wrong. He cursed Joe Lennox, staring at a street of dumb faces. Seconds later he was wrapped in a different kind of silence, his ears howling, his body covered in debris, a hero who had saved at least 150 people from the wreckage of a Shanghai bomb.

Memet Almas returned to his home in Astana, where he was seized by Kazakh police.

Five hours after paramedics and rescue crews had hospitalized the survivors in Screen Four, police discovered an unexploded bomb wedged beneath a seat in the back row of Screen Eight of the Silver Reel multiplex. A technical fault with the IED had prevented the bomb from exploding. Ansary Tursun was subsequently arrested in Guiyang on 17 June, his role in the attacks having been leaked to the Chinese authorities by a source in MI6.

The device planted by Abdul Bary in the metal bin on the sixth floor of the Paradise City mall was never found, because Bary had removed it at the last minute, having suffered a change of heart. Surveillance footage showed that he returned to the disabled toilet with his rucksack, then left the mall minutes later in the company of his wife and daughter.

He is still at large.

Joe Lennox was taken first to the Rui Jin Hospital in Luwan and then to a private room at the Worldlink on Nanjing Road. For the first thirty-six hours he was unconscious.

Waterfield had called me in Beijing late on the night of 11 June to tell me that he had been unable to reach Joe by telephone and was concerned that he might have been caught up in the Xujiahui bomb. At that early stage, the explosion at Larry's had not been linked to what had happened in Paradise City. For all anyone knew, the two incidents were unrelated.

I flew to Shanghai at dawn on Sunday and was at Joe's bedside by eleven o'clock. An undeclared SIS officer from the embassy— let's call him Bob—almost beat me to it, and before I had a chance to find anything out about Joe's condition I was being ushered downstairs to the canteen, where Bob bought me "a quiet cup of coffee" and proceeded to lay out what he described as "the respective positions of the British and Chinese governments."

"Here's the thing. It's obvious to local liaison that Joe was one of us." Bob was an overweight man in his mid-forties with a tense, persuasive manner. I thought that I recognized his face but couldn't place him. "They've got closed-circuit of RUN going bananas in the mall ten minutes before the bomb went off. There are dozens of eyewitnesses. At the same time, you've got a CIA officer going through the same routine in Nanyang Road. The Chinese are obviously keen to find out how the hell we knew what was going on."

I was about to speak when Bob silenced me with his eyes. A young Chinese doctor walked past our table. There was a smell of sickly sweet cakes in the canteen and I started to feel nauseous.

"What happened in Nanyang Road?" I asked.

Bob told me about Larry's. Until further notice, he said, the Chinese were calling it a gas explosion. Then there was an eyebrow, a half-smile, and he gave me what bureaucrats like to call "the bigger picture."

"Look. About nine hours ago a second IED was found in Screen Eight at the cinema. Unexploded. Rucksack. That makes what happened last night a co-ordinated terrorist strike on the Chinese mainland. And who tried to stop it? We did. The Brits did. One point three billion Chinese and not a single one of them knew what the hell was happening in their own back yard. Now it doesn't take a PhD in psychology to understand how that makes the Chinese feel. Embarrassed. Ashamed. Do you follow?" Bob must have thought that he wasn't getting through to me because he added, "I'm talking about a loss of face, Will."

I nodded. He was going to ask me to agree to something. It felt like I was getting out my cheque book for a plot of land I didn't want to buy.

"Joe is a bloody hero," he said, with what seemed like genuine professional admiration. "He's also *persona non grata*. The Chinese want him out of the country as soon as he recovers. Far as they're concerned, what happened at the Silver Reel was an isolated incident, a grudge. You've seen today's papers. They're blaming a single Uighur fanatic. Ablimit Celil. Apparently he's got previous. Joe Lennox, the second IED, the bomb at Larry's, all of them will be airbrushed from the historical record."

In the canteen, somebody dropped a tray of cups. There was a hole of silence into which we all turned. I had a sudden mental image of tapes being erased, of witnesses threatened, of surveillance recordings being consigned to a vault in Beijing. Everything would have to comply with the myth of modern China. Everything would be twisted, manipulated and spun.

Bob leaned forward.

"Over the past few weeks, Joe gave London a number of names which he believed were linked to Uighur separatism." He produced a crumpled piece of paper from his trouser pocket and proceeded to decipher his own seemingly illegible script. "Ansary Tursun. Memet Almas. Abdul Bary. We've now given these names to the Chinese authorities. Professor Wang Kaixuan as well. I'd bet my house they were responsible for what happened at Larry's and Xujiahui."

"And what does Joe get in return?" I was appalled that SIS were prepared to give up Wang before they knew the full story, but couldn't say anything about Joe's meeting with him in May because he had sworn me to secrecy.

"What Joe gets in return is a first-class air ticket to Heathrow and the chance to recuperate in London. What he gets is no awkward questions asked about a supposed employee of Quayler pharmaceuticals nosing around Shanghai under non-official cover. He's Beijing Red, of course, but there's not much any of us can do about that, is there?"

It was a typical British climbdown in the face of Chinese power. Don't upset Beijing. Think of the contracts. Think of the money. It made me intensely angry. Five floors above us was a man who had risked his life to save hundreds of innocent people, a man lying in a coma who was unable to play any part in negotiations which would effectively decide the next twenty years of his life. It seemed absurd, against the background of everything that had happened, that SIS were trying to protect the integrity of their operations in China at Joe's expense. Bob—and probably Joe, too—would have argued that the Office had no choice, but it still felt like a rushed and shoddy compromise.

"Don't look so upset," he had the nerve to say. "The Yanks are going through exactly the same routine with Moazed."

"What do you mean?"

"He realized what he'd done last night and got himself to the consulate sharpish. Nowadays, when a bomb goes off and you look like he does, there's only one direction the authorities are going to point the finger."

"Meaning?"

"Meaning that Shahpour is most likely already on his way back to Langley. His actions last night, perhaps Joe's as well, will be written about in Western blogs, reported in the Western media, but the story will be withheld from the Chinese. You don't need me to tell you that the government here doesn't give a flying fuck what the West thinks about China. Just as long as its own people are kept in the dark, Beijing is happy."

"And what about Miles Coolidge?" I asked.

"What about him?" Bob had reacted to the question as if I was being distasteful.

"Well, wasn't he involved in all of this? Isn't he obliged to leave China as well?"

"You didn't know?" he said, his soft, puffy face colouring with worry. "Did nobody tell you?"

53 | THE TESTIMONY OF JOE LENNOX

They came for Wang Kaixuan at night, when he was asleep in his bed. Six armed PLA stooges and a quartet of MSS officers sprinting down the damp, narrow alleys of a Beijing *hutong*, bursting through his front door with a single, well-aimed strike from the stock of a gun. Then torches in his face, handcuffs on his wrists, and a bewildered old man being led out into the Chinese night to face an imminent execution.

Joe regained consciousness at 10:25 on the morning of 13 June.

His first memory was of a conversation between two Chinese nurses standing in the corridor outside his room. He heard one of them saying something about being late for a seminar, to which the other replied, "I'll cover for you." Joe then became aware of an intense, brittle dryness at the back of his throat and called for water.

As luck would have it, I was downstairs in the canteen eating a sandwich when the younger of the two nurses telephoned and told me that Joe was awake. The doctors were going to run some tests, but I would be able to speak to him within two or three hours.

The Worldlink was swarming with MSS, so any conversation with Joe would have to be brief.

There was that same sickly sweet smell again as I made my way up to his room. An elderly Chinese man was dragging a floor polisher up and down the same section of the fifth-floor corridor, again and again. I looked through the small window in the door of Joe's room and saw that he was sitting up in bed, looking out of the window. He had a clear view of three unfinished skyscrapers, green-netted scaffolding capping their summits like mould. I knocked gently on the glass with my ring and his eyes were slow to turn towards me. There was a little more colour in his face now that he was awake. A nurse who was inside the room said, "Yes?" and then left immediately.

"You're up," I said. I was wondering how to begin, how to pace things. I didn't know where to start. A flicker of a smile passed across Joe's dried lips. He was glad to see me. "How do you feel?" I asked.

I looked at his left leg, raised from the bed and encased in plaster. A drop of blood had seeped through the bandages swaddling his scalp. Overnight, the doctors had taken him off the ventilator which had been running throughout Sunday. Whatever had fallen onto Joe in the cinema, whatever had partially crushed him, had also saved his life.

"I have a headache," he replied. "Otherwise I feel fine." Both of us knew that this wasn't going to be a conversation about his health. In an effort to find something to do with my hands, I started playing with a cord on the curtains.

"What happened?" Joe said quietly. It was a strangely open-ended question. I felt that he was giving me the opportunity to tell him what I had to tell him in my own good time.

"Shahpour saved everyone at Larry's," I began. His face flickered with relief. "He's on his way back to America. He's Beijing Red." A tiny nod of understanding. "You did the same thing at Xujiahui. They're estimating that there were about four hundred people in the cinema. Thanks to you, all but twenty of them got out."

"Isabella," he said immediately, the quietest, most desperate word I have ever heard. It was the door into Joe's future and I was the one who was going to open it.

"She made it," I said. "She's going to be fine." I remember making a conscious effort to look away at this point, because I thought that Joe would want to absorb the news without feeling as though he was being watched. Very quickly, however, he said, "Miles?"

I felt his eyes come up to mine and we met each other's gaze. It was immediately clear from his expression that he was hopeful of Miles's survival. I did not know how he was going to respond to what I was about to tell him. What Miles had done in the cinema was in many ways as brave as Joe's own actions; his instincts and courage had provided a kind of redemption.

"We think that Miles may have saved Isabella's life," I said. "The American consulate has been informed that he tried to protect her."

Joe asked me to explain. I said that Celil, upon hearing the alarm and seeing the audience streaming out of the cinema, had panicked and detonated his IED several minutes before nine o'clock. He had taken his own life in doing so. Miles, alerted by Joe's warnings, had pulled Isabella out of her seat and dragged her towards him. An eyewitness reported that he pushed his wife into Joe's arms with the words, "Take her, look after her," and then turned and ran back into the panic and gloom of the cinema, either to confront Celil directly, to try to prevent him from detonating the bomb, or to assist in the evacuation. Shortly after this point, the bomb went off.

"Miles is dead," I said. "You and Isabella were found very close together. You were shielding her at the exit. You did what Miles asked."

It was odd. On my way up to Joe's room, I had thought that the loss of Miles might in some way have pleased him, but of course there was only sadness in his eyes. Isabella had lost a husband. Jesse had lost a father. The rest was just politics.

"Who's looking after her?" he said. Something beeped on the cardiac monitor beside Joe's bed. I could hear the floor polisher going up and down in the corridor outside. I said that Isabella's injuries were not thought to be serious and that her mother had flown out from England as soon as she'd heard about the explosion.

392 / Charles Cumming

"That's good," he said, but his voice was very low and he seemed distracted. The energy was going out of him. "Will you tell her that I was asking for her?" His eyes were suddenly black with exhaustion. "Will you tell her that I'm very sorry for everything that's happened?"

A few days later we discovered the extent to which Miles had been keeping his masters at Langley in the dark. Lenan's murder, Celil's involvement with the cell, the plan to bomb the Olympics—all of it had been cooked up by a cluster of hawks in the Pentagon, most of them the same bunch of fanatics who had made such a mess of things in Iraq. It was at this point that Joe asked me to write the book, so I contacted my boss in Beijing and requested a six-month sabbatical. By the end of the month, Joe was well enough to leave hospital and Waterfield asked me to accompany him on his flight back to London. Isabella had already taken Jesse to the States to be with Miles's family. Nobody knew, at that stage, whether she had any plans to return to Europe.

On 30 June, eight years to the day since the handover of Hong Kong, Joe and I were escorted to Pudong International Airport by enough police and military to start a small revolution. Joe was waved through passport control and put onto our BA flight about forty minutes before any of the other passengers. A plain-clothes MSS man accompanied me to the check-in desk, passed through security and then sat by my side in the departures hall for a full two hours before making sure that I took my seat beside Joe. We barely spoke to one another during that time. As we were ordering drinks after take-off, Joe turned to me and said that he had not received a word of thanks, at any stage, from any of the Chinese authorities.

At Heathrow we went our separate ways: Joe to a safe house in Hampstead, me to the cottage I was renting near Salisbury, where I planned to begin working on the book. A week later, four brainwashed young British Muslims blew themselves up in the London rush hour, killing fifty-two people, and it felt as though the whole thing was starting all over again.

What happened that day forced some questions into my mind

which have never really gone away. What would have happened if SIS hadn't become involved with Miles back in Hong Kong? How would things have been different, for example, if Joe Lennox and Kenneth Lenan and David Waterfield had simply stayed out of his way? Without American interference, would Wang Kaixuan and Ablimit Celil and Josh Pinnegar and all the hundreds of other victims of TYPHOON still be alive today? Almost certainly. And would a small band of Uighur radicals have conceived, let alone executed, an attack on the scale of 6/11 without outside interference? I very much doubt it.

From time to time, during the long, complex process of researching and writing the book, I put these questions to its principal players. Had the security and wellbeing of British and American citizens been improved one iota by the activities of their respective governments in China? Who had really benefited from this new version of the Great Game, besides a few shareholders in the Macklinson Corporation?

Nobody, not even Joe Lennox himself, was ever able to give me a satisfactory answer.

ACKNOWLEDGEMENTS

Once upon a time, a man called Wang did emerge from the still waters of the South China Sea, but he was not a Chinese academic, nor did he encounter Lance Corporal Angus Anderson on the beach at Dapeng Bay. It was the mid-1970s. A young Gurkha patrolling Starling Inlet took him to see his commanding officer, General Sir Peter Duffell, who promptly sent him back to China. It is no exaggeration to say that Peter's riveting description of his brief encounter with Wang inspired *Typhoon*.

Many others played a part in bringing the book to fruition. A conversation beside a lake in Beijing with Oliver August led me to Xinjiang. I would urge you to read Oliver's excellent book *Inside the Red Mansion: On the Trail of China's Most Wanted Man*. Sebastian Lewis's knowledge of all things Chinese was as impressive as it was invaluable. Jeremy Goldkorn, Mark Kitto and Lisa Cooper gave up their time to show a stranger around Beijing. I would have got nowhere in Shanghai without the tireless efforts of Toby Collins. Christian Giannini, Richard Turner, Amina Belouizdad, Lina Ly, Zhuang Hao, Michelle and Bruno at M on the Bund and Josephine at Glamour Bar were also extremely helpful. Alex Bonsor, Ben and Katy Chandler, Dominic Grant and Ken Leung were first-class guides in Hong Kong. Captain John Newington showed me both sides of the Chinese economic miracle in Shenzhen. My thanks also to the mysterious Mr. Ignatius, who bought me dinner on the night train from Beijing.

Back in the UK, I was lucky enough to find a Uighur living in London. Enver Bugda was forced to leave his wife and children in Urumqi in 1998 after co-operating on an undercover Channel Four documentary about the impact of nuclear testing at Lop Nur. Enver was of great assistance to me and it has been a privilege to get to know him. I am also very grateful to Sacha Bonsor, William Goodlad, Belle Newbigging, Rupert Mitchell and James Minter, Simon Davis, Marcus Cooper and Davy Dewar at BP, Jemima Lewis, Jonathan and Anna Hanbury, Simon and Caroline Pilkington, Carolyn Hanbury, Ian Cumming, Milly Jones, Ed King, Trevor Horwood and Keith Taylor, Otto Bathurst, Mark and Gaynor Pilkington, James Loughran and Siobhan Loughran-Mareuse, Iona Hamilton, Bruce Palling, Simon Heppner, Xiaoqing Zhang, Katy Nicholson, Angus and Ali McGougan, Ian Frankish, David Jenkins and Kate Knowles, Richard Spencer, Mary Target, Rowland White, Tom Weldon, Carly Cook, Sophie Mitchell, Tif Loehnis and everyone at Janklow & Nesbitt in London, Theo Tait, Luke Janklow, Claire Dippel, Boris Starling, and the ruthless—but invaluable—Samuel Loewenberg. I'd also like to thank Keith Kahla, Kathleen Conn, and Rafal Gibek at St. Martin's Press. My wife, Melissa, knows how much I owe her. My children, Iris and Stanley, know how much time Daddy spent in his office.

Professor Wang Kaixuan's testimony in the safe house is based on documents assembled by Amnesty International. For further information, see: *Gross Violations of Human Rights in the Xinjiang Uighur Autonomous Region* at *http://www.amnesty.org.*

The following books, articles and websites were indispensable:

The Last Governor by Jonathan Dimbleby (Warner Books, 1997)
Black Watch, Red Dawn by Neil and Jo Craig (Brassey's, 1998)
The Dragon Syndicates: The Global Phenomenon of the Triads by
    Martin Booth (Carroll and Graf, 1999)

The China Dream by Joe Studwell (Profile Books, 2003)

The New Great Game: Blood and Oil in Central Asia by Lutz Kleveman (Atlantic Books, 2003)

Wild West China: The Taming of Xinjiang by Christian Tyler (John Murray, 2003)

The Cox Report at *http://www.house.gov/coxreport*

Beijing vs Islam by Michael Winchester at *http://www. asiaweek.com*

Wild Grass by Ian Johnson (Penguin, 2004)

Murder in Samarkand by Craig Murray (Mainstream Publishing, 2006)

Islamic Unrest in the Xinjiang Uighur Autonomous Region by Dr. Paul George (Canadian Security Intelligence, Unclassified) at *http://www.fas.org*

Hong Kong Diary by Simon Winchester at *http://www.salon.com*

Shanghai Baby by Wei Hui (Robinson, 2002)

Kowloon Tong by Paul Theroux (Penguin, 1997)

La Mortola: In the footsteps of Sir Thomas Hanbury by Alasdair Moore (Cadogan, 2004)

C.C.
London 2009